COLLIN IRISH

Messenger

For Amy, whose contributions can never be compensated. Although kisses and chocolate sometimes make a dent.

Galachian Empire
Talistave
Fromeathia
Flaenegor Mountains
Karpathode
Cleavicon River
Galathia
Ametrine Grasslands
Fenduer Forest
Talindrey River
Wrayan Mountains
Aeterna
Shinwate Forest
Aquerl Sea
The Frontier
Thurbush Thickets
Kelstone Mountains
Calonade
Vivigossic Ocean

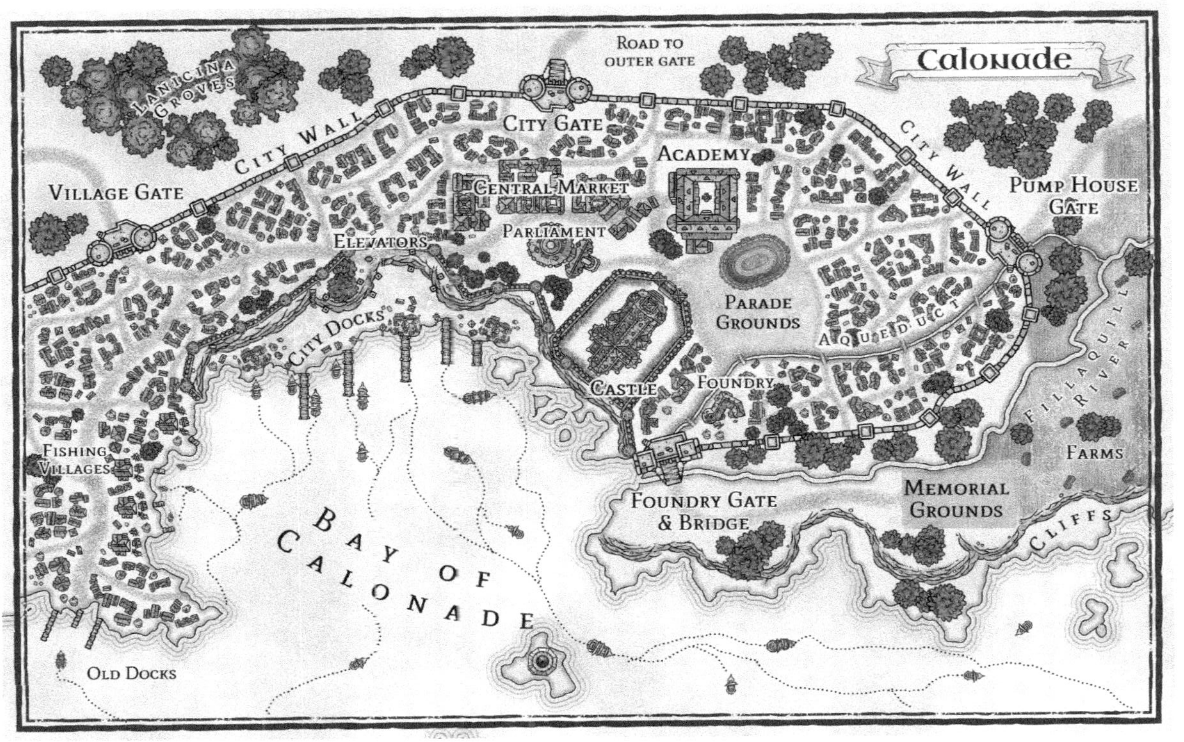

Calonade
Road to Outer Gate
Lanicina Groves
City Wall
City Gate
Academy
City Wall
Pump House Gate
Village Gate
Central Market
Parliament
Elevators
Parade Grounds
Aqueduct
Fillaquill River
City Docks
Castle
Foundry
Farms
Fishing Villages
Foundry Gate & Bridge
Memorial Grounds
Cliffs
Bay of Calonade
Old Docks

Milestones in
The History of Violet Sky Series

Stable AI developed — 2030

2177 — Earth's ecological collapse. Diaspora begins.

Genetic damage to humans documented. — 2301

2377 — Males endangered. Female growth is stunted.

Seeding planets with healthy humans begins. — 2411

2450 — Seeded Human Assets legally declared property.

New species declared: Homo faminae or Feminkind. — 2622

Alcott Station Clock

Urey Calendar

Sephy Alcott establishes Willacast Corp & space station construction begins. — 4080

Sephy Alcott disappears inside rogue black hole's orbit. — 4091

5000 — **Alcott Station Timeline Begins** — 0

0 — Myra is Maiden

Sephy Alcott establishes a transportation network. — 6865 — 5.1

Willacast Corp takes over galaxy-wide commerce transportation — 7192 — 6.0

1000 — Lillain becomes Maiden, Myra becomes mother.

Willacast Corp successfully blends nano-cyber technology with AI. — 8730 — 10.2

Willacast Corp becomes largest & wealthiest corporation ever. — 9022 — 11.0

1950 — Rafykin becomes Emperor of Galathia.

Melrayis Valdez discovers Urey. — 10555 — 15.2

2000 — Lillain becomes Mother, Kamur becomes Maiden, Myra becomes Crone.

Allcott & Valdez establish a secret retro colony on Urey. A triple nano-cyber automation system is installed. — 11286 — **Urey Calendar Begins** — 17.2

2200 — Rafykin builds Aeterna.

Sephy & Lakqwi — 13303 — 22.8

2973 — Nados "kidnaps" Izell.

2978 — Nados killed in battle.

Present Day — 14284 — 25.4 — 2998 — Present Day (Jay & Jurica)

Glossary

A glossary of terms used in Messenger can be found in the back of the book.

Chapter One

I own a planet no one wants.

   —from the journal of Sephy Alcott, Standard Galactic Year 10555.

Shinwate Forest, Day 021, Year 2017 local planetary calendar, Standard Galactic Year 13303

Sephy sat up, head spinning as she tried to focus. Several seconds passed before the swimming images settled into something coherent—a forest glen surrounded by tall trees. Damp leaves soaked through her jumpsuit. A slight mist penetrated the canopy from a violet sky, which looked as if it couldn't decide between rain and sun.

She shook her head, and her vision continued to float. She hadn't expected such a pastoral setting. The last time she visited this planet, she transported into the middle of a vast temple complex. Maybe this was a good sign. The point of this retro colony, after all, was to drop all influences of modern life.

Sephy's eyesight cleared, and she spied a single feminam youth staring at her from the edge of the circle. The girl stood, mouth open in shock, hyperventilating. Tall for a feminam, her face featured a light gray hue with the shallow wrinkles of youth.

"Hello." Sephy's voice came out as more of a croak than anything understandable.

The girl squeaked, turned, and ran, her hand-woven robe flapping behind her.

"Wait!"

The girl had already disappeared into the forest. Sephy levered herself to her feet. It'd been five years since her last field visit to this planet, with only a few other dirtside trips. The almost continuous desk work over that time had made her stiff. Urey's gravity didn't quite match that of the station. Getting knocked around by an old transit device, not properly calibrated, didn't help either.

Sephy activated her neural transponders with the flick of an eyebrow and got a healthy signal back. At least that worked. She sent out a ping and got an immediate answer from the trees surrounding the clearing. She shuffled over to one and leaned against it, still waiting for all the feeling to come back into her legs.

The tree, actually a sophisticated machine in disguise, answered her query with a standard password request. She mentally entered her pass codes, and the computer hidden under the base of the tree's roots allowed her access to its database.

She downloaded the activity logs into one of her neural file folders for examination later. Next, she needed to find the nearby Shinwate village and contact the chief. The reports from her former colleague, Melrayis, and her successors, showed the Shinwate thrived on Urey. At least until the reports dwindled to silence a few centuries ago on maintime.

Melrayis' meticulous habits had not translated down the generations, so Sephy had finally made time to check the status of her investment.

Keeping this odd planet off the books was Melrayis' idea. It would never sell on the colonization market because of its unstable blue star, but the financial oversight board had gotten cost-conscious lately, making it harder to hide her pet projects. Sephy might be the CEO of the Willacast Corporation, easily the most powerful business entity in the developed galaxy, but that didn't mean she was in charge. The mighty credit still held that title.

Sephy pushed off the tree and held herself rigid. Her balance back to normal, she left the circle and started down the path she presumed led to the village. The trees provided a pleasantly shaded trail, reminiscent of the many other seeded planets she had overseen. The blue star Urey orbited gave the flora a distinctive blue sheen. Light blue combined with deeper shades, along with a mixture of indigo and purple, on the leaves and flower petals. The foliage sported a lot less green and brown than with more common yellow star planets. Despite that oddity, it wasn't much different from the others. Many of the staple species of the galaxy had taken root, even if slightly changed by the environment.

A curious set of stones snaked through the underbrush at regular intervals. They weren't natural formations but ruins from an old wall interspersed with the remnants of stone foundations. Sephy paid little heed and concentrated on the thin trail winding through the thick growth.

As she walked, Sephy enjoyed her favorite part of fieldwork, breathing in the fresh air. Back at the office, the ventilators just couldn't compete, no matter how often they scrubbed the filters.

The ground shifted under Sephy's feet, and she stumbled a step before catching herself. A shadow cast over her from a tall tree that blocked her path. A long root emerged from the ground and slithered forward before plunging back into the earth. The tree slid through the soil, a step closer, leaving a furrow that filled in behind it.

Sephy's breath caught in her throat. She'd never seen a walking tree before. The part of her fascinated by the adaptation tried to figure out how it could happen on an Earth-modeled planet. A more risk-adverse part of her mind screamed with terror. She backed up a step, frozen between the two reactions—run or research?

The branches of the tree swayed left to right like arms opening. Sephy stared in astonishment at finding an adult Shinwate sitting in the tree. She straddled a saddle attached to a large branch near the trunk about halfway up. She wore similar rough-spun clothing to the girl, which blended in with the colors of the forest. Over her shoulder she carried a long recurve bow. A mask covered with a blue camouflage pattern obscured the top of her face.

The rider tipped the mask to reveal her gray skin tone and wrinkles. Definitely feminam, but taller than the norm. Was it a trend? The analytical part of Sephy's mind receded to the background as the rider, with an impressive athletic move, dismounted and dropped to the ground.

"Are you a slave?" the Shinwate asked in the native language.

Sephy's heads-up display identified it as Shin. Her neurals translated, and she got the meaning and several responses. Breaking away from standard Galactic was Melrayis' doing.

She had insisted on a new language for the start of a new existence.

"No," Sephy replied in Shin.

"You spoke Galathian to the attendant," the rider said.

Galathian? It took a moment, but Sephy remembered the capital city of the nearest large human civilization was once called Galathia. That must not have changed. Of course, the humans would name the dominant language after themselves. *They never fail to assume they're the center of the universe.*

"An unfortunate habit." The rider cocked her head and Sephy could tell she didn't quite have the accent right. "I'm not from here."

"I would know you if you were." The rider made no move for her weapon, but she kept her distance. "What is your name?"

Ready for this question, Sephy flashed her best smile. Melrayis had left a few keys to access the Shinwate culture. One of them was a name.

"Hukindi."

"You claim to be the prophet," the rider said.

Melrayis had evidently embedded a religious paradigm to preserve certain information. A popular way to do it, but it had some disadvantages. Like providing proof.

"Yes," Sephy said.

"You do not wear the traditional robes," the rider said.

"No, I'm afraid not." The observation illustrated another problem. Melrayis' files said nothing about acceptable clothing, likely because it was an adaptation in the belief system. Those could be troublesome. "What is your name?"

"My name is mine," the rider said. "You are a stranger and

not worthy to know it."

Sephy frowned. A suspicion of outsiders was a new adaptation as well. She wondered about the cause. "All right, Rider, what happens now?"

"I have a duty to kill you."

A *strong* suspicion of outsiders. This was definitely a problem. Sephy cast about for an idea. She could roast the rider with the disrupter hidden in her jacket, but that seemed extreme. The repulse setting was less deadly, but even a benign attack against a guardian of the village would start things off on a poor footing. Maybe she could do something with the trees, though they were far away. With hindsight, she probably should have stayed in the circle. She pinged them anyway, and an answer came from an unexpected location. The tree blocking the path wasn't a tree at all.

Sephy didn't have time to unpack that revelation. "Tell me about your mount." Sephy nodded toward the tree.

"This is my Yawa-lee."

Definitions of those terms popped up in Sephy's neural feed. The walking trees, Yawate, were thought of as semi-sacred sentient beings. The Yawa-lee were the Yawate that formed partnerships with their Shinwate riders. They were also disguised machines like the stationary ones surrounding the transit platform. Sephy had never heard of them, but she didn't keep up with all the nuances of planetary control.

"If you were Shinwate, you would know this." The rider unshouldered her bow.

The pass codes worked and Sephy had access to the Yawate's inner protocols. She parsed it quickly for a convenient command directory to access.

"I know this is your Yawa-lee," Sephy said with an air of

condescension. "Tell me about her."

With a flash, an arrow with a metal barb appeared in the bowstring. The rider aimed at Sephy's chest. Sephy raised her hands. "Whoa, there."

The rider took a step forward, with the arrow now pointed at Sephy's head. She winced. The expression probably didn't translate.

"The relationship between Shinwate and Yawate is sacred." Her eyes grew intensely wide. "It is not spoken of to strangers. I should kill you for blasphemy. I should kill you for speaking Galathian."

The bow shook ever so slightly in the rider's hands. Sephy could tell this Shinwate was an accomplished hunter, but not a killer. She only had a moment to work with and she reveled in it. Her plush office at the top of the heap, her position of unquestioned power in that other world, had stripped away the possibility of this feeling. An inch from death and everything depended on the next move. Sephy considered drawing it out but knew doing so would only end in disaster.

With a hand flourish, Sephy mentally activated a sequence of the Yawate's executables. It shifted, dropped a branch, and grasped the bow along with the arrow, snatching them from the rider's grip. The rider stumbled sideways in surprise, her head whipping around to watch the Yawate neatly place the bow into its saddle holster and the arrow into a matching quiver.

"Thank you, Yawate." Sephy bowed to the tree. It was the right move because the rider stared in astonishment, her expression no longer of a person about to take a life.

"How?" The rider's face flushed with embarrassed aston-ishment.

"I am Hukindi," Sephy said with a shrug. "Now, tell me your name."

"Lakqwi, First Daughter of Melrayis."

Sephy suppressed a snort of laughter and hid her amusement in a frown. Melrayis had based the religion on herself, of course. Even though Melrayis' egocentric approach was predictable, Sephy found herself pleasantly surprised. She wondered if *Daughter of Melrayis* referred to a tribal function or a statement of genealogy. Sephy could see the resemblance in Lakqwi's square jaw and intense eyes, but tragically, the laugh lines were missing. Sephy felt an overwhelming longing to see her friend again. Since Melrayis moved from the station to the dirtside timestream, it was far too late for that.

"Lakqwi," Sephy said in her most authoritative tone, "I should meet with your chief. I have been gone a long time and I feel there is much to discuss."

Lakqwi bowed. "It would be my honor, Prophet Hukindi. Would you prefer to ride?" She waved toward the Yawate.

Sephy's heart beat faster as she measured the climb to the Yawate's saddle. It was a tall perch, even for a stationary tree, and this one could move. With a sinking dread, Sephy wondered how fast it could go. Facing down a foe during a negotiation came easy. Physical prowess, however, had never been her strong point. Realizing a dramatic entrance into the village might be helpful with the colonists, Sephy suppressed a cringe and said, "Yes, but I fear it has been a long time, and I'm poorly dressed. You will have to help me up."

Lakqwi nodded and, with some awkwardness, helped Sephy climb and secure herself between the Yawate's trunk and Lakqwi's back. Lakqwi kicked the Yawate's trunk with her heel. It spun around and snaked a long root into the ground ahead of them. The Yawate swayed as it began pulling itself through the soil. Lakqwi tweaked a short branch situated like a throttle, and another root emerged from beneath the trunk, stretched forward, and plunged into the dirt. A few moments later, the Yawate roots churned through the soil and Sephy suppressed a scream of fear and delight as they rushed through the forest at the speed of a healthy gallop.

Chapter Two

I am Rafykin, Emperor of Galathia for the last 200 years. I have decided to chronicle my story. Perhaps you will find it as fascinating as I have.

—from Chronicles of Galathia by Rafykin, Urey, circa 2640 local planetary calendar.

Calonade, Day 288, Year 2998 local planetary calendar, Standard Galactic Year 14284

Tall and muscular, Jay's black warhorse snorted fiercely at the restraining bars. Havoc kicked the back of the starting stall, rattling the chains.

"Easy, boy," Jay said in a soothing voice. Havoc yanked the reins and shifted forward, half-rearing. Jay longed for freedom, too. The final event of his student-soldier career, and the only barrier to becoming Top Cadet, stretched out on the track before him.

Since the contest began years before, the winner had always been one of the Galathian occupiers. If he won, he'd be the first to break the tradition. Jay wondered how winning would feel. The thought of all Galathians forced to swallow their swollen pride warmed his heart. Even better, Calonadens would have to stop ridiculing his mixed ancestry and low station. Beyond the glory of adding his name to the winner's plaque, he'd earn the plum assignment and ride out of this cursed city as a freshly minted lieutenant of the Horse Division.

Twenty riders, the best of this year's academy class, lined up in the racing stalls, waiting for the starting gun. Jay brushed a stray strand of coiled copper hair out of his rust-brown eyes. A hash of pale blue plinum lines and starbursts decorated his deep blue skin, marking his mixed descent. But the accidents of birth didn't matter today. Only the rider, the horse, and fate had any influence on the outcome. Every fiber of Jay's being tensed to take a shot at a life far from here.

"A half-casting made the cut," a voice jeered. "That has to be a mistake."

To Jay's right, a stout Galathian sat atop his royal thoroughbred. Of all the contenders for Top Cadet, Jay ended up beside the person who constantly touted himself better than all others. Gilcres' plinum bands overlaid his features with orderly vertical lines, marking him as highborn. Gilcres sneered back at him through the iron bars that separated their racing stalls before flicking his pale eyes away from Jay with disdain.

Half-casting. Jay's blood boiled at the slur, but he held his tongue. He would soon prove he wasn't half-made or a flawed piece of machinery to be tossed away into the trash heap. He would show them he was far from broken or malformed.

"Shut up, Gilcres."

Gilcres sneered. "I suppose it's valiant to try, even though you can't win."

Jay appraised his opponent's sleek and well-muscled steed, bred for the track. The rider, however, didn't impress. Broad-shouldered and rotund, Gilcres had strength and skill with a blade, but he fared better at mounting a barstool than a racehorse. Jay was tired of his petty ridicule and blustering conceit.

Havoc tossed his head, flipped his tail, and lined up another kick, but Jay leaned forward and whispered into his ear. "He's going to eat our dust." Havoc snorted, flaring his nostrils, but held back his hoof. Jay needed him steady for a good jump at the starting gun.

They had transformed the academy parade grounds into a racing arena. Onlookers from all over Calonade filled it. Royalty, military brass, and Galathian merchants lounged in the upper tiers and gazed upon the proceedings as if they were a spectacle created solely for their entertainment.

Jay wiped beads of sweat from his face. The race meant more than a contest of speed. All the racers prepared for a test of resolve and a fight for survival. They rode in full kit, with saber and flintlock pistol, ready to face obstacles made to mimic battlefield conditions. As with any battle, the blood of both horse and rider could be spilled.

Fisherfolk, laborers, and artisans filled the lower stands and milled around on the grounds. Some even pressed against the track railing. The Calonadens came to see if one of their own could finally best the hated Galathian occupiers.

They didn't come to see Jay.

On Jay's left, Jortica, the only full-born Calonaden in the race, sat straight and proud on her blueblood mare. A thin white scar traced from the corner of her mouth, under her dark blue cheek, and back to her ear. It rippled as she clenched her jaw in concentration. A strand of black hair had escaped from under her short-brimmed cadet topper and fluttered in the breeze.

Jortica, the true competition, regularly bested anyone with sword and shot. For a person with deep fisherfolk roots, she rode a horse with true skill. Jay had never gone toe-to-toe against her, but he knew her reputation. She said little, just got the job done. If she won, the streets of Calonade would ring with long-sought triumph. It would prove that Calonaden's glory days were not twenty years past.

Though Jay would enjoy the wounded pride of the Galathians, he had to beat Jortica. If he lost, he could end up humping a pack up and down the Kelstone Mountains in the Calonade Foot or cleaning some Galathian officer's boots. Probably both. No better than a servant. Such a fate would make the castle kitchens, where he grew up as a cook's boy, seem pleasant.

Silence fell over the crowd as a team of cadets rolled out the starting gun wagon. They placed the monstrous antique brass cannon, stuffed with gunpowder and burdening its own axles to near collapse, in front of the starting stalls and pointed it crosswise to the track. One cadet touched the powder hole with a lit match cord.

The cannon let loose a deafening roar, flinging smoke and sparks across Jay's line of sight. The gates exploded open, and Havoc leaped with all his strength toward freedom. They burst through the plume and flew down the front stretch. Jortica claimed the lead, with Gilcres and Jay close behind. Hundreds of people crowded against the railing, waving their hats and cheering.

They rumbled through the first turn as an obstacle came

into view. Back straight, with perfect form, Jortica flew over the thin wooden fence. Her gray cadet's topper whipped off her head and her black hair bounced loose.

Gilcres' thoroughbred made it, dragging its belly over the top rail. Gilcres wobbled in the saddle but held on.

Jay dug his heels into Havoc's flanks. The broad and muscular horse, bred for battle not grace, surged forward. Splinters flew as Havoc leaped, crashed through the barrier, and pounded down onto the racetrack. A deafening roar rose from the crowd. Jay shook off the rough landing to see Jortica still in the lead.

He ignored the noise and crouched in the saddle. Havoc's steady stride meant he wasn't hurt, at least not badly. Jay breathed with relief at passing the first barrier unscathed. He steered into Gilcres' wake. Frothing as much as his thoroughbred, Gilcres slapped the sides of his mount with a whip to squeeze out more speed.

Trusting Havoc to run straight down the backstretch, Jay glanced back to see the rest of the riders far behind, their gray uniforms thick with dust. Ahead of him, along the last bend of the track, a lethal challenge waited. As he approached the turn, he faced a machine bristling with razor-sharp weapons.

A wide column of steel held dozens of metal tentacles looming over the racetrack. Blades on the ends of mechanical arms spun and reached out in all directions. The reek of oil and smoke filled the air as the deadly mechanism chugged along a circular course inside the far turn. Cogs and wheels spun to propel sharp spears and studded clubs into the path of the racers. Metal ground on metal. Gears whirred as spikes shot out and pulled back. Countless blades slashed and twisted, scissoring the air. Cadets called it the Barber.

Swinging wide meant trading speed for safety. Turning close meant risking a shave—or worse.

Jortica and Gilcres steered wide on the track, staying out of the machine's range. Gilcres slammed into Jortica's mount and pushed her farther off course. A howl of outrage rose from the crowd. Gilcres, not above cheating to win, left an opening.

Drawing his saber, Jay steered Havoc tight into the turn. He'd faced the Barber before, but this wasn't a practice run. For the contest, it wielded weapons sharpened to a deadly sheen. Showing the mettle of a Calonaden warhorse, Havoc thundered into the machine's notorious reach.

Calculating the machine's rhythms, Jay swung his sword hard and fast, cutting off the end of a spear before it skewered him. A heartbeat later, he ducked under a set of studded clubs. On the next stride, a cloud of gunpowder blasted Havoc's face, but Jay's seasoned mount didn't flinch. With a fiery burst of steam and a shriek of metal, the machine shifted and turned, blades cutting upwards to chase him. Jay flipped his sword back to block each blow, the impacts ringing to his shoulder.

They raced on, nearly out of the Barber's reach. Jay lifted his sword in triumph, but he celebrated too soon. A long, serrated blade sliced the back of his arm.

Jay gritted his teeth but didn't drop his weapon. A line of red welled up from a long, shallow cut, staining his gray uniform.

A close shave, as promised.

Jay flipped the sword under his arm and ignored the pain. Instead, he grinned at the view of the homestretch, smooth and open before him. Freedom within his grasp, the race distilled down to the wind in his face and the horse beneath him.

A moment later, the hair on Jay's neck stood up. He heard the pounding of hooves and glanced back to find Gilcres on his heels, his thoroughbred dredging up a burst of speed.

Gilcres swept by Jay, laughing. "Half-casting!"

Jay bit back his fury and pressed his body flat against Havoc's neck. With his ears laid back, Havoc rallied his strength and matched the racehorse's speed. Slick with sweat, he dug deep for the final leg. Hooves pounding and hearts racing, they flew over the track.

With thunderous strides and a blur of straining muscles, Havoc closed on the flying thoroughbred. He nosed past Gilcres' leg and gained inch by inch. Breath roaring with effort, Havoc drew past the thoroughbred's shoulder. They raced neck and neck. Eye rolling white and mouth frothing, the other horse lost a step. Stride by stride, Havoc pulled in front.

With the finish line in sight, pain lanced the back of Jay's neck. He flung up an arm and blocked a second blow. Undeterred, Gilcres whipped Havoc instead. Brutal swipes flayed the horse's flanks. Havoc shied, breaking stride. Gilcres pulled even, raising his whip for another strike.

"No, you don't!" Jay shouted as he lashed out with the pommel of his sword, hitting Gilcres in the chest. The stocky cadet flopped back, losing the grip on his reins, and sending his whip flying. The horses veered into each other with a rib-bruising crunch. They swerved wildly away. Gilcres flopped onto the muddy track. Jay hung on and yanked the reins to turn Havoc back on course.

Jortica flew by, her coat whipping loose in the wind. Graceful and powerful, her whole body stretched along the length of her sleek racer. To the thundering roar of the crowd, Jortica crossed the finish line first.

The sight took Jay's breath away. He didn't even notice the rest of the cadets racing by. As Jortica turned her horse to trot back around, she raised her fist and grinned. Her scar stretched along her jaw like a second smile. He had to smile, too. A Calonaden had finally won.

The moment didn't last. Jay dismounted to check Havoc. Bloody welts ran along his flank. Furious, Jay turned to tell off Gilcres, but the fool appeared right in his face.

"How dare you!" Gilcres shouted, dripping with mud. "I'm royalty."

Jay seethed. "You're a tin-striped cheat!"

"There are no rules on the battlefield." Gilcres quoted the academy maxim.

"So, you think *this* is a battlefield?" Jay gestured around the arena. The rest of the defeated riders slunk toward the exit, a few nursing wounds from the Barber. The crowd milled around the edges, waiting for the winner to appear on the pavilion. Jay glared at Gilcres again. "Believe me, if this were real, you'd be dead."

"I take it back. There is one rule." Gilcres pointed at himself. "Galathians always win. And you," he jabbed Jay with a finger, "you backwater, brainless half-castings always lose."

Jay squeezed his saber's grip. He stopped himself from cutting Gilcres' finger off. He smiled and held him in a glare powered by murderous anger. "It won't be a Galathian name on the Top Cadet plaque this year."

Gilcres blinked, stepping back before rallying, a sneer returning to his face. "I'll be declared the winner. Lord

Kendric will see to it!" He stalked away, swiping at the mud clinging to his uniform.

Gilcres was a fool. Always had been. Even back when they were growing up in the castle, he took on airs for no reason. Being the nephew of the deposed queen wasn't worth much in this occupied city, Galathian or not.

The feeling of satisfaction at rattling his old nemesis soured. Gilcres was right about one thing. Jay *did* lose. If he hadn't struck back and caused the collision, he would have won. His chance to ride out of Calonade with the Horse Division might be gone, but he couldn't let Havoc take a beating all the way to the finish line.

Shaking his head, Jay tended to his horse. He slipped a bundle from his saddlebag and applied a thick healing paste onto the cuts in Havoc's hide. Next, he pulled loose some splinters from Havoc's underbelly and treated those wounds as well. The big horse stopped pawing the turf and settled down. Jay rubbed the lanicin on his own wounds next, being careful not to overdo it. Jay didn't want to be overcome by the potent healing sap of the lanicina tree. He preferred to stay alert. As the throbbing from his arm and neck faded, Jay noticed no one on the raised stage in front of the judges' pavilion. Jortica should have been up there by now, surrounded by the judges.

In the stands, groups of Galathians in top hats and frock coats pushed for the exits against a sea of Calonadens wearing rough-spun clothing. Arguments broke out as the groups jostled each other. The fights would get worse if the judges declared someone besides Jortica the winner.

Havoc needed to cool down. Jay led him slowly along the track toward the pavilion. As they passed by, Jay got a view inside through an open flap. He stopped when he spied a judge.

Lady Izell wore her fair hair stacked on top of her head like a snow-capped peak, reminding everyone of her origins in the icy north. Being Fromeathian, her skin was almost all plinum, making it a blue so pale it was nearly as white as her hair. Perfectly vertical lines of thin blue showed the effects of highborn breeding taken to an extreme. Fans of feathers wove through her hair to provide shade for her face. She wore a white riding corset over a stiff, neck-high blouse. Royal brown riding breeches and the tall black boots of a Calonaden horse soldier completed her outfit.

Lord Kendric, Governor of Calonade, faced her, wearing Galathian red. Blood red because they ruled by spilling so much of it. A broad-brimmed hat protected his perfectly plinum-striped skin from the sun. He gestured emphatically, and the pale of his cheeks took on a pinkish tinge as he shouted.

Lady Izell stood ramrod straight, her expression cold and unflinching. Jay couldn't make out the words, as Lord Kendric, the second judge, tightened his grip on Lady Izell's elbow. She calmly pried Lord Kendric's fingers from her arm and pointed toward the pavilion's opening. Jay flinched, suddenly face-to-face with his headmaster and the third judge, General Saben. Only two plinum bands marching down his face broke formation to cross ranks. He wore a dark red double-buttoned military coat and an unlit pipe jutted from his mouth, clenched in his square jaw.

Hard, but fair to Galathian, Calonaden, and even mixed cadets, General Saben was the only Galathian Jay respected. The Calonaden cadets hated him because of the rumor he killed King Nados, thus paving the way for the Galathian occupation of Calonade. If true, General Saben had shed any bias from the past.

"Move along, Cadet," Saben growled. The tent flap snapped shut, revealing Galathia's sigil painted on the canvas. An arrogant golden sword impaled a crimson mountain.

* * *

Jortica vibrated with excitement as she held a rigid parade-rest stance. She could hardly believe she had won.

The first Calonaden to ever do it.

She felt just as shocked as everyone when the two fools ahead of her knocked themselves out of the race. She wanted to laugh, dance, and sing with joy, but she kept control.

A familiar rush of sound slowly faded from her ears as she calmed. The noise of the storm that nearly killed her as a youth forever lingered in the back of her head. It stirred like this, but never to the intensity of the day her home disintegrated around her, leaving her mother dead, her father blind, and a scar on her face.

She had become used to it, in fact. Expecting it even. During the race, the cheer of the crowd and the booming of the Barber had all been masked by her inner storm.

Just outside the judge's pavilion, Jortica stood with Calamity, her blueblood mare, letting her old friend cool off. She continued to feel buoyant, despite the debate between the judges unfolding within the tent. Jortica couldn't hear it all, but from the snatches she could make out, it appeared

Lord Kendric didn't like the results.

Lady Izell's assured voice leaked past an open tent flap. "An interesting proposal, Lord Kendric, but consider the ramifications. We cannot halt work for another day just to redo this trivial competition. If we did, we certainly wouldn't be able to harvest enough lanicin to meet the emperor's specifications."

Lord Kendric blustered something Jortica didn't hear, but it wasn't hard to guess at his embarrassment. A Galathian would not be the Top Cadet for the first time. Lord Kendric and his friends weren't used to losing. The Galathians bullied their way across the known world, expanding their empire into every corner. How could they possibly lose this race? Well, Jortica had shown them one way.

Everyone had seen it, except for her father. Quilum of Eventide, both blind and not in attendance, would hear about this, though. He'd have to admit a daughter of fisherfolk could fight and ride like anyone else. She didn't have to follow him into a life at sea and make up for what he lost with his sight.

The lowborn cadet from the race rounded the pavilion, leading his black horse. Everyone knew the horse. Havoc towered over all the other mounts. How had a lowborn secured such a creature? Luck of the draw, no doubt. The cadet's name was something simple, like Kay or Guy. She couldn't quite remember. He was lanky with plinum hash marks splashed across his sharp cheekbones. His hair was also an in-between color of brown with copper flecks. His arms and legs had grown faster than the rest of him, making him seem a bit too thin. He had an honest face, though, and was not bad looking.

He hesitated when he saw her, then screwed up his courage and came closer. He extended his blood-stained sword hand. "Good race."

Jortica grabbed his hand and pulled him close. She hadn't meant to do that, but she was still feeling punchy from the contest. "Shhhhhh," she whispered in his ear. "I'm trying to listen." She nodded toward the pavilion and the loose tent flap.

"Dammit, woman!" Lord Kendric shouted. "You're playing a dangerous game."

"I play no game at all." Lady Izell sounded bored. "It is the race that's a *game*, not the serious matter you imagine. What if a native Calonaden wins? Better to appease the populace than to risk unrest, don't you think?"

"How will I explain it?" Kendric asked.

"Gilcres was right," Kay whispered. Or was it Joe? "The Lord Governor is trying to fix the race."

"What's your name, again?" Jortica asked.

"Jay."

Jortica smiled at having sort of got it right. To his credit, he didn't look crestfallen or insulted that she didn't remember his name.

"Yours?"

"Jortica. I've seen you about but don't remember ever meeting." Full-borns like herself were less common than Galathians at the academy. She didn't know of any other lowborn cadets in the ranks besides this one.

"I would have remembered that meeting," he said.

Jortica felt a little tingle run down her neck. His hand was warm in hers. Sweat formed on her palm, and she let go abruptly. Jay didn't squawk at the sudden release.

Gilcres picked that moment to come trudging around the corner. Jortica knew him as the biggest blowhard at the academy. He had some weight on him, but it didn't impede him. In fact, his arms were thick and shoulders broad. Jortica knew from experience he could swing a saber well, but he didn't move as quickly as she could.

Gilcres fixed a scornful stare on Jay. He pointed and fumed but couldn't get out anything but a growl. He spun and furiously whipped open the pavilion flap. "Aunt Izell, I demand to be heard by the judges!" he shouted.

Lady Izell turned a withering gaze upon Gilcres. "Nephew, it isn't graceful to make demands on your superiors." She nodded toward General Saben, who had his back to the opening.

General Saben slowly turned and regarded Gilcres with a scowl anchored in distaste. "Cadet Gilcres, why don't you come in?"

Gilcres frowned, took a breath to say something else but thought better of it, and slunk into the tent.

General Saben's gaze passed over Jortica, giving her an uneasy chill. As the headmaster of the academy, Saben demanded perfection from every cadet, no matter their background or connections. His attention proved so unpleasant many cadets memorized his schedule to avoid him. The whispers of his career before the academy contributed most to his sinister mystique. If the rumors that Saben killed King Nados were true, Jortica didn't know how Lady Izell could be in the same room with him.

The general scowled. "Cadets."

Jortica and Jay snapped sharp salutes.

"You may join us. Be quick about it."

They marched into the pavilion and stood beside Gilcres at parade-rest. Gilcres sneered at them but said nothing. He didn't hold a rigid stance as he picked clods of mud from his uniform.

Suddenly aware of her own less-than-perfect appearance, Jortica wished she hadn't lost her cadet's topper. Her hair had sprung from her hairpins and hung around her shoulders. Nothing could be done about it now. At least Jay wasn't perfect either, with his blood-stained uniform.

Lady Izell continued her discussion with Lord Kendric as if they weren't present. "What would the emperor say if you returned home with his shipment of lanicin significantly light? If a native were declared the winner today, my workers could get back to work and, with newly inspired enthusiasm, provide a little extra harvesting. It could be a personal gift. Would that take the sting off?"

Jortica suppressed a frown to keep her face blank. The race had not ended on the track. The outcome had to be negotiated behind closed doors, or tent flaps in this case. These three foreigners debated over what everyone had witnessed. Her father had warned her about the ability of Galathians to obscure the truth. She'd never seen it done so blatantly.

As Lord Kendric considered, Jortica watched Lady Izell's impassive expression. Cold as ice, she waited for him to see hers as the only way. Jortica suppressed a smile. Lanicin, Calonade's tool to move the Galathians, and Lady Izell, its master.

Gilcres cut in. "My Lord, you can't possibly take that offer seriously. The pride of Galathia is at stake."

"Cadet," General Saben growled. "Mind your tongue."

"Easy now, General. The boy has a point. The half-casting

clearly cheated." Kendric focused on Lady Izell. "Your nephew is a victim of a breach of the rules. Surely, he should be declared the victor."

Gilcres sneered with triumph, but Jay ignored it, fixing his gaze straight ahead. The lowborn had some spine.

"I believe the maxim of our academy is," Lady Izell said with an icy tone, "there are no rules on the battlefield. Do I have that right, General Saben?"

"You do, M'lady." Saben scowled. Lady Izell didn't back down from his sour expression.

"This is a race, not a battlefield." The pale stripes on Lord Kendric's cheeks grew pink to match the tinge of his bulbous nose.

"Quite so," Lady Izell said, "but the principle still applies. What are your thoughts, Headmaster?"

General Saben's voice rumbled through the tent in a tone that was indisputable. "Cadet Jortica finished the course four lengths ahead of the next competitor. Neither of these two," Saben nodded toward Jay and Gilcres, "bothered to finish in good order."

"But there were extenuating circumstances," Lord Kendric sputtered. "Surely you see that. It's clear the half-casting cheated."

Jortica struggled to keep from rolling her eyes. The only cheater in the tent was Gilcres.

"Only one rider showed the skill necessary to win." General Saben shook his head in apparent disgust.

"We should re-run the race," Kendric said, his voice rising.

"The race is over." General Saben's tone allowed no further discussion.

"That's ridiculous!" Gilcres cried.

Saben rounded on him with a fierce glare. "I advise you to keep silent, Cadet." The general spoke in a low, bowel-threatening growl. "You may find yourself forced to repeat your academy training."

Gilcres' eyes bulged along with his cheeks, but he kept his mouth shut.

"I agree with General Saben." Lady Izell held her bland expression. "Jortica's service has been exemplary through-out her training at the academy. She ran the race clean and won it by not giving up, taking the initiative at the end. Very commendable. I think my nephew might benefit from a dose of humility and you can profit from a generous gift."

Jortica couldn't keep her expression blank. Her lips parted into a grin. She fought to keep control as tears of pride welled in the backs of her eyes. In Lady Izell's face, she perceived a hint of the same pride, much better disguised than her own.

General Saben crossed his arms and nodded to Lady Izell. "Cadet Jortica has earned the Top Cadet award."

"Will you make the announcement, My Lord?" Lady Izell asked Kendric.

"I won't do it!" Lord Kendric stormed out of the pavilion. Gilcres glanced at General Saben's implacable expression, opened his mouth to protest, thought better of it, and followed Kendric out.

"Very well," Lady Izell said. "General Saben, I believe it's up to you."

General Saben turned his gaze on Jay. "You're dismissed, Cadet Jay." He grabbed the tent flap and held it open. Jay stepped outside and took the reins of the two horses. He winked at Jortica before the tent flap fell back down.

Jortica drew herself up straight as Lady Izell and General

Saben escorted her out onto the pavilion's stage, facing the crowd. Most of the spectators milled about on the track. All waited to hear the declaration of the winner. As the three of them walked out onto the platform, the restless crowd hushed.

General Saben pulled a dangling speaking trumpet to his mouth. "People of Calonade!" he proclaimed, his rough voice blasting from multiple horns mounted on the pavilion's roof. "I present this year's Top Cadet, Jortica of Eventide."

The crowd roared as Jortica stepped forward. The sound washed over her like the pounding of surf over breakers. As she waved to the audience, the roar came again and again. Jortica rose with it each time, shining with pride.

Chapter Three

The natives call the planet Urey. They were seeded in the beginning of the post-diaspora before blue stars were banned.
  —from the journal of Sephy Alcott, Standard Galactic Year 10555.

Kelstone Mountains, Day 288, Year 2998 local planetary calendar, Standard Galactic Year 14284

The clockwork crow soared over a forgotten valley hidden at the foot of a range of mountains tall enough to be the spine of the world. Below, the mist-shrouded treetops obscured the ruins of a once great city. The crow descended into the haze, searching for landmarks. Dropping between vine-covered towers and toppled spires, the silver bird circled a long-dry fountain and followed a barely visible cobblestone path. It swooped under a cracked archway and landed in the center of a courtyard. Two huge and crumbling marble lions stood guard on either side of a tomb.

The entrance of the mausoleum, blocked by a huge stone slab, rose abruptly from the ground. Ancient symbols were etched around its edges. The clockwork crow examined the massive door. It pecked dead vines and pulled them aside. Under the debris protruded a hollowed-out shelf. The crow hopped onto it and peered at its symbols with bright obsidian eyes.

With the clicking of gears, a panel on the bird's breast swung open. Deep within the crow's springs and cogs sat a small stone, like an egg waiting to hatch. A lever pushed the stone out of the bird's ticking chest. With another whir of machinery, the panel snapped shut.

The crow picked up the stone and, with mechanical precision, placed it inside the niche of the shelf. It fit perfectly. A symbol carved on the tomb flickered to life. Then another awoke, glowing faintly. Tiny matching symbols appeared on the egg-shaped stone. The sound of gears turning emerged from deep within the tomb.

With a grinding wrench, the shelf shuddered and withdrew into the door. The crow jumped free and capered on the ground as the shelf disappeared. The bird cocked its head, listening to the sound of clicking gears receding far below the surface. As the sound died away, the crow waited in the stillness.

Every marking on the tomb flashed with power. Light burst from the ancient structure's seams and the stone walls groaned as they stretched outward. The crow ducked away and pulled a wing up over its head to protect its eyes from the brilliance. Just as suddenly, it was gone. With a final distant rumble, the tomb became silent once more.

Metal clinking, the clockwork crow fluttered its feathers into place and strutted back and forth in front of the threshold. It cawed again and again, its rusty voice echoing throughout the city.

No answer came.

As the crow spread its wings, its metal feathers rang with the sound of swords unsheathing. Up it rose, flying away from the ruins toward a tall mountain range whose peaks reached beyond the clouds.

Catching an updraft, the clockwork crow soared along sheer cliff faces. In the last of the day's light, its mechanical eyes focused with the whirring of tiny gears, examining the red and gray rocks that reached up like jagged teeth.

A crevice, darkened by soot, appeared as a streak of black among the stone slabs. The crow dove, wingtips sparking against the stone as the passage narrowed.

The crow emerged into a vast, smoky cave. Dark passages and rough tunnels led away in all directions. With the apertures of its obsidian eyes wide open, the crow flew on, a faint glow from its body providing the only illumination. Dodging between rock pillars and flying over still pools, the crow maneuvered through the labyrinth.

The crow entered a cavern filled with an eerie green light. Luminous stones lined the cave walls and revealed its contents. Statues and paintings, parchments and scrolls, treasures and trash, all stacked haphazardly, sliding into the mud.

On a raised wooden platform sat furnishings for a study, including bookshelves, a desk, and a coat rack. Stones submerged in murky water held the deck level. Its near corner rested on the shoulder of a huge stone bust of a helmed warrior, which protruded from the muck. The warrior's face was set in a fierce grimace to discourage any trespasser. A stairway carved into the stone rose into the darkness at the far end of the platform.

The crow cawed and circled the statue. Receiving no answer, the bird landed on top of it and gave it an experimental peck.

"It's not easy to take me by surprise." The raspy voice came from the stairway. "Yet you did."

Startled, the crow lifted off the statue and circled for a better perch. It settled on the top of the coat rack, ruffling its feathers. A light ringing of metal echoed through the cavern.

A woman, hunched with age, carefully descended the stairs and shuffled onto the platform. Her skin had a green tinge. Faded runes and symbols decorated her flesh like remnants of ancient parchment.

The crow bowed its head to her and clicked its tongue.

"How amusing." She chuckled. "A machine with manners. Don't worry about startling me. It's a pleasant sensation after all these years." She approached to get a better look at the crow. "So, what are you?"

The clockwork crow opened its wings, stretching them wide. Scratched into its metal underbelly were two glowing symbols, much like the old woman's tattoos.

"So that's why you are so stealthy." Her withered face hovered just inches from the crow's body. "Whose rough work is this? Who is looking out of those eyes?" She tapped the bird on its metal head.

The crow cried out and snapped at her fingers, but she whipped them away from danger with surprising quickness.

"Now, now, no need to be offended. I respect the mysterious. I am the Oracle, after all," she said with a sly smile. "At least tell me why you're here."

The crow refolded its wing and bowed again. It straightened and cawed loudly several times.

The old woman scoffed. "That cannot be. I would already know of it."

The crow ruffled its feathers and let out a single indignant squawk.

"Of course, I doubt you." She pointed at the crow with a crooked finger. "You give me nothing but a short message without an origin. What did you expect?"

The crow bobbed its head and screeched a challenge.

"Well, the looking is easy, but concealing the looking from other lookers takes strong magic." She eyed the crow warily. "You could be a lure for me to reveal myself."

The crow clicked its beak at her and tapped a talon on the stone.

"Fine, but if you lie, I'll pull out your mainspring and make you part of my collection. You look very ornamental."

The crow's feathers ruffled again, but the old woman didn't notice. She had already closed her eyes. Along her wrinkled arms, several faded symbols lit up. A rune on her forehead shaped like an eye blinked to life. It held a steady green glow, lighting her face and revealing a timeless serenity.

"Ah," she sighed. "The Vinctus Stone *has* been moved to the ancient city of Aeterna."

The magic faded, and she opened her eyes. "Why take it there? If you know the secret entrance to my hiding place, why not simply deliver it to me? That would have saved me some trouble."

The clockwork crow cocked an eye and squawked.

"Thought I was in league with my sister, did you? Ha!" The old woman crossed her arms and frowned at the mechanical bird. "Well, I suppose caution is wise. I want the cycle to turn as much as you, which is why the Vinctus Stone must wake.

Tell me, who bade you to steal it from my sister?"

The crow stayed quiet for once.

"Ha! Another mystery, eh?" She wagged a finger at the crow. "You've turned the tables on an old fortune teller. Still, you brought me the news I most desired. Thank you."

The crow bowed a final time and stretched out, flapping its wings. It rose into the air.

The old woman struck like a rattlesnake, gripping the crow's legs with one bony hand. The bird flapped and struggled to break free, but her grip held. The crow's screams of rage echoed across the cavern. Metal wings struck out to slash flesh but bent against the woman's skin.

The Oracle traced a glowing finger along a symbol under its wing, and the bird fell limp. She cackled. "No, little messenger, you shall not escape. I have a message of my own to send."

Chapter Four

By the 200th year of my reign, I had conquered all my enemies and forged a lasting peace throughout the empire. I didn't know peace could be so bloody.

    —from Chronicles of Galathia by Rafykin, Urey, circa 2640 local planetary calendar.

Calonade, Day 288–289, Year 2998 local planetary calendar, Standard Galactic Year 14284

Jay sat back, propping his chair against the wall. He stayed near the corner of the officer's mess hall to keep from drawing attention. As he watched, Jortica rose to stand beside the autonomous piano, which wound down to quiet. Other cadets surrounded her and held the newly updated Top Cadet plaque. Her smile glowed as bright as the plaque's embossed brass.

Jortica held it in place while the barkeep turned the thick screws. Once the plaque was affixed to the wall, the crowd's cheer echoed along the vaulted ceilings.

"To Jortica! For Calonade!"

Jay raised his ale with the others. He had to face it. She

won. The first Calonaden to take the prize was a momentous event. Jay swallowed a fair portion of ale to tamp down his disappointment.

He could only hope he'd put in a good enough showing to be considered for the Horse Division, but he'd probably be joining the Calonade Foot. That meant long days marching up and down the Kelstone Mountains, but at least he wouldn't have to go back to the castle.

Gilcres and a handful of unpleasant Galathians huddled around a table, glaring at Jortica as they drank their thick beer. They tried their best to drown out the good cheer of the others by toasting Gilcres and boasting of the glory that awaited him.

The double doors to the mess hall clanged open and Jay leaned to the edge of his chair to see a dozen riders from the Horse Division stomp inside, their black leather cloaks dusty from the road. Each carried a stack of packages wrapped in oilskin.

"Eyes front!" a voice sang out. Commander Kahela strode in behind her troops. Three circlets shone brightly on her collar. She carried a single packet.

Jay jumped to his feet along with everyone else, his heart beating fast in his chest. Commander Kahela, the toughest officer in the military and the highest ranking full-born Calonaden, led companies of horse soldiers beyond Calonade's Outer Gate every day, policing the Frontier. The Galathians considered it a hardship to avoid, but Kahela's riders were the best of the best, and Jay burned to join them.

Jay had only seen Commander Kahela from a distance. At nearly six feet tall, she almost met Jay's height. She had a sleek outline that was all muscle. Her steely eyes scanned the crowded room as she removed her riding gloves.

"Cadet Jortica Eventide, come forward," Kahela barked.

Jortica stepped up quickly and snapped a salute. Commander Kahela took a moment to look her up and down. Next to each other, both women stood strong and fierce.

Kahela nodded in satisfaction. "At ease, all," she said in a powerful voice. "Cadets, I came in person tonight both to congratulate Jortica and to personally deliver your commissions." She thumped the packet in her hands. "General Saben allowed me the honor."

Commander Kahela leaned in and spoke to Jortica in a low voice. Jortica laughed as they conversed. Jay couldn't help but burn with envy. Earning the favor of the Horse Division Commander was a hell of a way to start a career. Jay had come so close. He knew he should be proud of his fellow cadet, but he'd need a couple pints more to get there.

"Jortica of Eventide," Commander Kahela continued. "I am pleased to offer you a place in the Horse Division. Congratulations, Lieutenant."

"Thank you, Commander." Jortica held her chin high.

Jay felt another pang of jealousy as the commander handed Jortica the sealed paper and pinned a golden lieutenant's circlet on her collar. She saluted crisply. Jortica returned the salute, looking like she would burst with pride.

"My aides will hand out the rest of the orders." Kahela addressed the room. "And I believe there was something of a celebration. As you were." Commander Kahela motioned for Jortica to join her.

Jay muttered into his cup. "Great for her." He downed another gulp. He'd been denied plenty as someone of mixed descent, but he thought he had the race in hand. Still, a

Calonaden as Top Cadet was a change for the better.

One by one, the cadets were called forward to receive their orders, along with the symbol of their new rank. They ordered many of them to report to the Ship Division, which made sense because most Calonadens grew up sailing and fishing. Others received the dreaded Foot Division assignment.

"Gilcres of House Justinkeel," an officer called.

Gilcres swaggered over and grabbed his papers. He joined the other Galathians as they gloated over their assignments.

"Command Division." Gilcres' voice boomed over the crowd. "Only natural for the *true* Top Cadet." His friends chuckled and slapped his back.

"This one only has the letter *J* on it," a voice said from the front of the room.

Jay looked to see a Galathian officer in a Horse Division uniform—a rare sight. He was holding a packet of orders. Jay held his breath. His fate rested in those papers.

"Over there, Captain Fauden." Kahela pointed Fauden in Jay's direction.

"Oh, right, the orphaned half-casting. Thank you, Commander," Fauden said over his shoulder as he moved toward Jay. Plinum bands marked regular lines down his face except for a few which curved to accent his cheekbones. Not the perfect specimen of Galathian breeding, but he carried the rank of captain in a traditional Calonaden assignment. Working for Commander Kahela, no less. Might be more to this one than Galathia typically offered.

Jay held his face blank at hearing the slur. He wasn't really from anywhere besides the castle and he couldn't claim to be a member of any house of Calonade, no matter how modest. Leaving off a surname meant only one thing. Half-casting.

Malformed, broken, a mistake and worse. Except for the times they called him a *castle rat*, most Calonadens referred to him as *Jay of the Castle*, or *Jay Castle* for short. He'd been the tenth orphan to come along since the castle started taking them in. With the Galathians in charge of the documents, all he got was the tenth letter as a name.

Fauden dropped the packet on the table. "Here's your assignment, Lieutenant. Try not to disgrace yourself." He strode away.

Jay grinned. He only paid attention to one word: *lieutenant*. Not bad for a former castle rat.

Jay took the packet and tore open the wax seal. He held his breath, hoping to read the words *Horse Division*.

They weren't there.

Report to Captain Gaven of the Castle Guard.

The Castle Guard!

He read the words again, then a third time. He forced himself to read on, hoping it wasn't true.

You will receive training as a Castle Messenger. Jay's mind reeled. Shuttling letters for Galathian royals? How could this be?

Jay sat down, staring at the pages in shock. He had joined the military to leave the confines of the castle, and now he was forced to return. A sour taste rose in Jay's mouth, and his disappointment flared. If only he had won the race.

What would he tell Gran? She would probably be glad to have him back in the castle with her. However, she had insisted he join the academy four years before. *You can't be a cook's boy all your life*, she had said. *You can be more.* Looks like he wouldn't become much more than he was when he started.

A kick to his chair brought Jay out of his brooding.

"Hey, half-casting." A familiar voice barked in his ear. "Get me another drink."

Jay glared up at the face of the oaf who had ruined his chances. "I think you've had enough," he told Gilcres through gritted teeth.

Three Galathians stood behind Gilcres with nasty grins.

"Junior officers serve their betters in the mess hall. Get me another drink." Gilcres poured the remainder of the sticky Galathian beer on Jay's boots and thrust the mug at him.

Jay held himself in check and calculated his chances. Gilcres was taller and weighed more but was not a better fighter. It would be easy—and sweet revenge—to knock Gilcres off his self-appointed pedestal, then make him clean his boots. But that's why Gilcres had brought friends.

Against four, the odds weren't so good. He was headed for the castle, where he would be at the mercy of the royals—just another servant. Would anyone believe a Galathian had started the fight? Would anyone care? Things were bad for him now, but fighting would only make things worse. Gilcres, on the other hand, had nothing to lose.

Jay tried to keep his cool. "Let me remind you we're the same rank. You'll have to get it yourself."

Jay pushed the cup firmly back at Gilcres.

"Oh, really?!" Conversations around the room stopped as people craned their heads to look. "Let me remind *you*. I'm royalty. I've always outranked you, and I always will. I'm Galathian and you're not. In fact, no one really knows what you are, huh? Not even you, half-casting."

Jay flew forward, seizing Gilcres by the collar. He yanked the big man to his knees. "Don't ever say that to me again."

Gilcres' friends grabbed Jay. Two broke Jay's grip while the other forced him against the wall. Gilcres rose to his feet, his uniform askew but a smirk on his lips. Jay tried to lash out and wipe that expression off his face, but the Galathians had him pinned.

Gilcres reared back, and Jay braced, but the blow didn't come. Jortica sprang to Jay's defense, bringing a group of Calonade officers in her wake. Hands and arms crisscrossed Gilcres' gray coat, holding him back. Jortica stopped in front of Gilcres, steely-eyed, daring him to try something.

Jay tensed against the bodies holding him back, but no one gave him any room to move. Calls of "break it up!" came from the rest of the crowd.

"Let go of me, you raw-cast fools," Gilcres yelled. "It's over."

The Calonadens glared at Gilcres for the slur, but they let go. He brushed his wrinkled uniform and gave a curt nod to his friends, who released Jay.

"This loser ought to be tossed in the brig." Gilcres pointed at Jay. "Or hauled away to Karpathode—only place he's good for."

Without thinking, Jay started toward him again, but Jortica held him back, a hard hand against his chest.

"Stand down, Lieutenant," she growled in his ear.

Jortica's breath tingled on his face. His anger subsided as a new feeling rose, threatening an embarrassing response. Jay shifted his stance and shook his head to regain control.

For a moment, Jay and Gilcres glared at each other over Jortica's shoulders, both waiting for the other to make a move.

Gilcres held up his hands and backed away, chuckling. "It

makes sense now. I know how you almost beat me today.”

“Almost? Really?” Jay said.

“It wasn’t you. It was your horse.” Gilcres turned to the crowd. “His horse was faster, that’s all.”

The audience groaned. Everyone knew riding was far more than the horse.

Jay felt a finger of cold run down his spine. Gilcres was predictable, always ready with another insult, but this seemed different. He was up to something.

“I’m working for Lord Kendric now. I need a better mount and Havoc is the best.” Gilcres whirled back to Jay. “Tomorrow, I’ll take Havoc for myself.”

Jay froze. “Havoc isn’t yours to take.”

“I clearly need a bigger horse than you.” Gilcres looked down at Jay’s slighter form. The Galathians laughed.

Jay’s stomach turned over uneasily, but he stood firm. “There are plenty of horses for you to choose from. I’ve always ridden Havoc. He’s—”

“Yours?” Gilcres interrupted with a snort. “He’s not. That horse is Galathian property, just like everything in Calonade. We can assign any horse to anyone.”

“That’s a load of *horse manure*,” Jortica hissed. “Everyone knows Havoc is assigned to Jay.” The crowd muttered in agreement.

“Only for cadet training.” Gilcres sneered. “Training is over. Tomorrow he’ll be reporting to the Castle Guard. Won’t get any horse at all.”

The floor seemed to be falling out from beneath Jay.

“Impossible,” Jortica said. “A guard? Tell him, Jay.”

Gilcres mocked Jortica’s voice. “Yes, tell me, Jay. Go on and deny it.”

"That's enough, Lieutenant," a quiet voice said behind Gilcres.

Gilcres spun round to snarl a response but found Commander Kahela at his elbow. He looked straight into her eyes, but her glare still knocked the bluster out of him. "Y-yes, Commander."

Kahela's eyes were hard, and her voice harder. "Lieutenant, your choice of mount is of no interest to me. How you choose to conduct yourself is very important. Stay out of trouble this evening." She glared at everyone in the room. "This party is over. You are *all* dismissed."

Gilcres rallied and tried to stand his ground. "Commander, I'm Galathian royalty working for Lord Kendric. You best watch your step."

Kahela smiled. It was the kind of grin that greeted an enemy on the battlefield.

Gilcres faltered and turned away, but he found solace with his cronies as they swaggered out the door. The rest of the crowd dispersed soon after, but more than one officer shot a backward glance. Kahela gathered her riders and marched out.

"Is it true, then?" Jortica asked once the room was quiet. "You're assigned to the Castle Guard?"

Jay swallowed hard. "It's worse than that. I report to the Guard, but I'll only be a messenger."

Jortica started back in shock. "I'm so sorry, Jay. It should be you in the Horse Division, not me."

"No, we should both be there, and Gilcres should be at the bottom of the harbor. Don't ever believe you don't deserve this."

Jortica relaxed a little. "But Jay, if Gilcres asks for your horse, I think he can get it. Like he reminds us every five minutes, he *is* Lady Izell's nephew."

"I'm not worried," Jay replied.

Jortica gave him a skeptical look. "You seem worried."

Jay sighed. "All right, I am. Threatening Havoc gets under my skin, but it's more than that. Something else is going on."

"What?"

"I don't know. It's just odd. I got a lousy assignment out of the violet sky. How did Gilcres know? I just found out myself."

Jortica's eyes widened. "He must've had something to do with it. You can request a transfer. Once you're in good with your commanding officer; it's just a matter of time."

And some bribes. Jay knew Captain Gaven, but there would be a whole chain of command above him to navigate. No one would offer that kind of money to help a former castle servant. He didn't have much hope. "Thanks. I'll figure out something."

"Hey, this isn't goodbye yet. I'll see you before I ride out."

"Right," Jay agreed, trying to avoid thinking about it. In truth, he dreaded seeing her leave without him.

"Until then, Lieutenant Jay." She offered him a formal salute.

He returned it. "Until then, Lieutenant Jortica."

* * *

The next morning at dawn, Jay raced to the stables. Situated between the parade grounds and the academy barracks, it wasn't far. He hurried through the labyrinth of corrals to reach the barn that held Havoc's stall. Given yesterday's excitement, the stable hands weren't up and about. Jay understood because his head ached from too much ale and too little sleep, but he pushed the pain aside. He had to talk to Horsemaster Zabe before Gilcres showed up. There must be something he could do to keep Havoc.

As Jay entered the yard, he stopped short. Havoc stood outside the stables already fitted with Command Division tack.

"Good morning, Lieutenant," General Saben growled from behind him.

Jay snapped to attention as Saben approached. The general looked as polished as he had the day of the race.

"At ease." Saben stood next to Jay for a moment, jaw clamped on his unlit pipe. Jay held his breath, wondering if he would get an earful for eavesdropping outside Lady Izell's tent.

The general slipped his pipe into a waistcoat pocket. "That horse is a fine animal."

"Um, yes, sir." Havoc snorted at Jay's voice and ambled over to him. Jay reached out and rubbed Havoc's nose as the horse nuzzled his neck.

"We'll see if Gilcres can handle him."

Jay turned. "You know about that, sir?"

"Yes, Gilcres was here last night talking with Horsemaster Zabe. I just happened to overhear. Said I'd be here in the morning to saddle Havoc personally."

"Yes, sir." Jay nearly choked on the words. If General Saben was against him, then there was no way to stop Gilcres.

"I'm sure Gilcres will be along shortly."

Jay nodded but didn't respond.

"You know," Saben said, after a long, quiet pause, "I knew Havoc's sire."

Jay turned in surprise. "Sir?"

"A battle-tested warhorse. I rode with him many times. Havoc has the same lines." As he gazed at Havoc, General Saben actually smiled. He was known for showing no emotion, growling out his unquestionable orders with a heart of stone. Now, there was something different in his tone, something personal.

"Sir, did you fight at the Kettlebone Pass?" The question burst out before Jay could think better of it.

The smile disappeared from Saben's face. He stared off into the distance. "Yes, Lieutenant, I did."

Jay had never talked to someone on the Galathian side of the battle. At least not about personal matters. He knew by heart, like every cadet, the *official* version of the fighting. The rebel king held the Kettlebone Pass, but when he fell, the Galathians were victorious. Calonadens are good fighters, went the story, they just need leadership.

He took a breath to steel himself and went on. "One of the fallen in that battle was my father. A northerner like you. Did you know a soldier named Dunken?" He didn't mention that his father had deserted and fought for Calonade. Saben would probably call his father a traitor, and Jay didn't need to hear that.

The general considered his question as Jay held his breath. Saben shook his head. "Sorry, Lieutenant. I don't know that name."

Jay released his breath slowly. No one seemed to know much about his father, not even Gran.

"Ah, finally," General Saben growled. "Here's Gilcres now."

Gilcres had already gotten his hands on a new uniform. His golden circlet shone from the collar of a crisp red military coat, clearly tailored to fit. A broad-brimmed riding hat adorned his head in the Galathian style. He held a silver pocket watch with a handsome gold chain. It glinted in the morning light.

Jay forced himself to remain calm as his anger swelled. He would have to obtain a used coat previously worn by another soldier. The watch—he'd never have anything that fine. And the tin-striped, arrogant fool was here to take his horse.

"Good morning, sir. I see I'm right on time." Gilcres snapped the watch closed and offered General Saben a lazy salute.

"Might want to check that timepiece, Lieutenant. You're late."

"Sir, I assure you it's of the finest Galathian construction," Gilcres protested.

"Doesn't mean it's set correctly." General Saben arched an eyebrow.

Gilcres ignored the comment and slapped Havoc on the rump. "Isn't he a fine horse? I've requisitioned him for the Command Division. Did you come to see me off, sir?"

Jay's stomach tightened again. He couldn't watch Gilcres take Havoc, but if he tried to prevent it, he'd just be tossed in the brig. Either way, he'd never see Havoc again.

"One moment," General Saben said. "Havoc's assigned rider hasn't been decided yet."

"It hasn't?" The question burst from Jay before he could hold back.

"Quiet, Lieutenant," General Saben growled as he gave Jay a warning glare.

Jay clapped his mouth shut.

Gilcres shot a sneer of satisfaction Jay's way, then turned back to the general. "But it has, sir. The horsemaster promised me my pick of mounts."

"I'm sure he did," Saben said. "But Zabe seems to be detained. Likely sleeping off the rum you bribed him with."

"Sir, I didn't—"

"Save it," General Saben snapped. "Here's the deal. If you can ride him, you can have him. If not, the horsemaster finds you another mount. Got it, Lieutenant?"

Jay blinked in confusion. What was Saben doing?

Gilcres seemed unfazed by this new requirement. "Yes, sir. Won't be a problem, sir." He stepped into the stirrup and swung his large bulk into the saddle. Havoc reared up and screamed. Gilcres lost his grip on the reins and fell hard to the ground.

Jay leaped forward to calm Havoc, but the big horse settled down once Gilcres was off his back.

"What the—? Stupid animal!" Gilcres sputtered as he picked himself up. "Hands off, half-casting!"

Jay couldn't help smiling. "Good boy," he whispered to Havoc. Saben gave him another look of warning and he backed away.

General Saben turned back to Gilcres. "You all right there, son?"

Gilcres stammered. "Of course. I—I don't know what happened, sir. The dumb thing is still wild. Doesn't know how to handle a real rider."

Jay ground his teeth but kept quiet.

"Care to try again?" Saben asked.

"Yes, sir!"

Gilcres patted Havoc's neck and spoke softly. The tone was soothing, but the words were still full of malice. "Easy. Easy now, you dumb animal. Let me ride you or I'll turn you into fish bait." Gilcres eased himself up and slowly onto the saddle.

As soon as he sat down, Havoc reared again. The big horse thrashed the air with his forelegs. Gilcres tumbled off Havoc's back and landed with a thump. He grimaced as he rubbed his sore backside.

Once again, Jay leaped to Havoc's side and barely kept himself from laughing.

"It was him!" Gilcres pointed at Jay from the ground. "He did something to the saddle. Look at his face!"

"I saddled the horse myself, Lieutenant," General Saben said.

Gilcres pleaded. "Let me try again, sir. I'll break him."

"He's already been trained, son," General Saben said with a stern look.

Gilcres started in on more protests, but Saben held up a hand. "No, Lieutenant, it seems this is not the mount for you. He comes from a spirited line."

Gilcres' mouth opened in shock. Jay was pretty stunned himself.

"Hmmm," Saben pulled his pipe from his pocket and inspected it. "I think you need a tamer beast. Perhaps a gelding."

"But, sir, I—"

"You are dismissed, Lieutenant," General Saben said.

Gilcres rose and stared in astonishment. His mouth opened

and closed a few times.

"I said *dismissed*," the general growled.

Gilcres stalked away, muttering under his breath. "Sway back nag. Only good for fish bait." Jay remained where he stood, uncertain what might happen next.

General Saben tapped the pipe into his palm. "I was thinking," he said, "this horse should be assigned to someone who can handle him, or we'll end up with a lot of rookies with bruised rear ends."

"Yes, sir, you might." Jay dared to hope.

"I hear *you* can ride him. Is that true, Lieutenant?"

"Yes, sir!"

"Then he's yours. Permanently." Saben turned to go. "Oh, one more thing. When you change Havoc into Castle Guard tack, be sure and remove the burr that's under his saddle."

Jay barely kept himself from laughing as the general strode from the stables.

Chapter Five

The humans of Urey have evolved for over 8000 Standard Galactic Years without interference. They are perfect for my experiment.
—private communication from Melrayis Valdez to Sephy Alcott, Standard Galactic Year 10555

Calonade, Day 290, Year 2998 local planetary calendar, Standard Galactic Year 14284

A Galathian captain Jay hadn't met stomped through the cadet quarters shouting, "Last day! Make it a good one. Clear this place out." A rude way to wake, but it felt familiar. Jay would be glad to move on from this daily ritual.

Jay straightened his coat for the hundredth time. He had found a second-hand uniform in a barter shop in town. It almost fit, but the sleeves were short. It had cost all his coin. Still, the only slightly faded Galathian red wool looked sharper than the gray cadet uniform.

Jay shouldered the trunk and hurried to the door. He had transferred Havoc, his saber and pistol, and the rest of his riding kit to the castle stables the night before. Jay only had his cadet uniform, civilian clothes, and a few other items in the trunk.

Outside, four wagons trundled up to the cadet barracks, each with a placard: *Command, Foot, Ship,* and *Guard.* The first one looked like a royal carriage and was filled with newly minted Galathian officers. Jay could hear Gilcres' blustering laugh among them. The next two wagons were stout examples of Calonaden build, and the last sagged on its axles from age. Nothing testified more accurately to the prestige of each division of the army. The Horse Division obviously didn't bother with wagons.

Jay clomped down the barracks steps and headed for the last wagon. Before he got three steps, his foot caught, and he went down hard, spilling the contents of his trunk. He pushed himself out of the dirt to hails of laughter from Gilcres and his lads. The owner of the offending boot that tripped him was his favorite Galathian.

"Having a little trouble with your footing, half-casting?" Gilcres looked down at him with an evil smile.

Jay swallowed his first retort. Once again, Gilcres had the numbers. Jay dusted himself off and gathered his things with a brooding silence. Gilcres helped by picking up his cadet jacket and tossing it under the carriage. The carriage pulled away, and the Galathians hopped on, leaving Jay to scrounge his jacket out of the dirt.

By the time Jay carried his trunk to the wagon marked *Guard,* the driver waved him away. "Too full. You'll have to carry it yourself."

"Come on." Jay held up his trunk so one of the soldiers could take it.

"No room," a Galathian jeered. The Calonadens ignored him. The driver whipped the horses, and the wagon pulled away, leaving Jay standing alone.

Jay cursed. He wanted to see Jortica off, but now he wouldn't have time. Carrying the trunk, he probably wouldn't make it to the castle gate to report for duty with the rest of the new castle guards. Starting off badly on a new assignment might scuttle his chances of requesting a transfer. Jay ground his teeth, stooped, and wrestled the trunk onto a shoulder. Scowling with disgust, he started for the castle gate.

Jay felt like kicking himself again for losing the race. If he'd won, he'd be leaving this cursed city right now, riding beside Jortica, instead of going back to the place he dreaded most.

Gray slabs of rock carved from the Kelstone Mountains were stacked twenty feet high to make up the walls surrounding the castle. Wide towers with cannon emplacements rose periodically along its length. Galathian banners snapped in the breeze on either side of the looming gatehouse. All travelers passed through its huge twin cogwheel doors, currently rolled fully open. People stepped carefully across the slots for the gear teeth of the thick metal mechanism. Jay tried to blend in with the crowd as he moved through the gatehouse entrance and into the castle grounds.

"Hold up, there." A castle guard stepped in Jay's path. "Who might you be?"

Jay set down the trunk and saluted the Galathian officer. "Lieutenant Jay, reporting for duty, sir."

"Ha! Funny," the Galathian lieutenant said. "Don't make jokes like that, half-casting. It will get you killed. Now, state your business and tell me why you have on a guard's uniform."

"Excuse me, sir, what's your name?" Jay asked in his calmest tone of voice.

"A polite half-casting. That's nice. Dothery is my name."

"I have orders, Lieutenant Dothery." Jay reached inside his coat and produced his papers. He hoped to get through this hazing quickly to catch up with his unit.

"What's going on, sir?" Another guard approached. This one was Calonaden.

"Sergeant Matis, examine this man's papers while I keep an eye on him."

Matis shrugged and accepted Jay's papers. "Looks like orders to me." He handed them back to Dothery.

Dothery held the papers up to the light. "These are authentic. That's the old headmaster's scrawl, all right. We have a half-casting lieutenant here, Sarge. Joining our unit."

"Astonishing, sir," Matis said.

Dothery slapped the papers into his empty palm and scowled at Jay. "This a secondhand coat? Tailoring is a bit off. Suspicious. A disguise?"

"No, sir," Matis said. "Only garment he can afford, more like."

It was true, but Jay didn't have to admit it.

"Papers say he's assigned to us as a messenger." The lieutenant snorted the last word. "Well, Sarge, if you're going to make a half-casting an officer, he's probably best suited to be a messenger."

"Best thing for 'em," Matis said.

"All right, stand at ease," Dothery said to Jay.

Jay held his hand out to retrieve his orders.

Dothery slapped the papers into Jay's palm. "Try to stay out of trouble. Maybe rely on your Galathian half, 'eh."

Jay suppressed several non-polite responses to that ridiculous statement and stuffed the papers back into his pocket.

As he stooped to retrieve his trunk, a boot slammed down on it.

Dothery grinned. "You better leave that with us. Don't want you to enter your service with undue burdens."

Jay glanced at the trunk and decided it wasn't worth it. The cadet jacket had sentimental value because Gran had stitched it for him four years before. She'd forgive him for losing it. He should have left it all behind in the barracks.

"Does he look familiar, sir?" Matis focused on Jay's face. "The race. He's the half-casting that almost won the race."

Dothery stepped in close to Jay's face. "I think you're right, Sarge. He knocked our boy off the track and let the Calonaden girl win."

Matis glanced at Dothery but only said, "Tragic day."

Dothery stared into Jay's eyes, only inches away.

"Terrible day." Jay spoke in a voice laced with danger.

Dothery stepped back but then laughed, clapping Jay on the shoulder. "That's the spirit. I like it when everyone knows their place. Right, Sergeant?"

Matis nodded, but Jay saw his eyes roll. "Yes, sir."

"We're going to get a redo of that event," Dothery said. "The results will be much different, I think, if they keep the cheaters out of it."

"Yes, sir." Jay knew they didn't agree on who might be the cheater. But it didn't matter. Even if a rematch were held, Jay knew no second chance awaited him.

Jay marched away from the gate and headed into the guard mustering yard. Through the archway, he could hear Captain Gaven finishing his orientation speech. He was one of the few Calonadens to keep his position throughout the occupation. How many times had he heard this as a boy? It had once been exciting to pretend to be a guard. Now he felt condemned.

Jay slid into the courtyard at the back of the formation just as the new guardsmen were dismissed. He lined up to march to the barracks with the rest. Captain Gaven towered nearby. The Calonaden was as tall as a blue mountain pine with biceps as thick as branches. His usually thoughtful eyes blazed in anger as Jay came near. He blocked Jay's path and let everyone else go. Jay braced himself for a thorough, military-style reprimand.

"My office. Now."

Gaven spun and marched away. Jay jumped to keep up. They entered Gaven's office, and Jay tried to look sufficiently humbled. In the sparse room sat a rolltop desk and a chair. A couple of oil lamps adorned the walls. Papers lay scattered across the desk along with an ink bottle, a set of goose quills, and a burnt candle.

Affixed to the opposite wall was a rack of weapons. A dozen muzzle-loading muskets were neatly stacked alongside oiled and sharpened sabers. The brass handles of flintlock pistols and the blades of pikes gleamed in the sunlight. Several kegs of powder and shot were stacked nearby.

"You're late, Lieutenant!" Gaven thundered. He slammed the door shut and stood with his jaw jutting out at Jay. "Is this how they taught you to behave at the academy?"

"Sir, no, sir." Jay snapped to attention.

Gaven crossed his muscular arms and glared at Jay. "You missed my entire speech."

"I know it well, sir. 'It's a noble duty,'" Jay quoted, "'to serve at the very heart of Calonade.' You haven't changed the speech in years."

"That's because it's an excellent speech." Gaven's hand

knifed out toward Jay's chest. "Since you're such a know-it-all, you must already know what discipline you'll receive for your disrespect."

"Happy to muck out the stables, sir," Jay said with a genuine smile. At least in the stables, he'd have Havoc for company.

"It's *punishment*. You're not supposed to be happy about it." Gaven shook his head in disbelief. "But it turns out you won't be reporting to the barracks or the stables, because I have new orders for you."

The smile faded from Jay's face. Another change in assignment? What could be worse than a messenger?

"At ease, Jay." Gaven relaxed his own stance. "Don't look so worried. Castle messenger is not your assignment."

"So, it *was* a mistake, sir?"

"No. You're a messenger." Gaven lowered his voice. "But you've been assigned as a *private* messenger." Jay wondered what would make this clamorous man so quiet. "You'll be working for Lady Izell."

Jay's eyebrows shot up in surprise. He had never heard of such a position. However, working for Her Ladyship meant he wasn't at every simpering royal's beck and call.

"Don't assume you're getting off easy," Gaven continued. "You will report to Lady Izell's private council chamber immediately, and every morning hereafter. No days off. Plenty of extra training. That's not the hardest part."

So far, it didn't sound hard at all. He wanted to be saddle sore from riding Havoc all day for the Horse Division. He wasn't really an accurate judge of hardship.

"Now listen close." Gaven locked eyes with Jay. "Before I tell you the rest, you tell me if the time you spent at the academy brought out more Galathian in you."

"Excuse me, sir."

"You know, did they straighten out your stripes?"

Jay groaned inwardly but kept his face from showing his disgust. No full-born Calonaden would ever have to testify to the content of their blood. "No, sir, quite the opposite."

"Good." Gaven smiled. "Keep it that way, Jay. I should've known the way you threw the race to our girl, Jortica, but I had to ask."

"But I didn't—"

"You'll be under the direct command of Her Ladyship," Gaven continued. "However, if asked, you are to say you run messages for me."

"Can I actually say that to a superior officer?"

"No, but those are your orders."

Jay couldn't believe he was being ordered to lie.

"I know you have questions," Gaven said. "You'll get answers from Her Ladyship. Before you see her, I need to know you can keep your mouth shut. Because, if they find out, certain government officials will court-martial you and me both."

Jay guessed he meant Lord Kendric and his Galathian followers. Jay was no fan of Galathia and talked to his Galathian superiors as little as possible, but he never actually risked any disobedience. However, the assignment sounded a hell of a lot better than a regular messenger. Eventually, some back-channel string-pulling from the former queen might get him into the Horse Division.

"Yes, sir," Jay said, "I believe I can."

"You're a credit to your kind." Gaven strode forward, offering his gigantic hand. Puzzled, Jay reached out and had his hand shaken vigorously. "Jay, I've known you since you were a boy running around the kitchens, and I'm proud to see you back. Welcome home."

"Um. Thank you, sir." Jay tried not to cringe at Gaven's words. They were kindly meant, even if painfully misguided. Being welcomed back to the castle felt more like being owned than returning home.

It's just for now.

Captain Gaven clapped Jay heartily on the shoulder. "Good, lad. Now, report to Lady Izell. Best not to keep her waiting." He gave Jay's shoulder a final mighty squeeze and then strode out of the office.

A meeting with Lady Izell in her council chamber. Jay's head spun. Everything he had expected this morning had been turned upside down. With only one place to get answers, Jay headed into the castle.

* * *

Jay took a deep breath as he stood before the entrance to the room in which Lady Izell met government ministers, foreign officials, and Galathian overlords. A Fromeathian stood guard at the entrance, giving Jay a menacing stare.

"You're late, boy," growled Oryk, Lady Izell's bodyguard and manservant.

Jay controlled his instinct to flinch away. Oryk had tough, ropy muscles and possessed a sour face. Jay knew he had come to Calonade long ago with Lady Izell when she was a new bride to King Nados. He didn't seem to age; he just became surlier. Oryk had the meanest pinch in the kingdom. He used to draw welts on Jay's tender underarm for the slightest transgression.

"What's it to you, Sergeant?" Jay jutted out his chin, daring the man to try his pinch now.

"Ha!" Oryk burst out. "Look who's been made an officer." He shook his head in disgust. "Her Ladyship and your gran have been waiting for you, sir." Oryk spat out the last word like a sour pit as he held open the door.

My gran! Jay opened his mouth in surprise as he slipped past Oryk's notorious reach. *By the goddess, Gran is crafty.* He wouldn't be able to dodge her now.

Inside, he found the large, domed room brightly lit by skylights. A tray of Fromeathian crystal adorned a long conference table. The entire room sparkled, and the dazzle from the wine glasses hurt his eyes.

At the far end of the room stood Lady Izell, deep in conversation with his gran. No two could look more opposite from each other. Lady Izell, like most northerners, stood taller than Jay. She dressed in white to match her mostly plinum complexion. Her clothing glittered like ice under a bright sun. Gran was short, even for a full-born Calonaden, and wore the plain and practical garments of a servant.

Jay swallowed. He had been in this room a hundred times, but never as something other than a cook's boy. Today, he was a freshly minted lieutenant. The distinct possibility of getting a lecture from his grandmother in front of Lady Izell made him squirm.

"Ahem." Jay cleared his throat loudly, setting his shoulders straight, gathering his courage. "Lieutenant Jay reporting for duty, Your Ladyship."

"At ease," Lady Izell said in her smooth voice. She brushed a piece of lint off her long sleeve and nodded to his gran. "Before we begin, Sedia would like to speak with you."

Gran hustled past Lady Izell and stopped short of him, looking him up and down. *Here we go.*

Without warning, she hugged the air out of him.

"Ooof," he grunted. He couldn't tell if this was more or less embarrassing than being yelled at.

Jay looked over the top of Gran's gray hair to see how the former queen of Calonade would react. Lady Izell didn't pay any attention as she drifted serenely to a window and peered into the gardens beyond.

Close to his gran's ear, Jay quietly asked, "What are you doing?"

She pulled away. "I had to see you. Now, how are you, child? I imagine things aren't as expected?" She held his hands in her own. They were just as he remembered them, wrinkled yet strong. He didn't want to meet her eyes, but Gran didn't give him a choice. A warm and knowing expression held its familiar place on her face. As usual, Jay couldn't keep anything from her.

"I messed up at the competition," he blurted. "When I didn't win, I thought it didn't matter. I thought I'd still make you proud. Instead, I'm back here." Jay's eyes burned with shame.

"Hmph." Gran shook her head at him. "Jay, you *did* make me proud by standing up to that bully. Your actions during the race are why you're here today. And by contriving to lose, you made it easier to explain your new assignment."

"Wait, you know about my assignment? Gaven said to keep it to myself."

"Who do you think got you the job?" Gran replied with a mischievous smile. "Now, 'Zell will explain it all."

'Zell? Jay raised his eyebrows. He had never heard the former queen referred to by a nickname. She seemed far too proper. Lady Izell made no objection as she crossed the room to Gran and put a hand on her shoulder.

"Lieutenant. May I call you Jay?" Lady Izell asked him in her calm voice. Though she seemed reserved, she regarded him with intense interest.

Jay nodded.

"You come highly recommended. I'm glad to have you assigned to me."

"Thank you, M'lady." Jay didn't know what Gran had gotten him into.

Gran nodded to Lady Izell. "You two will get on fine, you'll see." She turned and gave Jay another quick hug. "You'll have a lot to do, but you can do it." She clapped her hands together and smoothed her prim apron. "Now, I need to get back to work. I'll check on you later."

As his no-nonsense grandmother bustled out of the room, Jay felt even more nervous. He wished she wasn't leaving him alone with Lady Izell.

For a long moment Lady Izell just looked at him, standing so stiff and erect in her white layers she seemed to float above the granite floor. It was like being examined by a Fromeathian glacier. The silence soon became uncomfortable.

"M'lady? Are you ready to discuss my assignment?"

She blinked as if waking. "Of course. Will you sit with me?"

Sit? With Lady Izell? He had never even relaxed around a superior officer, much less royalty. Stranger and stranger.

"Yes, Your Ladyship."

As he said her title, Lady Izell's face briefly hardened, but it was quickly gone and replaced by her usual unruffled expression. "We are going to need a different relationship than most people." They sat down on either side of a writing desk, and she continued. "In public, I will remain *Your Ladyship*, and you will simply be another lieutenant, as anyone would expect. In private, it will be less formal. I want your observations, your insights. I need us to speak openly, as I do with Sedia."

"Begging your pardon, M'lady," Jay said, "but I never knew you talked to her about more than food."

Lady Izell nodded. "That was our intention. For us, it will be similar. Only five people, including myself, will know you work for me. To all others, you will be a low-level courier delivering messages from the castle. Because of this, people may let down their guard. You may see things, hear things, and make observations."

Jay leaned forward. Making observations sounded a lot like eavesdropping. "M'lady, where exactly will I be making these observations?" Did she mean he would be on horseback outside the castle walls?

"In every part of the kingdom. Beyond the kingdom and into the Frontier should it be necessary. That is one reason you are right for this job. You are the best and fastest rider I've seen since, well, for a long time," she said with a small smile.

Jay couldn't contain his grin. He wasn't confined to the castle. He would get to ride Havoc, leave Calonade, and even see Jortica. Jay almost jumped up with excitement.

"Easy, Lieutenant. You'll have to contain yourself. This is a serious job."

"Yes, M'lady." He forced himself to keep still.

"I can't assure you it's safe," Lady Izell said in a hushed tone.

Don't forget I'm the man who cut it close with the Barber.

"Emperor Staukard grows restless with us," Lady Izell continued. "He wants our soldiers to fight his wars. I have resisted his entreaties thus far, but I fear they will become more forceful."

"I heard rumors to that effect at the academy, M'lady. The Galathians didn't like paying for their losses with their own soldiers when much less valuable assets could be made available." It made Jay want to spit in disgust, but he controlled the urge for the sake of Lady Izell's immaculate floor.

"The inherent risks are another reason you were chosen," Lady Izell said. "At the competition, you showed your ability to defend yourself. This is a gravely important job. The royal House of Justinkeel and all Calonade depends on your speed, your skill, and your discretion. Do you understand?"

Jay's eyebrows shot up at the mention of Calonade and the former royal family house. She hadn't said anything about the Galathian Empire benefiting from his service.

"Permission to speak freely, M'lady?"

She nodded.

Jay took a breath to calm himself. "I would warn you not to trust anyone this much, so fast. Even if you consider my gran your friend, you don't really know me."

Lady Izell gave him another small smile. "That's exactly the kind of advice I want from you. It's quite true. I don't trust you that much—yet." She slid the Fromeathian tray of wine to the side, revealing an envelope hidden underneath.

"This is for the Minister of Science. Do you know where his lab is located?"

Jay knew Minister Kaloby well. "Yes, M'lady, dungeon level. He tutored me there when I was a boy."

"He once tutored all the castle children, not just the cohort you grew up with, but Lord Kendric declared it unnecessary." Lady Izell paused for a moment as she gazed into the distance.

Jay knew what she really meant. Kendric had forbidden it because Kaloby taught what really happened rather than the Galathian version of history. Lady Izell seemed indifferent about it, but Jay wondered if her chilly exterior was real. What actually went on behind her serene mask?

"I believe you also know the castle layout," she continued. "What is the quickest, most *private* way to his quarters?"

Jay knew exactly what she meant. "Your private courtyard, M'lady. There's a servant's entry on either side. The far one opens to the boiler room coal lift."

"Very good. Let's see if you can deliver this without revealing the true nature of your new position. A small test."

Jay stood and had to stop himself from snatching the envelope out of her hand in excitement. Instead, he took it carefully and slipped it inside his coat.

"Is your assignment clear now?"

"Yes, M'lady." He bowed.

It was as clear as Fromeathian crystal. He had just been recruited to be Lady Izell's spy.

Chapter Six

In a fit of madness, I dressed as a beggar and wandered the breadth of my empire. I liked that better than ruling it.
—from Chronicles of Galathia by Rafykin, Urey, circa 2640 local planetary calendar.

Calonade, Day 290, Year 2998 local planetary calendar, Standard Galactic Year 14284

Jay stood in front of the service entrance to Lady Izell's private garden, a small door in a deserted servant's corridor on the ground floor. It wasn't marked, but all the staff knew where it went. During Izell's time as queen, a guard would ensure security of the inner garden, but currently it remained unwatched. Jay stepped through.

He waited, listening to the trickle of a water fountain, birdsong, and the occasional buzz of insects. Like every visit as a child, the garden stood empty.

Well, not *completely* empty. Castle guards walked the tops of the walls every fifteen minutes. Jay crept forward and peered through a curtain of thorny vines. Precisely cultivated hedges, flowerbeds and trellises created a winding path through the courtyard. On the walls, two guards in red coats marched by and out of sight.

Jay darted toward a second hidden door on the other side of the garden. He dodged around the fountain's curved base and skidded to a stop.

"Commander Kahela!" Jay scrambled to make a proper salute.

Commander Kahela—the key to his transfer to the Horse Division—stood right in front of him. Jay gawked in amazement. Like the night after the race, the commander wore her riding uniform, complete with saber and pistol. Not the clothes an officer would don while relaxing in a garden on leave.

Could he appeal to her now? Considering his new assignment, did he want to ride with the Horse Division? Of course he did. A lifelong dream doesn't die in a single afternoon, but the words caught in his throat. His mind snapped back into focus. Why was the commander of the Horse Division here? Her serious face proved impossible to read.

"You seem surprised, Lieutenant," Kahela said. "Lady Izell sent me to retrieve a message packet for her."

For an instant, panic caught hold of Jay. Was his cover blown so soon? He quickly removed all emotion from his face and jerked his hand away from the bulge in his coat. "What packet, Commander?"

"The one you're taking to Minister Kaloby. I'm afraid you compromised your assignment."

How had he given himself away? Jay went over every step, every word, since leaving Lady Izell's chamber. He couldn't think of a thing. This could be part of the test. Lady Izell may have sent Commander Kahela to confront him and see his response.

"Well, I'm a messenger now." Jay inched away. "Reported for duty at the castle today. My first message is for Captain Gaven. Just taking a short cut, ma'am."

"Then you won't mind handing it over. Besides, Gaven's office is the other direction."

Jay cringed. He'd have to lie better in the future. "Can't do that, ma'am. *Eyes Only* for Captain Gaven."

"I outrank you both." Kahela rested a hand on her pistol grip. "Hand it over. That's an order, half-casting."

Jay's hand twitched toward his own pistol, but he kept himself under control and tucked his fists into tight balls at his side. "I'll be keeping the message, Commander."

"Will you?" Before Jay could react, Kahela drew her pistol and aimed at Jay's heart. "Pull out your pistol, Lieutenant. Slowly."

Jay remained very still as he spoke. "Ma'am. I'm not giving up the message. Are we done with the test?"

"What test?" Her voice made his blood run cold. Jay gulped and followed her directions, wondering if anyone would ever find his body. "Drop your pistol and kick it away."

As he did, Kahela holstered her gun. She unsheathed her saber and rolled her shoulders a few times. "Draw your steel, Lieutenant."

Jay drew out his saber, his heart pounding. Was this a test, or was it real? It sure felt real.

"Let's see what the Galathians taught you." In a flash, Kahela attacked.

Her blade flew at him straight as an arrow and just as fast. It was not a slashing strike taught at the academy.

Surprised, Jay barely parried her blow while stumbling back

blindly. Thorns caught his uniform and blue petals scattered as he crashed into a rosebush and rolled to the side.

He righted himself quickly and lunged at Kahela. She knocked the blow aside and spun out of his reach. As he moved to pursue, she parried his swing and jumped back again. *Goddess, she's fast!* He knew Kahela could continue to dart in and out, using her speed to keep him off balance. He wouldn't last long unless he did something unexpected.

Jay turned and made a dash for the door.

Kahela had to jump over a shrub and sprint after him, but she still cut him off. She moved in with a series of rapid strikes, keeping him away from the door by pressing him back into a wall. Jay blocked every swipe, their blades ringing. The door stood just out of reach.

He feinted to one side and then tried to slip by on the other. Kahela's sword whipped up, blocking his path. Jay rammed his shoulder into her, trying to use his weight to force her out of the way.

She turned the contact against him, upsetting his balance and smashing an elbow into his nose. Pain flared and his eyes watered, but he brought his sword up to protect against her next blow.

Kahela slid her blade under his guard, ripping open his coat. The packet fell to the ground, and Jay felt the sharp edge of Kahela's sword press against his ribs. With her free hand, she pinned his sword arm by the wrist and bent it backwards. Jay's blade clattered to the pathway.

Jay grimaced in anticipation of the backslash that would end his life, but the death blow didn't come.

Kahela withdrew her sword in a slow, fluid motion. "Stand down, Lieutenant."

It was over, and Jay was alive. At least his life wasn't at stake, but what was? Jay regained his feet and used the back of his sleeve to wipe a trickle of blood from his nose.

"Does this mean I've lost the position, Commander?" Jay rubbed his wrist.

"Pick up your charge."

Jay bent and picked the message packet out of the dirt.

Commander Kahela stepped back and looked him over. "Lieutenant, your attacks were predictable, your reaction times barely passable. I was in control throughout."

Another failure. Jay ducked his head as the heat of shame flooded his face.

"Yet you lasted an entire minute," she continued. "Not bad for a raw officer on his first day."

Jay looked up in surprise. "Ma'am?"

She gave a short, harsh laugh. "General Saben isn't allowed to make real soldiers at that school of his. You'd be a threat to Galathia. Which is exactly what you will be when I'm done training you. Seeing how well you protected that packet, you're going to need it."

"I'll be training with you, Commander?"

"That's right, Lieutenant." She sheathed her sword with no hint of expression.

Jay breathed a tremendous sigh of relief. Few could boast of living through a sword fight against Commander Kahela. Then again, he couldn't either, but maybe someday he would hold his own against her. Learning directly from her was an exciting prospect, maybe better than riding in the Horse Division itself. "I'll be in touch. Minister Kaloby is waiting for you. Your day isn't over yet."

"Another test, Commander?"

"Carry on, Lieutenant." The commander turned and strode out of the garden.

* * *

Jay gave the coal lift gate another yank. Metal screeched as he forced it open. *So much for stealth.* Perhaps the old stone stairway at the far end of the castle would have been a better approach.

While trying to keep the copious layers of coal dust from smudging his uniform, Jay peered into the gloom. The heat from the castle's vast boiler pressed against him. The huge cast iron chamber groaned and rattled as the flames changed river water into steam power for the castle. Luckily, the coal tenders were busy elsewhere. Jay had done his time with a shovel down here. It wasn't fun.

Jay dashed through and pushed open a heavy metal door. It clanged shut behind him as he emerged in the long under-ground corridor that ran the length of the castle. Steam pipes ran along the damp stone walls and ceiling. They clicked and popped as the heated water burst through to every room above.

As he crept along the deserted passageway, Jay wondered what his old tutor had in store for him. He kept his pistol drawn and ready. After Commander Kahela's duel, he would not be taken by surprise.

Kaloby could have anything planned, and no one would know. Could that be why the old man had chosen such an odd place to work? When Jay had studied here years ago, the *school* had been a dimly lit, cramped dungeon overflowing with books and papers. He had never looked in the individual cells beyond the main room or considered what all the clutter could be hiding.

Jay turned a corner, passed under an arch, and came down a set of stairs, recognizing the aroma of parchment and wax. Underneath, he caught a whiff of something smoky and metallic, like burnt gunpowder. Slowly, he peered around the archway leading into the dungeon.

Everything he remembered was gone. All the chaos had vanished. Every book was neatly shelved, and every scroll stored away. Oil lamps illuminated the room, magnified by sets of reflecting mirrors.

The middle of the room housed a ring of stones surrounding a modest fire. A large, enclosed cook pot with legs was placed over the flames. Copper coils emerged from its top and looped into a set of glass beakers held on a tray. The whole thing rattled as its contents boiled. A metal hood positioned over the contraption funneled the steam and smoke outside.

"Hello?" Jay called, his voice echoing through the long chamber. He made his way around laboratory tables, tall stools, and racks of equipment. The room seemed empty, but so had the courtyard.

"Minister Kaloby?"

"Back here." The voice came from behind a glass-fronted cabinet displaying botanic specimens. Shiny blue beetles and purple butterflies were pinned and labeled next to samples of lanicina bark. Jay passed the case and found the old man sitting next to a pile of books. His hair and beard had faded to nearly white, contrasting with the deep blue, almost black, skin tone of a southern islander. His smile had not changed.

It was still wide and warm.

Minister Kaloby closed the book he was reading and eyed Jay's drawn weapon, bushy eyebrows raised. "Has Her Ladyship ordered my execution?" Kaloby asked in an amused voice. "If not, you can put that away."

Kaloby hadn't planned another test of his physical skills. Jay holstered the gun, and Kaloby stood to shake his hand. As Minister of Science, Kaloby wore practical clothes, his lab coat with a dozen pockets carelessly thrown over a chair. His waistcoat buttoned tightly over a white shirt with rolled up sleeves.

"Jay. It's good to see you again," Kaloby said. "I knew you'd make it."

Jay smiled in return. "Just barely, sir."

Kaloby chuckled. "Commander Kahela takes her assignments seriously. I, on the other hand, have only one test for you—the package, please."

Jay pulled it from his coat, knocked the dust off, and handed it over.

To his surprise, Kaloby examined the seal on the package but did not break it. "Very good," he said, handing it back to Jay. "I knew you could be trusted."

"Thank you, sir. Aren't you going to open it?"

"Oh no, my boy. It's for you. Have a seat and read it."

Jay sat and turned the bundle over in his hands, examining it for the first time. The seal was simple wax, stamped with an elaborate J for the royal House of Justinkeel. A royal message for him? Before this morning, that would have seemed impossible. Jay broke the seal and opened the package. It contained a set of papers.

"Dear Candidate," Jay read. "I regret to inform you that you have failed to meet the privacy requirements for a messenger position."

"Oh, you can give me the top letter." Kaloby reshelved the ancient volumes he had been reading. "Standard dismissal letter, should you get curious and open the packet. Read on."

Jay turned to the second page and scanned through it. The content was the same information relayed to him by Captain Gaven and Lady Izell, with orders to burn the papers once they were read. What was this? His living arrangements were reassigned—to the *dungeons?* There had to be a way out of that. "Won't this look suspicious, sir? Not being quartered in the messenger's barracks?"

"Captain Gaven is covering your tracks." Kaloby put away the last of the books. "The guards will believe you're bunking in the barracks, and the messengers will think you're staying in the guard house."

It was all worked out. Jay's face fell. Knowing Kaloby, his days would be filled with studies rather than adventures. Being stuck in the castle was too much like his childhood.

"Ah, you're disappointed," Kaloby said. "You think you've lost your free time? Well, you're right, but it's for a good reason. You'll have extra studies with me, using all the new resources I've acquired. You may have noticed them on your way in."

"Hard to miss, sir."

"This, for example," Kaloby stepped over to the miniature boiler in the middle of the room, "is my ongoing study of lanicina bark. I've been experimenting with the distilling process, using some new tools. I'm investigating how to best enhance lanicin's healing properties and reduce the possibility of overdose. The by-product," Kaloby pointed to a glass jar filled with a dark liquid, "does just the opposite. Also useful under certain circumstances."

"Oh, and my personal steam system powers the whole process." Kaloby turned a valve and vented a jet of steam into the air. "Most compact in Calonade. I had to tinker with metalworking. Fixed it up myself."

"I hope you asked Gran for permission for the cook pot," Jay said as a joke.

Kaloby chuckled. "Oh, believe me, I did. It took quite a speech on the advancement of science to get it out of her. Wouldn't you like to stick around and learn how it works?"

Jay had to admit he was curious.

"And you'll be busy with extra training with Commander Kahela," Kaloby added. "Don't tell me you'd pass that up."

Jay sighed. "You're right, sir. This is all far more interesting than life in the barracks." Maybe even better than the Horse Division, but he wasn't sure yet. This was still *the castle*.

"Jay, there is one final reason for your new quarters." Kaloby looked directly into his eyes. "Your job is very sensitive. No one can know what you're really doing. Lives are at stake due to the secrets we keep. This housing arrangement will help prevent you from revealing your assignment to your friends. You'd just be putting them in danger."

Jay frowned. He didn't have any friends. Except for maybe Jortica. She had his back in the officer's mess. That said a lot about her. Kaloby was right. He'd probably tell her without thinking. His stomach tightened at the thought of keeping a secret from her. He probably wouldn't get the chance anytime soon. Her training with the Horse Division would take her far into the Frontier.

The stuff about secrets and risk had him puzzled. Everyone seemed so concerned. So far, the only danger he'd found was the usual slur tossed his way. He was used to that. Jay wouldn't mind if someone thought of a new insult to break up the monotony.

"What danger, sir? Lady Izell hinted at my clandestine role, but peeping through keyholes doesn't seem all that risky. And why do it? Galathians are as predictable as they are deplorable."

"The emperor needs soldiers. We believe the emperor plans to dispense with Lady Izell and take command of our forces," Kaloby said without a blink.

Jay's eyebrows shot up in surprise. *That would be a new approach.* "I see. There would be an immediate rebellion."

"The emperor seems to think there's already one going on. And he's right. The only thing keeping the emperor from marching on Calonade, besides not having an army to do it, is the threat of interrupting the flow of lanicin."

Kaloby sat beside Jay. "Do you remember our thought experiments from when I was your tutor?"

"Yes, sir." Jay recalled them fondly, and his ability to think through a question had served him well in the academy. He sailed through countless verbal exams, much to the chagrin of many a Galathian schoolmaster expecting less of a mixed student.

"Try it now. Put yourself in Emperor Staukard's shoes. How would you force Calonade to send troops to the front?"

Too easy. "All the emperor needs to do is divert his army from the front to take our city. Then march back once Calonade is secure." A terrible sentiment, but it's what a Galathian would think.

"Galathians don't retreat. They would lose every foothold in the east they have gained in the last two decades."

"Perhaps it's worth it to them in the long run," Jay said.

"Galathians don't think long term. Besides, Lady Izell would burn the groves at the first sign of an invasion."

Really. Jay hadn't heard that before. Though brutal, it was a sound strategy. The emperor would never put his only source of lanicin at risk. However, it would also devastate the Calonaden people, many of whom depended on lanicin for their livelihood. "I guess it's a stalemate, then."

"For the moment, but there are rumors, hints, and whispers something is afoot." Kaloby's eyes sparkled as he said this. "This is why we need all the peeping through keyholes, as you put it."

It *did* sound dangerous. "What are the rumors?"

"My informants tell me an agent of the emperor disembarked from a Galathian steamship yesterday under the guise of an imperial inspector. Legate Armone has temporarily slipped through my network, but we will locate him soon. His agenda includes meeting with key members of Parliament. More than those necessary to inspect our lanicin shipments."

"Shall I track him down, sir?"

"No, I have other people for that. For now, your assignment is to get settled. We have set your bunk up in cell number four. I cleared it of bookshelves and had a bed and basin placed within. I have a similar arrangement across the way. Food will be brought to us, so our work will not be disturbed. Since you've missed the noon meal, you'll have to get something from the kitchen. I believe you know the way."

Jay smiled at Kaloby's joke. They both knew he could get back to the kitchen with his eyes closed.

"Once you've filled your belly, your next assignment will be to get some decent rest."

Jay started to protest, but Kaloby raised a hand to stop him. "You can sleepwalk through the academy and still come out as Top Cadet, but for *me*, you'll need your wits about you. From now on, no ale, and no fighting. Not even completely justified fighting with a certain ostentatious lieutenant."

Jay shifted uncomfortably. He wasn't the only spy in Lady Izell's service.

"I know that won't be easy either," Kaloby said. "Perhaps a brief history lesson will help you curb yourself. But first, try my new lanicin tea. It's quite rejuvenating."

Kaloby hopped up and stood by his steam apparatus, turning the valves in sequence. "Under that specimen case, you'll find the cups and saucers. Yes, there, in those drawers."

Jay pulled out the wooden drawers. Below the trays of leaves and insects, he found the old earthenware dishes from Kaloby's teaching days. Jay retrieved two familiar mugs and handed them to Kaloby.

Kaloby balanced the mugs in one hand like a barkeeper. He turned a spigot with his other hand, releasing a steaming golden liquid. It smelled wonderful, not like bitter lanicin at all. Kaloby placed the mug in front of Jay.

"Now tell me, what did your military academy teach you about King Nados?" Kaloby sat down on his own stool, propped his elbow on his knee, and gave Jay his full attention.

Jay sipped the tea and considered Kaloby's question. He had been forced to learn the so-called history of King Nados for his first-year military exams. It was all Galathian lies, of course, but to continue at the academy, a cadet had to correctly repeat the information word for word or be threatened with treason and a prison sentence in Karpathode.

"Did you add something to this, or take something away?" Jay considered as the warmth of the tea spread throughout his body. The usual sharp bite was gone, replaced by a sweet and spicy taste. He suddenly felt much more alert.

"Both!" Kaloby answered. "It's quite remarkable actually—ah, but you won't distract me that way! Quit stalling, now, and answer the question."

Jay swallowed another mouthful and cleared his throat. "King Nados Justinkeel reigned in Calonade, without sanction from the emperor of Galathia, for five years," Jay recited. "He led an unsuccessful uprising against the empire's forces and died at the Battle of Kettlebone Pass. A year after his death, his wife, Queen Izell, signed a peace treaty and swore fealty to the emperor. The treaty reduced Lady Izell to her current rank and appointed her to manage Calonade as an independent colony for a transitional period, under the oversight of a Galathian governor. King Nados had no offspring, so this arrangement will last until Lady Izell's death. At such time, Calonade will become a territory of Galathia under parliamentary governance."

It sounded hopeful for a conquered land, but everyone knew the Parliament was full of Galathian stooges and collaborators. The emperor's agent must have plenty of friends to visit.

Kaloby nodded and sipped from his own mug. "Now, send your mind back to what I taught you. That was quite a different perspective, don't you think?"

"A different *perspective*, sir?" Jay gave him an incredulous look. According to Kaloby, his gran, and any other elder Calonaden, they had grown up in a sovereign nation of fisherman and farmers. Until the emperor decided he wanted their lanicin, that is. "Begging your pardon, sir, but one story is the truth, and the other is lies."

"Some truths are considered treason. As are some actions." Kaloby leaned forward. "You know some treasonous truths, and thus far, you have kept that knowledge to yourself. Can you continue to stay silent? Can you remain unnoticed by Gilcres, for example, who seems determined to undermine you? Both your words and your actions are now very important."

Jay nodded. "I can, sir."

"Good. And remember, truth is a tricky thing," Kaloby said, "but it's something you may finally be ready for. Now finish your tea."

Chapter Seven

Urey revolves around a nearly vertical axis, which means it has no seasons like most life-supporting worlds. The climate is stratified and so are the people.

    —from the journal of Sephy Alcott, Standard Galactic Year 10555

Calonade, Day 290, Year 2998 local planetary calendar, Standard Galactic Year 14284

Calamity crested the final rise before Calonade's Outer Gate without breaking stride. She might be smaller than the average Horse Division mount, but she was one of the strongest. It had taken most of the day to climb the switchback road up the side of the Kelstone Mountains. Jortica patted Calamity on her sweaty neck. Her horse would need water and time to cool before they trekked into the Frontier.

Only Captain Fauden had beaten her to the Outer Gate. Commander Kahela had tasked him to bring up the new Horse Division recruits to the Frontier rally point. He dismounted and gave his horse over to the head stable girl. Jortica followed his lead and did the same.

Fauden strode to the ridge, looking down upon the road and the city below, and frowned. Jortica joined him, giving him some distance as seemed proper for the officer in command.

The climb up the Kelstone switchbacks wasn't a small task, especially carrying a full saddle load of water, food, powder, and shot. Thirty new Horse Division troops, including five of Jortica's fellow academy graduates, strung out in a ragged line along the road.

"Not everyone is ready for this," Fauden said.

"Yes, sir."

Captain Fauden turned and regarded her closely. "You've shown some pluck getting up here in good order. Not your first time, I take it?"

"Correct, sir. I've been up here before."

Fauden arched an eyebrow. "Part of a training exercise? I've been pushing General Saben to include a run or two up to the gate as part of the curriculum."

"No, sir. In my free time." More than once. She hadn't gone home on breaks, and it got boring in the barracks. She'd taken to exploring, and the Outer Gate held a lofty allure. She hadn't felt a need to share these jaunts with anyone. Some might question her about traveling this far from the academy without orders. The stricter Galathian officers didn't even like having cadets off the academy grounds. Jortica wasn't sure what kind of officer Fauden might be.

Fauden turned back to the straggling riders coming up the final turn in the road. His scowl deepened. "Initiative. A positive trait in some, but it's gotten your kind in trouble in the past. Try to keep it reined in, Lieutenant."

Fauden pivoted and strode away.

That answers that question. "Yes, sir," Jortica said to his back.

Past her sweating colleagues and their beleaguered mounts lay all of Calonade proper. The foothills of the Kelstones blended into the lanicina groves and other farmland and small townships before a stout wall rose to mark the boundary of the city. The cobblestone streets, laid out in a more uniform grid, led the eye to a central market and the brick buildings surrounding it. These included the Parliament House, a formidable stone building that housed Calonade's current version of government. It could no longer be described as a bastion of democratic rule under the occupancy of the Galathian Empire.

The academy and its parade grounds stretched away to the east. The Fillaquill River meandered through the farmland and just outside the city wall until it dumped into the bay with a colorful spray of blue and purple mist. The aqueduct, seemingly under continuous construction, ran into the city proper, providing irrigation, power for mills, and fuel for the new steam boilers popping up here and there. A few smokestacks belched black smoke, but the breeze dispersed it well enough to preserve the view. Coal-fired steam power originated from Galathia, and it was well known soot filled the skies of the empire's capital. Jortica hoped such a fate would never befall Calonade.

Her eyes lingering on the academy, Jortica wondered what happened to Jay. He'd promised to see her off but had not appeared at the mustering grounds. Maybe he found a way to get excited about guard duty, though that sounded unlikely. Jortica frowned a little, recalling his disappointment. Hopefully, he had more character than to be envious of her.

Opposite the academy, cliffs dropped to the old fishing

villages, tucked into the fertile crescent between rock and shore. Jortica smiled toward her home, Eventide, one of the oldest districts in Calonade. In a seaside cabin lived her father and sister, likely mending fishing nets this time of day.

That would have been her fate too if her father had any say in the matter. Her presence at the Outer Gate of Calonade and riding to join the Horse Division in the Frontier indicated how little influence he had over her.

The most impressive part of the view drew Jortica's eye—Calonade Castle. Built on the cliffs overlooking the sea, it stood behind a second and much more imposing wall enclosing the keep and its courtyards. Its spires reached high above the city, with stained glass windows gleaming in the sunlight. Only an occasional stream of black smoke issued from a chimney of the castle's steam furnace.

The castle sat like a jewel on the ring of the Bay of Calonade. The bay glistened at the foot of the cliff where the docks provided haven to the elegant wind-driven ships of Calonade and the large and imposing steamships of Galathia. A ship not made to harness the wind looked wrong. They sailed nonetheless, though without the grace of her own people's seafaring vessels.

Beyond the bay, the sea stretched south to a blurred purple line that blended with the violet sky. Jortica breathed in the air, crisp with the salt spray even this far from the surf. Or was the sensation in her head, lingering from her childhood as a daughter of the sea? Well, if that were the case, then it would soon end. Her life no longer centered around the perpetual grind of seas against shore. She need no longer fear the sea when it changed from calm to perilous. Now, she would ride into the Frontier. The place of solid rocky ridges, tall blue pines, and a sky occupied by the birds of the forest.

* * *

By the time the Horse Division recruits ventured from the stables, a moonless dark had descended on the Outer Gate, leaving only torch light to see by. Jortica had never been through Calonade's most formidable fortification.

The walls on the outer side stood three tiers high, with can-nons on each layer. Their barrels pointed into the Kettlebone Pass, the only land entrance into Calonade. The formidable Kelstone Mountains made all other routes fruitless. Wall sections protruded at intervals to create crossfire killing zones.

Even though Jortica couldn't see much of it in the dim light, she could feel the place ran thick with ghosts. The endless history of warfare on this strip of ground made it the most infamous battlefield of the empire. Here, Calonade and Galathia had clashed many times before the Galathians finally prevailed. Here, King Nados, the last true sovereign of Calonade, died to save his people. It was hallowed ground to all Calonadens and sacred for the Horse Division.

Torches along the top of the Outer Gates revealed guards moving along the walls. The gloom of the pass felt like a weight, and the column hushed until they entered the forest beyond.

The riders perked up as they saw lights ahead. Jortica felt relief to be away from a place so haunted by the weight of history. The lights came from Thurbush, the town on the outskirts of the Frontier that served as their rally point. Already erected tents greeted their column as they rode into the open pasture of a farmhouse. No stable hands served here, so the riders had to put their own horses up for the night.

After staking Calamity, Jortica went in search of her bunk assignment. She found Captain Fauden in the command pavilion talking with a Galathian official who wasn't wearing a uniform. In fact, he was quite an odd-looking creature for the setting. He stood tall in a black cloak with gold brocade and a hood drawn down around his shoulders. Clearly civilian garb. As he paced in and out of the firelight, Jortica glimpsed his greasy hair, lanky limbs, and sharp face. She approached and felt something amiss by the tone of their voices.

"Captain Fauden," the cloaked Galathian said. "Perhaps you have been poorly trained in this backwater fishing village the natives think of as a city, but in the heart of the empire, command is carried out by those who hold the highest rank."

Jortica noticed many Galathian horse soldiers. Far more than she expected. It was said only Calonadens served in this so-called hardship duty. At least a dozen lingered within the firelight, wearing fur-lined boots and coats as if they expected to ride to a colder climate.

"I assure you," Brocade-Cloak continued. "A writ directly from the emperor himself far outweighs any, and I use this term loosely, *command structure* you have out here."

Fauden started to protest, but Brocade-Cloak pressed on. "You, in fact, make my point, Captain. Did it not take you two hours more than it should have to get here tonight? The vaunted Calonade Horse Division hasn't lived up to its reputation."

"Those were the new recruits, sir." Fauden noticed Jortica

approaching. A quick shake of his head told her to stay back. "They haven't been trained yet."

"Were they not the best your academy has to offer, Fauden?" Brocade-Cloak spun to glare directly at Jortica. "In fact, Captain, do I see the winner of the race here with us now?"

Fauden grimaced. "Yes, sir."

Brocade-Cloak came closer as Jortica snapped to attention. "The Top Cadet, am I right?" he asked Fauden. "Gracing us with her presence."

Jortica had it drilled into her head to never speak to a superior officer without express permission, so she kept her mouth as tight as her rigid stance.

"A woman, no less." Brocade-Cloak stared at Jortica but spoke to Fauden.

"Yes, sir," Fauden said. "I believe you know Calonade allows women to serve as soldiers."

"I *did* know," Brocade-Cloak said, "but it's hard to believe unless you see it yourself. What is your name, soldier?"

He addressed the last question to Jortica as he loomed over her. Just about every male in Calonade had tried to intimidate her, both Galathian and Calonaden, so she was used to it. She thought of several ways she could bend this fool in half and teach him some manners—a little pastime of hers that inspired her combat training. In four years as a cadet, she had gone from shaking in her boots, to anger and contempt, to downright boredom at the lack of originality. She also knew just how quickly rash action would get her discharged, and likely after a long stint in the brig.

Brocade-Cloak's pathetic attempt at intimidation didn't scare her. Her insides turned to water at the thought of the long walk back to her daddy's door in disgrace. It would end with his sightless expression of disappointment mixed with knowing he was right. He would say, in his soft voice, she never belonged anywhere else but with him in the fishing village. That possibility frightened her far more than anything any other man could conjure. "Lieutenant Jortica, sir," she answered crisply.

"I know who you are," Brocade-Cloak said. "You were *declared* the winner of the race for Top Cadet, though I dispute the result. It was blind luck on your part rather than any skill. It's too bad this rotten excuse of a Galathian colony doesn't have better leadership."

Jortica remained silent since that wasn't a question and officers who gave speeches never asked for commentary from lowly lieutenants.

"Isn't that right, Fauden?"

"If you say so, sir."

Jortica kept her expression blank but was impressed by Fauden's pluck, giving a response as close to insubordination as any officer could get when addressing a commander. Then again, Fauden was Galathian, so it really wasn't all that surprising.

Brocade-Cloak gave Fauden a glare but didn't respond. That would have been a lashing if said by a Calonaden officer. He turned back to Jortica.

"As you can see, I'm well informed about the officers under my command, Lieutenant Jortica," Brocade-Cloak said. "Let's see if you are just as prepared. Do you know who I am?"

"Sir, no sir," Jortica answered without hesitation. It wasn't the time to lie.

"Tell her, Fauden."

Fauden sighed. "This is Legate Armone, formerly the Warden of Karpathode, but now assigned as Commander of the Horse Division in Calonade."

The bottom dropped out of Jortica's stomach. She barely kept herself from saying, *what about Commander Kahela?* Her eyes darted between the two of them and she struggled to remain expressionless, but the Horse Division under the command of someone other than Kahela was inconceivable.

"Witnessing the lack of discipline among your troops, I feel Commander Kahela's performance borders on negligence and perhaps insubordination." Legate Armone sneered at them both.

Fauden stepped up to face Armone. "Commander Kahela has always credibly served the interests of the empire. She is an expert at defending the Frontier and passing along the skills and knowledge required to her junior officers and even the common horse soldiers. It will be difficult to replace her."

Armone stretched taller as he pointed his hand like a knife at Fauden's chest. "We shall see how you do, Captain." He flashed a predatory smile. "In the morning, you are to take your recruits and any other horse soldiers formerly under Kahela's command on a sweep of the Frontier along the entire length of the Talindrey River. Understood?"

Fauden blanched a little. "Yes, sir. You won't be coming, sir?"

"No, Captain. I have other duties to attend to." His grin transformed into a scowl. "Dismissed."

Fauden turned and ushered Jortica out ahead of him. She stopped out of earshot of the tent. "What the hell was that about, sir?"

"Commander Kahela received a new assignment earlier

today and was summoned back to Calonade Castle. Legate Armone has taken command."

"Why, sir? It makes no sense. How can a former jail guard command the most elite mounted force on the continent?"

Fauden sighed and rubbed his forehead. "The former warden of Karpathode is hardly a jail guard, and this smells political. However, it has nothing to do with our orders, Lieutenant." Fauden stared Jortica in the eyes. "Stow your questions and get some rest. We ride out in the morning."

Jortica could tell Fauden would accept only one answer. "Yes, sir."

Fauden stomped into the dark, muttering under his breath.

The Galathian uniforms suddenly made sense. The oddly equipped horse soldiers weren't outfitted to go to a colder climate; they had come from one. Armone had brought his own men with him, and he meant to send all the others with Fauden on a long trek far away from Calonade. A cold feeling crept up Jortica's spine. This was not the plum assignment she had been hoping for.

Chapter Eight

During the diaspora we sought out and seeded every Earth-like planet we could find. The genetic damage from the environmental disaster ran deep and we grasped at any remedy.

—from the journal of Sephy Alcott, Standard Galactic Year 10555

Shinwate Forest, Day 021, Year 2017 local planetary calendar, Standard Galactic Year 13303

After a brief but invigorating ride on the Yawate, it slowed as they neared the Shinwate village. The walking tree stopped at the outskirts and let Lakqwi and Sephy dismount. It lumbered back into the forest. Lakqwi took the lead as they stepped onto the street made of uneven cobblestones.

The village, smaller and far more primitive than Sephy expected, had thatch roofs built over uneven brick walls. The trees pressed up against the boundaries of the village. Sephy estimated between a hundred and two hundred people lived here.

The civilization she had left behind, something like five years ago, had numbered in the thousands and built much more sophisticated architecture. She did the conversion in her head. Five years on the station rounded out to around two thousand years in local time. Things had changed. Was this Melrayis' doing? She had expressed a desire for a more primitive existence, both as a retreat from the rigors of their technocentric world and as healing for the genetic price they paid for it. Even though many of her people had volunteered to live a simpler life, Sephy hadn't expected to arrive in the Stone Age.

Several villagers carried water in clay pots. A set of craftsmen shaped bricks from soil, leaves, and pebbles to repair a hut. A pair of hunters strode past carrying bows and arrows. The weapons were not bone or flint. The presence of metal arrowheads revealed signs of metallurgy. They all wore a combination of animal skins and simple hand-woven garments. Only a few accessories hinted at more advanced textiles.

This made her self-conscious about her own clothes. She'd put on a nondescript technician's jumpsuit with a utility jacket. Though a perfect disguise for remaining incognito back home, it looked alien here. She'd have to figure out a way to explain.

Continuing her survey, she found threshing bins and squat storage silos for grain, but no machinery in view. These Shinwate lived as an agricultural and hunting society trading with the more advanced people of the planet. They were far from the dominant culture.

Sephy frowned. That wasn't the plan. At least not hers. When she last checked, the Shinwate competed for dominance, and she had activated measures to assist them in their rise. They should have been well on their way to controlling at least this region of the planet, if not the globe. Had Melrayis changed something vital? Maybe she had transported into a primitive sect?

"Stay here," Lakqwi said to Sephy. "You can wait by the fountain." She gestured toward a short, circular wall surrounding a sculpture at the center of the village. "I will meet with the village chieftain."

Lakqwi marched into a large hut with ancient brick walls, leaving Sephy to entertain herself.

The weather had warmed, and the signs of rain had passed. Hot from the ride, Sephy examined the fountain, hoping to cool off. Marks on the stones of the dry basin revealed it had a healthy flow in the past. Rising from the far wall, a statue of a young feminam poured water using a pitcher. Not Shinwate or human, she represented Melrayis' dream with a long lithe body, a muscular physique, and a face free of wrinkles. The statue modeled an ideal figure with the scars of the diaspora healed and the evolution from human complete. What feminam were supposed to be and would someday become, at least according to Melrayis.

On the back side, Sephy discovered a hand pump. After pushing the lever arm up and down for a few minutes, a stream of water, barely more than a trickle, emerged from the pitcher. Sephy took a handful to cool her face. She hesitated to drink it. Unfiltered well water, no doubt. Who knew what the pH rating might be? Still, going native, even if briefly, might be worth it. She drank a hand full. A tad gritty, but fresh.

Tasting the water brought back a memory of this fountain from her last visit. It had been automated, with a continuous flow. Examining the village again, she estimated the distance to the remnants of the walls, taking in the remaining cobble-stones and the placement of the fountain. She spun to stare in the direction she and Lakqwi had taken to get here.

A faint pattern betrayed uniformity in placing the trees and the space between them. A section of a stone wall reduced to rubble amongst the vegetation receded into the forest. Ruins in the trees meant this wasn't a new place. She *had* landed in the temple. She stood in the courtyard entry to the fortress that had once surrounded it.

Sephy's jaw dropped open. Once the center of Shinwate civilization, the temple complex had covered several city blocks with domes and towers. They had built it to impress with elaborate wall reliefs, gold inlay, and stained glass. Dismayed, Sephy stared at the jungle that had risen to take the place of Melrayis' city on a hill. The beacon of enlightenment and healing for the feminam had crumbled to unrecognizable ruins. Its few inhabitants were shadows of what they were meant to be.

Sephy fought the growing panic rising inside her. This had to be a primitive sect. They had taken over the old temple and let it crumble. She would have to find the rest of her people elsewhere.

The files! Sephy accessed the data from the Yawate at the temple circle and sorted through it for answers.

Halfway through a disturbing set of reports describing the height of the conflict between the Shinwate and the Galathian Empire, she felt a tap on her shoulder. She stopped the feed and looked up to see Lakqwi peering at her curiously.

"Are you well, Prophet Hukindi?"

"Yes, sorry. It's a message," Sephy said, a little breathless from the string of revelations. Somehow, the seeded humans had turned the tables and reversed the power dynamic. A series of conflicts had ensued with seeded humans dominating the Shinwate colonists.

"Do you need more time?" Lakqwi asked. "Privacy perhaps? Forgive me, even though I am First Daughter, I am unsure of your methods and needs as the Prophet."

"There's no need." Sephy steadied herself. "Will the chieftain see me?"

"Yes, she is eager to meet you."

"Let's go then," Sephy said. "I have many questions."

Lakqwi nodded and led the way into the central hut.

Sephy entered a thatch-roofed meeting hall sprawled out haphazardly between mud-caked stone walls mixed with brick and mortar. A cast iron wood-burning stove sat idle in one corner while an elaborate stone hearth resided on the other side. Embers within the latter glowed as several villagers tended to cooking duties. A steaming copper tea kettle hung from a wood tripod to cool.

It was a curious combination of historical eras mixed into one dwelling.

Several Shinwate villagers lounged within the room, tending fires and drinking from fired-clay cups. In the center, an imposing figure lounged in an elaborately carved wooden chair draped with a blend of old upholstery and animal skins. The Shinwate had long braided hair and wore similar hand-woven clothing except for a swath of silk around her neck. A twisted circlet of bright metal rested on her brow. At first it seemed to be gold, but signs of tarnish betrayed its true material to be brass.

Lakqwi bowed to her, and Sephy did her best to mimic the gesture. "High Chief Tanimundi, I present the Prophet

Hukindi." Lakqwi spoke in a booming, authoritative voice.

A large feminam with broad shoulders, Chief Tanimundi possessed a hefty belly. Her ample figure didn't make her look unhealthy or weak. In fact, her well-contained bulk made her seem even more powerful. She regarded Sephy with a wary expression, her arms folded and resting on her belly. "The prophet, you say?" Tanimundi asked in a low and rumbling voice.

"That is her claim," Lakqwi replied.

Great. Now more proof is required. Sephy felt a tick up in adrenaline with the rising stakes of the moment. If the chief didn't buy her act, she might as well go home. If she got the chance, that is.

"You do not wear the traditional robes." Tanimundi waved a hand at Sephy. "Is this the new Galathian fashion?"

The audience tittered at the insult, but Sephy ignored them. "No, this is what the prophets wear now." No one could dispute her since she was the only prophet around, at least as far as she knew. If these people suddenly produced another prophet, her goose was cooked.

Tanimundi ignored her statement. "How is the weather in the capital city?" She slouched and smiled in a manner that screamed indifference, but her eyes keenly focused on Sephy.

"Truth is, I've never been to Galathia." She had sent a team there to establish the dominant religion of the empire, but she had never visited the place herself. "I arrived here today in the center of the old temple. By the way, what happened to it?"

The smile vanished from Tanimundi's face. She slowly sat up to glare at Sephy with a new intensity. "You *arrived* in the Temple of the Daughters?" Tanimundi looked at Lakqwi, who nodded.

"Yes," Sephy said. "The Temple of the Daughters." *Melrayis had restricted access to the transit portal using her invented religion. Nice.* "It protects a doorway to Willa, or the Underworld, as you know it. Last time I was here, it was an impressive spectacle of advancement. This area," Sephy gestured around them, "was simply an entry courtyard and trading market that stood outside the gates. The destruction of the temple complex puzzles me. How is it the Shinwate have lost their influence in the world?"

Sephy must have struck a nerve because Chief Tanimundi scowled. Hopefully, she hadn't laid it on too thick. Still, the loss of the temple and the clearly depleted civilization of the Shinwate needed an explanation more detailed than the sporadic and unclear reports left in the Yawate's database.

"How do you know of the Heart of the Temple?" Tanimundi asked. "Its ancient secrets remain in the keeping of the Daughters of Melrayis."

"I am the Prophet Hukindi," Sephy said with a shrug. "You are going to trust me and tell me what you know, or I will leave you to your own devices for another millennium or two."

Tanimundi frowned, and Sephy realized *millennium* hadn't translated. The chief must have gotten it through the context because she didn't ask what it meant. She sat back again, and deeper creases formed on her face, revealing a long-standing grief.

"The goddesses abandoned us." Tanimundi's voice dropped low and breathy. "It is true we were once a proud people, thousands strong. We dominated the woods from here to the west and over the Wrayan Mountains to the Fenduer Forest. A vast network of cities stretching south to the sea, east to the desert, and north to the frozen wastes. The soil was deep, and the trees were tall."

A glint of pride flickered briefly in Tanimundi's eyes, but it extinguished just as quickly by a tide of sadness. "We lost it all. The Galathians came, and they had the favor of the goddesses. We fought them for centuries, but they always gained, and we always lost. Now we are fractured and defeated. The forests are lost to us, except for a few isolated places."

Conditions had deteriorated far more than Sephy thought. An entire thriving civilization of feminam reduced to a few tribes. The reports from the Yawate had hinted at the decline, but now Sephy grasped the full weight of the destruction. It was breathtaking in scope and, once again, humans were to blame. Sephy felt the shame of the common origins between *Homo feminae* and *Homo sapiens*, but she couldn't let that stop her from finding out how it happened. The tri-goddess arrangement put in place to govern the inhabitants was supposed to prevent exactly this result.

"The goddesses didn't favor you?" Sephy asked.

"No, the Maiden has not fostered peace, the Mother has not provided nurturing, and the Crone has not offered wisdom. At least not to us. They all reside with the humans and provide us with no comfort or succor."

This was puzzling. The three Willacast goddesses of Urey had been put in place to favor the interests of the Willacast Corporation, which meant the interests of the Shinwate tribes in this case. Even within this non-traditional situation, it should have worked without any oversight. Something had gone terribly wrong.

The phrase about comfort and succor sounded familiar.

Sephy ran a search on it through her neural database and a result appeared in her display. A phrase popped up from Melrayis' journal, which described a change to the tri-goddess instructions: *provide the Shinwate with no comfort or succor.* An appeal to self-determination and independence from outside interference had been misused somehow. Melrayis felt self-sufficiency would better support the genetic healing the feminam needed. Had her colleague inadvertently doomed their colony?

Sephy clenched her fists and had to concentrate to keep from cursing. That hadn't been the deal. Melrayis had agreed a dominant feminam culture with generous reproductive resources available from the seeded human population to be the top priority. Genetic healing goals ranked lower than colony viability. Melrayis must have reversed the Willacast priorities. *Damn.* Sephy hadn't noticed until now. *Double damn.*

Lowering her head into her palm, Sephy felt like kicking herself. Leaving a mainstream colony unwatched for five years was a huge mistake. Leaving it all in Melrayis' hands was another one. Melrayis was an idealist, and now Sephy could see Melrayis had needed her own pragmatism for balance.

Sephy may have come too late and lost it all. She could blame her inattention on the demands of her job. Sephy struggled to organize this clandestine trip, disguised as a vacation, without arousing suspicion back at the office. None of those excuses would fix anything. She had wrapped too much into this blue planet to write it all off and had to reverse this blunder. But how? Well, there was one way. Undo what Melrayis had done. That would take a personal touch.

"Chief Tanimundi, I've come to fix the problem." Sephy mustered her confidence. "I enjoy considerable influence with the Willacast Goddesses. An audience with one of them will set things straight."

"An audience with a goddess," Tanimundi said. "How will you achieve such a feat?"

"I am the prophet," Sephy said with a shrug.

"Travel to Galathia where our kind are enslaved on sight?" Tanimundi asked with a skeptical frown, which looked better than the weight of sadness that had burdened her expression before.

"Well, in that case, I'll need your help," Sephy said as if it had been decided. "First, however, I'm tired and in need of refreshment, a bath, and a change of clothes. Could I ask from you the hospitality you reserve for your special allies and friends?" Sephy guessed the culture would offer accommodations for important traveling dignitaries or religious icons.

Tanimundi's frown hovered on her face and then broke away to let the lazy smile return. "You intrigue me, Prophet Hukindi. I will not have you slain just yet."

Sephy nodded her thanks, wondering how close she'd come to a blade in the back or some such ending.

Tanimundi grinned, but in a more predatory fashion than friendly. "We have what you need, including a SHA if you desire."

Sephy forced herself not to grimace at the thought of what an unwashed male human might be like in this primitive jungle, even if properly conditioned. However, an examination of the current conditions of this colony, depleted as it was, needed to consider every detail, including the health of this village's Seeded Human Assets. "Of course. I await your guidance."

Tanimundi waved to Lakqwi, and the warrior led Sephy out of the hall. They headed into the part of the village that occupied what was once the market district. Sephy couldn't help but wonder what kind of adventure her so-called vacation was turning into.

Lakqwi escorted Sephy through the entrance of a hovel made from the ruins of an ancient hotel lobby. The concierge's granite desktop had survived and served as the dining table. Sephy could vaguely recall a lecture from Melrayis about abandoning the crutch of technology to facilitate true healing of feminkind while they were standing almost in this exact spot.

She and Melrayis had quite the debate. Sephy shook her head at the memory, which seemed to be only five years ago. Melrayis had put her vision into practice while no one else was watching. Whether she won the argument was yet to be determined.

"You will be assigned an attendant to see to basic needs and requests. Let me know if you require anything beyond what is needed for your comfort." Lakqwi ducked out, letting the hide flap fall across the threshold.

Not much for conversation

Sephy spent a minute surveying her surroundings. The construction used mud and brick for the walls and a thatched roof supported by cut timber. The ancient mortar mixed with a more recent handmade variety. A wicker chair graced one corner, and a box filled with hay, which Sephy reluctantly identified as a bed, occupied the opposing corner. A stout hearth, situated against the back wall, held glowing embers and a cook pot. Sephy raised an eyebrow at the food that might portend. The granite desktop in the middle of the room remained the only other remarkable piece.

The tent flap rustled and pulled aside to reveal a young feminam. She bowed and stood just outside the door. Sephy swore she could see the poor girl trembling. It was the same young one she had surprised at the temple circle.

"What's your name, child?"

"Havaqwi," she peeped.

Sephy noticed the similarity with Lakqwi's name. Were they related? Mother-daughter pair perhaps? Was the local religion a family business? "You must be my attendant."

The girl nodded and fidgeted. She didn't quite know where to put her hands. They ended up at her sides, gripping her robe between her fingers. She might be about twelve years old by most feminam standards. Some wrinkles formed in her face, but the smoothness of youth was still present. Her color was a light gray, as with any feminam of her apparent age.

"How old are you?" Sephy asked.

"Thirteen fastings," Havaqwi said.

Fastings. A new term. Sephy blinked as the neurals attempted a translation, but nothing to do with duration came up.

Might as well just ask. "What is a fasting?"

"Daughters of Melrayis and their attendants follow the ancient traditions," Havaqwi recited. "The end of fasting season is when the year renews."

Fasting season. Urey didn't experience seasons like Earth once did. The planet's lack of tilt left no seasons to speak of. *Does fasting season translate to winter?* Sephy pondered this discovery. "What are the seasons?"

Havaqwi's eyes widened. Sephy guessed she hadn't been expecting a quiz on her faith. Nevertheless, she rallied.

Ticking them off on her fingers she said, "Fasting, Renewal, Feasting, and Preparing."

Sephy immediately saw the parallel with Earth's seasons, but why would people of Urey even care? *Melrayis!* It had to be something she came up with. It made sense, knowing her old colleague's way of thinking. Melrayis wanted the feminam living on Urey to mimic, as closely as possible, the lifestyle they once had on Earth. Her friend had invented seasons within religious practices. If you want to reclaim a genetic disposition from the past, simulate the conditions in which it evolved. Seasons exerted an extensive influence on the physiology of *Homo sapiens*. Melrayis had successfully planted the practice within the feminam society. Brilliant, but did it work?

"Very good, Havaqwi," Sephy said with a purposely warm smile. "Are you familiar with a practice called a medical examination?"

The translation of the last words came out as something like *scrutiny of the priestess.* Sephy cringed, hoping it didn't come out wrong, but Havaqwi simply nodded as if such a thing were expected. "Would you let me examine you?"

The last word again came out as *submit to scrutiny*, which also sounded weird to say, but Havaqwi simply nodded. She kneeled, bringing her hands together, palms to her chest and her head bowed.

Sephy waited for a moment, but when Havaqwi didn't rise, she asked, "What's that gesture?"

"A prayer, Prophet Hukindi, for a successful examination,"

Havaqwi said, standing.

"Well done." Sephy tried to maintain her pretense as an instructor.

Havaqwi bobbed her head to Sephy and hopped up on the table. She lay down on her back with her arms at her sides.

"You've done this before," Sephy said.

"Attendants are trained to know how to serve the priestess. We practice receiving scrutiny every change of season." She spoke calmly while staring at the ceiling.

Sephy scratched her head and wondered what a thorough physical examination on a young feminam would involve if Melrayis had written it into gospel. Didn't matter, because Sephy didn't need to know everything. At least not yet.

Sephy possessed a basic knowledge of feminam biology, but not enough to be effective without help. She summoned a diagram of several key anatomical features on to her neural display. Sephy examined Havaqwi's skin along her arms, face, and neck. She had Havaqwi pull up her undershirt and pressed into key areas of her abdomen. She pulled a penlight from a jacket pocket and looked into her ears and throat. Havaqwi seemed a bit startled by the light, but otherwise didn't react to the probing.

Sephy stepped back and Havaqwi pulled loose the tie that held up her trousers. Sephy patted her hand. "No need, dear. That's enough for now." Havaqwi shrugged and tightened her garment.

"What's for dinner, if I may ask?" Sephy said in a casual tone.

Havaqwi hopped off the table and checked the contents of the cook pot. They apparently didn't meet her standards, and after some confused explanations, she bowed and scrambled out the door.

Sephy supposed she'd be back. In the meantime, she pulled out her journal, an old-fashioned kind made of paper. The penlight also served as a pen. She started writing out her thoughts. As she got them organized, she entered them into her neural log. Physical writing, though unnecessary, relaxed her. After thousands of years of evolution, Sephy detected a few subtle changes in feminam physiology in her first case study. One data point meant nothing, but it could be a sign Melrayis' experiment had merit. If this planet turned out to be the key to healing feminkind, Sephy would have to preserve it.

Chapter Nine

Why would an emperor leave his palace? What drove me to despair? Why, love, of course. It's always love.
—from Chronicles of Galathia by Rafykin, Urey, circa 2640 local planetary calendar.

Calonade, Day 328, Year 2998 local planetary calendar, Standard Galactic Year 14284

After a trot through the city streets, Jay dismounted at the dark stone pillars in front of the Parliament House and hitched Havoc to a post. Havoc nickered with pleasure, but Jay could tell he needed a real run to stretch out his legs. He couldn't get up to a healthy gallop through the city streets packed with wagons, carts, and carriages. A ride in the country wouldn't do Jay any harm, either, as the daily routine of running Lady Izell's messages back and forth wasn't exactly satisfying.

A bulky steam carriage trundled past, spewing acrid smoke as it wobbled over the cobblestones. A shrill whistle of steam escaped from a poor seal along the side of the boiler. It sounded like the Barber, and Jay half-expected hidden blades to poke out of its metal sides. Drivers cursed as the noise spooked their horses, but the Galathian steering the monstrosity with a wheel like a ship's helm ignored them all with an oblivious smile on his face. Jay shook his head at the foolishness. Calonade's occupiers insisted on building bigger and uglier toys for themselves.

Behind him, the stone building rose tall and formidable. Pillars held up a huge copper dome that featured a giant Galathian clock. Built in front of the marketplace, it blocked the view of the castle.

Though Calonade Castle once held the seat of sovereign power, it was now firmly within the walls of the Parliament House. The governor had quarters in both places, but he spent most of his time in an opulent suite of floors in this building.

As a boy, Jay visited to watch people come and go. Above, krikes flew in and out of the dome. They carried messages to and fro all over the empire. Jay could see a healthy flock of black-feathered birds with red eyes flitting about the aviary.

Jay used to sneak inside the Parliament House and listen to the speakers. Bombastic Galathians and determined Calonadens went at each other with cultured words—most of the time. Sometimes the verbal exchanges weren't so civilized. Not that he had understood much, but it was better than fetching water for Gran all day.

In his red uniform and black messenger armband, Jay had free access to the Parliament House halls. Despite his official capacity, most Galathians and a few Calonadens gave him a glare as he passed by. A particularly suspicious Galathian guard demanded a look at his package. Jay complied and when the guard saw the royal seal, he relented, muttering about how the world was coming to no good with half-castings being put in uniforms.

Jay had endured a lifetime of this treatment. The guard stopped no other messengers. In fact, people made way for them in every other instance as they hurried by. Having a secret purpose beyond messenger lessened the sting.

Jay rushed down a set of back stairs and through a hall filled with printing presses. The acidic tang of hot ink on paper greeted his senses. The steam-powered machines vibrated as freshly printed papers emerged, featuring heroic descriptions of the latest Galathian victories in the east. For having so many victories, it sure was taking the Galathians a long time to conquer their latest foes.

Jay quickly found the correct room and delivered his charge. Not long after, he was out on the street again.

Just as he was about to mount Havoc, he saw Gilcres standing on the Parliament House steps. He spoke heartily with a balding Calonaden man wearing the gaudy red frock coat of a parliamentarian. The representative clearly wished to be included in the grandeur of Galathian court. A guffaw from Gilcres echoed over the square as he laughed at something the man said. Jay noticed Gilcres had two golden circlets on his collar. *Unbelievable! How had he been promoted to captain already?*

Gilcres looked his way and caught him staring. With a nasty smile, he strolled toward Jay, absently fingering his pocket watch.

"Well, well, *Lieutenant*, what a lovely little armband you're wearing. Being a messenger suits you."

"Good morning, *Captain* Gilcres." Jay gave the required salute in deference to the rank, not the man. Reaching the rank of captain usually took years of exemplary service or exceptional conduct on the battlefield. He was sure Gilcres had done nothing to earn it.

"I suppose I could give you an order." Gilcres sneered. "An order to hand over your horse would be fun."

Jay stood at attention, waiting for the taunting to stop. He kept calm by remembering how Gilcres had flipped heels over ass off Havoc. He was too much of a coward to try that again.

"I'm just not in the mood," Gilcres said. "I'm too busy these days with my appointment to the Parliament as an adviser."

Yep, the tin-striped idiot won't try it. Probably still bruised. "Begging pardon, sir, who are you advising?"

"A member of Parliament, you simpleton. Were you even listening?"

Jay bit back a rude reply. "Yes, sir, just wondering which one."

"The Deputy to the Adjunct for Logistics." Gilcres puffed his chest with pride.

Jay mentally pictured Kaloby's extensive chart on the Calonaden government. A minor post, though Gilcres obviously didn't know it. All about shipping logistics of lanicin to foreign ports. Jay tried to remember the name of the representative. It was something like Tober. He was from one of the family houses that represented the interests of the trading guild. The post languished in the corner of the chart somewhere and sounded like a vanity position for Gilcres to avoid any actual work.

"He is merely a raw-casting, the poor fellow. This is just my first step. *I'm* in the game." Gilcres gloated. "The grand contest, if you will. And what are you doing?" He stopped and looked at Jay with a savage glee. "Answer, Lieutenant."

Here it was, the very instance Kaloby had warned him about. Jay was tempted to knock the smug grin off his face.

"Castle messenger, sir."

Gilcres guffawed. "*Castle* messenger. Well, that suits you at least. Born for the role, one might say. You better get back, so you don't miss any important messages from your powerless ex-queen."

Jay clamped his jaw tight. *If the Galathians thought Lady Izell was powerless, why did they want to get rid of her so badly?* More interesting, however, was this new sentiment from Gilcres. Usually, he bragged about being related to Lady Izell and thereby close to power.

"Aren't you her nephew, sir?"

"What did you say?"

"It just stands to reason, sir, if she had the power to get you this position, then—"

"Izell had nothing to do with it," Gilcres spat. "She's related to my family through some foully conceived marriage I imagine, but I am pure Galathian. If anything, she's a hindrance to me."

"If you say so, sir." *A new perspective indeed.* Gilcres had been listening to his new Galathian friends who heaped disdain on anything aligned with Calonade. Gilcres would have to conceal the fact that his Fromeathian mother was Lady Izell's sister, Lady Marzell. The poor woman had died in childbirth. The *foul* part of the marriage was likely Gilcres' Galathian father.

Still excited by the chance to brag, Gilcres went on with his self-aggrandizing monologue. Jay struggled to keep from rolling his eyes as he wondered if Gilcres knew anything about a plot against Lady Izell. Kaloby said he had people investigating, but did they know about Gilcres? Would anyone trust this pompous fool with their secrets?

Jay looked over Gilcres' shoulder. Several Galathian members of Parliament, along with Tober, were gathering around a Galathian dressed in a sweeping black frock coat with gold brocade. Only one kind of person wore a gold pattern like that—an agent from the emperor. *This must be Legate Armone.* The group moved up the steps and into the building.

Gilcres probably knew nothing, but his friends might.

Jay interrupted Gilcres' boasting. "That's great, sir. Quite a lot to do. In fact, I'm late for my duties. By your leave, sir." Jay didn't wait for a response. He leaped onto Havoc and rode as if the goddesses themselves had summoned him.

* * *

Jay steered Havoc around a corner and down an alley, out of sight from the Parliament House. He entered a little stable yard tucked into the end of the side street, where he pressed a silver coin into the hand of the stable boy.

"An oat bag for my friend, if you please."

The stable boy nodded, and Jay left Havoc in his care. Jay dashed back the way he had come. He slipped into the Parliament House through the servant's entrance and made his way to the upper floor. Snaking through various crawlways, he wasn't sure which of the many halls the group might end up in. When he heard Gilcres' distinctive guffaw, he followed the sound. He emerged on the balcony overlooking the main auditorium.

Below, all the Galathian representatives mingled along with Gilcres. Tober remained the only Calonaden skulking among them. They stood around the room in clumps. Legate Armone drifted among them, shaking hands and clapping men on the shoulder. Jay worked his way down to the edge of the balcony railing while remaining in the shadows.

"Are the servants and clerks excused?" Armone sounded cold, hard, and in command. "Good. Secure the doors."

A bustling followed the sound of doors locking shut. Jay's heart began beating fast. His instincts had been right. This meeting might yield valuable information. Jay wondered if any of Kaloby's people knew about it. Well, one did, training or no.

A series of voices overlapped as everyone spoke at once, shouting questions. Then someone called for silence.

"Come now, Armone. Tell us what you know!" one man said.

"Are the rumors true?" Tober asked. "Are you here to deal with Izell?"

They all talked over each other. Then Gilcres' voice boomed out, "Gentlemen! Let's hear what Armone has to say!"

"Yes, if I may have your attention," Armone said, and everyone fell silent. Jay risked a quick glance over the railing. The man had a long, sallow face with withdrawn cheeks and a wolfish expression.

"In a short time, Lady Izell will no longer be a problem, I assure you," Armone said. "Do not concern yourselves with her."

The group shifted about again as several spoke.

"Gentlemen!" Armone barked. They quieted to listen. "We

have other concerns to address here. Namely, I need your help to make sure Izell and Nados have no heir."

Jay rolled his eyes. Everyone knew Lady Izell's only child with Nados was stillborn. She had no heir with the late king nor any other children from anyone else.

"As you know, we have been keeping track of all the young half-castings. And yes, it is time to implement the next phase of our plan," Armone said.

More commotion followed this statement, along with the rustle of papers. Then the voices were too low to hear. Jay chanced another look. The group stood huddled together in the middle of the room, reading several sheets of parchment.

"What's this?" Gilcres cried in disbelief. "You're considering Jay, the cook's boy?"

Jay ducked down, holding his breath.

"We have to consider them all," Armone replied.

"He's too young," Tober said, "by at least a year."

"The rumors may not be accurate," Armone said. "We've expanded the project to all half-castings."

"All of them?" one of the men asked.

"Yes, we have to be thorough," Armone said.

"The cook's boy you're watching is no longer a servant, eh Gilcres," Tober said. "Graduated the academy."

"Ha!" Gilcres snorted. "Nothing going on between the ears, if you catch my meaning. He was made a messenger, the lowest position for an officer. He's a halfy simpleton."

Tober countered. "He nearly won the academy race, if I recall. A bit embarrassing. Isn't that right, Captain?"

"It was close, but only because he cheated," Gilcres replied. "He certainly couldn't win a fair race. I'd rule him out."

I cheated? Jay clenched his fists. The outcome of the race still felt raw, but he had to concentrate on the actual issue.

"Not one will be ruled out, Captain," Armone said with a stern tone of voice. "The emperor rewards diligence. All right, you have your assignments. Go out and find them all."

The group broke up and headed out the doors.

Find them all. That sounded ominous. What if the emperor believed the rumors of a secret heir? Did the emperor truly think that anyone of mixed descent could rise to challenge him like in the fairy tales? If so, Lady Izell wasn't the only one in trouble. Every person of mixed ancestry, including himself, was in danger of being part of a purge fueled by paranoia.

Jay made his way through the shadows and out the back of the room. He slipped back through the crawlways and servant corridors, returning to the stables without being seen. Once there, he checked on Havoc, who was happily munching on oats.

"Sorry, boy, we have to go." Jay removed the feed bag.

Havoc snorted with irritation but seemed eager to stretch his legs again. Jay rode out of the marketplace and straight for the castle. The road was no clearer than before and he was forced to flow along with the traffic.

The congestion gave him time to think. Galathians were known for their prejudices, but having secret meetings and ominous plans was new. And Gilcres had been set to watching him. *That must be how he knew my orders so quickly.*

Finding every mixed civilian would take some doing. Jay and his kind were rare enough to be singled out in a crowd, but Calonade was a large city. Many townsfolk made up the crowds of people in the marketplace. Residents of the surrounding farms and groves counted for not a small number.

"Ho! Lieutenant!"

Jay found himself at the main entry to the castle. From the wall above, Captain Gaven looked down at him.

"Yes, sir!" Jay snapped a salute.

"Would you like to pass through or just sit there all day?"

Jay realized Havoc had stopped to nibble on a tuft of grass beside the gate.

"I'll pass through, sir." And added quietly to Havoc. "Always thinking with your stomach, eh boy."

"Very good. Get a move on, Lieutenant. You may go slowly, but the rest of the world will not."

"Yes, sir." Jay considered the advice. While he dawdled, who knew what damage Armone and the other Galathians could do? Kaloby needed to know of their plan at once. There was not a moment to lose.

Chapter Ten

Urey's orbit is in the green zone of a massive blue star. One revolution takes about fifty standard galactic years. With the lack of seasons and the imperceptible slow movement of the stars, we imposed a standard calendar on their dominant culture.

—from the journal of Sephy Alcott, Standard Galactic Year 10555

Calonade, Day 328, Year 2998 local planetary calendar, Standard Galactic Year 14284

Jay ran down the steps to the dungeon and found Kaloby gathering papers. He wore his royal brown dress coat and matching neck cloth.

"Where are those maps of the front you were memorizing?" Kaloby didn't look up. "I need them for a meeting with Lady Izell."

"Sir, I need a minute—"

"Not now, Jay," Kaloby interrupted, locating the map. "After the meeting, I will have plenty of minutes. As of now, I'm five minutes late. The emperor is pushing once more to send our troops to the front." He shook his head. "Folly for all."

Kaloby gathered a few select papers, straightened his suit, and headed for the stairs. Jay knew he had to say something.

"Wait! Sir! What is Legate Armone planning for mixed children?"

Kaloby stopped in his tracks. "What did you hear, Jay? Quickly, now."

Jay relayed the overheard conversation. Kaloby rubbed his beard as he listened but didn't change his expression.

"Are you certain, Jay? It was the emperor's agent, and he's looking for Lady Izell's heir."

"Yes, sir. They have a list. Of people like me."

Kaloby nodded, looking serious. "That was risky, Jay. I have trained people in place to do that sort of thing."

"Then where were they? No one else was in the room."

"You didn't *see* anyone else." Kaloby shook his head. "Well, no harm was done, and it is timely information. I admit you are the first to bring it to me. Would you like to brief Lady Izell yourself?"

Jay's heart leaped. "Yes, sir!" He started up the stairs.

"Hold up, my boy." Kaloby grasped Jay's arm. "We should not be seen tearing off together to see Lady Izell. We'll take the steam tube instead."

"The old coal cart lift in the boiler room hardly works anymore," Jay said. "There's still a long way to go from there to reach Lady Izell's council room."

"We'll meet with her in a more private place." Kaloby waggled his bushy eyebrows. He led the way to a dusty corner in the back of the lab. Putting one finger to his lips, he pulled a loose stone from the wall, revealing a knob. He yanked it and the whole wall shifted, rotating outward. Jay had never seen the concealed door before. It opened, revealing a circular chamber lined with smooth bricks. Kaloby ushered Jay in, handing him an oil lamp. There was just enough room for them to stand beside each other on a metal floor. Jay looked up to see a tunnel rising straight up into the flickering shadows above.

Between them, a manual gearshift jutted upward to waist level. It had a steam gauge attached to it. Kaloby tapped the gauge. "A healthy charge."

"What's this?" Jay stared in amazement at the secret room and its mechanism.

Kaloby handed his papers to Jay. He pulled the door shut and grabbed the handle of the gearshift. "Brace yourself." He squeezed the handle and pushed the gearshift to a position marked with the number three—the highest setting.

The floor lurched and rose as steam blasted from under them. Jay stumbled but recovered his balance. The air was wet and stifling. The floor rose faster and faster until Jay's stomach was in his throat. They had gone well beyond the ground level of the castle when Jay called out, "How far up are we going?"

"To Lady Izell's quarters," Kaloby shouted.

What? That was at the top of a castle spire—a place he never dared go. The rush of steam lessened as the lift stopped in front of a new doorway. Kaloby yanked the gearshift back into its original position and the floor settled to a stop. Kaloby pushed the portal open, and they stepped out into a large room. Kaloby brushed water droplets from his coat and Jay shook warm moisture from his hair.

The circular chamber filled half the width of a castle spire. Arched windows let in the breeze from the sea below. Sparsely decorated, the room gave an expansive feel. A canopy bed, with its drapes pulled shut, dominated the far half. On either side of the bed, two large banners hung from the wall. One contained a white castle on a blue background—the sigil of Fromeathia featuring its ice palace, said to be carved out of a glacier. The other was much more stirring to Jay.

The Calonaden sigil of a lanicina tree stood on a royal brown background. The leaves of the tree intertwined with its roots to form a net. An anchor reached down from the heart of the trunk and into the earth. A gold crown hovered over the top of the tree.

Jay stared for a moment. He had never seen a Calonade banner in person—only sketches in his military history books. His respect for Lady Izell rose a notch. She was brave to display such a symbol of Calonaden sovereignty. Although few would see it here in her private bedchamber, it was still inspiring.

Across the front two bed posts hung a shaft with a shining blade affixed to its end. Its finely honed edge gleamed in the candlelight. "What's that?" Jay pointed toward the weapon as Kaloby collected his papers from Jay.

"A Fromeathian battle spear. An antique. Family heirloom, I imagine."

Impressive. She keeps it sharp.

Jay turned to see they had emerged from the backside of a pivoting section of a large bookshelf.

"How long has this been here?" He gestured toward the steam tube.

"The escape tunnel was built with the castle. It used to feature a ladder and a daunting climb. The steam elevator is a more recent addition. Not many people know of it, so please keep its existence a secret." Kaloby pushed the door shut. "Come along, let's find Her Ladyship."

Kaloby led Jay down the length of the bookshelf and through another archway. The other half of the chamber spread out before them. The arched window on this side showed the rising slopes of the Kelstone Mountains. Situated under the open window sat a large desk filled with parchments, inkwells, and writing quills. Lady Izell sat at the desk, scratching on a piece of paper.

"Ah, there you are, Kaloby," Lady Izell said, "and you've brought Lieutenant Jay. Very good."

"Good day, M'lady," Kaloby said with a curt bow.

"I heard the steam chute. Letting the lieutenant in on our secrets, I see."

"Yes, well," Kaloby said, "he should know about it for your safety."

Jay tried to keep his expression bland, but a hint of a smile betrayed his pride at being trusted by Lady Izell.

"I agree," Lady Izell said. "What is on your agenda today?"

Kaloby nodded, and Jay launched into his report. The description of Legate Armone and his search for a secret heir got particular attention.

"Well, the emperor has been trying to get rid of me for a long time, so that isn't unusual. This fiction about a secret heir is new. And rounding up people of mixed ancestry is simply unacceptable. What can you add, Kaloby?" Lady Izell asked.

"Not very much, I'm afraid, M'lady," Kaloby said. "This visit from Legate Armone wasn't announced. Usually there are many message krikes sent to the governor's aviary, letting him know of such an arrival. Not a peep this time. In fact, I don't think Kendric knew about the visit until Armone reported to him in person. We certainly didn't know until he stepped off the boat."

"Perhaps Staukard is losing trust in Kendric," Lady Izell said.

Kaloby shrugged. "Possibly. If so, that's a bad development for our intelligence gathering."

"What do you think, Lieutenant?" Lady Izell asked.

"Begging your pardon, M'lady," Jay said, "but a search for a fictitious heir is going to get people hurt. We need to warn them."

"We don't want a panic either," Lady Izell said. "We need to find out more about this Legate Armone. Perhaps he can be redirected."

Jay frowned. Armone, Gilcres, and their friends seemed awfully enthusiastic about their mission. Jay wondered if Lady Izell's typical tool of persuasion—lanicin—would have any effect.

"I can look into it, M'lady," Kaloby said.

"Thank you, Minister Kaloby. Anything else?"

"I brought the latest maps of the front." Kaloby laid them on the desk. "The Galathians continue with their ill-conceived conquest—"

With a screech and a clatter, a large silver bird landed on the window ledge. It hopped onto Izell's desk, scattering papers, ink, and quills. Jay reached for his hilt and grabbed air. He forgot he had to be unarmed while acting as a messenger in the city. He recovered and lunged forward to protect Lady Izell as she stumbled back from her desk.

Kaloby appeared at Jay's shoulder, holding a small palm pistol pointed at the machine shaped like a large crow. Under its steel feathers and contained within its metal chassis, wheels and gears whirled and spun. A silver glow emanated from the bird's undercarriage that gave it an aura of power. The clockwork crow made a rusty, barking caw and folded its wings. It stood, staring at them with its obsidian eyes.

"Hold!" Lady Izell shouted. "I know what this is."

Jay froze in front of Izell, staring into the bird's dark eyes and wary of its sharpened feathers and gleaming talons.

"What is it?" Kaloby asked, still aiming his palm pistol at the bird.

The crow bobbed its head and peered at them like a natural crow would. Cocking its head, it pecked at an errant quill lying askew on Izell's desk.

"The one I saw was a toy in the Galathia court some years ago," Izell said. "This one seems much more sophisticated. I believe it's a messenger."

As if on cue, a panel in the bird's chest briefly opened and a rolled parchment flopped out onto the desk. The crow pecked and nudged it closer to its audience. It gave a rusty caw and hopped back onto the window ledge. Before Jay could react, it leaped into the air and soared away from the castle spire. Jay leaned out the window to catch a final glint of sunlight off steel.

"It's gone," Jay said.

Kaloby opened the parchment. He had returned his palm pistol to its hiding place.

"A message from the Oracle for you, M'Lady." Kaloby placed it in her outstretched hand and leaned over her shoulder. They both read the scrawled ink intently.

Jay blinked in surprise. The Oracle, an old woman who lived in the Kelstone peaks above the city, was said to be either a gifted seer or crazy, depending on who you spoke to. After a few moments of silence, Jay couldn't help himself. "What does it say?"

Kaloby glanced at Izell, leaving her to answer the question. She read aloud, "*Greetings Lady Izell*, some pleasantries, a warning that my position of influence is at risk, but she knows that I know. Here's the meat of it: *I bring news that Aeterna is awakened by the return of the Vinctus Stone. Now is an auspicious time to collect it and use it against our foes. Send a message to me when you are ready, and I will prepare the way. Delay only serves our enemies. Sincerely, Myra, Oracle of Urey.*"

Izell handed the parchment to Kaloby, who produced a magnifying glass from a pocket and examined the writing. Izell glided to the far side of the room, lost in thought.

Jay hadn't heard of a Vinctus Stone, but Aeterna sounded familiar. "Isn't Aeterna an ancient mythical city?"

"Yes, from the fairy tales." Kaloby focused on a nuance of the message. "It actually exists, but few know how to find it." He looked up at Jay. "It's hidden by magic."

Jay had learned to read using the tales of the half-cast prince and how he left Aeterna to go on adventures. Though he couldn't recall all the details, he remembered them fondly. He never thought aspects of the stories might be real. Could the magic in the stories exist as well?

"Magic?" Jay asked.

"I'm afraid science can't explain everything," Kaloby said. "Many such unexplained phenomena are associated with the Oracle. For instance, no one has ever found the city of Aeterna without the Oracle's permission despite centuries of searching. However, all the past sovereigns of Calonade have visited it once, receiving admittance."

"All save one," Lady Izell said.

"Pardon me, M'Lady," Kaloby said. "I meant no offense."

"In my short tenure as sovereign, I didn't have time to visit," Izell explained to Jay.

"King Nados went?" Jay asked.

"Yes, he was the last to visit," Kaloby said. "Just before he became king."

"Why, M'Lady?" Jay asked. "What's important about Aeterna?" In the tales, it was the home of the half-cast prince between adventures, but not much more.

Lady Izell's serene expression dissolved into a somber mask, and she turned her focus to the parchment. Jay realized too late that invoking the king's name reminded her of the tragic past.

"Minister Kaloby," Lady Izell said in her formal tone. "Please take the lieutenant back to your lab and explain what he needs to know. I need to consider this message and how to respond."

"Of course, Your Ladyship," Kaloby said with a bow. "Come, Lieutenant, let me show you how to operate the steam tube." They left Lady Izell holding the parchment with a far-away look.

* * *

After they returned to the lab, Kaloby showed Jay how to set the steam tube to recharge.

Jay hoped he hadn't offended Lady Izell by bringing up King Nados. That had to be a sore subject. Jay shook his head in disgust at his lack of tact.

Kaloby must have sensed his brooding. "More questions on your mind, no doubt."

"Not sure where to start. I'm still a bit startled by the flying bird machine. Throw on that a mythical city become real and its magical seer stone." Jay shrugged.

"Visiting Aeterna is a test," Kaloby said. "A formidable one with a useful reward. No one seeks admittance into Aeterna without serious preparation. The ritual has never been widely shared, though key leaders from the old days know about it. With the occupation, it passed into obscurity. I'm surprised it's come up again."

Jay stared at Kaloby. If Aeterna was real, were the fairy tales true? Did a half-cast price once ride the Frontier? If so, maybe he could too.

"The Vinctus Stone," Kaloby continued, "is a whole other level of obscure. Very few people know of its existence. It's only mentioned in a few old remnants of ancient texts. Until now, I had written it off as lost, an exaggeration, or not real at all."

"What does the stone do?" Jay asked.

"It's connected to the Oracle and Aeterna," Kaloby said. "Though it is not clear how. Since the Oracle closely guards the city, perhaps the stone is kept there. Inside lives a ghost who imparts prescient wisdom to a successful entrant. Such legitimacy and knowledge have allowed the rulers of Calonade to be successful in challenging times for many generations. If they follow the advice, that is."

Better and better. Mystical ghosts and magical stones. How many more revelations would this day bring? Jay's head spun a bit. Not just from the new information, but from who brought it. Kaloby, the Minister of Science, had gone further afield than he let on.

"Holding the Vinctus Stone," Kaloby said, "is like having a prescient adviser with you all the time. Imagine a battle commander who can see the future, or even better, a ruler who has such insight."

Jay sat down on a bench near a bookshelf heavy with dusty tomes. "With Legate Armone stirring up trouble, Lady Izell, her loyal followers, and all those of mixed descent are in jeopardy. I can see the usefulness of the magic stone, if it's real, but why does the Oracle want to give it to us?"

"An astute question." Kaloby nodded. "One that has inspired many conversations with Lady Izell and King Nados before her. We haven't been able to understand the Oracle's motivations. Her generosity to Calonade must be part of a greater agenda, but thus far, we haven't discovered what it is."

"Do the Galathians know about it?" Jay asked.

"We don't know. They have access to more books than I do." Kaloby gestured around the room at his collection.

Jay raised his eyebrows in surprise. "You have the most books I've ever seen."

"Galathia has many libraries that make my collection seem paltry. It's possible they know much more than we do."

Kaloby frowned, and Jay felt his longing for the unattainable knowledge possessed by their Galathian foes.

"What if it's a race?" A tingle shot up Jay's spine. "We should go to Aeterna as soon as possible." The exciting prospect of thundering through the Frontier on Havoc as he hurried to beat an army of Galathians to Aeterna captured his imagination.

"Slow down, soldier," Kaloby said. "It could be a lure to draw Izell out of Calonade. We don't know yet the best course of action or even if the Vinctus Stone is real. Besides, you need to get ready for tomorrow."

"Tomorrow?"

"You will have your first training session with Commander Kahela in the morning."

At last! Jay's excitement shifted to a new track. "She's visiting from the Frontier, sir? That's wonderful!"

"I'm glad you're looking forward to it, but be warned, she won't go easy on you. I have more errands. Get some rest." Kaloby climbed up the stairs, leaving Jay alone in the dungeon laboratory.

Chapter Eleven

I applied everything I learned from leading an empire through unending conflict to conquer love. War was easier.
—from Chronicles of Galathia by Rafykin, Urey, circa 2640 local planetary calendar.

Thurbush, Day 328, Year 2998 local planetary calendar, Standard Galactic Year 14284

After hundreds of miles of riding, Jortica could honestly say she'd never get used to saddle sores. The dust of the Frontier caked her uniform, not to mention her face, in too many layers to count. Thurbush, after almost forty days on patrol, was a welcome sight, until she rode into the heart of town.

A pall of dread hung over the place. None of the daily sounds of people tending to their duties and chores could be heard. The town, abandoned of its folk, only harbored Galathian soldiers. They swaggered down the street, leaned on the hitching rails, and lounged in the saloon. At a glance, there seemed many more present than when she left.

The Galathians didn't act at all happy to see their fellow Horse Division soldiers. They spat and sneered. Some turned their backs, while others scowled. One even shouted a slur. He ducked down before Jortica could get a bead on him.

Not surprised by the behavior of the Galathians, Jortica felt more apprehension from seeing so many of such poor disposition in one place. In Calonade, the natives outnumbered the conquerors in any gathering or group. Within the Horse Division, Galathians used to be rare. Now, they were everywhere. It made her hackles rise.

Captain Fauden gathered the squad leaders. Four remained of the six who had started the trek. Not everyone was cut out for the Horse Division. Their force had dwindled by nearly half since the first day. None were deserters as far as Jortica knew, but Fauden made no attempt to encourage the disaffected riders to stay. He sent them home without comment.

"Have the troops picket the horses," Fauden said. "I'll check in with the commanding officer to see about lodging and our next assignment." Wincing from the same hard riding they had all endured, Captain Fauden dismounted and marched toward the manor house at the end of the lane that had been requisitioned as headquarters.

Jortica steered Calamity to her squad of three riders gathered a few paces away. "We stay here."

"I hope the Cap can get us bunks," said Eason, the skinny townee. "Been a long time since I slept decent."

"You had a whole life of sleeping in a bed, Eason," said Samos, the tall and beefy farmer. "A dry bale of hay in a barn would do just fine. Let the Cap know, LJ."

"The stables and corral are full," said Kessa, the overeager lanicina grove tender. "But the Galathians look to be getting ready to ride out. Maybe we can put up the horses there after they leave, Lieutenant."

Jortica read the weariness on their faces. It had been a long ride, but her squad had stuck together. They could handle another night. "We'll stake the horses and get the saddles off their backs. Set up camp here for now. I'll check around for better accommodations."

"Ma'am, yes, ma'am," Kessa answered.

On the long road, Jortica had gotten to know her squad pretty well. Though she still thought of them by their childhood origins, they were full-fledged Horse Division riders now, just like herself.

As the horse soldiers set up camp, Jortica wondered when the Galathians would leave for their tour of the Frontier. Hopefully soon. The natural charm of the place suffered from their presence.

Jortica spotted an odd wagon parked across the main street at the front of the jailhouse. It had a barred cage built over the bed. A moaning sound came from inside. Two Galathian sergeants sat on the seat, passing a bottle back and forth.

Jortica approached from the rear and peered in at the cargo. A couple of kids huddled around a man lying in his own blood. Half conscious, the man had a bloody gash across his forehead.

"Sergeant! What is going on here?" Jortica snapped in Galathian.

One sergeant whipped his head around and reached for his sidearm. His face looked as if made of bricks. His bald head, marked with uneven plinum bands and prodigious scars, shone in the moonlight. The other sergeant peered over his shoulder with less concern. He sported a graying and scraggly beard, far from regulation.

"Lieutenant." The bearded sergeant patted his partner on the arm. The other man let go of his grip on his pistol. "No need to worry. The halfy is subdued, and the kids didn't put up much of a fight. We'll get 'em processed right quick. Prolly send the kids back, but the big fella will get some attention."

Frowning with disgust at the treatment of the Frontier citizens, Jortica stepped around to look the sergeants in the eye. The disheveled uniform and wrinkles of the older one revealed a career of low expectations. The younger and bigger one followed his leader's example, but with dimly lit eyes compared to the first. "Are these people criminals, Sergeant?"

"Naw, they just halfies," the bearded man said. "Rounded 'em up this morning down by Clem's farmhouse. He held 'em for us."

Jortica clenched her fists and forced her voice to be steady. She sent the next words like rifle shots. "What's your name, Sergeant?"

"It's a woman," the other one muttered with raised eyebrows.

The bearded one glanced at his partner. "My name is Nackers, and this is Lunt. We drive the Welcome Wagon." He smiled and gestured to the cage. "We specialize in picking up the drunk and disorderly soldiers and providing them with a nice ride to lockup to cool off. Lately we been rounding up halfies for the Legate."

"It's a woman," Lunt repeated.

Nackers gave his partner another look. "I think the *lieutenant* knows she's a woman, Lunt. In fact," Nackers returned his gaze to Jortica, "this is none other than the winner of the race. First Calonaden to win, I hear, and first woman ever."

Jortica glared at Nackers' attempt at flattery. The one and only Galathian to acknowledge her victory had to be this pathetic example of a human being.

"A woman *officer*?" Lunt asked.

Jortica shifted her glower to Lunt. The way his plinum bands crisscrossed up over the top of his head and down his face made her wonder about the dividing line between high and lowborn. This man's appearance wasn't all that different from the people he abused.

"I apologize for my friend here, Lieutenant. He has trouble with new ideas," Nackers said. "Took him a week to understand we're rounding up halfies instead of drunks."

"I can hit 'em harder." Lunt grinned.

"That's right, my friend," Nackers said. "We have to be polite to soldiers."

The sheer magnitude of outrage rising in Jortica became too much to express. The wind in her mind picked up along with her anger. She stood flabbergasted as the two Galathian clowns continued their banter. Her mind focused on the next step rather than the current abhorrent circumstance.

"What do you mean by process them, Sergeant?" Jortica asked.

"The Legate questions all the male halfies," Nackers said. "Not sure what he's after, but he sure is thorough. Then he tosses them in the jailhouse. Problem is that it's getting full. Somebody's gonna hafta come up with a new place to put 'em."

"There sure are a lot of 'em," Lunt said.

"Yep, jail's full to brimmin' with 'em. More halfies out in the woods than in town is my understanding," Nackers said.

"Show me," Jortica said.

"The jail?" asked Nackers. "We don't got—"

"Show me, Sergeant. That's an order," Jortica snapped.

"All right," Nackers said. "Follow me. Lunt, keep an eye on things out here."

He levered himself down off the wagon and lumbered up the steps to the jailhouse. After a few words with the Galathian soldiers inside, he ushered Jortica in.

The first thing that hit her was the smell. The stink of the unwashed hovered like a thick fog. Jortica surveyed the three jail cells that took up the back of the building. They were packed with men. Some were lying on the floor, others curled up in the corners. Some leaned against the walls or the bars. Stripped down to their trousers, all of them were bruised and bleeding. Jortica spied some wounds that had begun to fester.

There were old ones, young ones, and in between. They all had one thing in common. Their skin had patches of light blue over dark. Some had streaks and others had freckles. Many had blotches over uneven patterns. They all had light-colored hair, some lighter than others, and a few almost as blond as a Galathian. They were all lowborn.

There had to be thirty of them stuffed into the three cells meant for one or two prisoners at most. All of them kept quiet with their heads down. Only one nearby seemed to notice her as different from the rest. His eyes lit up with hope, and he reached through the bars until a guard slapped his hand with a riding crop. The guards chuckled as the man groaned and dropped his eyes to the floor.

Jortica turned to Nackers. "Who told you to do this?"

"The Legate," Nackers said. "He's the commander, ya know."

Jortica dug her thumbs into her belt. How could anyone let this stand? A half dozen Galathians were treating the citizens of the Frontier worse than cattle. These were the people the Horse Division had sworn to protect.

Her expression must have been like a bonfire of disgust because Nackers stepped in close and bent to her ear. "You might wanna take a minute, Lieutenant," he said with a smile that edged into a sneer, "and get used to your new surroundings. I know you're a smart one and there ain't nothing you can do about this."

Jortica knew Nackers saw her as a green lieutenant who would back down if given a strong suggestion from an experienced sergeant. She could tell he also expected her to have no spine, being a woman. Jortica had sized up dozens of men like this, stuck in their own stale opinions of a world changing around them.

"Sergeant Nackers, you will immediately release these people from custody and allow them to return to their homes." Jortica glared at Nackers, daring him to contradict her.

A dark frown crossed his face, but it dissolved just as quickly into a tense smile. "Ha! Good one, Lieutenant," he said, glancing at the audience of Galathians surrounding them. "But I know you're joking because we're all just following the Legate's orders."

Jortica didn't budge as she sized up what she could do against six Galathians with one shot and a sword. She noticed two of the more sober Galathians watched her closely, their hands hovering over weapons, hoping for an excuse.

In the back of her mind, she heard the rush of a wind rising. It came up quiet and low, but Jortica knew if she let it brew, it would grow into a raging storm.

"Lieutenant Jortica!"

Jortica spun to see Fauden standing in the doorframe. "Sir," she saluted by instinct. The Galathians shrank back.

"Come with me, Lieutenant." Fauden turned and strode away.

Jortica glared at the sergeant and his fellows. "This is not over."

She hurried out of the jailhouse to catch up with Fauden. "Did you see that, sir?" She pointed back at the tragic spectacle behind them.

"Yes," Fauden said. "And it's none of our concern."

"How is that none of our concern, sir? Those people are being abused in there."

Fauden stopped and gave Jortica a long look, forcing her to wait. "We have our orders and they have theirs," Fauden said.

"They are not criminals, sir. Those are citizens. Orders to detain people for no reason besides their skin coloring are illegal and immoral."

Fauden glowered at her. "When a Galathian Legate of the empire gives an order, that's the new law and the new morality. Besides, they're just half-castings. The Legate wants them rounded up and contained. He's working on better quarters for them and should have a camp on the outskirts of town ready for them in a few days."

Fauden wouldn't see reason, which really didn't surprise her given he was Galathian. Maybe she could shift things a different way. "What about medical attention? What about food and water?" Jortica asked, her voice rising. "How can you stomach this?"

"Calm yourself, Lieutenant," Fauden said in an icy tone.

"I know it's not what you're used to. I'm not either, having served under Commander Kahela, but times have changed. The emperor wants something, and Legate Armone is here to get it. The best thing we can do is help get it over with."

Jortica seethed. "I refuse to round up innocent people."

"Good, because those are not your orders, Lieutenant," Fauden snapped. "We ride out again in the morning."

Jortica shook her head. She had been expecting a few days of downtime and maybe leave after so much riding. "Where?"

"Same tour," Fauden said. "The length of the Talindrey. The Legate wants to weed out those that can't endure it."

Jortica's mouth dropped open in shock. A second later, she snapped it shut because she knew the Legate's objective was a lie. "He wants us out of the way."

"Lieutenant, no one is getting killed, just detained. This will pass, and they'll go home. You are a promising officer. Don't force me to do something I don't want to do. There will be a great future for you if you follow your orders now. Commander Kahela would expect nothing less."

Jortica nodded. She could tell Captain Fauden wouldn't give in. She also knew Kahela would never put up with this, which is why she'd been sent away. Jortica had to do something but was outnumbered right now. She saluted and marched away to give the orders.

A small fire spread its glow over the camp. Her squad waited with four sleeping rolls laid out around it and the horses picketed beyond. Three other circles of riders and their mounts dotted the meadow. Eason stirred the contents of a cook pot. Samos peeled four potatoes, and Kessa cleaned a rabbit carcass.

Eason smiled up at her. "So, LJ, no room in the inn

tonight?"

Jortica shook her head, only half listening to the young man.

"We got potatoes and two hares at the market." Kessa matched Eason's good cheer. Samos remained quiet.

"What's the word, ma'am?" Eason asked.

"We ride the Talindrey again. Start in the morning." Jortica repeated Fauden's orders without inflection. The haunting images from the jailhouse still lingered.

The smiles melted off Eason and Kessa's faces. Only Samos seemed unmoved.

"Why?" Eason fired off the demand for an answer without thinking. Most townees behaved this way. She'd yet to discourage it enough.

"Those are our orders." Jortica knew she lacked her usual crisp tone. She couldn't get the jail out of her mind, except the faces kept changing from the lowborn to her family. Her little sister behind the bars. Her father staring sightlessly at her wondering why she did nothing. The Galathians would never stop at a few disadvantaged people. They'd keep pushing until every Calonaden languished in prison.

Jortica's attention returned to the little camp where Kessa and Eason argued over the value of their orders. "Eyes Front!" All three horse soldiers jumped to attention.

"Listen to me. We will follow our orders."

Eason started to protest. "But we just rode—"

Jortica cut him off with a gesture. "For now."

Kessa's turn: "But orders have to be—"

The same gesture stopped her. "There's going to be a time when we won't." All three of them stared in silence as she told them about the jailhouse. "Those people are innocent, and we'll do something, but not yet. We can't charge in there the four of us and rescue those people."

"We have help." Samos gestured to the other camps.

"Still not enough," Jortica said. "They have over a hundred troops itching for trouble. Even if we made it out, we'd be hunted down, and they'd be killed or captured again. There will be a time when we fight. I'll tell you when."

All three nodded. The firelight carved deepening shadows into their faces. Jortica felt a new pressure landing on her shoulders. The storm in her head kept brewing at a slow boil. None of them knew how to face this injustice, and yet they had to. She could feel her squad's need for her to lead them. She just hoped she'd know what to do when the time came.

Chapter Twelve

The technology on Urey has advanced to an equivalent of classical antiquity on Earth. If human progress is not checked, it will continue along the same trajectory to ruin.

—from the journal of Sephy Alcott, Standard Galactic Year 13280

Calonade, Day 329, Year 2998 local planetary calendar, Standard Galactic Year 14284

"Damn!" Jay swore as Commander Kahela knocked him to the ground for the hundredth time. The walls surrounding Lady Izell's private courtyard spun for a minute. As he picked himself up, ripped vines and shredded roses fell from his uniform. It seemed heartless to rough up the garden again. But as their new training yard, it would have to get used to a regular beating.

The castle guards no longer patrolled above them. Gaven must have arranged for more privacy. A new structure stood in the courtyard, looking like a fancy shed. It even had decorative trim and woodwork to match the surroundings. Unlocked, however, it revealed racks of every kind of weapon:

heavy swords and pikes used by old-style footmen, riding sabers and lances for cavalry, and every flintlock available, from long-range rifles to palm-sized pistols.

Jay liked the variety and to have weapons on hand. As a messenger, he didn't carry a saber or pistol unless he traveled to the Frontier, which he hadn't been allowed to do yet. Jay badly wanted to try the glaive. It had a sword blade on a long handle. A rider could use it like a long sword from the saddle and as a bladed staff from the ground. For now, he was stuck with basic swordplay using a heavy blade instead of the lighter one he was used to. At least until he could get past Kahela's guard. A goal that seemed impossible since he'd never seen moves like hers before.

"Prepare yourself," the commander called out in Calonaden.

Kahela insisted on using only native language during their training. He had to get accustomed to it again after not using it much since his childhood. The hardest part was relearning all the names of the weapons.

She came at him with a wide range of attacks. He parried swiftly, barely meeting an overhand chop toward his head, followed by a low swing aimed at the inside of his sword arm.

"Better." She panted as she attacked. Maybe he was wearing her down.

The thought gave him enough fire to try a counterattack. Kahela fell back, barely blocking his swings in time. Jay felt victory within his grasp and pressed forward. Their swords met with a sharp ring, and he held her with all his might.

With a lightning-fast swipe and twist, Kahela sent Jay's sword flying out of his hand. A moment later, she swept his feet out from under him with a kick. Jay landed on the ground, looking up at the point of her blade.

"Did I seem exhausted?" She pulled the blade back. "Things aren't always as they seem. Let's go again."

"Yes, ma'am." Jay groaned and climbed to his feet, watching Commander Kahela warily as he groped for his weapon.

The commander looked amused. "I won't come at you while you're unarmed, Lieutenant. At least not yet."

After a long, embarrassing moment, Jay pulled his sword from a tangled bush.

"Prepare yourself." Kahela charged again.

Instead of pushing forward, Jay waited. Kahela feinted right and shifted to a chopping blow to his left. For once he didn't go for the feint. Instead, he countered the chop with his blade and found a small opening. He threw a weak left-handed punch. Jay's fist caught the commander in the ear as she ducked. They both staggered back, staring at each other. It was his first hit.

"Very good, Lieutenant." Kahela smiled as she rubbed her ear. "Shall we call it a day?"

"Yes, Commander." He headed for the tool shed to store his weapon.

"Not so fast, Lieutenant. Sit." She pointed to the rim of the fountain. "Drink some water. That's an order."

Jay punched the sword into the earth and sat. Kahela joined him and waited while he cupped his hands and drank from the fountain.

"You seem to be learning," Kahela said. "Shows you have a mind in there. You've earned the right to ask a few questions. If they're good, I might answer them."

That sounded like another warning to prepare for battle. Jay considered his words carefully. "Thank you, Commander.

Where did you learn to fight like this?"

"On the battlefield. You learn fast when your life is at stake." She laughed a little. "I don't think you're quite that motivated yet."

"It *feels* like you're trying to kill me," he grumbled.

She considered him with a serious eye. "If I were, you'd *know* it."

Kahela stood and stretched. Her sleek form rippled with muscle. "The empire conscripts most of their soldiers from the lands they conquer. Each culture has its own favored weapons and combat style. To fight the empire, you need many disciplines to survive."

Jay studied the commander's stern face. She was one of the few Calonaden officers to return from fighting for Galathia on the eastern front. Rumors at the academy described slave-like conditions, suicide missions, and the systematic destruction of entire villages. It sounded horrid, but no one knew how to fight the Galathians better than Commander Kahela.

"But ma'am, I won't be on a battlefield. I'm a messenger."

"Is that a worthy question, Lieutenant?"

"Begging your pardon, ma'am." Jay scrambled for words. "I mean, why exactly is a messenger receiving extra training?"

"Better. About how many assassination attempts do you think have been made on Lady Izell?"

Jay stared at her in shock. "I didn't know there were any."

"There have been four. All unsuccessful, obviously. Three in the first few years after Lady Izell's surrender. The last one was just over forty days ago."

Jay's jaw fell open. "Who's behind it?"

"Various factions stand to gain from her death, but the most likely candidate is always the emperor."

"Is that why the Legate is here?" Jay blurted out before he could stop himself.

Kahela gave him a hard stare. "Could be. We don't know."

"He could be an assassin. And I'm going to be around her a lot." The pieces were falling into place. He could see why Kahela pushed him so hard.

"Correct. You may be the last line of defense for her someday. Your skill will determine the outcome of such an encounter. You have a long way to go to be prepared. It's a good thing my time has suddenly opened up."

"It has, ma'am?"

The commander rose and took Jay's sword. She returned it to the tool shed. Jay couldn't see her face as she snapped closed the lock on its door. "Until further notice, you will study with Minister Kaloby in the morning and train with me in the afternoon. Every afternoon."

Kahela sounded calm, but she still didn't turn around. Jay remembered Gilcres' threat to reassign Kahela. Had he succeeded?

"How can they spare you from the Horse Division for so long, Commander?"

"Someone else will be filling in."

"A Galathian?" Jay guessed.

Kahela spun around, her eyes blazing. "Things are in motion, Lieutenant. The empire doesn't like the few freedoms we still hold, but we'll be watching. We'll be ready."

"Ready for what, ma'am? What are they planning?"

Kahela looked at him with a grim expression. "Think. What do you know?"

Jay turned the puzzle pieces over in his mind. Assassination attempts followed by Kahela's removal from the Frontier. A secret Galathian conversation about mixed kids. Renewed pressure from the empire to send Calonaden soldiers to the front. "I honestly don't know what it all means, Commander," he admitted.

"It means war." Without further explanation, she changed the subject. "We shall begin with the long sword again tomorrow to see if you retained anything from today's training. If you have, then we will progress to a lesson on the glaive. Dismissed, Lieutenant." The commander turned to leave.

Jay's eyebrows shot up. *War?* A million questions scrambled through his mind.

"Wait, ma'am, wait! Before you go, can you tell me, is being Lady Izell's messenger a new position?"

"No." Kahela considered him from the end of the garden path. "She has always employed a private courier who received special training."

"What happened to the messenger before me?"

"Roughly forty days ago, let's just say, the position opened up."

Jay gulped, considering the timing of the last assassination attempt on Lady Izell.

"I hope to see you again tomorrow, Lieutenant." Kahela turned and exited through the servant entrance, leaving her words hanging in the courtyard.

Chapter Thirteen

I gave my heart to the Maiden Goddess, and she became the Mother, but then she wanted more than I could give.

—from Chronicles of Galathia by Rafykin, Urey, circa 2640 local planetary calendar.

Calonade, Day 365, Year 2998 local planetary calendar, Standard Galactic Year 14284

It always rained on Remembrance Day. Not the whimsical sprinklings from a purple sky, but more like a gray blanket, heavy with wet. The endless dark clouds rolled in over the mainland, blocking out any view beyond the white caps dancing along the shore. Jay tightened his borrowed frock coat against the damp. He'd rather wear his wool uniform coat, but Kaloby had allowed a day off and Gran had insisted she needed his company as her grandson rather than as a soldier.

He'd tried to explain the two were the same—soldier and grandson—but she would have none of it. *"Are you still the cook's boy too?"* That shut him up. He'd put on Kaloby's second-hand coat, deep blue with black trim as per custom for visiting the dead. The sleeves turned out short, but it sufficed for the required mourning look.

Jay and Gran walked arm-in-arm across Sorrow's Path along the cliffs over the sea, as proper mourners should. Gran carried a pair of bouquets in the crook of her free arm, much like many of the bereaved. A quiet procession of Calonadens trudged through the rain in a long column of blue and black.

Noise came from the road nearby. A hundred or more carriages trundled over the cobblestones just to the inland side of Sorrow's Path. Galathians also had a holiday the same day to pay respects, but they did it differently. Their parade was more a display of wealth than an expression of grief. They rushed to the Galathian portion of the cemetery, around a circular road, and out again. Jay imagined them tipping their hats as they whisked by the graves. Thus was the extent of their respect, even for their own.

Jay didn't begrudge the Galathians their ways. How they pushed aside the customs of others delivered the insult. An illustration of the conflict came into view where Sorrow's Path and the Galathian road had to share a narrow passage around an outcropping of the cliffs. Galathian soldiers took up stations at the crossroads to regulate traffic, which meant making the Calonadens wait in the rain for the carriages to pass.

"Hold up." A Galathian guard held out his hand, blocking the path. As Jay and Gran waited, he waved three carriages through. Jay recognized his old friend, Lieutenant Dothery. Jay hoped the gate guard wouldn't recognize him.

Behind Jay, a deep voice muttered. "Bloody Galathians." Jay glanced back to see a tall and bearded Calonaden in a frayed blue coat frowning at the guard. "No proper way to honor the dead." Though an older man, the strength of his youth still showed in his shoulders. He leaned on Horsemaster Zabe, a smaller man who swayed to brace his weight. They were both drunk.

"You said it, Vinset," Zabe drawled. "Buncha racket."

Both were the right age to have served during the last war against Galathia. Maybe they had fought at the Outer Gate along with Jay's father. If true, they had lost a lot of comrades in the ultimate battle.

Gran turned and gave the two gentlemen a scowl. "There's no need to join them."

"Join 'em?!" Vinset shouted over the noise of a passing carriage. "You and the half-casting here are the ones that joined up with 'em. Let 'em in the gates and let 'em in your home."

Jay shifted to a protective stance slightly in front of Gran. "Horsemaster Zabe. Vinset." He nodded cordially to both. Zabe seemed startled to hear his name, but Vinset glared at Jay. "A good Remembrance Day to you and yours."

Zabe reached to tip his hat but missed the brim and did a clumsy pantomime of the gesture.

Vinset pointed an accusing finger at Jay. "Ain't you in the wrong place, half-casting? Ain't you supposed to be in a carriage to give respects to your tin-striped daddy?"

Heat rose into Jay's face. "My father fought for Calonade, sir."

"Did he now?" Vinset waved a hand around and took a step toward Jay, leading with his finger like a blade. "Ain't it interesting that every half-casting says that until the Galathians march by? Then they change their story."

Dothery glanced at them and chuckled. Vinset's voice

carried over the rattle of the carriages. Jay bit back a retort as Gran squeezed his arm. "Lieutenant!" she called over her shoulder. Jay groaned inwardly, hoping to escape the guard's notice. Dothery peered at her as he waved through the last of the three carriages. "These gentlemen will cross next." Gran stepped aside and pulled Jay with her.

Zabe nodded his thanks and guided Vinset along as they stumbled over the cobblestones and back onto Sorrow's Path beyond. Vinset craned his neck to glower at Jay until they made it around the next bend.

Jay and Gran waited until the next opening to cross.

"That's funny." Dothery nodded toward the two men passing out of sight. "A half-casting in a carriage." He shook his head. "Foolishness." He turned back to direct the traffic.

Gran kept silent and Jay felt his heat turn cold as he ground his teeth. Picturing himself in a carriage riding through the cemetery *was* ludicrous, but he didn't like agreeing with Dothery. Too many Calonadens thought mixed people were privileged. Most Galathians hated his kind even more. Those of mixed descent didn't fit in anywhere.

A break in the traffic allowed them to cross, and Gran pulled Jay closer. "I'm glad you're with me today."

Jay relaxed. The one place he fit was with his gran. That would have to do, and Jay had to admit it did him nicely.

Jay and Gran entered the cemetery through an archway built between two tall trees. A field of simple white stones, each etched with a name, spread out beyond. At the far end, near the cliffs, a tall memorial to the fallen king of Calonade stood proudly among the tombstones. The sea crashed against the rocks below.

Jay and Gran walked along a familiar part of Sorrow's Path

as it diverged through the cemetery woodland. Murmurs of *blessed day* and *sorry for your loss* spoken in Calonaden could be heard throughout the grounds. Some families exchanged greetings with Gran and Jay, while others avoided them. Jay could hear the occasional whisper of *half-casting* as they drifted out of earshot. Comments about his ancestry weren't new, and Jay didn't let any reaction show on his face.

As they neared the graves of his parents, Jay's mood darkened, and Gran must have noticed his frown, because she squeezed his arm again.

"For Dunken, a brave soldier, who fought for what is right." Gran placed a bouquet. She said the same thing every year, since that's about all she knew. "For Olivia, my beautiful daughter. Ah, how your quick wit made me laugh. You are remembered." She placed the second bouquet and lingered over his mother's grave, brushing away tears. Jay looked away.

"Any words to share, Jay?"

Jay shook his head and rubbed an ache in his chest. The empty feeling always came up when he thought about his lack of parents.

"It's all right to feel sad," Gran said. "You didn't deserve to lose them."

"I don't feel sad, Gran." Jay spoke low enough only she could hear. "I never knew them, so I don't really feel a loss like you do. It hurts because on Remembrance Day there's nothing for me to remember."

Gran peered into his eyes, her own still misty. "I'm sorry. I can't offer you much more than you already know." Her eyes welled with tears. "Please believe me, I would if I could."

"I know, Gran." Jay pulled her into a hug.

Gran patted him and said, "Also, Remembrance Day goes beyond your own personal losses. Everyone buried here did their duty just like you will when the time comes."

Jay nodded. He knew that, of course, but hearing it was comforting. Maybe, in the end, this would be the place where he belonged most. "Thanks, Gran."

While Gran arranged the flowers just so, Jay scanned the crowded field. Calonadens gathered at the grave sites and strolled the walkways, many women carrying drab umbrellas. In the distance stood the king's memorial, a white granite tomb with a life-size statue towering over the flat grave-stones surrounding it. The noble visage of King Nados looked toward the Kelstone peaks. Beside the memorial to the old king stood a modest plain grave spire for his unborn son.

Jay wondered what it had been like nearly twenty years past as Lady Izell, the former princess of Galathia's most senior vassal state, Fromeathia, and King Nados, leader of one of the oldest families of Calonade, expected a son of mixed ancestry. Did people curse them for begetting a bad omen? Did they mutter the mixed prince would embody treachery and loss of purity? Perhaps the poor child had found a better fate by never drawing his first breath.

"Lieutenant," a voice said in greeting. "Sorry for your loss."

Jay turned to find Commander Kahela in full dress uniform, Galathian red, not Horse Division garb. Several conspicuous metals were pinned to the front lapel.

"Blessed day, Commander." Jay snapped to attention with a crisp salute.

"At ease," Kahela said. "You're off duty."

He couldn't help wondering why she was on duty. "Ma'am,

could I be of assist—"

"Relax," Kahela interrupted him. "That's an order."

"Yes, ma'am." Jay watched Commander Kahela march toward the memorial to King Nados, nodding to the mourners as she went. In front of the tomb, she stopped and surveyed the grounds.

From the opposite direction, another soldier in a bright red dress uniform caught his eye. Not a Calonaden soldier. General Saben strode toward Kahela.

The crowds stopped talking and parted before him. Some ladies even gasped. Only Commander Kahela seemed unaffected. At the memorial, she and Saben exchanged salutes. General Saben crossed his arms and glared at the gathering.

The whispers spread through the crowd, and several people looked openly hostile toward the general, but no one did anything overt.

"Poor man." Gran shook her head. "He knows what they say. It's just shameful."

"Well, he is Galathian." As much as Jay respected him, he didn't think Saben should have come to the Calonaden burial grounds. "Why is he even here?"

"Jay," Gran said in an incredulous tone. "Don't you know? He fought at the Kettlebone Pass."

"I know. It's said he killed the king. He put the man in the grave he's standing beside."

Gran's eyes opened wide in anger. "Young man," she whispered. "Saben did not kill King Nados. He fought on *our* side. He was one of the most loyal of the king's men. Saben helped outsmart the Galathians countless times. They called him the *Turncoat Captain*."

Jay stared at her in astonishment. "That was a ploy to

get close to the king. He's the headmaster of the bloody academy!"

People turned and looked at him, and Gran hushed him.

"He's one of *them*," Jay whispered. "Everybody knows it." Galathians even suspected of helping Calonade were pushed down like the natives. Only a loyal Galathian would be allowed such a position.

"People accused Saben of murdering Nados because he was nearby when the king died," Gran hissed. "'Zell put him in prison because the Parliament demanded it. He was still there when Galathia took over."

Jay blinked and shook his head. He had never heard this tale. The official Galathian version merely stated the king was a casualty of the battle. Rumors at the academy put their frowning headmaster at the center of the intrigue. "He didn't do it?"

"By the Three Sisters!" Gran swore under her breath. "You try my patience, child. Of course not! He did his best to prevent it, but the blessings of the Willacast Goddesses were not with him that day. Nor with King Nados or the rest of us. When the Galathians found him accused of the king's death, he became a hero to them."

Jay could not reconcile his previous idea of the man to this current story. "Did he deny it?"

"As far as I know, he never spoke of it at all."

Jay's head spun. On the one hand, Jay knew him to be the most demanding officer at the academy, always expecting perfection and doling out extra work. On the other hand, he had helped Jay keep Havoc. No true black-hearted Galathian would have done that.

Jay opened his mouth to ask another question, but Gran

silenced him with a look. Several castle guards hurried to Saben and Kahela's position. Jay recognized Captain Gaven in the lead. They spoke briefly with Kahela and spread out. Gliding through the cemetery threshold came Lady Izell, escorted by five more castle guardsmen.

In the fashion of Calonaden mourning, she wore deep blue garments. Slowly she wove through the crowd, expressing sorrow for the loss so many had sustained. Jay realized Lady Izell would pass by them, and he tried to fade back, but Gran gripped his arm with fingers like iron.

"Hello, Your Ladyship," Gran said to Lady Izell. "I am so sorry for your loss."

"Blessed Remembrance Day, Sedia." Lady Izell spoke in fluent Calonaden with her usual calm expression. "I am sorry for your loss as well. And who is this?"

Do I look so different without my uniform?

Gran gave a sad smile. "My grandson, Lieutenant Jay, M'lady. Orphaned by the war."

"Ah yes, he's the new messenger in the castle." Lady Izell gazed into the distance. "Sorry for your loss, young man."

"Sorry for your loss, Your Ladyship." Jay played along. Izell nodded and drifted on to the next family.

"Good job," Gran whispered, finally releasing his arm.

"You were worried?"

"Frankly, yes," Gran said in her no-nonsense way. "Now you've passed the test, we know how you'll do in the future."

Jay shook his head. *Another test, of course. Would they ever end?*

He watched Lady Izell glide away from mourners and up toward the memorial to her husband. She placed flowers and then stooped over a smaller gravestone nearby. She bowed low over the tomb of the prince who died in her womb, along with all hope for an independent Calonade.

The castle guard surrounded Lady Izell at a discreet distance, while Kahela slipped in behind the former queen. Kaloby strode into view and joined them. He had donned his good coat for the occasion. Jay watched with interest as they conversed. Lady Izell seemed to keep her distance from Saben, giving him a frigid look. Was that an act? Did Kaloby and Lady Izell trust Saben or had the headmaster been assigned to watch them by Lord Kendric?

Jay longed to talk to Kaloby. The old man clearly held more secrets he hadn't yet shared. Jay felt an almost irresistible pull to join the conversation, but Kaloby didn't give him a signal. With great reluctance, Jay stood still. He had passed another test and surely would be allowed deeper knowledge. But when? Could he ask Kaloby tonight? How long would he have to wait?

A dark figure brushed past Jay, giving his shoulder a bump and shifting him off balance. Jay recognized Vinset marching toward the king's memorial.

"That's trouble." Jay undid his arm from Gran and sprang forward to block Vinset's path.

"Hold on, Vinset." Jay caught up to the big man. "You don't want any part of that crew."

Vinset turned his red-eyed stare onto Jay. "Shut up, half-casting. I got business with the old queen." He reached out to shove Jay from his path. Jay dodged, captured Vinset's outstretched arm, and pulled him off-balance and off the path. Vinset growled as he swung his free arm at Jay's head. It would have hurt had he been sober enough to connect. Jay outmaneuvered him again by dodging the wild swing, sweeping a leg, and sending Vinset down onto his substantial butt.

Vinset howled and tried to push himself upright, but Jay had a boot on his shoulder and enough leverage to keep him planted on the ground. Vinset struck with sudden speed into Jay's hip and sent him stumbling back. The big man heaved himself upright and bared his teeth in a fierce snarl. He balled his fists to charge, but two burly castle guards appeared on each side. They had him bound up tight in their grip before he could take a step.

"What's all this?" boomed the commanding voice of Captain Gaven.

Vinset's eyes bulged at the sight of Gaven. He shut his mouth, looking widely around for a way to escape the scrutiny of the Captain of the Castle Guard.

Zabe appeared and stumbled to a halt, breathing hard. "He took off on me," the Horsemaster said, as if Vinset were an ornery steed.

"Captain Gaven, this is Lieutenant Vinset formally of the Calonade Foot." Jay guessed at the position, but it was an educated one. Vinset had the disposition of a man used to climbing mountains to get to his quarry, and he had the initiative of an officer, albeit misguided on this day. By Vinset's sudden focus on him, Jay knew he got it right.

"I'm familiar with Vinset." Gaven leaned into the big man's face. "You knocked his rank down a notch, Lieutenant Jay. Vinset is a retired captain. Battlefield promotion and retirement with honors."

Jay shrugged. He'd been close.

"I wonder what he's thinking, being drunk and disorderly on Remembrance Day in front of the brass." Gaven tilted his head toward the group of officers with Lady Izell.

"Just gonna tell the queen what I think of her occupation," Vinset said through the arms of the guards that held him tight. His voice was much less animated from the pressure.

"Do you think that's wise, sir?" Gaven asked.

Vinset sighed. "No, it probably ain't, but somebody ought to."

"Let him go," Gaven said. The guards released their grip and stepped back. "You're gonna go home, Vinset, and sleep it off. That way you can keep your pension and not end up in the city jail for making a nuisance of yourself."

"You can't tell me you're on her side." Vinset's voice came out more like a sigh. The fight was out of him, but the grievance remained.

"Well, I'm not on yours, Vinset, until you get sober and wise up." Gaven spoke with a calm and serious intensity that made junior officers wet their pants. "We clear?"

"As Fromeathian crystal," Vinset said.

Gaven nodded toward Zabe. "Take him home and make sure he sleeps it off. I'll send a guard by later tonight to check on him."

Zabe made a sloppy attempt at a salute. "Yez-sir."

"You might want to sober up a bit yourself, Horsemaster," Gaven said.

"Yez-sir," Zabe said as he got up under Vinset's shoulder to guide him out of the cemetery. "Yez-sir," he repeated with every step as they trudged away.

"Good job, Lieutenant," Gaven said to Jay. "That was quick thinking to stand up to Vinset like that. I'd hate to see him end in a bad way 'cause of one mistake."

Jay beamed with pride. "Thank you, sir. Glad to help."

Jay joined Gaven in a survey of the grounds and noticed Lady Izell had finished her vigil. Kaloby, Saben, and Kahela went with her, leaving Jay to stand beside his grandmother.

"Well done," she said to him with a smile.

"Do people really think Lady Izell brought the occupation down on us?" Jay asked in a voice just above a whisper.

"Some do," Gran said just as quietly. "But they're wrong. Once King Nados was killed, the Galathians were coming. It was inevitable. After the war and the last stand at Kettlebone Pass, there were precious few left to fight. Vinset was one of the wounded and your father one of the dead. Lady Izell had no other choice."

Jay watched Lady Izell glide over the grounds and back toward the entrance, nodding to her people. She stopped to chat with some and took their outstretched hands in her own as they shared tears.

"It must have been hard," Jay said.

"You have no idea," Gran replied with a sudden grim expression, but it faded quickly. "Come on, escort me home and I'll bake you a pie."

Jay smiled and took her arm again, happy to leave the saddest place in Calonade.

Chapter Fourteen

Melrayis believes we can heal our genetic scars if we immerse ourselves in this new planet. I wonder how much, if any, of ourselves we can recover.

—from the journal of Sephy Alcott, Standard Galactic Year 13280

Calonade, Day 001, Year 2999 local planetary calendar, Standard Galactic Year 14285

Kahela charged toward Jay. He spun and struck the target dummy behind him and then tried to turn back, but a sword struck him in the back of the knee, sending him sprawling in the dirt. Jay rolled over and thanked the goddess once again that they practiced with wooden blades.

"Why am I doing it this way?" he asked. "Seems like I shouldn't turn my back on the most notoriously skilled sword wielder in Calonade."

Kahela offered a hand to help him up. "It's not the one in front you have to worry about."

"You're the one putting me on the ground over and over," Jay said.

"We're working on your speed as well, but the principle holds," she said. "Hit the one behind you first, then see what's next. Let's go again."

Kahela returned to her spot against the opposite wall of the garden, and Jay stood with his back to the target dummy. He had to figure out a way for his sword swing to help him turn to face Kahela.

"Go!" Kahela charged.

Jay spun and swiped the neck of the dummy and let the flow of the swing pull him around in a full circle. With a triumphant thrill, he blocked her strike but missed the elbow that followed it. It smacked him in the eye, and he went down again.

"Ouch! What was that?"

"Pain helps the memory." Kahela offered him a hand up again. "You succeeded. Don't forget it. Let me see your eye."

Jay stood as Kahela prodded his bruise. "A bit of lanicin and this will be fine. However, I want you to fight wounded for the rest of the session. You won't always have lanicin immediately available."

"Fine." It was true, but Jay didn't have to like it.

"Let's try some Talistavvi wrestling moves."

"Some *what*?" Jay asked.

"You won't always have a weapon," Kahela said. "You need to know how to fight without one. The Talistavvi are the best at that sort of combat."

"You fought Talistavvi pirates?"

"No. I was one for a while." Kahela didn't smile.

"Holy Goddess Triumvirate," Jay said. "That's amazing."

"Flattery won't help you in a fight," Kahela said, still not smiling. "We start with elbow strike and move on to vaulting."

"Vaulting?"

Kahela's elbow flew at him, and he ducked just in time to avoid a second bruise on the same eye.

"Good dodge, but you want to get in close. Deflect the blow with your palm and step in for a strike to the chin." Kahela showed him the move. They practiced it over and over for a few hours.

* * *

Jay rubbed his tired and bruised muscles as he stared at the map spread out on the table in Kaloby's dungeon lab. He should have been studying Calonaden battle code by matching old battlefields with their cipher. Instead, his focus kept drifting to the edges of the empire. Galathians had penetrated north into the frozen glaciers of Fromeathia. They had pushed south, skirting the impenetrable Fendeur Forest, marching through the mountainous Frontier to occupy Calonade. They had crossed the Aquerl Sea to the far shores and contested those lands with the native long boatmen. Then they expanded eastward along the extensive Cleavicon River valley and into the Ametrine Grasslands, where they fought a continuous war against the nomadic inhabitants. A bloody conquest in all directions.

Kaloby hurried down the dungeon stairs, holding a tightly rolled scroll. Jay recognized a message from a Galathian krike right away. Kaloby plopped the scroll onto the table. "Translate this." He pulled a small book from his waistcoat and set it beside the scroll. "Book cipher. The date on the message tells you the page to use." He hurried off to the back of the dungeon and searched through his collection of dusty tomes.

"A Pocket Guide to Galathian Grammar?" Jay picked up the little book.

"The key is its size and apparent innocuous nature," Kaloby said from the book stacks.

Jay put a hand to his head and winced as he brushed the bruise over his eye. It needed some lanicin.

The parchment contained mundane inquiries after lanicin production written in Galathian. Had to be from one of Kaloby's spies. Jay applied the cipher like he'd learned in the academy. Once Jay worked it out, he called Kaloby over.

"*Unrest rises from within. Staukard withdraws forces from the east. He will not let Calonade stay out of the fight. Beware of attempt on the queen*," Jay recited from his translation of the message.

Kaloby scratched his beard thoughtfully, his brow furrowed with concentration. "The emperor wishes to force our hand. Even though they have no motive, he'll blame the east for Izell's death and use it as a pretext to take over Calonade completely."

An icy chill ran through Jay as he recalled Kahela's warning about war and the longevity of the former queen's messengers. "How do we make it unsuccessful?"

"Done," Kaloby said. "We already have the assassin in custody."

Jay breathed a sigh of relief and then wondered why he had translated out-of-date information.

Before he could ask, Kaloby went on. "He was rather

clumsy, as is typical with Galathian thugs, but what puzzles me is the fact the ruffian was not aware of the presence of the emperor's agent. The emperor must have a multi-prong approach."

Jay looked around the dungeon. He hadn't noticed any prisoners, nor bars or gates, either. The instruments of torture must be stored in one of Kaloby's many drawers. "Where are you holding the assassin?"

"Certainly not here," Kaloby said. "We have secret places throughout the city, hidden and unknown by any Galathian."

Jay raised his brows. He hadn't heard that before. Kaloby wasn't just a professor of clandestine conflict, he was a practitioner. There was more to his old tutor than Jay had ever known.

"Why not pick up the Legate?" Jay asked. "Question him for a bit?"

"Such an action could start a war. An assassin works in secret and is denied if discovered. The emperor's agents are quite the opposite. A more subtle approach is needed."

"If we're trying to avoid a war with Galathia, why not fight for them in the east?" Jay asked. "It's what we've been trained to do."

"That was the thinking about fifteen years ago. We sent what we had left from the war to fight with the Galathians to prove our loyalty." Kaloby gave Jay a long and sad look. "Few returned, and the tales they told were horrific. They were treated no better than slaves and lives were tossed away as if worthless. Izell vowed to never make such a deal again."

"Kahela is a survivor," Jay said.

"One of the few," Kaloby said. "She is a remarkable soldier, and she almost didn't make it home. When the Galathians demanded more, we reported there was no one else to send. An effective argument, but with the establishment of the academy, we have built up our forces."

"And the emperor knows it," Jay said.

Kaloby nodded. "When Governor Kendric came to press our troops into service a few years ago, we threatened a strike that would stop the flow of lanicin to the empire. It worked. The emperor let us be for a while."

"But it's not working anymore?"

"I'm afraid Lieutenant Jortica's victory at the academy race has been the latest pretext to argue Calonade is ready to support the empire's efforts at the front," Kaloby said.

Jay wrinkled his nose as if smelling Gran's cooking vinegar. Jortica would hate that. It was also another reason to keep things from her.

"We have threatened a renewed strike," Kaloby said. "The emperor knows Lady Izell is the lynchpin of our resistance. She is in constant danger."

"What do we do?" Jay asked.

"The best tools to fight tyranny are politics and strategy."

Politics and strategy? Jay groaned. "I practice every day with Kahela to learn a more direct approach."

Kaloby smiled. "I know, I know. You want to ride into the Frontier to face an enemy head on. However, there's nothing we can do outright. All assassination attempts on Lady Izell have been covert, and there is no gathering of clearly hostile forces. There's no imminent threat to stoke a rebellion, so we cannot strike back."

"So, there's nothing we can do?"

"Hmmm." Kaloby casually pulled off his lab gloves, then worked on the buttons of his coat. He seemed distracted, but the actions masked the turning gears of Kaloby's mind. "Perhaps today is a good day to put into practice your training."

Jay hoped he meant something more interesting than studying maps. "Do you mean eavesdropping again? On the Frontier this time?"

"I mean gathering information directly, without the subject knowing. Actual spy craft."

Spy craft! It was the first time anyone training him had said the word *spy* out loud.

"Excellent! What do we do first?" Jay jumped up from the table. "Disguises? Camouflage? Where do you keep the spy gear?"

Kaloby chuckled. "Hold on," he said, pointing at the chair for Jay to sit. "The only gear you'll need is your ears and what's between them." Kaloby pointed at his own head and then toward Jay's.

Kaloby poured them both a mug of lanicin tea and sat down across from Jay.

"The biggest trick is to get another person talking, someone with valuable information. You listen and learn without giving anything away to them. You gain their trust, pretend to be their friend." He winked and clicked his mug against Jay's. "And if they *do* ask for some detail, you make sure it's something you want them to have."

"You mean lying," Jay said with an uncertain smile as he took a sip of tea.

"If necessary, yes." Kaloby rubbed his chin thoughtfully. "But keep in mind, it's easy to lie to the enemy. It's not as easy to lie to your friends, but sometimes you must."

Jay's smile disappeared. "But it's the Galathians we have to trick. We can trust the people on our side, right?"

"Perhaps, but have they been trained to conceal and deceive? Do they understand the risks? Are they prepared for the danger?"

"But—"

"Think about it." Kaloby held up a cautionary hand. "An enthusiastic friend may reveal your purpose accidentally. Think of yourself just after Lady Izell gave you this assignment. Would you trust that version of you to go out into the field on a mission?"

"No." Jay had to admit he'd learned a lot about discretion recently.

"We must appear different than we truly are. Being a spy sometimes means gathering information without seeming to. Concealing part or all the truth." Kaloby paused and gave Jay his most calculating gaze. "And sometimes, a spy must trade a secret for a secret. Doing so is very dangerous and only done with a mixture of finely honed skills and desperation."

Kaloby leaned back to sip his tea. "The ability to deal with information is critical to spy craft."

"How do you know what to reveal and what not to?"

"Practice," Kaloby replied. "Lots of practice. And that's what I want you to do today. Take a day off from your training and go somewhere plausible."

"Oh, I know. The royal offices in the Parliament House. I could sneak into Lord Kendric's quarters."

"You won't find anything useful there," Kaloby said.

"The aviary! I could intercept some Galathian messages." Jay's excitement rose.

"Already covered," Kaloby said. "Think of somewhere else."

Jay paused but couldn't think of anywhere else he could

find secrets.

"Somewhere you would be expected to go on a day off."

"You mean like the officer's mess hall?"

"Perfect. It's a place for people like yourself to take time off. Go talk to people. Find out something we don't know. Try not to reveal anything yourself and report back tonight." Kaloby got up to leave. "I'm off to give my findings to Her Ladyship. I will inform Commander Kahela you won't be joining her. See you for dinner this evening."

"Wait." Jay jumped up after him. "Those are your instructions? Just go talk to people?"

"These are people you know. They'll be relaxed and genuine if you seem the same. Much easier targets than a watchful enemy, but still a good place to start."

With a small wave, the old man departed, leaving Jay alone in the lab.

That's it? Just go out and be a spy? Jay suddenly appreciated his training with Kahela much more. She had more direct methods, which made sense because of the nature of war: allies and enemies, kill or be killed. Battle made for clear divisions. With the arts of politics and espionage, nothing was certain.

Chapter Fifteen

When the cycle turned and the Maiden became the Mother, a new Maiden was born. I was unprepared for how begetting a goddess would change me.

—from Chronicles of Galathia by Rafykin, Urey, circa 2640 local planetary calendar.

Calonade, Day 001, Year 2999 local planetary calendar, Standard Galactic Year 14285

After she hitched Calamity onto the front rail of the Calonade officer's mess hall, Jortica shook miles and miles of dust from her Horse Division uniform. She couldn't brush off the dread she felt. In the last several weeks, she had ridden the length of the Talindrey River with the Calonaden Horse Division soldiers for the second time. Captain Fauden gave the exhausted team a one-day leave. He ordered them not to enter Thurbush under any circumstances. Fauden escorted their unit personally to the Outer Gate, sending them home with the dourest expression she'd seen on him yet.

A few more horse soldiers had washed out, but not nearly as many as the first round. She'd kept her squad together. Kessa,

Samos, and even Eason, the fidgety townee, had stuck it out with her. They had dispersed at the city entrance, leaving Jortica on her own. She couldn't help but wonder how many would decide to stay home. Such an outcome didn't tempt Jortica. She didn't want to go anywhere near her home.

Calamity could use some tender loving care from the academy stables. The mare had tossed a shoe during the last go-round, and Jortica's makeshift repair wasn't holding up. She patted her mount's flank. "Horsemaster Zabe will see to it, girl, but I need a drink first."

She strode into the mess and noted the place had changed very little. A few Calonaden officers mingled, drinking ale and listening to the autonomous piano. It spewed Galathian ditties, which normally would darken her mood, but the familiarity of it reassured her this time. Galathian officers gathered in clumps, sipping their bitter beer. The ones that bothered to look up turned away, scowling. Jortica smiled inwardly at her reputation but kept her expression bland. She didn't want to get into an argument today.

Jortica sat down at the bar and ordered an ale. The bartender, a Calonaden cadet Jortica hadn't met, took her order and then nodded toward the wall. "We'll get that fixed, ma'am."

The engraving of her name on the Top Cadet plaque had a mark scratched through it. She shook her head. "Doesn't matter," she said to the barkeep. "Everyone knows I won."

The cadet set down a full mug of ale. "It ain't right. We'll get it fixed."

"Thanks." Jortica reached into her waistcoat for a coin.

"On the house." The cadet went back to work.

Jortica scooped up the mug and headed for a quiet corner

table away from the rest of the patrons. She didn't feel social.

Two satisfying sips into the ale, Jortica had just started to relax when a Calonade guardsman wearing a messenger shoulder patch burst through the front doors. He scanned the place. When his eyes locked onto hers, his face lit up in a beaming smile.

"Jortica!"

It took her a second. Jay, the lowborn who put on a show at the race. If he hadn't been such a fool near the end, he'd be the Top Cadet. That would have wrought twice the scandal of her victory. Havoc, his big black horse, was especially memorable. How could he lose riding that monster? Well, he and that royal Galathian idiot, Gilcres, found a way.

He'd also stood her up on the day she rode out of Calonade, which felt like a long time ago. He strode over and sat down without a by-your-leave. "It's been a while."

"It has." Long enough for this one to get into decent shape. He had looked lanky when they first met just after the race. Now he looked in solid fighting shape, having put on twenty stone of muscle. A bruise over one eye revealed he'd been brawling again. Maybe he'd finally punched Gilcres in the nose. Naw, if that had happened, he'd be stuck in the brig because of his mixed ancestry, no matter how much Gilcres deserved it. The thought of it reminded her of the jail in Thurbush filled with tortured lowborn. She had to suppress a shudder. Maybe that madness hadn't spread into the city.

"Here ya go, Jay." The barkeep dropped off a mug of ale at their table.

"Thanks, Mika." Jay slipped her a coin. She nodded, glancing back and forth between the two of them before getting back to work.

"You in here a lot, Jay?"

"Um, yeah," Jay said. "A couple times a week. Riding messages around town gives me a chance to stop in."

He took a healthy sip of ale and then focused on her with a curious expression, as if trying to solve a puzzle. She wondered what this meant.

"What happened to your eye?" Jortica asked.

"Oh, uh." Jay touched his face and hesitated for a second. "I forgot to put lanicin on that. Caught an elbow in the face while going through the kitchens the other day. I must look frightful."

"Not really," Jortica said. "You look like you've been in some intense training. Are the castle guards paying more attention to fitness lately?"

Jay laughed. "No, not much has changed with that outfit. I'm just doing a lot of work."

He seemed uncomfortable as he shifted in his seat. His amiability hit a headwind of nervousness she'd seen a dozen times before. Even though fraternization among officers was against the regs, it didn't stop boastful young men from making advances on young women in alehouses who preferred to be left alone. He hadn't crossed a line yet, but Jortica drew up her defenses to protect her flanks.

"Have you heard about the rematch?" Jay asked.

Maybe he wasn't so easy to read. "What rematch?"

"The Galathians are talking about a rematch for Top Cadet. They insist on leaving the Barber up and ready on the racetrack."

"That's ridiculous." It really didn't matter all that much. The Galathians could race around all they wanted. She wouldn't be joining. She had a job to do. Her shoulders dropped a bit thinking of it. Riding with the Horse Division hadn't turned out as she'd pictured. "Maybe you'll win this time."

"It's not happening. The pride of our striped friends is easily wounded, but that's not enough to bring the entire city to a halt for another day. Besides, we already have a worthy winner." Jay tapped his mug against hers.

Jortica smiled. He was definitely charming, but she was scheduled to ride back up to the Frontier in a few short hours. A solitary bath and bed still had him beat.

"What about you?" Jay asked with a hopeful grin as he gestured toward her uniform. "You've clearly been riding a good bit. How are the Frontier and the Horse Division?"

Jortica glanced down at herself and cringed at the state of her appearance. Her uniform showed a fair amount of wear from miles of riding over rough trails and dusty roads. She wasn't the spit-and-polish ready-for-muster soldier of her cadet days. Beneath the uniform lurked a layer of weariness beyond what the miles bestowed. Under Jay's sincere gaze, she couldn't keep up the façade of normalcy anymore. "I've been riding the Frontier," she answered. "This is my first leave." She stared down into her mug with a frown. "It's not what I thought it would be."

"I heard Commander Kahela got reassigned," Jay said, "but it hasn't changed all that much, has it? It's still the best of the best."

Jortica put down her mug but continued to stare at it. The images of the jail in Thurbush wouldn't leave her mind. She could easily imagine Jay imprisoned with the others. Shame burned her cheeks. She'd done nothing about it. Jortica had left those people, the ones she should have protected, in the hands of the Galathians. She'd promised to stop it but couldn't think of a way that would work. The wind in the back of her mind stirred. She tried to ignore it.

Jay leaned in. "That bad, huh?"

Jortica nodded and looked around the mess hall to make sure no one sat within earshot. "The new commander is a Galathian civilian given a fancy title," she said in a low voice. "They call him a Legate, but he's more political than military. He's a greasy agent of the emperor."

Jay gazed at her intently. Maybe he could do something. Maybe he knew someone in the castle. Or maybe all she had to do was tell what she saw. It was a long shot, given his rank and circumstances, but she didn't know of anything else to try.

"A lot more Galathians have been assigned to the Horse Division. They came in with the new Legate. Then he separated out the Calonadens, except for Captain Fauden." Jortica told him about the grueling patrol over the last eighty days. "I noticed the Galathians were busy while we were gone."

"Doing what?" Jay asked.

Jortica stared into Jay's eyes. Flecks of gold graced the deep brown layers, much different from the black of most Calonadens. How many people in the jail cell had eyes like Jay's? She had to warn him.

"The Galathians are holding people. About thirty," Jortica said. "They've got them crammed into the little jailhouse in Thurbush. But they haven't committed any crimes. They all have only one thing in common, Jay—they're all like you."

Jay's face was blank for a moment, but then he realized what she meant. His open expression faded behind a shadow of grim distaste, and his eyes flickered away from her face.

"Sorry, Jay." She reached out and touched his forearm. "The Legate has his patrols going around the Frontier gathering up the lowborn. They're in awful shape and I don't know what to do for them."

Jay's focus returned, his jaw clenching. Jortica could kick herself. It wasn't the best move to point out racial differences with someone who seemed to be becoming one of her only friends. He noticed the arm touch, though, glancing at the spot twice.

"The whole town is quiet," she went on. "Except for the Galathians. They fill the streets and the tavern. I think they're roughing people up. Stealing. It's bad. Captain Fauden ignores it. I don't know what to do."

"Fauden." Jay shook his head.

"What?"

"Nothing. You said there's a Legate in charge," Jay said. "Do you remember his name?"

"Yes. It's Armone."

For an instant, Jay's face blazed with triumph. Why was that important?

"Do you know about him?"

"Not really." Jay seemed distracted, as if thinking hard.

"What about Commander Kahela?" Jortica grasped for a new idea. "Have you seen her? She'd never put up with this."

Jay's attention snapped back, but his eyes flickered back-and-forth, giving him an uncharacteristically shifty look. "Um, I've passed her in the corridors."

"Could Kahela find out what's going on with gathering up the mixed-descent people?" Jortica asked. "I'm not sure anyone outside of Thurbush knows about it."

"I can ask," Jay said. "I end up in the same places as some important people."

He smiled with admirable confidence, but she didn't feel as sure. Legate Armone seemed determined and, if he had the backing of the emperor, the trouble might not end in Thurbush. "Be careful, Jay." Jortica touched his arm again. "I don't know what all this means." She noticed the hard muscles under his skin. He'd definitely been training. Maybe he decided to make something of himself.

Jortica stared down into her mug and noticed Jay doing the same. She'd shared a lot and felt better, though not as good as doing something about it herself. She still had no idea what that might be. At least the threatening storm in her mind had subsided.

"Can I get you another ale?" Jay asked.

Jortica pushed her mug away. "No, it's making me feel worse. I've had enough."

"Do you want to get out of here?"

"Goddess, yes. Oh, I need to get my horse into the stable."

Jay's face lit up again. It was contagious, even with the dark news she carried. Jortica matched his smile. "Let's go."

* * *

He really is very sweet.

Jortica finished rubbing down Calamity in one of the academy's stable stalls. She snuck a peek at Jay as he strolled up and down the aisle, helping the stable hands get their charges settled. Horsemaster Zabe had been more than happy to lend them a stall, and her mare dug into an oat bag.

Jay had hitched his big black monster to a post outside. Havoc had a regular stall inside the castle stables and wouldn't be staying here. Jay helped anyway. Jortica had already spent long hours doing the care and feeding of her mount on the Frontier and didn't feel like doing anything beyond what her horse needed. Jay, however, seemed to relish the work. He definitely knew his way around the animals. Townees have their uses.

After Calamity was put up snug and dry, they left the stable, strolled off the academy campus, and walked through the city toward the sea. All around them, the city buzzed with activity. Down the street to one side resided the center of the marketplace and to the other side stood the castle gates. Horse carts trundled by as merchants hurried to pursue their errands. A few steam-powered carts showed off the Galathian's proud and noisy invention. Acrid smoke spewed from smokestacks. The salty breeze from the sea spared the city the worst of it. The smell of day-old fish covered the rest.

City life wasn't her favorite, having grown up with the fisherfolk in the lower part of town. Shore life felt more familiar with its quieter pace, but the sea had a treacherous side when a storm came to fill every sense with terror. The rush of the wind suddenly picked up, but Jortica felt no breeze on this calm day. Instead, the sound of the storm blew in her mind. The veritable storm had upended her life ten years before. Its harsh memory rose when she needed to fight hard or because of a feeling of being trapped, hurt, or wronged. This time it brewed for those poor people in the Thurbush jailhouse. Since the storm, she longed for the solid safety of the mountains looming behind her. Now, she knew the

Frontier also harbored danger.

Jay moved along beside her with a confident stride and an optimistic smile. He carried the same expression on their first meeting just after he'd lost the race to her. Jortica's darker thoughts dispersed, and her spirits rose. Even if Jay was a townee, he was a pleasant one. He made no advances, like many of the young men she'd met before. It felt nice to spend time with him.

The bustle eased as they reached the cliffs and stepped onto the walkway overlooking the water. The path led away from the castle onto the cliffs that rose above the harbor. Along the wall, two dozen inactive gun emplacements marked regular intervals—the cannon barrels were lashed down and the priming vents capped.

Newer steam lifts chugged alongside people heaving at older mechanical elevators. Hundreds of barrels of goods lifted to the city or dropped to the docks.

Ships packed the harbor as usual. A few Galathian steamships bobbed along with the tidal swell, their massive paddle wheels dormant. Calonade vessels rigged solely for wind power took up most of the docks. The *Victory*, a mighty Calonaden thirty-gun frigate, moored opposite the Galathian steamers. The wind-powered ships easily outmatched the steamers in aesthetic beauty.

The bay curved away to the east and Jortica had a commanding view of the fisherfolk towns along the shoreline. Clumps of shacks and bungalows made up the various fishing villages. Just out of sight near the far end of the bay was her home in the seaside village of Eventide. Sails of Calonade fishing boats dotted the horizon. If she had a spyglass, she might pick out a few of the crews she knew. None would be her father, though. He was once a well-known fisherman, but now he simply repaired nets with Jortica's little sister, Mils, to look after him.

Jortica put aside the sad things—her broken father, the abused lowborn—and concentrated on the good things. The pleasant view and the handsome man beside her. Maybe it was the ale or maybe the need to quiet the inner storm, but she slipped her arm into the crook of Jay's elbow. He smiled at her and gripped her arm with his free hand. The storm in her mind subsided, and Jortica felt on course again.

She also noticed the pattern of calluses on Jay's right hand. Her hand possessed a similar pattern of hard flesh. Such tokens only came from one thing—extensive use of a sword. Jortica's eyebrows raised at the discovery. Jay wasn't merely working out; he was training for combat. Her estimation of Jay rose a notch along with her questions. Simple guardsmen didn't need to know the art of the sword. Why did he?

Jay moved closer, and Jortica realized she might be leading him on. She would not end up with a townee, no matter how well put together. He'd started off in the castle—even worse than a townee—and Jortica figured he was content to end up there. But what if that wasn't true? His training had gotten him into solid fighting shape. He'd almost won the race for Top Cadet. Turning it close to the Barber took real courage. He'd talked about joining up with the Horse Division, though that wouldn't work now. Did he have plans? The sword calluses must point toward something.

Jortica gazed at the sea. "Jay, you never came to see me off."

"What?" Jay asked.

"You know, when we left on assignment."

"Oh, right." He cringed. "I got held up after the final muster by Gilcres and his friends. They made me late reporting for duty."

Jortica frowned. A townee late for duty, not surprising. "What's next for you?"

Jay hesitated, looking surprised at the question. "Um," he started, then stopped to rethink a response. His eyes shifted around again. "Not sure. As you saw, I kept Havoc, though I hardly ride him beyond a trot into town and back. Gilcres got too busy to take him again. He's actually getting fat. I mean Havoc, not Gilcres, of course. Gilcres was already fat."

Jortica frowned instead of laughing, as Jay clearly expected. Gilcres was a fool, but he wasn't fat. He was built strong, and Jay had better know the difference or get bested again. "So, you're still feuding with Gilcres. Have you met any new people? Been involved in any castle politics?"

Jay's eyes popped wide, and he actually gulped, but he recovered his nonchalant attitude after a second. "Oh, I wish. There's been nothing at all interesting. I'm still going to put in for a transfer."

Jortica had seen that expression too many times from townees. She knew Jay was lying. She wasn't sure about what, but it was clear he didn't want to tell her something, so she withdrew her arm from his and watched his face closely. "Where are you going to transfer to? What's your plan?"

"Plan? I don't know," he stammered. "All I've ever wanted to do was ride."

No ambition. This didn't bode well. Was Jay just a boy who wanted to ride his horse? Was he a townee liar? What was he hiding? *Damn townees and their intrigue.* Jortica wanted no part of it. The carefree joy he exuded ran deep. Although initially dazzling, it didn't make up for a lack of aspiration.

"Hey, that's an idea," Jay said with a tinge of desperation in his voice. "Let's go out for a ride. Havoc could use the exercise. I could too."

Jortica gave him a weary look. "We just got Calamity put up for the night."

Jay slapped his forehead and winced as he hit his own bruise. "Oh right, forgot about that." He blinked, trying to recover. "We could—"

"No thanks. I have to report back for duty in the morning. This is my one day off."

"Oh." Jay deflated.

Jortica sighed. Townee through-and-through. At least she spotted it early. "Walk me back, Lieutenant." Jortica turned and made a beeline for the academy barracks. Jay caught up to walk beside her. His brow furrowed, overtaking his usual optimistic look. He was a good person, just out of his depth with her. Still, he'd calmed her storm. Maybe he was worth a final push.

She stopped in front of the barracks. "Jay, we're out of the academy now. It's time to take military life seriously. You must think of your career. If you don't, someone else will. There are rumors Galathia wants to conscript Calonade soldiers to the front again. You don't want to end up there."

"No." Jay shook his head. "That'd be bad. I had a career plan to get into the Horse Division, until a few minutes ago. I'm open to suggestions."

"Have you considered the Ship Division? That would get you away from the castle and out of Calonade without fear of a transfer to the front lines. On the sea, no one will care who your parents are."

Jay stiffened, clenching his jaw. He had a haunted look for a moment. "Naw, the Ship Division isn't for me. I can't swim."

Jortica almost laughed, thinking it was a joke, but realized he was serious. "You can't swim?"

"No. Never learned."

Oh, my goddess! Townees! Jortica tried to keep her expression bland. He was a soldier of a seafaring nation. Did he think all the fighting would be on dry ground? She decided not to argue the point. "What's your plan? To hang around the castle like you always have?"

"No. Well, it wasn't," Jay said. "What's *your* plan?"

"I'm where I'm supposed to be," she grumbled. "It's not exactly what I dreamed of, but Galathia is in charge. I will have to make the best of it. Maybe change things from within."

Jortica knew she sounded disappointed and angry because she was. But no matter how bad it got, she'd never give in to her father's wishes and join the Ship Division. Nor would she ever go home and take up tossing nets into the sea. Even with the saddle sores and strange politics, the Horse Division remained a far sight better.

"Jortica—" Jay started.

"Enjoy your ride, Lieutenant, and good luck with your plans." She turned and marched into the barracks without looking back.

Chapter Sixteen

There are rules prohibiting what I'm going to do on this planet. I know because I wrote them.

—from the journal of Sephy Alcott, Standard Galactic Year 11275

Calonade, Day 001, Year 2999 local planetary calendar, Standard Galactic Year 14285

Jay watched Jortica disappear through the threshold of the barracks and had to keep from kicking himself. The irony burned his stomach. She hadn't even blinked at his mixed ancestry like most women. When it came up, her words were all compassion instead of the usual insults. A new and very welcome feeling.

On the heels of that glorious moment, she had rejected him for his lack of purpose. Him. The one serving Lady Izell as her spy. The one learning spy craft directly from the master, Kaloby. The one being tutored in combat by the legendary Commander Kahela herself.

He wanted to shout it all back at her, but he knew he couldn't because then it would all be over. Spying on his friend felt horrid. Jortica had seen through his evasions and chalked him up as a fool. He was going to throttle Kaloby when he got back.

And yet, he had succeeded. He had come to gather information and had done so. Good luck for Jay the spy. Bad luck for Jay, friend of Jortica.

Jay trudged back to the stables to gather up Havoc. The revelation Armone had taken control of the Horse Division probably wasn't news to anyone. It explained why Commander Kahela seemed so serious and grim. However, Armone using the Horse Division, suddenly stocked with Galathians, to round up mixed folk, was big and ominous news.

Jay mounted Havoc and headed out of the city. His horse needed a long run through open country and Jay needed to vent.

"So unfair," he fumed. Havoc felt his frustration and snorted in reply. What were his *career plans*? Jortica had basically called him out for having no ambition and dismissed him as not being worth her time. He had been working night and day, but he couldn't say a word about it. Nor would he because he *was* career-minded. He didn't want a meaningless career under the Galathians, rising in the ranks using bribes and political connections. What he did looked like that by design, but it wasn't. And it was far better than riding in the Horse Division.

Well, he wouldn't lose the trust placed in him or put anyone in jeopardy because of bragging. If Jortica doubted his dedication, she didn't know him at all. Jay ground his teeth in frustration and pointed the eager Havoc toward the outskirts of the city. They both needed some air.

The scenery changed from the crowded cobblestone streets

of the city proper to the farmland beyond. Havoc stretched his gait into a canter, and Jay felt himself stretch out too. It wasn't long before they were galloping along a sparsely populated road surrounded by lanicina groves. Cultivated trees merged with the wild forest climbing up the mountainside.

The twenty-foot-tall mature lanicina trees, planted in rows on either side of the road, reached out with their deep purple branches, spreading their broad blue leaves skyward. Sap welling from their spongy bark filled the air with a tangy scent. The grove tenders kept the trees trimmed and the ground clear of undergrowth.

For some, the pungent smell meant relief, healing, and pleasure. People across Urey steeped the leaves to brew healing teas and boiled the roots for remedies. Some smoked bark shavings in their pipes and added sap lumps to their ale. The bark could be chewed raw, cooked into pie, dried and ground into powder.

For others, lanicina meant profit. Every part of the tree could produce a form of lanicin, and Calonade was the only place the lanicina trees grew. Everyone in the known world wanted it, which led to the dark side of the substance. A person could go too far and end up with an unrelenting addiction. You can't treat an ailment if the problem is also the only medicine.

For Jay, it smelled like home. It reminded him of Gran's kitchen. She used lanicin in many ways, Jay's favorite being her muffins and tea. Growing up a cook's boy to the best chef in the land taught Jay the power and danger of lanicin.

Jay drove Havoc into a full sprint, skirting the boundary between the thick woods and the farms. He pressed himself along the length of Havoc's neck and felt every hoofbeat in his own body. Every part of him felt alive. The big horse nickered with pleasure, and Jay had to grin. They'd both been stuck in the stables for too long.

Jay spied movement in the distance. A cloud of dust quickly became a group of mounted soldiers blocking the road. Jay reined in and brought Havoc to a stop to let them pass. Havoc shook his head in impatience, ready for more.

"Steady there." Jay patted Havoc's neck. "We'll get another good run on the way back, I promise."

As the group grew closer, Jay noticed all four were Galathian riders of the Horse Division, each with plinum bands as pale blue as sea mist. What were they doing here? The Horse Division patrolled the Frontier. Had they been given a few days off like Jortica?

He saw another Galathian, not wearing a standard red uniform, riding behind them. Jay swore under his breath as he recognized the black coat with gold brocade. Legate Armone.

"Hold up!" one of the Galathians shouted.

"Who are you?" another called.

"Messenger, sir," Jay shouted with a salute that hopefully blocked his face. One-handed, he directed Havoc to the side of the road. Between his fingers he got a better view than from the dark balcony.

Jortica was right, Armone was *greasy*. His limp and stringy blond hair hung down around his eyes, which gleamed pale and sharp with malice. He grinned as he yanked on a rope.

At the far end of the rope, Jay spied a young mixed boy, about twelve years old, on foot with his hands tied. He stumbled forward with a look of terror. Jay dropped his salute in shock.

"It's another half-casting!" A third Galathian drew a pistol.

Jay reached for his weapon, but it wasn't there. He had ridden out of the castle as an off-duty officer, which meant unarmed. All these men were armed.

Fortunately, he had other skills under his belt. Jay pulled the reins to turn Havoc about and dug in his heels. The big horse leaped in the direction they had come from, almost immediately reaching a full gallop.

Jay looked back to see all four soldiers in pursuit, which was good, since his plan wasn't to outrun them. He veered Havoc off the road and jumped the fence into the lanicina grove. To Jay's relief, Havoc didn't have to break through this one, built shorter than the race obstacle. Two of his pursuers' horses balked at the jump.

"Shoot him!" Armone shouted in the distance.

The crack of their pistols echoed in the air, but Jay knew he was far out of range.

"Cut him off!" Armone bellowed.

After a few moments of swift riding, Jay checked over his shoulder. The remaining two pursuers came on strong, while the others headed down the road.

Keeping the Galathians in sight through the dappled leaves, Jay turned Havoc. After a few moments, he turned again and rode deeper into the trees. The two men stayed on him as he wove through the lanicina branches. *Perfect.* Every tree looked the same and created an illusion of an endless grove. They couldn't tell Jay had led them in a wide circle. After a few minutes, he had them turned around and heading back to where they'd started. Jay slowed Havoc's pace to let his pursuers think they were gaining.

"Best to give up, halfy," the beefy Galathian in the lead yelled. "It'll go easier for you."

When Jay knew he'd come full circle, he turned Havoc to one side and poured on the speed. The fence came up fast, but Havoc jumped it with ease and even managed the ditch beyond. Then they were on the road once more.

Behind him, the first rider lost his mount on the jump, falling hard against the fence. The other reined just short of the barrier.

Jay sent Havoc full speed down the center of the road. As he came over a small rise, he saw them. Armone stood tall in his stirrups, looking in the other direction. The boy looked toward Jay, eyes wide. Jay steered Havoc to cut between the agent's horse and the boy. He leaned to one side and held out an arm, hoping the boy would be brave enough to take the chance.

At the last moment, Armone heard Havoc's approach and tried to turn, hand on his sword, but too late. The boy jumped and Jay had him. The impact nearly tore his shoulder out of its socket, but he held on. Havoc shouldered Armone's mount into a staggering stumble and the rope holding the boy whipped out of Armone's hands. They thundered away.

Jay swung the boy behind him, and they rode for a long while. The boy wriggled free from the rope and wrapped his arms around Jay's waist, his head pressed into the small of Jay's back. Jay turned onto crossroad after crossroad until he knew none of the riders were chasing them. He directed Havoc off the road and into a clump of bushes for cover. They caught their breath.

"Looks like we're safe now." Jay spoke in Calonaden as he slipped off Havoc and helped the boy down. "What's your name?"

"D–D–Dale, sir," the boy stammered.

"Let me see your wrists." They were red and raw, which made Jay sick to his stomach. *How could anyone do this?* He wanted to go back and kick some answers out of Armone, but he had to stay calm and get Dale home safely.

"How about I take you home, Dale?" Jay asked with a smile. "Think you can show me the way?"

Dale turned around, his eyes dazed and his hands shaking. "I don't know."

He must be in shock. Jay cut loose a rough piece bark from a lanicina tree and offered it to Dale. Jay knew it would taste terrible, but the boy popped it into his mouth without protesting.

While he waited for Dale to recover, he rubbed lanicina sap onto his own sore shoulder. Dale weighed more than he looked. As the pain ebbed away, Jay spread sap into scrapes on Havoc's hide from tree branches. The big horse snorted with relief. Jay finally remembered to spread some on his bruised eye.

Jay offered Dale his canteen, and the boy drank like he was parched.

"Thank you," he gasped. "Your horse goes fast!"

"That he does," Jay said. "Dale, do you know your way home now? I'd like to get you there."

Dale peeked through the bushes, looking up and down the road. "We can cut through the farms and stay off the road."

"Sounds like a splendid plan. Lead the way."

Jay gave Havoc's bridle a pull and the big horse followed along through the trees. "Do you know why that man was holding you prisoner?"

The boy gave him a sideways, suspicious look.

"I'm like you," Jay said to reassure him. "They're after me too."

Dale kicked at the dirt as they walked. "Well, the fella in the fancy gold coat kept asking me questions 'bout me ma and pa. Where they was from. He got real twitchy when I said they should let me be 'cause I know the half-cast prince."

"You mean from the story?" Jay asked.

"Yeah, no one messes with him. He has magic. Anyways, Fancy Coat wanted to know where to find him. Real bad."

"And what did you say?"

"That the prince is in Aeterna, a'course."

Aeterna, mythical home of the half-cast prince and now the Vinctus Stone, according to the clockwork crow. How much of the tales were based on truth? "I bet he didn't like that," Jay said.

Dale just shrugged. "He didn't like it much when I called them all rusted-to-the-core, tin-striped hollowware, either."

Jay snickered. *The kid could deliver an insult.*

"Anyway, that's when he got out the rope. He let the others knock me around, call me a half-casting. Nothing I ain't heard before. But Fancy Coat held the rope." The boy looked up into Jay's face. "He was the scariest."

Jay nodded in agreement.

They walked on, and it wasn't long before the back of a farmhouse came into view. A Calonaden woman was working in the garden.

"Wait, Dale. Those soldiers, do they know where you live?"

"No, sir. Picked me up on the road."

"Then I think you'll be safe. But you're going to have to

stay inside for the time being. Let your parents know why. Now go on home."

Dale did not have to be told twice. "Yes, sir!" He pelted toward the house.

Armone, using the Horse Division both in the Frontier and in the farms around the city to capture mixed people, went beyond looking for a possible heir to Izell. Why would Armone care about a young boy? Why were they holding people in the Thurbush jailhouse? Armone had said they were expanding the search. Did he mean not only to find all the people of mixed descent, but to imprison them too? It sure seemed like it the way they chased after him.

Jay mounted Havoc. "All right, boy, that's enough information gathering for one day. Let's follow the same advice as we gave. It's time to go home." Kaloby needed to hear what he had found out on his first spy mission.

Chapter Seventeen

The day Melrayis left Willa Station for the last time, she made me promise to watch over our settlement on Urey. I wish I had done a better job.

—from the journal of Sephy Alcott, Standard Galactic Year 13303

Shinwate Forest, Day 021, Year 2017 local planetary calendar, Standard Galactic Year 13303

A vegetable much like an old Earth potato garnished a seared piece of protein. Sephy guessed it to be lamb. She washed it all down with a light mead beverage and finished her meal with a sigh of pleasure.

The cooks at the station did their best with genetically replicated food and the infrequently delivered dry goods, but the real thing tasted so much better. Maybe the cure to the ails of her species lived in the simple fare of primitive cooking. Sephy would have to make a note in her journal. She got it out and began writing on the topic.

Havaqwi entered and cleared the dinnerware. "Are you ready to see the SHA?"

Sephy snapped out of her reverie. "Yes, bring it in." As Havaqwi stepped out, Sephy quickly cleared the stone slab for business again.

Lakqwi came in, leading a male human by a rope tied around its neck and looped through a ring in its nose. At nearly six feet tall, it stooped to fit into the cabin. It looked gaunt and had wrinkles that rivaled her own. Wrinkles like this on a human indicated it was approaching the end of its life cycle. It wore only a loincloth. A curious pattern of alternating dark and light blue bands of skin pigment ran up and down its body. Dead eyes and a blank expression met her curious gaze. The stench of its unwashed flesh drove the pleasant smell of dinner from the room.

Sephy frowned. She hadn't expected a young, handsome, or even clean SHA, but this was disappointing indeed. "Is this the only specimen?" The last word didn't translate well, and Lakqwi hesitated before answering.

"This is our SHA."

Sephy sighed and waved an arm at the stone table. "Put it up there."

Havaqwi, who had followed the SHA into the room, gasped and flung her hands over her mouth.

Lakqwi cocked a brow but didn't move. "Surely you don't mean to have the SHA service you on the sacred examination table."

"No." Sephy gathered her patience. "I plan to examine it on the examination table." The word examination kept coming out of the translator with the same odd religious connotation. Why hadn't Melrayis simply taught these people science and called it science? Seems it would be a lot less complicated.

Havaqwi squeaked with distress again.

Lakqwi continued in a tone suggesting she also summoned her patience. "Prophet Hukindi, you must know the sacred examination table is only for the Daughters of Melrayis."

Sephy, with much effort, kept from slapping her palm to her own face. *No, I didn't know that, damn you, Melrayis.* Sephy took a breath. She had to remain diplomatic rather than resort to her CEO style of communication, at least for now. "Where do you examine the Seeded Human Asset?"

Lakqwi and Havaqwi stared at her with blank expressions. Sephy realized her translator had pronounced the full acronym. The Shinwate probably used only the word SHA and didn't know its meaning. With a few flicks of her eyebrows, she adjusted the vocabulary. "Where should I examine the SHA?"

Lakqwi glanced at Havaqwi, who simply trembled with fright. "Prophet Hukindi, we do not allow the SHA to participate in the ritual of examination. We only permit those of the tribe who require healing."

Oh my God! A horrid sensation grabbed Sephy's stomach, which threatened the stability of the just-ingested meal. The myriad of terrible consequences of that revelation marched through Sephy's mind. She rapidly retrieved any data on the population growth of this colony of Shinwate from the Yawate report. Statistics on this tribe and several others showed a trend of decreasing population. In some places, including this tribe, the numbers fell alarmingly low.

"Tell me, Lakqwi, what is your tribe's reproductive rate?"

Lakqwi stared at her blankly again.

Sephy realized that didn't translate at all. "How many babies have you had lately?"

"The Mother Goddess has blessed us with one this year,"

Lakqwi answered with a frown.

The baby Lakqwi noted popped up on the Yawate report. "Yes, and how many the year before?" The report showed zero.

"We were not so blessed last year," Lakqwi said.

"You should be having more. Could it be your SHA," Sephy swept her hand up and down the male standing passively nearby, "is not up to the job?"

Lakqwi furrowed her brow, clearly trying to work out the connection.

Sephy spent a long second wishing for a quick method of infusing a primitive culture with vital scientific information. Just in the area of health would make a big difference.

"It could be sick," Sephy said. It certainly didn't look in tiptop health. "Its seed could be spent."

Lakqwi glanced at the appropriate location for male human seed storage. She stood straight and looked into Sephy's eyes. "This is our only SHA. It is the best we have."

"Why haven't you acquired more?" Sephy suspected she knew the answer, as she imagined a male human abduction scenario with the tribe's primitive technology. A high-risk endeavor.

"Galathians build walls around their cities. They rarely stray from protection." Lakqwi glanced at Havaqwi. "Few Daughters remain who are capable of the hunt."

A quick search of the data log revealed failed missions in the past. The Shinwate casualties and losses left a negative balance. The tribe made do with what they had. Sephy shook her head. She'd let Melrayis down. The colony was almost beyond repair. Imagine if she had waited another few weeks to take her "vacation." These people would have been doomed. Time to turn this situation around.

Sephy locked eyes with Lakqwi. "I'm going to examine this SHA and find out if it's done. There's only one way to do that properly. I'm sorry if this will offend your beliefs or change your doctrine, but it's got to happen. If it doesn't, your tribe will die a slow death."

Lakqwi stood for a moment, staring at Sephy. She didn't appear angry or afraid. Her expression became one of resolve. "You are the Prophet Hukindi."

Could Lakqwi see reason, or did she decide the prophet knew best? Either way, it worked.

Lakqwi led the SHA to the table, had it sit, and then lie down. Its legs drooped off one end. Lakqwi walked out the door, gesturing Havaqwi to follow. Left alone with a nearly naked male human, Sephy took a breath, wondering at the lengths she had to go to in service of feminkind.

* * *

After Sephy was done with the exam, the SHA seemed content to lie on the table. It snored a little while later as Sephy took notes in her journal. Poor thing was tuckered out. The elders must have increased their odds of success by raising the frequency of attempts at reproduction. Since this one had long ago lost the ability to protest, likely through the customary psychological break, it couldn't refuse. Its organ was purple with bruises, not desire. It was also out of seed. At roughly sixty years old, a long life for a human on a primitive planet, it no longer had value and should be retired from service.

This SHA's skin coloration stood out from most humans Sephy had experience with. Human pigment tended toward shades of pink, brown, and black from their origins on Earth and its yellow star. Most colonized planets were the same, but this one, with its blue star, produced a unique result in human skin melanin. The alternating colors must have evolved over the years to provide protection from the local star's ultraviolet radiation.

Sephy wondered if intentional breeding contributed to the uniform pattern. It seemed likely from its lack of randomness and the odd importance primitive humans placed on their skin color. Starting with humans seeded from a yellow star planet, this result spoke to an environmentally driven evolution combined with a generationally controlled breeding program.

Sephy couldn't recall a mention of this phenomenon. During her previous visit, she had spent no time with the human population. An exobiologist had likely described it in an obscure report. The SHA stock on Urey had to be worth something, though. Not this particular example, but a younger, more fit male could fetch some attention. Something to consider later. There were more important priorities at the moment.

A knock on the door pulled Sephy's attention from her writing. "Come," she said in Shin.

Lakqwi came in, frowning down at Sephy. She held a spear blade up and dug the blunt end into the dirt floor. "Chief Tanimundi wishes to speak with you."

Havaqwi scampered in and woke the SHA. It grunted as it rose and slid off the table. It followed the young feminam out the door.

Sephy glanced between Lakqwi's hard expression and the menacing blade. "I'm guessing this request can't be denied."

Lakqwi shook her head. "I have chosen to respect you, Prophet Hukindi, and offer you escort. However, you cannot refuse." Lakqwi twisted the spear just enough to get the point across.

Sephy smiled. "Good. I want to talk to Chief Tanimundi as well." She stood up. "Please lead the way."

Lakqwi nodded, looking a bit relieved, and stepped out the door, holding the flap open for Sephy. As Lakqwi led Sephy from the cabin, two more muscular Shinwate guards took up positions behind Sephy. The chief was serious.

Glancing behind her, Sephy liked the look of the guards. Similar to Lakqwi, they showed signs of a vigorous life. They seemed taller and a touch less wrinkled than most feminam. Were her observations uncovering a favorable trend? Could Sephy allow herself to hope Melrayis' wild experiment on this forbidden planet wasn't a waste of time?

Did she have time for such a favorable outcome? The reason Sephy couldn't sell the planet for the seed stock also made it a poor incubator of the future of feminkind. The blue star it orbited was too unstable. It would provide between five and ten thousand more years of sustainable life on Urey. Blue stars were banned for seeding because the risk outweighed the chances of recouping the capital investment costs. This one had been populated before the ban and then claimed by Melrayis for her research.

Sephy shook her head at the audacity of the decision and its potential results. She had to admit her own stake as well. Melrayis had made this retro tribe of feminam her baby and that meant they were Sephy's adopted children. She couldn't let them perish at the hands of humans. Plus, if these people held the key to reversing the effects of the genetic damage afflicting her species, it would be big. Potentially bigger than Willacast Corp. It was early in the experiment, only a few thousand years in. Another five to ten thousand years and she might have something to show. If the planet lasted that long. If the Shinwate survived that long.

Sephy looked around as she strolled toward the chieftain's pavilion. Clean air and water. Plenty of food. High-tech sentinels and capable hunters. Melrayis' obsession with the place made sense. Sephy had to ensure its safety.

Sephy strode into the Shinwate meeting hall with her escort. The scene hadn't changed much from her first visit, except more of the tribe was present. Chief Tanimundi sat in her chair, surrounded by her attendants. The benches around the fire filled with feminam. More leaned against the walls and lounged in the dark corners. A set of heavily wrinkled feminam, with white hair and deep gray skin, sat in a row at the front near the chieftain's throne.

Sephy raised her brows at a row of seven elders. They were clearly at least twice her own age and Sephy wasn't even close to a nubile young thing anymore. Though the genetic scars of her people became more pronounced with age, this collection of feminam spoke to the planet's potential for longevity. Further reason to save it.

"Chief Tanimundi," Sephy said before Lakqwi could announce her. "I'm glad you invited me to speak to you and your people. I have much to share with you and an offer to make."

Tanimundi leaned forward and frowned down at Sephy, her

muscular bulk rippling. She embodied the best example of Shinwate strength, which Sephy took as a sign of hope for the experiment rather than intimidation. Also, Sephy had negotiated with far more formidable opponents in her role as CEO of Willacast Corp. This time, however, the stakes were personal.

"Prophet Hukindi, I understand you've been using the sacred examination table for our SHA. If this is true, you are blaspheming against the Daughters of Melrayis." The chieftain glanced at Lakqwi, who nodded. "This is a serious offense. What say you?"

"Well, unlike you, I knew Melrayis. It wouldn't bother her to know a SHA received a medical exam." Once again *medical exam* came out in a religious context, but Sephy pushed on. "What would bother her is the grave danger in which you've placed this tribe. Your reproductive rate is appallingly low. Your tribe's territory is shrinking. You've lost the Temple of the Daughters. The same is true for all the Shinwate. This, Chief Tanimundi, is a far greater offense to Melrayis than anything I've done. What say *you*?"

Tanimundi sat back, eyebrows raised in disbelief. "You dare rebuke me in my own long house?" Her voice rose to a booming baritone.

Sephy had to admit the chieftain had an effective presence. Sephy shrugged. "I'm the Prophet Hukindi." Sephy wondered how long that comeback would work, but Tanimundi drummed her fingers as she considered Sephy under a deeply furrowed brow.

"What say the elders?" Tanimundi kept her glare on Sephy.

The elders looked at each other, and they all nodded toward the one in the center. She had to be the oldest of the tribe.

Braided white hair flowed down the length of her squat body and her eyes almost disappeared into her wrinkles. Despite her age, she pushed herself to standing. An impressive feat for someone who had to be nearly a hundred and fifty years old. A rare but possible age to reach in a modern feminam society. Six more elders of comparable age sitting near her made it remarkable.

"Something must be done," wheezed the feminam elder in a reedy voice. Everyone in the long house held still to hear her.

"I agree, Elder Fornaqwi," Chief Tanimundi said. "We cannot let this interloper disrespect us even if she is the Prophet Hukindi."

The crowd erupted in comments. Some shouting in support of the chief and others protesting the decision. Many of the tribe had noticed the falling rate of births. The younger feminam adults of child-bearing age showed the most concern. However, a louder contingent didn't like Sephy flaunting the old ways, prophet or not.

Damn. Sephy thought she had them. She couldn't afford to get stuck in this place, but she still needed help to pull off her plan. Sephy slipped a hand into her jumpsuit and fingered her disruptor. She hated to use it, but she might have to. A hostile takeover wouldn't be the best solution, but it might be the only one.

"Daughter Lakqwi," Tanimundi said. "Take the prophet into custody, then we shall—"

"No, Chief Tanimundi," Elder Fornaqwi interrupted in her airy wheeze. The tribe hushed and Fornaqwi waited until they quieted before continuing. "Chief Tanimundi, despite her irreverent behavior, we see the prophet's wisdom in this matter." She steadied herself and took as deep a breath as she could manage. "We need to listen to her. We are not growing as a tribe. None of the Shinwate are. We were once a proud nation, rivaling the Galathian Empire. We once had many SHA to choose from. Many babies were seeded. This is no more."

A groan of longing and grief erupted from a group of the younger feminam in the crowd. Havaqwi buried her face in her hands and sobbed. Others comforted her and even the forceful religious contingent fell quiet with empathy for her sorrow.

"We have lost our land and our temple. We have lost too much." Elder Fornaqwi reached a soothing hand toward the grief-stricken young feminam. "We must make a change or perish." She nodded toward the chief and took her seat.

"I see. You speak with the best interests of our people at heart, Elder Fornaqwi, and I hear you." Tanimundi rubbed her chin in thought. "Perhaps I've been hasty in judgment." She peered toward Lakqwi, who remained impassive.

Chief Tanimundi turned her gaze onto Sephy. "Let's hear what the Prophet Hukindi has to say."

Sephy eased her grip off the disruptor and clasped her hands behind her back. She settled into the stance she always assumed when negotiating with powerful leaders. In the past, the stakes were trillions of credits and thousands of years. These terms were different, but Sephy could feel the weight of the words she had to utter next. The thrill she never grew tired of coursed through her body.

"This is an easy problem to solve," Sephy said to the crowd. "All I need is an audience with the Willacast Mother Goddess."

The villagers gasped, but Chief Tanimundi's expression

didn't waver. "You've said this before. It is impossible for Shinwate to travel into Galathia. We are killed or enslaved on sight. The Mother Goddess lives within the Galathian palace, the heart of our enemy's capital. Even if you could speak a word to the goddess and solve our problems, how will you get there?"

"I have a way to travel to the center of the mountain to the north of the city using the same method by which I traveled here," Sephy replied. "From there I will reach the Mother Goddess."

Chief Tanimundi peered down at Sephy as if she were mad. "You wish to enter Rolotundra, the Hollow Mountain, the home of the Well of Ages, the most sacred place of the Galathian Empire, and strike up a conversation with their most powerful deity? You must pardon me, Prophet Hukindi, if that sounds preposterous."

The Hollow Mountain, which Galathians called Karpathode, was an extinct volcano. It housed a device of similar technology to the remnants of the temple. Sephy's files identified the Well of Ages as the local name for Urey's main transit device. Its custodian, the Mother Goddess, would monitor it day and night.

Sephy ground a foot into the hard dirt of the long house. "She is our deity, not theirs, Chief Tanimundi. The Well of Ages belongs to us. I am the Prophet Hukundi, and it is my duty to set this straight."

"Duty is irrelevant if you can't get there," Tanimundi replied.

"Oh, I can get there." The problem was pulling it off without being detected by the Willa transit technicians. The transit portal she used to arrive in the temple connected to an abandoned transport platform on the station. No one knew it was operational. Thus, her ability to have a secret vacation. The Well of Ages didn't have such a clandestine bypass. Using it might be noticed by the system monitors. They worked for her, but she didn't want the personal attention she was giving this planet to be known. Such a revelation, no matter how well controlled, would lead to a disaster. This would have to be a silent operation.

"You and what army?" Tanimundi flung an arm toward an audience low on soldiers.

Sephy peered around at the surrounding feminam for effect. She already had someone picked out. Her gaze stopped on Lakqwi. "I just need one capable person to accompany me."

Chief Tanimundi laughed in a deep and booming guffaw and her audience joined in, thinking it a joke, but Lakqwi looked into Sephy's eyes without smiling. She twisted her spear, grinding the butt end into the dirt. She knew it was not a joke. She nodded to Sephy. "You are the Prophet Hukindi. I will follow you."

Chapter Eighteen

Betrayal on the battlefield leading to loss and retreat is a bitter pill to swallow. Betrayal at the hands of one's own family is far worse.

—from Chronicles of Galathia by Rafykin, Urey, circa 2640 local planetary calendar.

Calonade, Day 001, Year 2999 local planetary calendar, Standard Galactic Year 14285

Neither moon had yet risen, and clouds pushed inland to obscure the stars. Jay used the cover of darkness and back roads to reach the castle without detection from roaming Galathian horsemen. When he arrived, he rode casually past the castle gate, swaying a little in his saddle. Even though he felt the urgency of the information he carried, he sought to appear as if returning from a night on the town.

As soon as he stabled Havoc, Captain Gaven appeared.

"Sir." Jay saluted. "Reporting for duty."

Gaven glanced at the guards stationed at the gate. "Walk with me to my office, Lieutenant. I need to send a message."

Gaven shut the door, and concern shaded his face.

"What is it, sir?"

"Not sure, but Lady Izell wanted to see you as soon as you came in, which was supposed to be before nightfall." Gaven lifted a piece of blank parchment from his desk, scribbled an innocuous note, folded it, and handed it to Jay. "You better get moving."

Positive he was about to get wire-brushed on top of everything else that had happened today, Jay hurried up the stairs of the castle entry and headed straight for Lady Izell's private meeting chamber. Oryk glowered as he approached but said nothing and opened the door for Jay.

Inside the large room, a set of candles lit the central table. Shadows played across the faces of Kaloby, Commander Kahela, and Gran, who stood next to the seated Lady Izell. They all studied a map spread across the table.

Jay froze in his tracks. He'd been invited into Lady Izell's most inner circle. *Finally!* The thrill of it made his heart beat against his chest. Jay forced himself to keep moving as he straightened his uniform jacket by force of habit.

When Gran saw him, she crooked a fist against her hip and clucked her tongue. Jay had seen the gesture a thousand times. He *was* about to be chewed out in front of everyone.

"Lady Izell sent for you hours ago, Jay." Gran used her I'm-about-to-whoop-you-with-a-spoon tone.

"Sorry, ma'am." With a touch of relief, Jay noted she didn't have her thick soup-stirring spoon in her hand. That one hurt.

"Now, now, Sedia," Kaloby interjected. "I sent him on an information-gathering mission for his training. It had an open-ended time frame. Please report, Lieutenant."

Jay snapped to attention. "Begging your pardon, but I

have news." Given the trouble he was in, Jay got right to it. "From a reliable source, I learned the emperor's agent, Legate Armone, has been using the Horse Division to control the Frontier. He detains people of mixed descent without cause in Thurbush. Today, I found him leading a group of armed Galathian Horse Division riders in the lanicina groves. He tried to kidnap a mixed boy."

Gran gasped. "Were you hurt? Was the boy?"

"The boy is safe. There was an altercation, but it turned out well." He gave Kaloby a significant look. "Given I was unarmed."

"What?" Gran turned, hands on hips, to glare at Kaloby across the table.

"Ah, yes." Kaloby straightened the cuffs of his sleeve, unable to meet Gran's eye. "He was technically on leave."

"Fine time for it," Gran snapped.

"He was on a special assignment. He had to look the part," Kaloby said.

"That's not the point," Gran said. "You shouldn't assume—"

"Enough." Lady Izell's lips pressed together in a thin line. "Regardless of the risk, his information confirms our suspicions. Please show Lieutenant Jay the map."

Jay had to take a breath. He'd never seen his Gran address any of these people with anything less than deference. Of course, he'd never been invited to join the inner circle, either. He knew Gran was upset by something other than his late arrival. Also, Lady Izell rarely expressed anything beyond serenity. Her show of annoyance surprised Jay. "What's happening, M'lady?" Jay stepped up to the table.

"Shore observers spotted four Galathian steamships maneuvering in front of the harbor. They appear to be forming a blockade." Kaloby pointed to the mouth of Calonade Bay, where four markers showed the positions of the ships. "If Armone's new Horse Division is also inside the city, it's hardly a coincidence."

Jay stared at the map in disbelief as the news sank in. These maneuvers represented much more than the machinations of one power-hungry Legate. He glanced at Commander Kahela, remembering her warning about a coming conflict. "What's our next move?"

"Patience," Lady Izell said, back to her calm demeanor.

"What about the prisoners in Thurbush?" Jay asked.

"While Legate Armone controls the town, we can't do much about it directly," Lady Izell said. "But we have control over lanicin production. A threat to the supply of Galathia's favorite commodity can protect the people of Calonade and the Frontier."

"Always an effective way to influence the emperor." Kaloby looked Jay in the eye. "We'll set our people free soon enough."

"These activities indicate a tightening of the empire's grip," Izell said, "but they are not acts of war. They suggest a plan in motion. We need to get word to General Saben to be watchful for Galathian troops approaching from the north."

Jay frowned. Lady Izell wanted to check in with a Galathian about other Galathians? Not just any Galathian, the headmaster of the academy himself. Jay remembered Gran's story about Saben's innocence of the death of King Nados and his defection to join their fight. Knowing the man's reputation made it hard to believe. He could be a spy for Lord Kendric. "How can General Saben keep watch for an invasion, M'lady? Isn't he at the academy?"

"He's been running drills up at the Outer Gate since Commander Kahela was relieved of duty," Kaloby said. "We needed reliable eyes up there."

Jay turned to stare at Kaloby in disbelief. The spy master trusted him, too. This was getting truly bizarre. Maybe there was something to it, but Jay's years of dodging the headmaster kept him wary.

"If he's late to report in," Jay said, "I could ride up to the Outer Gate tonight, stay undercover, and report back when they make their move."

Kaloby rubbed his chin, thinking. "We need a fast rider—"

"It won't be him," Gran said. "Not again."

Jay glared at his Gran. Now that he was included, she wanted to push him right back out.

"Sedia," Lady Izell said, warning in her voice.

"Don't you *Sedia* me." Gran crossed her arms and glared at Lady Izell. "You all need to wake up. Galathia is about to take over for good."

"Thank you for your opinion," Lady Izell said. "I believe we all need to wake up a little and would benefit from Kaloby's new lanicin tea. Would you be so kind?"

"Hmph." Gran headed for the door, letting it close with a bang. Jay cringed. It was never a good idea to anger the cook.

"Now, Lieutenant," Lady Izell said to Jay, "you have indeed ridden much today. Are you prepared for a second adventure?"

"Yes, ma'am!" Jay couldn't wait to prove himself worthy to serve with Lady Izell's most trusted.

"I require a messenger to ride to the Oracle and return with her advice," Lady Izell said.

Finally. Jay barely held his excitement. Lady Izell meant

to try for the Vinctus Stone. Maybe the Oracle already had it and just needed him to retrieve it. "Outstanding. I could ride up to her dwelling in the Kelstone peaks tonight and be back before dawn."

Kaloby frowned, and Kahela raised an eyebrow. Izell must not have shared this part of the plan with the others. Did anyone else besides Kaloby and himself know about the Vinctus Stone? Jay looked to Kaloby for guidance, but he didn't appear to notice.

"The Oracle provided me with a warning this day might come. I'd like to find out if she knows more," Lady Izell said.

A chance to ride out of Calonade proper was the moment Jay had been waiting for. He could barely keep himself from dashing to the stables to prepare Havoc this instant, but he knew he had to at least get the message first.

Kaloby scratched his beard, and Kahela took a long look from Lady Izell to Jay and back. Jay could tell they doubted him, but he wasn't worried. With Havoc, he could best anyone who tried to chase him. He'd proven it yet again today.

"I will draw up a letter after our meeting and charge you with its delivery, Lieutenant," Lady Izell said.

"Yes, ma'am." Jay couldn't keep from grinning.

"Now, let us consult the map, Minister Kaloby." Lady Izell returned her focus to the projected courses of the Galathian ships.

Jay vibrated with eagerness to ride into the mountains. He could check up on General Saben on the way. Maybe visit the Outer Gate to see for himself what was going on. Would he meet Jortica there? He'd probably beat her up the mountain since she wasn't scheduled to ride back until morning. Even if he couldn't tell her the details, she could guess his purpose and rethink her opinion of him.

The Oracle lived in a cave along the peak-to-peak trail. The Calonade Foot sent scouts along its windy path to patrol the edges of the kingdom. Perilous trails were the norm of the journey, but Jay could ride Havoc most of the way.

Oryk abruptly swung the door open. They all looked up and Jay started in surprise as General Saben himself entered, dusty from a long ride. Behind Saben, Gran bustled in with a tray in her arms. She began pouring tea as Saben snapped a salute.

"At ease, General. Have some tea," Lady Izell said.

"We were just discussing your position." Kaloby tapped the map. "We have news that suggests the arrival of Galathian troops is imminent, most likely moving by stealth through—"

"Begging your pardon, Minister Kaloby," Saben interrupted with a growl. "But they already have. This morning, just after dawn."

It felt like a bolt of lightning shot through the room. *This morning?* Why was Saben reporting it now, almost a full day later?

Gran nearly turned over the tea service in shock. "I thought we'd have more time."

Kahela glared menacingly at the map where the offending army currently resided but said nothing.

Jay's excitement curdled. If the enemy held the Outer Gate, he'd be riding straight into them. Jay could feel his long-awaited assignment sift through his fingers. He'd still do it. Insist on doing it, in fact, but it wouldn't be a carefree jaunt.

"We received no signals of an approaching force," Kaloby said.

"The signal crews were relieved of duty before the Galathians came into sight. At least a legion of Galathian soldiers arrived from the north." General Saben stepped up to the table and Jay made room for him next to Kaloby. He pointed to the only land entrance to Calonade. "They took over the Outer Gate. They did it quietly. No commerce has been disrupted, no exchange of fire. They simply took command."

"Just like the Horse Division," Kahela said.

Saben nodded, his face grim.

Kaloby's hand came down on the map with a resounding blow. "Stealth instead of an assault. This changes everything."

"The emperor has finally lost patience with my refusal to send troops to the front," Lady Izell said. "And he must feel he has sufficient control over Parliament to maintain the lanicin trade. This is a coup."

"They won't use that term, but, yes," Kaloby said with finality. "You will be removed from all power, symbolic or otherwise. When they reach the castle, they will take you into their custody and escort you to Karpathode. Or worse. Lady Izell, we must get you to safety. Now."

Jay's assignment was dust. He'd be accompanying Lady Izell, no doubt. Jay peered at the map, trying to work out the best escape route. With the bay blockaded and the Outer Gate in the hands of the enemy, there weren't many places left to go. Could they fight? A legion was a lot of Galathians. Four steamships carried even more. It wouldn't be an easy win.

Lady Izell did not stir from her chair, nor did her face betray any fear. "General Saben, how long do we have until the troops reach the castle?"

"They're quartered at the Outer Gate, sleeping off an

evening of celebrating. I spent a pretty penny on wine and lanicin to make sure of that. We have the night to prepare a counterattack by sea."

"The harbor is blocked by four Galathian vessels," Kahela informed him, "and any frigates trying to escape will be fired on. The new Horse Division has been busy inside the city. I'm sure orders to deploy the harbor guns will be countermanded."

"Damn," Saben muttered. "I'm sorry, Lady Izell."

It was a tight spot. Jay sipped from a cup of tea, considering. If only they had known earlier. It seemed odd that Saben didn't send word of the loss of the Outer Gate sooner. His suspicions of the old headmaster nagged his mind.

"Escape is the only option now," Kaloby said. "If commerce is not being interrupted, we have a chance via the old fishing village docks."

Escape to sea in fishing boats! Jay shivered and wished he'd learned to swim. What else could they do? They were about to be outmaneuvered by the empire unless they could run for their lives.

"How risky is that?" Lady Izell asked.

"In the past, I would say not at all. Lately, however," Kaloby gestured to the map in frustration. "They may have anticipated the move. But assuming we make it in the fishing boats, we'll be divided and vulnerable. We need a safe harbor."

"Commander Kahela, who is at sea right now?" Lady Izell asked. "Beyond the blockade."

"Admiral Filcor is sailing the Vivigossic Ocean trade routes on the *Liberty*," Kahela said. "His frigate and a few escort ships are out beyond the blockade. That's about all, ma'am."

"There's something else to consider." Kaloby frowned. "Some people may see this retreat as cowardice. Others will lose hope, feel defeated."

"We don't have time to explain our actions," Commander Kahela countered. "This is a military move."

Lady Izell held up her hand to stop them. "You are both correct. Thank you. Thank you, everyone." The time for discussion had ended. She stared out the darkened windows for a moment. Jay wondered at the thoughts spinning behind her distant eyes.

"It came sooner than expected," Lady Izell said, "but it has always been inevitable. Minister Kaloby, I believe if the treaty is broken, then I am the Queen of Calonade once more."

Jay looked at her with astonishment. She was right. With the treaty gone, she was the sovereign of Calonade.

"Yes, yes, of course." Kaloby bowed his head. "To many, Your Majesty, you have been nothing other than our queen."

Jay and the others bowed as well, but Queen Izell stopped them. "We will skip any ceremony for now," she said, "but I will need to be publicly recognized as the queen once we're safe. That will help us negotiate with allies for support against the Galathians."

"You plan to fight." Commander Kahela smiled with a look of grim satisfaction.

"Yes. Our uneasy peace has ended. Now we will try war."

Everyone nodded. The room tingled with anticipation.

"Shall we follow through with our threat to the emperor, Your Majesty?" Kaloby raised a questioning eyebrow.

"Burn the groves?" Queen Izell didn't blink as she spoke.

Gran sucked in her breath. Jay cringed as he imagined such a disaster. Everyone stared at the queen for a long heartbeat.

"No. Our people will need them. Plus, I plan to return, turn out our oppressors, and reclaim our home. We will need them even more then," Queen Izell said.

Everyone released a collective breath.

"Prepare our escape by sea," the queen commanded. "To everyone who helps us, spread the word. The future of Calonade is at stake."

"For Calonade," Commander Kahela said.

"For Calonade," Jay repeated with the rest of them.

Jay tried to feel the hope and courage in her words, but a moment later, his stomach knotted at the idea of a small dark boat bobbing over an endless sea.

Queen Izell turned to Gran. "Quietly gather the loyal servants. Have them pack light and meet in the kitchens. Prepare stores for a sea voyage to attempt a rendezvous with the *Liberty*."

Gran grasped both of Queen Izell's hands in her own, her eyes brimming with emotion. "Yes, Your Majesty." The way she said it seemed even more personal than a nickname. Then Gran hustled around the table and hugged Jay fiercely. "Take care. May the Three Sisters bring us together again soon."

Jay hugged her just as tight, then reluctantly let her go and suppressed a shudder. Worse than his own fears, he didn't like the idea of his gran in a tiny boat fleeing enemy forces.

"Commander Kahela," Queen Izell said. "Prepare the castle guard. Hand pick your soldiers and put them in civilian garb. They will pair up with the servants and leave in shifts. Pass the word to any loyal officers and soldiers to slip out of the bay if they can. If they can't, give permission to leave their Galathian assigned posts and lie low or resist if opportunities arise. We'll contact them through Kaloby's network."

Commander Kahela saluted and left the room without a word.

"Parliament?" Kaloby asked.

"We do not have the time or the resources, I'm afraid. They will have to hunker down with the people. I hope it will not be for long."

"Yes, of course, Your Majesty. Now, about provisions. We'll need more than we have on hand for a long sea voyage. We could *ask* Calonadens to give up such supplies, but perhaps it would be better to spread some coin. That will ensure it all stays quiet. And our allies are more interested in partners than beggars. Shall I raid the treasury?"

Jay thought nothing could surprise Queen Izell, but this did. "Really? Can you do that? Kendric never let me have a key."

Kaloby grinned. "That's why I made a secret copy."

"Very good," Queen Izell said with a matching smile. "Pack quickly and make it so."

Kaloby hurried out of the room, muttering to himself about the important papers he needed to gather.

Only Jay and General Saben remained. Queen Izell contemplated them both for a moment. Jay felt her gaze on him, and he straightened up tall, showing as much courage as he could muster. A bit more than he felt. Nevertheless, he felt proud to be a trusted aide for the Queen of Calonade, however long her reign and wherever she might go, even on the ocean if necessary.

"General Saben, I need you to ride again tonight," Queen Izell said.

Jay's ears perked up. Where would Queen Izell send Saben? Could he be trusted knowing about their escape plan?

Saben saluted. "At your service, Your Majesty."

"I have an important message that must be delivered, and time is of the essence. While you prepare two horses, I will draft my message. Lieutenant Jay will meet you at the stables with the package. Since you appear to be an ally to the Galathians, I believe you are uniquely equipped to ensure the safety of the package."

"Yes, Your Majesty," Saben replied. "What is the destination?"

"You and the lieutenant will ride to the Oracle's dwelling in the Kelstone peaks. We must seek her aid."

At first, Jay felt profound relief. He'd get to ride out of Calonade after all. It was dangerous, but far better than throwing up in front of the queen. The feeling soured an instant later when he realized he'd be sharing his assignment with Headmaster General Saben. How many push-ups would he have to do on the way up to the peaks? Jay opened his mouth to protest but paused. The general stood frozen, staring at Queen Izell with eyebrows furrowed. Perhaps he was forming a protest of his own.

"Do you have an objection, General?" Queen Izell asked, her voice icy.

He started from his brooding. "No, Your Majesty." Without another word, he marched out.

Once the door swung shut, Jay couldn't keep quiet. "Permission to speak freely, M'lady, I mean, Your Majesty."

Queen Izell picked up a lit candle and glided to her writing desk. "Of course. One moment."

Jay watched her ready a parchment, quill, ink, and her royal seal. She sat with her back to Jay and dipped her quill until the nib was black with ink. "Now, what is on your mind?" She began to write.

"Are you sure you can trust General Saben?"

Queen Izell paused, quill hovering over the parchment. "Why do you ask?"

"Why didn't he report the loss of the Outer Gate sooner?" Queen Izell frowned, her face flickering in the candlelight. Jay went on. "If he had, you might be out of danger by now."

"Ah." Queen Izell continued her writing, her words flying across the page. "General Saben didn't know the harbor was blockaded. Observations during war are like trying to solve puzzles with missing pieces. I've known General Saben for a long time. I'm certain of his loyalty."

"But—"

"Stop." The queen turned to look directly into his eyes. "I understand you are being taught to think like a spy, but Saben is useful because our people are prejudiced against Galathians. He even plays the part of the oppressor for me. I need you to see beyond these appearances to his true intentions."

Jay's face burned with embarrassment. He knew what prejudice felt like. "I'll try."

Queen Izell finished the letter and dusted it with sand to dry the ink. She folded the parchment and dripped wax from her candle onto the crease. Jay knew it would cool and harden quickly. For the final steps, Queen Izell pressed her seal into the wax and placed the letter in a sturdy oilskin wrapper. It reminded Jay of the message she had used to test him when he first started as her messenger.

"Be sure this does not fall into enemy hands." She rose from her desk to give him the package. "Deliver it to the Oracle personally."

"Yes, Your Majesty." He stuffed the package under his uniform coat. "Where will I rejoin you?"

"I don't know, Lieutenant. We will be far at sea by the time you deliver the package."

Jay frowned. "What about the Vinctus Stone? Don't you want it delivered as soon as possible?"

Queen Izell regarded Jay with a cool expression and paused, as if choosing her words carefully. "Don't worry about the Vinctus Stone just yet. We don't know what it is. Delivering the package to the Oracle is the priority."

"I figure the Oracle might have it ready for you."

Izell cocked her head. "I hadn't thought of that. If she does, then bring it back with you."

"What about a reply?" Surely, the advice of the Oracle on how to proceed was just as important, if not more, than the note asking for assistance. Jay could arrive without the package and simply tell the Oracle the queen needed her help.

"You must rely on the Oracle. She will advise you on how to find me."

Jay recalled Kaloby's reservations about the Oracle. "Begging your pardon, ma'am, but Kaloby told me to be on my guard with her."

"She is far too mystical for a scientist like Kaloby." Queen Izell shook her head. "You must trust her. Whatever her instructions, follow them as if they were my own. She will know my plans."

"Does she really know so much?"

"I believe she sees all."

Jay wondered if the Oracle knew something about the emperor's agent. "With your permission, I'd like to ask the Oracle about Legate Armone. There must be a reason he's seeking to capture and question those of mixed ancestry. I think it goes beyond an obsession with finding your fictitious living heir."

Queen Izell sat at her desk and pulled out another piece of parchment. She sighed as she began a new message. "If you wish, Lieutenant, but I think simple prejudice explains the Legate's actions. The Galathians have always had odd notions about the importance of nationality and parentage. Using such differences to divide people is an age-old tactic."

"Could we use that predilection to our advantage?" A plan sprang into his mind. "I could draw them away, Your Majesty. Tell them I'm the heir to King Nados and ride to the Outer Gate. I'm close enough to the right age, at least from a distance."

Queen Izell turned to face him as he spoke.

"I could dare them to pursue me into the Frontier." Jay's excitement grew. "Armone has already seen me ride Havoc. He'll take the bait."

"Lieutenant." Queen Izell shook her head.

"I've studied Kaloby's maps. I could lead them on an epic chase while you escape." Jay knew he could do it. He burned to do it. It was his dream come true. It was better, in fact. He wanted to ride out of Calonade. Now, he could do it with a glorious purpose.

"No, Lieutenant," Queen Izell said calmly, but her eyes were wide with alarm.

"Don't you see, Your Majesty," Jay went on, "it's a way to make sure you survive. You saw me in the race. You know I can do it."

"No, Lieutenant." Queen Izell raised her voice as she stood.

"But I'm just a messenger. I can ensure that you get away. I can create the perfect distraction."

"No, Jay." Queen Izell reached out and put a hand on his shoulder.

Icy fear pricked Jay's insides. "My gran." An image of his grandmother pursued by enemy ships, fighting ocean swells, and being dragged down by the waves sprang into his mind.

"She will be fine. She'll be with our best people, right beside me. I need you to go to the Oracle."

Jay took a breath and cleared his mind. "Please, Your Majesty, send General Saben to the Oracle. I'll ride Havoc out into the Frontier." Jortica was in the barracks. Would she come with him? "I'll make sure—"

"I'm sending you both because I *do* have an heir." Queen Izell spoke with an icy calm voice, but her eyes pierced him with a fiery intensity.

"An heir?! With King Nados?"

"Yes. My son lives. The Oracle knows where he is. I need you and General Saben to take my message to her."

"But the grave," Jay stammered, thunderstruck by the revelation.

"The one for my stillborn child? There is a baby in it, in case some foul Galathian ever got curious, but the poor thing is not mine."

Stunned, Jay barely kept his feet. "There *is* a half-cast prince!"

"Yes. He has lived in secret for a long time." An expression passed over Queen Izell's face Jay couldn't read. Jay was sure it was masking deeper emotions.

"It is the most closely kept secret of the realm," Queen Izell said.

"Who knows?"

"Kaloby, the Oracle, and now you. I need you to go to the Oracle. To protect my child." Queen Izell's eyes entreated him to understand and obey. Before he could reply, Jay heard a commotion in the hall.

The door flew open, and Governor Kendric swaggered into the room, dressed in a red and black robe, as if he were in his own sitting room. Oryk followed him, hovering behind with an uneasy grimace.

Jay snapped to attention.

"Ah, there you are," Kendric said in an oily voice. "I saw your light in the window and thought I'd pay you a visit. We have a few things to discuss."

"Lord Kendric." Queen Izell moved to stand in front of the table. "What a pleasant surprise."

"I'm sorry, M'Lady, he pushed through," Oryk grumped, looking flustered.

"It's all right, Sergeant Oryk," Izell said. "I'm done working for the evening, and surely I need no guard while I am with the Governor."

Kendric chuckled, looking far too pleased. "Of course not, my dear. Send your servant elsewhere."

Oryk seemed doubtful, but Izell waved him toward the door. "No need to stay at your post. I believe you intended to have a late meal?"

Realization dawned on Oryk's sour face. Gran must have informed Oryk of the plan to head to the kitchen.

"Yes, M'lady." Oryk retreated out of the room.

"May I invite you to partake of some late-night refreshment?" Izell gestured to the tray Gran had brought up, ignoring Jay's presence.

"No, no. I am feeling quite well for now." He eased himself into a chair, slouching as if he were in his own chamber and Queen Izell was his servant. Jay burned with hatred for the man.

"Are you sure? A new product has been developed. Twice distilled lanicin. I'm told it's refreshing and quite potent."

"Potent, you say?" Kendric's interest piqued.

"I have some freshly brewed right here." Izell picked up a carafe from the tray, one Jay had assumed was milk. She opened the cap and offered it to Kendric. A powerful fragrance filled the room, far stronger than the tea. This must be the opposite of Kaloby's less-intoxicating brew.

Kendric couldn't resist. "I suppose a taste wouldn't hurt."

Queen Izell served him, standing next to him as he sat. Her subservience was painful to watch. Lord Kendric sipped from the glass Izell offered. Then he took a significant swallow, his eyes closed as he savored it.

"What a splendid development." He swirled the golden liquid in his glass. "This is perfect for a celebration I have in mind. In your honor, of course." He took another drink. "I'm here to talk it over with you."

"Of course. Perhaps we should speak privately?"

Kendric followed Izell's gaze over to Jay, apparently noticing him for the first time. "Ah, who is this?"

"A castle messenger," Queen Izell said. "He was about to leave when you arrived."

Kendric rose to examine Jay, leaning in close, his eyes bleary as he blinked. He squinted as if he detected something puzzling about Jay. The odor from his breath could knock out an ox. He had partaken plenty of wine before his visit. Jay had to keep from turning his face away.

Kendric turned a bit unsteadily toward Izell. "He's a half-casting then?"

Queen Izell's expression became almost imperceptibly harder. "He is of mixed ancestry, yes."

"Splendid." Kendric's smile broadened. "Another one for Armone."

Jay stiffened with anger but held himself in check.

Queen Izell stepped between them. "Excuse me, my Lord, but I must get this message on its way. Then we can talk. You know how servants are." Without waiting for permission, she said, "Follow me, Lieutenant," and stepped to the doorway.

Jay followed her into the hall.

"Please deliver these reports to Minister Kaloby, and wait outside my door for more instructions," she said loud enough for Kendric to hear. Then she whispered, "Find Saben. Go to the Oracle. Stop for no one."

She squeezed his hand hard and then spun back to Kendric. "Another glass, Governor? I'm intrigued by this celebration you're planning."

Their voices faded as Jay turned and hurried toward the castle stables. He couldn't believe it. The half-cast prince was real.

Chapter Nineteen

Upheaval from disasters, whether natural or created by men, brings irreparable change to the landscape. The most devastating changes to my inner landscape came with the gain and then loss of a daughter.

—from Chronicles of Galathia by Rafykin, Urey, circa 2640 local planetary calendar.

Calonade, Day 002, Year 2999 local planetary calendar, Standard Galactic Year 14285

Jortica could feel Calamity faltering as they took a switchback turn on the road to the Outer Gate. Her horse hadn't gotten near enough rest and neither had she. Calamity's sweat foamed around the saddle, and she breathed with a harsh rasp. Jortica didn't like to abuse her mount, but orders were orders. She'd insist on a long rest for Calamity at the Outer Gate stables and ride another horse if necessary. Drop a coin or two on the stable master to ensure excellent treatment. Wouldn't be the first time.

Jortica spoke into Calamity's drooping ear. "Only a few more turns."

Captain Fauden had rousted her out of bed in the middle of the night, giving her orders to gather the Calonaden Horse Division riders on leave with her and lead them up to the Outer Gate to await further instructions. He didn't explain and simply walked away, expecting it to be done. She found the other squad leaders and, to their credit, they didn't question her. Like her, they mustered their riders for the long climb up the mountain.

Jortica felt a wash of pride to be officially acting in Captain Fauden's stead for the first time. A sense of dread rose to replace it once she realized leave was over and another hard ride awaited her. A horse soldier in service to Calonade was never truly on leave, so the saying went.

To Jortica's relief, they topped the last rise and entered the seaward courtyard of the Outer Gate without too much trouble. Two of the Kelstone peaks loomed on either side of the stone fortress walls. A central tower provided an overlook of both the mountainside back down below to Calonade and over the other side of the walls into the Kettlebone Pass. An iron portcullis blocked the way into the inner courtyard of the keep.

Calamity let out an exhausted snort upon reaching level ground, her head drooping. Jortica dismounted and pulled a lump of lanicin sap from her saddlebag. She pushed it into Calamity's mouth for her to chew. The lanicin would take care of the immediate pain, but she needed water, a good brushing, and oats. Jortica turned to wave for a stable hand, but one had appeared by her side already.

Jortica slipped her a coin, and she led Calamity away. Poor thing needed a couple of days rest at least. As the other riders topped the switchback road, it was plain their horses weren't in any better shape. All fourteen riders would have to change out their mounts.

Jortica swept a critical eye over the remaining Horse Division riders. These were the truly dedicated horse soldiers of Calonade. Of those still in the outfit yesterday, only two stayed in the city. Jortica felt a whiff of pride that her entire squad made it, though not in the best of shape.

Eason managed a weary smile but had no sarcastic quip this time. Kessa drooped in her saddle but snapped a salute as she passed. Samos appeared solid but grim. All the horses were spent. The one under Samos looked bushed. Carrying the big farmer up the mountain was no simple task. Jortica wondered if the Outer Gate stables had enough to spare. Likely not, since these stables were a civilian waystation, more for draft horses than military mounts.

Jortica waved Kessa over. "Make sure all the horses are stabled tonight." Jortica dropped a few coins in her hand.

"Ma'am, yes, ma'am."

Eason stuck out a hand for coins, but Jortica knew better than to let the townee have any spare change. "No gambling dens here, Eason."

"That's too bad, LJ." He grinned, looking a little more like himself after peeling his thin frame out of the saddle.

"Lieutenant Jortica, I presume." The rough voice came from the other side of the portcullis. As the gate rose, Jortica got a better view of the speaker and immediately wished she hadn't.

"Sergeant Nackers," Jortica said. "Sergeant Lunt." The two men nodded back, and Lunt even doffed an imaginary hat, though he wasn't wearing one to cover his scarred head. "What brings you away from your scurrilous duties?"

Nackers chuckled and Lunt looked confused. "What is squirrelious?"

"Like it sounds, lad. Like it sounds," Nackers said to his friend. "We been sent by Legate Armone to pick you up." Perhaps his smile was meant to be friendly, but it looked a little too cunning.

"Really? In your wagon, I suppose." Jortica nodded toward the wagon's iron-bar cage.

"Well, we are the welcome wagon, after all," Nackers said with a mischievous grin.

"We'd rather march to Thurbush. Besides, our orders are to wait here," Jortica said.

Nackers pulled a parchment from his tattered waistcoat. "Got some new orders for you. From the Legate hisself."

Jortica took it and read through the scratchy Galathian script.

"What's it say, LJ?" Eason asked.

"The Legate wants all of us in Thurbush by dawn?" Jortica peered at the eastern sky. It took on a light purple of the rising sun. "That's only a few minutes from now."

Nackers tapped the plank on which he sat. "Hence, the Welcome Wagon, darling. We'll have you there in a jiffy. Right, Lunt?"

"In a twinkle," Lunt said.

Orders were orders, but these didn't feel right. Jortica watched two more wagons trundle up to load the squads. None of them had bars around the sides.

"In a trice," Nackers said.

"What's a trice?" Lunt asked.

"Like it sounds, lad. Like it sounds."

The Calonaden riders stood in a sagging group around

Jortica. They looked as whipped by the endless riding as their mounts. A march to Thurbush wouldn't happen tonight. What could she do? Orders were orders, even if they came from a Galathian Legate. Still, Jortica didn't have to do it their way.

"All right," Jortica said, "we'll go, but only if you're disarmed."

Nackers growled in a low voice. "Excuse me, Lieutenant."

"You heard me. Toss your weapons in the back with us. We're in friendly territory, Sergeant. You shouldn't need them." Jortica glared at Nackers until he blinked.

"All right, Lieutenant, have it your way. I'm just trying to get you to your next post on time. That's all." Nackers tossed his sidearm into the wagon and gestured to Lunt.

"You sure, boss?" the big Galathian asked.

"She's the boss right now, lad. Just do it."

Lunt shrugged and tossed his sidearm down too.

"And pull off the back gate." Jortica pointed to the rear bars of the welcome wagon. "None of my people will sit in a cage. I'm going to sit up front with you. Lunt can join my squad."

Lunt shrugged again and unsheathed a long knife. He deftly flipped the bolts from the hinges and lifted the barred gate off the rear of the wagon. He tossed it onto the ground. "Gonna have to come back for that."

"It's alright, lad. Anything to keep the troops on time." Nackers' glare faded into a friendly smile. "We'll do it the lady officer's way."

Jortica scowled at Nackers. "You will refer to me as an officer or lieutenant from now on instead of *lady officer*, Sergeant Nackers."

"Yes, ma'am," Nackers said with a grin of triumph. "It will be my pleasure."

"Why is that?" Lunt asked Nackers.

"Because it's a pleasure to serve, lad," Nackers said, still smiling.

Lunt shrugged as if to say he didn't see much pleasure in it but stepped into the back of the wagon and sat heavily on a side bench. He waved a meaty hand at Jortica's squad. "Come on, then."

Jortica nodded, and the tired Calonadens clambered into the wagon and took seats on the side benches. Samos sat beside Lunt and gave him a sizing up. Jortica swung herself into the seat beside Nackers, giving him a suspicious sidelong glance but made no comment.

After all the Galathian drivers had given up their arms, Jortica waved to the other squads to mount their wagons. Nackers, still grinning like a cat who snagged a fish from the net, gave the reins a snap. He took up the rear position in their little convoy as the horses pulled the wagons past the portcullis and into the landward courtyard of the Outer Gate.

The broad stones of the gate stacked layer upon layer to produce the most formidable fortification known in Calonade and the Frontier. Soldiers patrolled the tiers of the walls, walking past ramparts and cannon emplacements. A long, fortified tunnel provided the only passage through the wall. Goddess help anyone who tried to enter without an invitation. The edges of the man-made structure interlaced with the jagged sides of two Kelstone Mountain peaks, each one towering above them on either side of the gate, reaching higher than the clouds.

It was said the Outer Gate was built with magic and that no

army could break it down because the cannon balls simply bounced off the stone. People say a lot of things, and Jortica put little stock in relying on magic. Still, the place seemed like it might stand for ages.

Nackers steered the wagon into the wall passage without a comment. The guards working the doors must have seen him coming. Jortica could make out a lot of striped faces on the walls today. Seemed like more Galathians on duty than usual.

The horses shied in the tunnel, but Nackers had no compunction in giving the animals a touch with the whip for encouragement. The horses calmed as they passed back into the light on the outer side of the gate.

In the light of day, the scars of past battles dominated the Kettlebone Pass. Only moss and sparse scrub brush dared to grow within the range of the cannons. Even the exposed soil seemed dark, as if still soaked with blood.

Everyone relaxed as the wagon trundled onto the forested road beyond the pass. Even though Jortica felt bone tired, she couldn't catch a nap. First off, she didn't trust Nackers enough to close her eyes anywhere near him. Second, he was the worst wagon driver to ever attempt the trade. The road to Thurbush had always been heavily trafficked during times of both war and peace, which showed in the road's condition. Nackers put a wagon wheel into every rut along the way. She wasn't surprised when they got stuck.

The wagons ahead of them stopped to wait. The road cut a straight path through a thick stand of trees. Forest loomed on either side.

Nackers cursed and whipped the horses, but they couldn't pull the wagon free. "Lunt, get out there and see where we're stuck," he yelled over his shoulder. The big man stomped between the rows of exhausted horse soldiers and jumped down onto the road.

"Go with him, Samos," Jortica snapped.

"Aye." The big farmer stood beside the equally sized Galathian.

"Well, give it a push, you lumps," Nackers shouted.

They grunted and rocked the wagon, but it remained stuck.

"Must be the front." Nackers leaned to his side. "It's not this one." He nodded to Jortica. "Check yours."

Jortica leaned over the side of the wagon. The wheel nearest her sunk deep into the mud, but she couldn't tell if it was the one holding them up.

Jortica straightened to find Nackers holding a long knife to her chest.

"Don't move, Lieutenant," he said, no longer smiling. He reached into her gun belt and took her riding pistol.

A shout made Jortica whip her head around to see Lunt standing at the back of the wagon, holding a knife to Samos' throat. Eason and Kessa reached for their weapons.

"Don't!" Lunt pulled the knife tighter against Samos' neck.

"Take aim!" a voice shouted. A row of Galathian foot soldiers stepped out of the trees on either side of the road. They leveled long rifles at the wagon train.

Everyone froze.

Nackers pointed Jortica's own gun at her face and pulled back the hammer. It was primed and ready to fire just as Jortica had stowed it. "Now," he said sharply, so all could hear. "Toss out your weapons or your officer won't ever give another order."

Samos growled but held still when Lunt drew a trickle of

blood from his neck.

"What do we do, LJ?" Eason's panicked voice echoed through the valley. He'd gotten his pistol halfway out of his holster.

Kessa's wide-eyed terror shifted between Nackers and Jortica. She'd drawn her saber, but it shook in her grip. "Ma'am?"

All the other Calonaden horse soldiers stared down the barrels of the Galathian guns surrounding them, frozen in the moment.

Lightning crackled in Jortica's mind, just like the time the storm ravaged her childhood. Time slowed like it does as a storm approaches. Only one destination awaited their surrender. The jailhouse. She shivered. She'd led her team into a trap. No, Captain Fauden had handed them over to Legate Armone like a wrapped present.

"This is a life-changing moment, Lieutenant." Nackers voice echoed over the rumble of the coming storm. "Make a wise decision today and you get to make another one tomorrow." His toothy grin dominated her vision. He enjoyed this. He loved taking freedom and dignity from his captives.

"What are you doing, Nackers?" The rising wind muffled Jortica's voice.

The cunning smile grew wider. "Just following orders, ma'am."

"Are your orders to shoot us or take us prisoner?"

Nackers shrugged. "I think that's up to you."

No Calonaden would choose chains. They would fight against them until death or victory. Why extend the suffering? Besides, the people of Calonade must know. People like

Jay had to be warned. Doing so was the sworn duty of the Horse Division. Someone had to escape and now was the only chance. She'd told her squad the time would come to disobey orders.

All the lives on this road hung in the balance. Jortica's heart pounded under the weight of it. The rush of the storm grew in Jortica's ears, blotting out all else. Nackers said something, but Jortica could only see his lips moving around his ever-present sneer.

"Fight!" The storm parted before her scream and her squad sprang into action. Eason drew and fired. Kessa charged out of the wagon, saber pointed at Lunt. Samos smashed the back of his head against Lunt's face.

Jortica punched Nackers' wrist and the knife flew into the air. Gunfire erupted all around them. Nackers fell backward off the wagon seat, firing the pistol harmlessly into the air. Jortica leaped after him and they ended up tangled in the mud. Jortica kicked Nackers hard in the stomach and pulled free of his grasp. She crawled off the road, away from the wagon.

A Galathian soldier rushed toward her, leading with his bayonet. He reared back to stab down. Jortica kicked his ankle and sent him over onto his back. His musket flopped on the ground beside her. Grabbing the weapon, Jortica leaped to her feet and stabbed the Galathian in the chest. Behind her a Galathian cursed, and he frantically reloaded his musket. Jortica pulled out her saber and charged him. She slashed with all her strength and felt the blade rip into flesh, but she didn't look to see the result.

She spun just in time to see a second volley of shots hit the wagon, ripping holes into it and its occupants. Samos had fallen on Lunt. Both were bloody and struggling in the mud.

Samos' body jerked as two shots hit him. He didn't move after that. Eason, slumped against the side of the wagon, riddled with shots. Kessa sprawled in the mud, her saber broken under her body.

The other wagons met the same fate. All the Calonaden horse soldiers were dead and dying.

"No!" she screamed at the Galathians as they reloaded. She gripped her sword, wanting to kill them all. She would rage down upon them like the storm in her head and blow them into oblivion with retribution's thunder. A rational part of her mind still held control. There were at least twenty of them and no one left but her to fight.

"One more near the trees," an officer shouted, standing across the road. He pointed his sword at her as the Galathians readied their next volley.

Jortica stared them down, the wind in her head reaching a terrible tempest. Two fired before the rest, and bark erupted from the tree beside her. She ducked and ran into the forest. The sound of the rest of the shots joined the rush of the storm blowing fiercely at her back.

Chapter Twenty

History proves, time and again, that when humans are allowed to strive beyond their moral capabilities, suffering is the only result. Our hard-won evolution beyond the limitations of Homo sapiens is the only thing that protects us from a similar fate.

—from the journal of Sephy Alcott, Standard Galactic Year 13303

Calonade, Day 002, Year 2999 local planetary calendar, Standard Galactic Year 14285

Jay rushed through the servant's passageways of the castle, his heart pounding. *The half-cast prince is real.* Queen Izell had an heir, and the Oracle knew where to find him. That must be what the message from the clockwork crow was all about. It was a secret that Kahela didn't know, Saben didn't know, hell, Gran probably didn't know. Jay knew Gran would have told him if she knew.

But I know!

He really needed to talk to Kaloby. There was no time, however. With Kendric traipsing about the castle, planning to oust Queen Izell, Armone could be on his way even now.

They had to move fast to stay a step ahead.

Jay made his way to the kitchens, which he found stripped of supplies. The yawning cupboards and empty pantries seemed unnatural, as if the invasion had already happened. At least he knew for sure Gran was on her way. A harrowing journey through the shadows of the fishing village and the fickle sea was her only obstacle to safety now. Jay couldn't let himself think about it. He had to focus on his mission.

As he exited the castle, he made no pretense of being casual. He ran for the stables at full speed and burst through the doors in a headlong sprint.

He skidded to a stop. In front of Havoc's stall stood two Galathians wearing castle guard uniforms. One of them he recognized from his first day of duty. Lieutenant Dothery.

"There you are." Jay spun around to find Gilcres standing in the doorway. He pushed the stable doors closed.

"Going somewhere in the middle of the night?" Gilcres made a show of checking his silver pocket watch for the time.

Jay's training flashed into his mind. *The one in front of you isn't the problem*, Kahela's voice said. He had to worry about the two behind him. Jay ducked and slid sideways as the guards tried to grab him. They tangled with each other. Jay crouched and swept their legs with a kick. Dothery went down on his butt and the other stumbled back a few steps.

Jay sprang up and grabbed the nearest object, a pitchfork. He put his back to a wooden beam next to Havoc's stall. The Galathian, still on his feet, drew a sword and charged. Jay caught the blade between the tongs and twisted. The tongs broke, but the sword flew from the Galathian's grip. Jay flipped the handle of the tool and bashed the Galathian on the top of the head. His eyes crossed, and he fell flat.

Turning to face Dothery, he stopped short to stare into the barrel of a flintlock pistol. Jay could see it was primed and loaded.

"Hold still, half-casting," Dothery hissed. The barrel of the gun shook as the Galathian stared at Jay with a burning hate.

Jay froze, dropping the pitchfork. "Easy now."

Dothery grinned as he kept the gun on Jay. "It's the half-casting who cheated you out of winning Top Cadet, Captain Gilcres. I finally get to kill him." He shifted sideways to lean against the stall gate.

"Not just yet, Lieutenant." Gilcres smacked his lips as he leaned against the far wall, savoring the moment. "I knew I'd find you here, eventually." He snapped his pocket watch cover shut and shoved it into his waistcoat. "Poor messenger Jay. Scurrying here and hurrying there, all day long. It's hard work for a dumb half-casting like you. Why don't you let me take that message and deliver it for you?"

"What message?"

Gilcres pointed at his chest. Jay realized his jacket had come open, revealing the package he was carrying. *Damn!*

"Hand it over," Gilcres growled, pointing toward Dothery.

Dothery nodded toward the package. "Drop it."

Jay felt a shift in the air from inside the stall just in time to cover his face. The stall gate crashed open slamming Dothery onto the stable floor. The pistol went off, and the shot flew over Jay's head. Havoc burst from the stall with a fierce scream of rage. He stomped with a foreleg on Dothery's hip. Bone crunched, and the man screamed in terror and pain.

Jay shouldered Havoc back into his stall. "Easy, boy." He didn't need the big warhorse kicking in this confined space.

Havoc sputtered and whinnied but settled down.

Gilcres held back, keeping his distance from Havoc, and Jay feared he'd draw a weapon. His eyes flicked down to where a holster would be. Empty. While off duty, Gilcres remained unarmed like him, per military rules.

At his feet, one Galathian was out cold, blood dribbling from a scalp wound. Dothery moaned as he squirmed into a corner, trying to protect his head from a stomping horse no longer there.

"I'm going to put down that mad horse," Gilcres said.

"No, you won't," Jay said. "You don't have the guts."

"Come out of that stall and we'll see."

Jay stepped out. No need to upset Havoc anymore. Jay needed him fresh for the climb up the mountains. He could just mount up and ride because Gilcres wouldn't stand in the way, but he had no supplies, no weapons, not even a saddle. Gilcres wouldn't stand around watching him prepare for a journey. Besides, doing so might give away his intent. No, he had to deal with the problem. Jay set himself, relaxed but ready, just like in training. "All right, Gilcres. What's it going to be?"

Gilcres smiled, pressing a beefy fist into the other meaty palm. "I'm going to break you, half-casting." Gilcres lumbered toward him.

The insult burned, and Jay forgot his training. He broke from his stance and charged, leaping to deliver a flying kick to Gilcres' head, but missed and hit him in the shoulder, which didn't budge. With his follow-through fouled, Jay landed off-balance, flung an arm up to block Gilcres' answering punch, missed, and took a hard hit in the breastbone.

Gilcres got his weight behind it and Jay went down on his

back, his breath exploding out of his lungs. Gilcres crashed down and pinned him. Jay floundered, unable to catch a full breath.

"Eat dirt, halfy!" Gilcres snarled as he pushed Jay's head into the stable floor. The acrid smell of horse piss and stale straw filled his nostrils, but he breathed it in greedily. He twisted and squirmed out of Gilcres' hold for a moment, but Gilcres shifted back and had him again, pushing down, crushing Jay's back and neck.

Jay reached out with a free hand and found the pitchfork handle. He whipped it backhanded and connected with Gilcres on his ear. The big man roared with pain and let go.

Leaving the handle behind, Jay rolled and crawled. He scrambled free and got to his wobbly feet. Gilcres was already up, blood trickling down the side of his face. He charged with a howl. Jay, still unsteady, stepped to meet him with a fist, but Gilcres blocked Jay's weak punch and smashed him up against the stable walls. The boards above them rattled with the blow. Jay's lungs emptied again.

Gilcres peeled Jay away and tossed him back onto the floor. Jay's head and elbow cracked on the hard surface. His arm went numb, and his head spun. Gilcres jumped on him again, pinning his good arm and shoving a knee into his stomach. Jay felt like he might burst at the seams. Havoc whinnied a warning and shifted in his stall but didn't come out this time. Jay was glad because anything Havoc could do would likely hurt him, too. He had to get out of this himself. Who knew Gilcres was such a good fighter?

With no way to catch a good breath, Jay was spent. He had to try something else. "Why do you hate me so much?" Jay rasped through his raw throat.

Gilcres' grip eased just a fraction. "Hate," he snarled, "doesn't even describe it. You are nothing. Garbage." Gilcres spat the last phrase with a voice full of contempt. He shifted a forearm across the side of Jay's head and pushed his face against the floor, painfully twisting his neck.

"We were friends once, in the castle as kids," Jay said to buy time, though for what he wasn't sure. With Armone and his soldiers coming in, it wouldn't be long before Gilcres had a lot of help.

"Ha!" Gilcres sneered. "We were never friends. You were a half-cast cook's boy and still no better. I'm Galathian royalty. To me, you didn't exist. Still don't."

In his fury, Gilcres tightened his grip, and Jay couldn't move. "Why are you trying to kill me then?" he choked.

"Because the Legate seems to think a half-casting can be royalty." Gilcres pushed Jay harder into the muck. "He's very mistaken but cannot be convinced that you and your ilk are nothing. You. Are. Nothing." Gilcres pressed him down more with each word.

Gilcres leaned down close to Jay's ear, his hot breath assaulting Jay's face. "I would be related to a child of Izell. By the holy goddesses, I will never allow a half-casting to claim such an honor. I'll kill them all, starting with you."

Jay's free arm tingled back to life. With his spinning head and heart pounding, Jay held it hard as a knife and jammed it into Gilcres' neck, right under his wounded ear. The big man reared up and Jay took the sweetest breath of his life.

Gilcres roared and punched Jay in the eye. It felt like a hammer blow and his vision went dark. Jay flung up his good arm to deflect the next blow from his head. Gilcres punched him in the chest. Already bruised, Jay felt his ribs give way as pain lanced up and down his spine. Another crack and pain exploded across Jay's cheek. Jay flailed, unable to see where the next blow would hit him.

"Captain!" A barking growl cut through the haze.

"Headmaster Saben?" Gilcres answered. "What are you—?"

"Stand at attention, Captain."

"But I—"

"Do it!" Saben demanded. "Eyes Front."

Gilcres' weight lifted and Jay could breathe again. Ribs and face throbbing he turned on his side. His watery vision slowly came back.

Gilcres stood at attention in front of the general. "I was dealing with the half-cast traitor, sir."

"I see that. I'll take over now."

Jay rolled over onto his stomach, his ribs aching. Maybe they weren't broken after all, but they sure hurt. Blood dripped down his face from a cut over his eye. His jaw felt loose, but no teeth were knocked out, thank the goddess.

"But, sir, the Legate assigned him to me," Gilcres pleaded.

"To *watch*, Captain," Saben said, "not to kill."

"Half-castings are better off dead, sir." Gilcres' tone rose to a whine. "Especially this one."

"Murder is not a part of your orders," Saben said.

"Murder? Killing a traitor—"

"Without due process is murder." Saben leaned into Gilcres' face. "I was once accused of being a traitor. Would you have me executed without trial?"

"No, sir, but—"

"You're dismissed, Captain," Saben snapped.

"But sir—"

Growling, Saben took Gilcres by the lapel and pulled him close. He wobbled off balance in Saben's grip, his eyes wide with surprise and fear. "I don't care who your aunt is. You never talk back to me, Captain Gilcres. Do you understand?"

"Yes, sir," Gilcres squeaked.

Saben let him go but stared him down with a withering glare. "Report back to the Legate. I'll take care of this." Saben waved toward Jay and the Galathian lying unconscious on the floor. Dothery must have crawled out during the scuffle.

"Yes, sir," Gilcres said, and he hurried from the stable.

Saben stood over Jay.

Jay blinked at the stoic general. He was about to find out if Queen Izell's faith in General Saben was well-placed. If not, he'd likely pay with his life.

Saben bent to offer Jay a hand. "Sorry I'm late." He pulled Jay to his feet and then picked up Queen Izell's envelope, which must have fallen out of Jay's jacket during the fight. "Can you ride?"

Jay accepted the package and grinned. He immediately regretted it as his face throbbed with pain. "Yes, sir," he said and spat out a glob of salty blood.

Saben examined his face. "A couple of good hits, but I've seen worse. Might help with what we have to do tonight."

"What's that?" Jay asked.

"Sneak past an invading army."

They led their horses out of their stalls, and Jay quickly got Havoc saddled and packed.

"I picked up a few things you'll need." Saben holstered his pistol and checked his mount. "Take a look."

Jay unrolled the blanket and found a flintlock pistol, primed and ready, and a riding saber freshly oiled.

"Thank you, sir. I was feeling naked."

Saben chuckled. "Mount up, soldier. And eyes front! We may meet with more trouble along the way."

Chapter Twenty-One

The price of our evolution is the necessary moral challenges upon which our survival depends. Some say the cost is too much, or our claim to have evolved is false, and we should strive to recover the full humanity of our past.

—from the journal of Sephy Alcott, Standard Galactic Year 13303

Calonade, Day 002, Year 2999 local planetary calendar, Standard Galactic Year 14285

Saben led Havoc along by the reins. Jay sat in the saddle with a strip of cloth over his mouth and his hands tied. At least, that's the way it looked to the passersby. He appeared to be an unfortunate half-casting caught by a Galathian. He even looked unarmed. He hid both sword and pistol from sight, but within easy reach. Spy craft, at times, boiled down to the tactical placement of a rolled blanket.

They didn't have to bother with much subterfuge along the streets of the city. No one paid them any heed. Galathians and Calonadens alike raced by, not even looking up. A challenge, however, awaited at the city's outer wall. Saben headed straight for the main city gate.

"Wait," Jay whispered past the loose gag.

Saben held up and let Havoc come alongside his mount. "Yes, Lieutenant?"

"Shouldn't we try to sneak through?"

"I prefer the direct approach. If you look like you're hiding and sneaking, people get suspicious."

That didn't endorse Jay's finely honed stealth abilities at all. "Won't it look like you're friendly with a prisoner right now?"

Saben struck out with a fist and grazed Jay's cheek. Jay reeled back, his eyes watering from the sting. The gag fell away and his split lip from Gilcres opened, dribbling blood. He hung on to the rope around his wrists.

"No, Lieutenant, I don't believe anyone will think that." Saben pulled forward without looking back and led Havoc to the gatehouse.

"Wow," Jay whispered as he flopped forward in the saddle, trying to look the part of a beaten captive. "That could've really hurt."

"What we got here?" One of the Galathian guards called out with a thick northern accent.

From his subservient posture, Jay noticed the guard was wearing fur-lined boots. He must have just arrived with no time to dress for the milder climate.

"A halfy prisoner," Saben replied.

"Holding pen is the other way, General," the guard said.

"This one is taking me to find more, Sergeant. We'll pass through."

"Yes, sir." The guard signaled, and the gate creaked open. Saben urged his horse toward the opening.

"General Saben." An oily voice spoke from the dark. "Isn't that right?"

Jay squinted through the gloom to see Legate Armone emerge from the shadows. He wore the brocade cloak and a black cloth covered a bundle he balanced in one hand.

Jay's heart froze, and he ducked his head down more, trying not to be recognized, while keeping Armone and Saben in view.

"Ah, yes." A smile flickered over Saben's face. It didn't seem to belong there, but he forced it to remain. "You're the emperor's agent." He dismounted and approached Armone with a hand outstretched. "Have we not met?"

Armone returned the handshake with a wolfish expression. "I don't believe I've had the pleasure, sir. I am Armone, former warden of Karpathode, but now I serve the emperor in a more direct manner. There's no mistaking you, of course. The Rebel King Killer."

Saben waved this off. "I only do my duty to the empire."

"Yes, don't we all." Armone pulled free the cloth to reveal a bird clamped to his left arm. It had black feathers and ominous red eyes. Jay recognized a Galathian message krike. A small leather pouch was bound under its breast.

Armone loosened its ties, and the bird leaped from the agent's grasp and flapped away into the darkness. "Good news for my master," the greasy man said with a grin.

"Quite so. What brings you so far from Galathia?" Saben asked.

"I've managed a change of scenery, shall we say." Armone peered at Saben intently. "Why is it I have never seen you in the Galathian court? We all owe you a debt. Why do you not reap the rewards the empire offers its heroes?"

Saben's smile took a harder set as he looked directly into Armone's eyes. "I'm no hero. I am merely a servant."

"Humble words that do you credit." Armone smiled to show yellow-tinged teeth that looked sharper than they should. "Or is the credit misplaced?" Armone arched an eyebrow at Saben.

Saben simply returned a stone-faced stare.

"Tell me what you have here," Armone said, changing the subject.

"A halfy spy."

Armone reached out and yanked Jay's head back. Jay kept his expression blank and broken. He moaned in pain, which he didn't have to pretend. Armone had a cruel grip.

"I think I know this one," Armone hissed with satisfaction. "Yes, he looks familiar, and this horse is unmistakable." Armone drew forth a serrated blade. "Shall I dispatch him now?"

Jay whimpered, still playing the part, but he really felt scared. He could reach his own weapons in time, but to attack now would mean death a few moments later from one of the nearby Galathian guards. Saben stood out of range to stop a quick death blow from Armone.

"It would do more harm than good." Saben kept his tone even. "He's taking me to more of them."

Armone slammed Jay's head back down, eliciting another moan of pain, which wasn't false either.

"Where?" Armone asked.

"Beyond the city gate."

"Ah, of course." Armone sheathed his knife. "That's where I saw him. Very good. Bring as many as you can to the holding pen."

"I will," Saben said.

"Better yet, send someone else to do it. You'll get no trouble from this one. I'm sure his companions will be no more of a challenge for a few Galathian fighters. You could join me as we take the castle."

"I don't think that will be necessary," Saben said.

"You don't agree with this course of action?"

"No, Legate, I don't. I believe Lady Izell is essential to maintain the supply of lanicin to the empire."

"As directed by the emperor himself, I understand," Armone said.

"Yes, those instructions came from him. Which is why I strive to keep Lady Izell in a position of influence despite the efforts of the factions against the emperor."

"Are you making an accusation, General?"

"No, just noting a sudden change in a long-standing policy." Saben kept a calm but hard tone.

"I assure you the emperor has changed his mind. He has accumulated a surplus of lanicin in case of an interruption in supply. You must have received word about this."

"No. Not a whisper."

"An oversight, I'm sure. Izell is no longer needed. The time is right for Galathia to take control here. Now come along, I do insist." Armone waited for Saben's answer, watching him closely.

"All right," Saben said. "Let me brief a few officers regarding the prisoner and then I'll meet you there."

Distant shots echoed across the gatehouse yard. Both men turned toward the noise.

"That's from the bay," Saben said.

"Ha, ha!" Armone barked. "Izell has some fight in her,

after all. Tell me, General, would you like to finish her off tonight?" he asked with a gleeful edge. "You could be the hero twice over."

"I will defer the honor to you, sir." Saben bowed to Armone.

A volley of flintlock fire echoed from the direction of the sea. The smell of sulfur drifted over the breeze. Armone salivated like a predator smelling blood on the wind.

"Come then, join me as we crush this sad rebellion." Armone licked his lips in anticipation.

"You go ahead, Legate," Saben said, seeing his eagerness. "I'll catch up shortly."

Armone nodded and strode away to a waiting horse. He mounted and led most of the guards away with him. The Galathians itched to fight. Saben mounted and without another word led Havoc through the open gate and out of the city.

Once they were out of sight, Jay sat up in the saddle. "I need to know what that was about, sir."

"Wait 'til we're in the groves."

One after the other, both moons had risen, their hazy light pried through the gloom. They reached a row of lanicina trees and Saben signaled for a stop. They dismounted and Saben examined Jay's wounds, applying raw lanicina sap to each one. The one on his lip left a bitter taste.

Saben slapped a piece of bark into Jay's hand. "For later, if you need it."

Jay put it away. He stood quiet for a moment, studying the old headmaster while he slashed off a strip of bark for himself. He was headmaster no more. Not after tonight. At some point, Armone would discover Saben's deception. If Galathia won, he had just given up his rank, his career, and possibly his life.

Once the throbbing stopped, Jay asked, "Sir, was it true what you said to the Legate?"

"Yes, as far as any Galathian knows. It's part of my cover story."

"Did the emperor really tell you to protect Izell?" Jay watched Saben's face closely in the moonlight to detect any sign of deception.

"Emperor Staukard wanted uninterrupted flow of lanicin. I told him he needed Lady Izell securely in place for that. He agreed."

"When was this?"

Saben's brow creased as he remembered. "Staukard visited Calonade about a year after our surrender."

"I didn't know that."

"He came in secret to see Lady Izell and make me governor. He thought, like everyone else, I killed Nados." A sour expression flitted across Saben's face, but it was quickly gone.

"You refused."

"I almost told him the truth. I was sick to death due to the loss of my friend, but Lady Izell stopped me. She ordered me to lie so she could take advantage of the emperor's trust."

The truth dawned on Jay. "You argued for the stability of Calonade to spare her."

"I didn't think it would work. It has for twenty years." For a moment, Saben looked weary, but that expression soon vanished beneath his stony visage. "In the end, they asked me to start the academy and chose a more political animal for governor."

Jay shook his head in astonishment at the audacity of it. Queen Izell leveraged the death of her husband to save herself and her people. And perhaps someone else.

"Did you know that Queen Izell has a child?"

Saben considered the question carefully. "No, but it's possible. Queen Izell was pregnant at the second battle of Kettlebone Pass."

"Wait, you're admitting there were two battles?"

"Of course. I was there. I fought in the first and observed among the wounded during the second."

"You've never said that before."

"We're not in a Galathian classroom, Lieutenant."

"We won them both, you know."

Saben sighed. "Yes, I know."

"It's just. Well, as headmaster you've never actually…"

Saben glared at him. "They weren't true victories. We lost the king and then we lost the country."

Gran had told him the story at least a hundred times. What the Galathians claimed as a single decisive victory was anything but. Losing King Nados on the Kettlebone Pass had been almost enough to deliver victory to the enemy, but Queen Izell rallied the nation. She led a band of women to the defenses while pregnant herself. That moment of glory bought Calonade a year and allowed a negotiated ceasefire.

"So, the child wasn't stillborn. Then what happened, sir?"

"I don't know. I was imprisoned by Parliament for a long time. Once the Galathians released me, Lady Izell was no longer pregnant and there was no baby. I was told the child didn't survive the birth. If that isn't true, then such a child would be in grave danger."

"That's why we're going to the Oracle. Queen Izell told me the Oracle knows where he is hidden."

In the moonlight, Saben's face looked hard and impassive,

but Jay felt something else. Something hung over the man's hooded eyes. Jay pressed for the truth. He slipped a hand to his sword hilt in case he needed to use it.

"Why do people think you killed King Nados, General?"

Saben blinked. His rigid stance dropped slightly, as if he suddenly felt a deep ache in his body. "I served as a personal aide to King Nados. When he fell, I fought to reach him, but there were too many. I couldn't. They overran us. I saw the fatal blow." This time the pain remained on his face, drawing his features down.

"You were blamed because you're Galathian. Then, when the invaders found you in prison, they thought the rumor was true and trusted you right away."

Saben nodded. "I have used that trust ever since in the service of Calonade."

Jay relaxed, and a realization struck him like lightning. "That's why you voted for Jortica to win the contest."

"No." Saben straightened, and his impassive expression returned. "She won because she deserved it. You came very close, Jay, but she won even though Gilcres prevented you from winning. Can you tell me why?"

Jay repeated the mantra. "There are no rules on the battlefield."

"That's right, Lieutenant."

In the distance, the crack of flintlocks continued to disturb the night. Both Jay and Saben listened.

"The castle?" Jay asked.

"Perhaps. This battlefield is changing as we speak. Let's get moving."

"Yes, sir." Jay followed without hesitation, understanding why Queen Izell and King Nados trusted this man. He was willing to risk his life for Calonade.

Chapter Twenty-Two

Perhaps our humanity is lost forever and should be consigned to the past where it belongs.

—from the journal of Sephy Alcott, Standard Galactic Year 13303

Kelstone Mountains, Day 002, Year 2999 local planetary calendar, Standard Galactic Year 14285

Saben and Jay rode high into the Kelstone Mountains. Even though Jay had traversed the steep trail before, moving over a narrow path with sheer cliffs on one side and a dizzying drop on the other was difficult. It forced Jay and Saben to dismount to keep the horses from stumbling.

Below them, a battle raged in the harbor. Cestra Peak loomed above, blocking out the light from the moons. Bright flashes followed by thunderous noise still reached them along the cliffs. Even from this distance, Jay could smell the pungent odor of black powder smoke on the wind. Jay borrowed Saben's spyglass when they stopped to rest.

A Calonaden ship slipped past the invading fleet and sailed to the mouth of the harbor. There, instead of escaping, it blazed away at the Galathian warships. Several steamships maneuvered to counterattack, their paddle wheels digging into the water.

"I think that's the *Victory*," Saben said.

Jay nodded. He'd seen it during his stroll with Jortica. "It's burning." The bow and forward sails were ablaze, lighting up the harbor. A burning mast fell onto the nearest Galathian ship. It quickly spread the fire. "I thought Queen Izell ordered everyone to escape quietly. Do you think they're on board?"

"No. This looks like Kahela's doing. It's likely a distraction so the queen can escape. Do you see our boats pulling away on the other side?"

Jay caught the flashes of oars beyond the burning wreck of the Calonaden frigate. "Yes, sir, but the guns are still firing. Did someone stay behind?"

"Those are probably using timed fuses. The queen and her escort are likely already at sea in fishing boats from the old docks. The burning wreckage will block the harbor channel nicely and encumber pursuit. A smart plan."

Jay swung the glass away from the battle and toward where the fishing village stood. All was dark there. He hoped the calm weather would hold.

"Tell me what you see on the trail below us."

Jay peered down the scrabble rock trail. He saw movement. The flash of another salvo from the harbor lit up the source.

"Several men on horseback are coming up the trail behind us," Jay reported. "They're dismounting. All in Galathian uniforms but one." The remaining figure came into view with his familiar gold brocade cloak. "Legate Armone."

"He didn't fall for my act for long," Saben said. "Probably ran into Gilcres and they put it together. Still, I'm surprised he's missing the battle."

Jay watched Armone through his glass. He pointed up the trail and waved his arms. A flash of triumph swirled through Jay. His plan had worked. He'd drawn Armone away from pursuing the queen. With his free hand, Jay felt a hard corner of the packet he carried under his uniform coat. Had Armone found out about the message? Or was he chasing who he thought was the half-cast prince? Either way, he'd be relentless.

Jay had beaten him once. This time, though, the stakes were higher. If he failed, Armone would surely take the message. Did it reveal the queen's plans or the true location of the half-cast prince? Jay considered reading the message and then destroying it, but that went against all his training. He'd just have to beat Armone again.

Jay watched the soldiers as they left their horses behind and climbed up the trail. "They've seen us."

"We'll have to leave our horses here to stay ahead of them," Saben said.

Jay looked up at the general, alarmed.

"They'll be fine. After we get away, they'll just take them back to the castle stables. Come help me hobble them, so they don't make a misstep and get hurt."

Jay, reluctant to leave Havoc's fate in the hands of some heartless Galathians, returned to the glass. They were indeed hurrying up the treacherous trail. He and Saben couldn't outrun them while pulling their mounts along.

Jay noticed one soldier kneel.

A bullet ricocheted off the rocks near Jay's head. Jay ducked down and then he heard the report of the gun. "One of them has a rifle."

"We're out of range," Saben said. "Only a lucky shot would hit us."

"That one was pretty close," Jay muttered.

"We need to go."

Jay snapped the glass shut, and they quickly picketed the horses. Jay rubbed Havoc's nose. "I'll come back for you."

Another bullet zinged off the nearby cliffs, followed by the thunder from the shot echoing over the mountainside. Jay climbed up the rough trail as fast as he could to draw the Galathian fire away from the horses. Saben came huffing along behind him.

* * *

After hours of scrambling over the footpath in the uncertain light, they reached a wide overlook backed by a towering cliff. Jay took a moment to observe the city below through the glass. Fires lit the castle windows.

Beyond the center of the city, torches burned along the piers. Enemy soldiers marched beside the shore wall and through the city streets. A pallor of smoke rose from the burnt-out ships blocking the harbor. Calonade had fallen firmly in the hands of the Galathian Empire.

Jay swung the glass back down the trail. Having thrown caution to the wind, the Galathians had gained ground on them. Jay could hear Armone's echoing curses meant to encourage their speed. Jay snapped the glass shut. "They're right on our heels."

In front of them, a large cave opened as if the mountain

gaped in shock. The trail led into its mouth and descended into pitch darkness.

"The Oracle better let us in, or we're done," Jay said. "Have you been here before, sir?"

"Yes, once with King Nados, though this is as far as I got. I haven't been inside."

Jay swallowed. "How do we go in?"

"I suppose we follow the path until we're greeted by our host." Saben pointed out a set of flat stones leading into the cave.

The bark of a flintlock sounded behind them, and a bullet whizzed past.

"I hope you're right, sir."

Saben drew his pistol. "I'll guard the rear. You lead, Lieutenant. Eyes front."

"Yes, sir." Jay drew his pistol and moved forward into the dark.

The flat stones became steps as they descended into the mountain. He felt his way along in the fading light, but after a time, the heavy darkness lifted. A faint glow compelled him to go deeper. Saben followed along behind.

The air grew thicker as he descended. The smell of damp rock mingled with a familiar fish odor. At the end of the stone stairs, an ordinary whale oil lantern on a pole burned vigorously. It lit a doorframe built into the sheer rock wall. It could have been a front door from a house in the city. A traditional bell string hung where one would expect.

Jay looked back to Saben.

The general shook his head. "No pursuit." Saben holstered his gun and stepped up to the door. "Have you seen the like? A house door in the middle of a cavern."

Jay put away his weapon, too. "I guess we ring the bell."

Saben nodded and gestured for Jay to do the honors.

Jay pulled the string, and a bell tinkled faintly on the other side of the door. Then it was quiet for a long while. Jay shrugged and pulled the bell again.

"One minute, one minute," a cranky voice said from the other side. "Keep your pants on."

The door unlatched and creaked open to reveal a woman bent with age. Gray hair with white streaks flowed down until it nearly touched the floor. She peered past a crooked nose and a face mottled green with gray splotches. A collection of faded tattoos, looking like runes, decorated the exposed skin of her arms and face.

"Soldiers." She squinted at them.

Each of her eyes, dark and deep, resembled the depths of a well. Jay had never seen a more gruesome and interesting old woman.

"Have you come to take me away, or is this a social visit?"

"Neither," Jay said. "I am here to deliver a message to the Oracle."

"Oh, a message. A message!" She turned and shouted over her shoulder, "Bernard, the post finally came and it's for me!" She looked back at them. "Who is it from?" She held out her hands.

Jay peered at her. "If you're truly the Oracle, then you should know."

The old woman's eyes twinkled with delight. "Izell has reclaimed her crown and run off with it, has she? Well, that's the way it goes some days."

Jay suppressed a start. Maybe this odd creature really did know all. How could she know the events of the last few hours without such powers? Jay retrieved the envelope from under his jacket and placed it in her hands.

"It's the package I've been expecting, Bernard," she called over her shoulder. "Come in, come in." She opened the door wide. "I haven't had company in a great while. You'll have to excuse the mess. Bernard and I aren't the best housekeepers."

"Ma'am," Jay said, "we were being chased."

"Bah. They won't find you now," the Oracle said. "Come on in."

Jay looked over his shoulder. No one pounded down the steps in pursuit. They entered a tidy home one might expect to find in Calonade city. The antique furniture smelled of beeswax polish. Several shelves held a variety of knick-knacks, including ivory-carved figurines, porcelain dolls, and elaborate dishware. Some items looked familiar to Jay, while others originated from unfamiliar cultures. A few had an otherworldly cast. Another shelf stored a collection of leather-bound parchments that would pique Kaloby's interest. A fire in the hearth and several candles placed in tall holders lit the room warmly. Curtains blocked what could only be false windows.

A finely carved clock hung on the wall, its inner workings visible through a glass face. It had two sets of numbers at each hour mark. Jay could only read the Galathian numbers. He didn't know the language of the second set.

In the corner sat an odd statue of a life-sized man on a wooden chair. The details of its face included neatly trimmed facial hair and stately wrinkles. The entire thing seemed to be made from a deep brown glazed clay. It had a few runes carved into its skin which looked like the Oracle's tattoos.

"A very nice home, Ms... What do I call you?" Jay asked.

"Myra," she said, smiling. "And you are Lieutenant Jay with your mentor, General Saben."

"Yes, ma'am," Saben answered. "How did you know the queen escaped?"

"I'm the Oracle, aren't I?" She chuckled. "Wouldn't be much good if I didn't know such things, would I? But where are my manners? Bernard, fetch us some tea."

For a moment, Jay wondered to whom she spoke, but then the statue twitched, and a green light lit up behind its eyes. It slowly stood up. Startled, Jay moved back. The figure made a whirring mechanical sound as it took a step.

"Bernard, please remember our guests," Myra said with an exasperated tone. "This is Bernard, one of my husbands. A copy of him, anyway. Not quite the real thing, but the best an old woman can do."

The moving statue raised an arm and stuck a hand in Jay's direction. Both Jay and Saben reached for their pistols. A strange noise emanated from deep within the statue.

A quiet voice wheezed, "How do you do?"

The automaton stuck its hand toward Saben. "How do you do?" the faraway voice said again. When neither Jay nor Saben reacted, the statue dropped its arm and turned toward the kitchen. It slowly trudged around the corner. After a moment, Jay heard the clinking of teacups.

"Magic," Jay said, amazed.

"Some magic, some machine. He takes some getting used to, but he's good company. Maybe even better than the original." Myra cackled. "Now, why have you come? Oh yes, the message. Let's have a look."

Myra tore open the envelope and peered at the parchment

it contained. She perched a pair of reading spectacles on her nose. "Interesting," she commented as she read.

"I'm happy to return with a reply for—"

Myra held up a finger, and Jay kept quiet. After a moment, she finished reading. "Oh my, well. That's that." Taking the note, she strode over to the fire and cast it in the flames. It was gone in a moment. "Now, what kind of tea do you boys like, eh?"

Jay watched the message he risked his life to deliver slowly turn to ash. Delivering it completed his mission, and he felt a moment of relief until he recalled the danger surrounding everyone he knew.

"No need for tea. I'd appreciate it if you would craft a reply to Queen Izell. Her need for a response is immediate." As Lady Izell's messenger, Jay had many weeks of practice speaking to lofty officials and projecting a sense of urgency. This time, he really meant it.

"I'm sure Queen Izell will have no trouble conducting a war. She hasn't needed my help in the past," Myra said. "Now, I don't have as grand a collection of tea as you're probably accustomed to, but I think we have a hyacinth that is only a few seasons old."

Jay looked to Saben, who shrugged. He was no help. Jay needed the Oracle to tell him where to go to rendezvous with Queen Izell. And he shouldn't show up there without a key insight or undiscovered secret. Perhaps the whereabouts of the Vinctus Stone or even the artifact itself.

Kaloby's words came back to him. *Make your target reveal important information while keeping your own secrets.* Jay had done it with Jortica. To do the same with the Oracle seemed like a tall order. He had to try.

"The queen said Calonade needs your help, but she didn't tell us how. What can you do to help us?"

"I'm not sure what you mean, young man. The message didn't mention any need for assistance." Myra held a bland expression, but Jay felt her sharp eyes on him.

Jay's eyebrows shot up in surprise. He wanted to snatch the message from the flames, but it was too late. "What did the message say?" he blurted.

"Oh, it simply asked me to take care of two guests," Myra said. "I presume she meant you two. Ah, here's Bernard."

The automaton bumped into the sitting room, carrying a dusty tea service. Jay accepted a cup of tea without pulling his focus from Myra. Saben frowned and waved Bernard away. Rusty gears squeaked as he turned back around and trudged out.

Jay sat back and took a sip of tea. It had a pleasant bitter taste which sweetened after he swallowed. He was certain the message said more than Myra let on. Kaloby had warned him about trusting the Oracle. She clearly was toying with him. It evoked a familiar feeling from his rounds among the self-important Galathians of the Calonade court. Myra, however, really was important. If she knew where to find Izell's heir, the Vinctus Stone, or both, he needed her cooperation.

"Look, Myra." Jay leaned in. "You're right. Queen Izell probably doesn't need advice on how to win a war, but she has entrusted you with an important charge." Jay took a breath, realizing he had to divulge his own knowledge of the best kept secret of Calonade, which didn't follow Kaloby's advice, but he couldn't think of another way. "Queen Izell has revealed the existence of her heir. Is her child here?"

Saben raised an eyebrow but didn't say anything.

Myra stared straight back at him, unflinching. "Look around. Do you see any children here? Of course not. I'm no wet nurse."

"He would be an adult by now." Jay's eyes narrowed. He was determined not to be tricked.

Myra shrugged and gestured around her humble home. "No one is here but us."

Jay crossed his arms and held Myra's gaze. "The queen said you know where he is. If he's not here, then where is he?"

"My dear boy, I have no more information on that question than you do," Myra said with a sweet smile. "Why do you think Izell sent you to me?"

"It's my job, ma'am." Jay felt defeated but tried not to show it. If Myra really knew where the half-cast prince was hiding, she wasn't telling.

"What about the Vinctus Stone?" Jay figured he might as well go all in. "Your message to Queen Izell said you had it."

Myra's laugh didn't feel as disarming as before. "My message said the Vinctus Stone has been safely locked away in Aeterna, which is far from here. More's the pity."

Nothing more would come from this meeting. Jay set down the teacup and stood. "Unless you'd like to write a message to Queen Izell right now, we'd best be moving on, ma'am."

"Oh, I can probably come up with something useful, since you're here," Myra said. "But I'm afraid you cannot attempt a delivery right now."

"It's my duty to try, ma'am."

"Oh, I know. However, it seems you won't be leaving so soon. Look out the window." Myra nodded toward the curtains.

Jay rose and pulled the curtains back. Instead of looking at a blank cavern wall, the scene near the cavern's mouth un-folded before them. Twenty Galathian soldiers and Armone stood just outside the windowpane. Saben started up and Jay reached for his weapon.

"Take it easy, gentlemen," Myra said. "It is a magical window that shows me what is on my front doorstep, so to speak. We are far below them and they will not be able to detect the entrance."

Legate Armone marched furiously back and forth in front of what Jay imagined was a blank wall from his point of view. He gestured violently at the cave and then back toward Calonade. After a while, he left most of the soldiers to guard the cave as he hurried down the mountainside.

"That maniac has my horse," Jay whispered. He could do nothing about it but stare out a false window.

"It looks like you'll be my guests," Myra said, "at least for a little while."

"Oh, I think it will be a long while," Saben replied. "I know a jail when I see one."

Chapter Twenty-Three

It's hard to be the father of a deity. It's even harder to be married to one.

—from Chronicles of Galathia by Rafykin, Urey, circa 2640 local planetary calendar.

Shinwate Forest, Day 022, Year 2017 local planetary calendar, Standard Galactic Year 13303

Sephy held open the tent flap to let Lakqwi enter her quarters. The Shinwate hunter carried an impressive array of animal skin bags and cloth bundles. "What's all this?"

"It is a long journey to Rolotundra, the Hollow Mountain. We must gather supplies."

Behind her entered Havaqwi carrying more bundles. She dropped them onto the floor and bent over them, panting. Lakqwi, not even winded from carrying about twice as much as the girl, sorted through the pile.

"These are gifts from the chief and the elders. I will organize them so we can carry as much as we can." Lakqwi began a tally.

"Well, aren't you two resourceful?" Sephy probed a bag

with her toe. "Nice work, but we don't need it."

Lakqwi straightened. "Please excuse me, Prophet Hukindi, but what we have here is not enough. We will be rationing food and water the entire trip. It will not be pleasant."

"No, excuse me, Lakqwi, but who is the prophet around here?" Lakqwi stared down at Sephy, not finding her humorous. Maybe she didn't understand. "That would be me. I have a better way. Won't take much time at all if you trust me."

Lakqwi's expression didn't change as she considered Sephy for a long moment. "Trust is earned."

"I know." Sephy grinned. "I trust you, Lakqwi, to be entirely too serious, and I trust Havaqwi to stay safe in the village while we're gone."

Havaqwi squeaked and pressed her hands against her mouth. "It is my duty to go if you need me," she whispered while shielding her mouth from view.

Sephy gave a side look to Lakqwi. She reached out and took the servant girl by the hands. "Of course, Havaqwi, but we need someone to stay here in case they're needed. Leaving the village entirely without guidance from Melrayis is unwise."

Havaqwi nodded and breathed a huge sigh of relief. "I will serve as best I can."

"Great." Sephy winked at Lakqwi. "No such luck for you." Sephy caught Lakqwi staring at Havaqwi with tremendous relief on her face. Maybe the Daughter of Melrayis position ran in the family. For a moment, it seemed apparent Lakqwi looked upon Havaqwi as more than a junior acolyte, but it passed and Lakqwi's impassive expression returned.

"Havaqwi remaining behind will help with supplies," Lakqwi said, "but what about facing the Galathians? Havaqwi's training includes bow and spear."

"We need stealth over fighting," Sephy said. "I have a way to get us to the Hollow Mountain, as you call it, without schlepping across the continent."

Lakqwi stared again and Sephy realized the old Earth word didn't translate. She ignored the confusion. "We'll only need enough for a few days. It's a quick mission. In and out, no fuss."

Lakqwi nodded. "You are the Prophet Hukindi." She bent and sorted through the bundles again, pulling out two packs. She stuffed them with food, water, and other useful items.

"I wonder if it's possible to find a new journal here?" Sephy considered her own supplies. "Oh, and a spare pen. That could be the tall order."

"Where are we going that is so close?" Lakqwi asked as she considered water skins, picking two of a more manageable size for their packs.

"The temple circle where you found me."

Lakqwi paused and rubbed her chin in thought. "You plan to travel to Rolotundra, the Hollow Mountain, the same way you traveled to our village from the Underworld, using the Heart of the Temple."

"Something like that," Sephy said.

"Will you teach me this traveling prayer?" Lakqwi asked.

"Let's not get ahead of ourselves, my friend. I'm not entirely sure it will work, but I have high hopes."

Lakqwi continued packing, looking as if hopes had never reached a status she considered high, which could be a good point. A lot could go wrong with Sephy's plan. The old transit device in the temple ruins might not work. Connecting to the portal in Karpathode could be an issue. She felt she could work out those problems. The real risk was transporting from the temple to Karpathode without being detected back at the station. Melrayis had made sure this planet didn't appear in the database. It was a delicate find, full of market potential, if handled discreetly. And Sephy didn't want Melrayis' medical experiment interrupted. Becoming a power broker for the key to healing feminkind could work out nicely if she could set the Shinwate back on a safe path.

"Do you wish to bring back a prisoner to make a SHA?" Lakqwi held a stout coil of rope.

Sephy raised an amused eyebrow. "Well, that's ambitious, but no, not this time. I assure you what I'm going to do will make it much easier for your tribe to acquire SHA later on."

Lakqwi packed the rope anyway. Within a few minutes, she was ready.

"Shall I call for my Yawa-lee?" Lakqwi handed Sephy her pack and stamped the butt end of her spear against the ground. She carried a bow and quiver across her back, looking ready to hunt or do battle as needed.

"No." Sephy rubbed her backside, still sore from the last ride. "Let's walk."

"You will need better shoes." Lakqwi nodded toward Sephy's technician booties.

Perfect for a stabilized artificial environment, Sephy wore them all the time and had forgotten she had them on. "Good point."

"Better clothes all around," Lakqwi said.

Sephy nodded, thinking it prudent to blend in better. Here she had her status for protection, but anywhere else she would be a target in her jumpsuit. "All right, Lakqwi, let's see what you've got."

* * *

Puffing by the time they reached the circle of Yawate guarding the transit platform, Sephy realized she had to get into better shape to spend a lot of time here. Her plan would demand more fieldwork than her current desk job.

Gray mist blanketed the forest, and heavy clouds rolled over the landscape. The trail grew soggy in places and Sephy had a fair collection of mud on her borrowed boots. They weren't as comfortable as her station booties, but those would be soaked through by now. The leather trousers, tunic, and fur pullover, however, effectively staved off the cold.

The platform, hidden under years of dirt and undergrowth, responded to Sephy's ping from her neural receptors as operational. Not bad for hundreds of years of neglect. The Yawate surrounding the little clearing were alert as well, each one sending a status to her inquiry.

Lakqwi and Havaqwi dropped their packs and knelt at the perimeter of the clearing. Sephy didn't bother to keep up her pretense and strolled out to the center of the roughly twenty-foot circle.

This transit portal connected to a part of the station that had been abandoned after renovations. It was supposed to be deactivated, but Sephy had brought it back online herself and kept it disconnected from the primary systems governing transit processing. Systems existed to track and disrupt unauthorized transit devices, which is how this one would be categorized if detected. Sephy had to prevent such an outcome and still get it to work.

Sephy unshouldered her pack and did a quick tour of

the clearing. Data from the Yawate revealed a layer of stones under the dirt and grass, which had to be the temple floor. Below that, a reinforced steel container protected the sensitive electronics and computer systems of the transit device. The Yawate linked their roots around the whole thing to keep it intact and stable. A thorough piece of engineering, which brought Melrayis to mind. She designed an isolated colony but had provided a way to get back to the station. At least until she decided not to return.

Sephy wondered why Melrayis committed her life to the development of Urey. She could have taken a generational viewpoint. Collected data on the Shinwate as if they were fruit flies. Instead, she decided to live and die with them. The time difference gave such decisions an unforgiving permanence. Perhaps she found the idea of retiring into obscurity appealing.

"Lakqwi, what do you know about the history of this place?" Sephy turned to see both devotees of Melrayis' religion, still kneeling with heads bowed. "Uh, ladies?"

Havaqwi kept her head down. Lakqwi looked up with a puzzled expression. "We await the invitation of the guardian Yawate to enter the Heart of the Temple."

"Really?"

Lakqwi simply bowed her head in response with her hands against her chest.

Sephy sorted through the interface subroutines of the Yawate and found nothing that would provide an invitation. *Must be another adaptation in the belief system. No one goes in the sacred space except the head honcho. It could be a safety precaution set up by Melrayis to keep people from meddling with the transit device.*

"I am the Prophet Hukindi. You have permission to enter." Sephy used her most official CEO voice.

Havaqwi trembled but kept her head down. Lakqwi looked up again. "No one has ever entered this sacred circle except for Melrayis herself many generations ago."

These people are hardcore. "What would convince you that it's okay?"

Lakqwi shrugged. "It has never happened."

"All right, hang on." Sephy rummaged through the files of the Yawate standing beside her companions. "Here we go. Try this." Sephy activated the speaker system of the root software package and then rebooted the core code. Even after hundreds of years, it worked. The computer at the base of the Yawate played the Willacast Corp start-up ditty. Sephy had the volume up to make sure they could hear it from underground. Cheerful music blasted out of the tree. Its quick pattern of notes only lasted a few seconds, but it echoed through the forest with eerie distortion.

Havaqwi squeaked and ducked lower, but Lakqwi stood and gazed at the singing Yawate. She gently reached out and touched the machine's bark. "That has never happened according to the texts of the Daughters of Melrayis."

Sephy had to suppress a laugh. No reboot required for hundreds of years. Her IT department would appreciate the feedback. Maybe she would tell them someday.

"So, good enough?" Sephy asked.

Lakqwi nodded. "After we're gone, please record this in the book," Lakqwi said to Havaqwi as she pulled her to her feet. Arm in arm, they stepped into the circle, looking all around as if expecting more music or lightning strikes from a vengeful goddess. Neither happened, and they relaxed a bit.

Both jolted back to alertness as thunder rumbled in the distance. They looked at Sephy with wide eyes.

"That was ten miles away at least," Sephy said. "A natural storm is brewing. Nothing to do with us."

They relaxed again as rain pattered onto the clearing. The storm could be a problem if significant lightning rolled over them while operating the portal. The electronics were vulnerable in power-up mode. Sephy needed to get moving, which meant she couldn't do all the configuring with just her neurals.

"I've got to use some magic to get this thing operational," Sephy said. "Don't be alarmed. It's normal prophet stuff."

Lakqwi set her stance as if preparing for battle. Havaqwi inched behind her taller companion.

"Havaqwi, you should probably wait outside the Heart of the Temple. This shouldn't take too long," Sephy said.

Havaqwi looked to Lakqwi, who nodded toward the edge of the clearing where they had knelt before. Havaqwi scampered off the platform and sat down in the same place Sephy first saw the girl upon her arrival. *Creatures of habit.*

Sephy engaged her neurals and activated a virtual hologram. A set of controls appeared near her hands. A set of square displays materialized in the air. Willacast symbols marched across their screens. Sephy spread them out in front of her like her workstation back in her office. The neurals worked for easy stuff, but sophisticated programming still required a more traditional interface, at least for her. She started typing on the controls, manipulating a multifunction knob, and watching the results on each floating screen.

Out of the corner of her eye, Sephy caught Lakqwi staring in amazement. Over on the edge, Havaqwi matched the disbelieving expression. The light of the symbols reflected off the looming circle of Yawate to give the clearing a mystical glow. Sephy felt the delight of impressing her companions. Admittedly, it was cheap theatrics, but it worked. She could get used to this prophet gig. She reluctantly put the feeling aside to concentrate on her work.

The portal connected to the station hub network without any problems. Sephy entered a transit code that disguised its signal and made it look routine. The time difference made the few seconds here only milliseconds on the station. As long as no one specifically looked for this pirated code, it would go unnoticed.

Sephy pinged their destination portal, but got no immediate response, which was odd. It should have been active, being the primary hub connection to this planet, even though it had been removed from the transit database. After a minute, her retry failed to connect again. The Urey portal could be down for maintenance, but that was rare. An access code update provided the only other explanation. Sephy used her executive privileges to get into the operations code through a back door. This maneuver added a bit more risk if an admin were monitoring her access log, but she had standing orders for that to only happen with her permission.

Sure enough, a security code update. Bad luck. She might be sunk. Sephy didn't relish the long journey to Karpathode Lakqwi had promised. Sephy paused to think of another way.

Lakqwi touched her shoulder.

"Prophet Hukindi," Lakqwi shouted over the wind. "The storm!"

Sephy's attention returned to the clearing. A hard, icy rain fell, and lightning flashed across the sky. The storm would be over them in the next few minutes. "Let me try one more thing," Sephy shouted back.

"Hurry!"

Sephy dived back into the world of station coding. She had developed the early version herself and knew its flaws. Layers of security patches had been added, but if she could find a dormant subroutine, she might get in. The risk was tripping a warning.

After a couple of false leads, she found something. A basic diagnostic program had been replaced but not uninstalled. Sephy punched through the firewall in a few seconds of reprogramming. She should have been appalled at the ease at which she had hacked her own system, but she only felt the thrill of beating the security, bringing back nostalgic memories from her youth. One didn't become the CEO of Willacast Corp without street cred.

Sephy fired up the connection to the portal at the heart of Karpathode. It pinged back *ready* along with an unfamiliar countdown timer. To her horror, Sephy realized she had sixty seconds of mainstream time until the access code cycled. That, without a doubt, would get her caught. Sephy's feeling of triumph soured. Her security people were better than she thought.

"Here we go!" Sephy shouted over the storm to Lakqwi. "Brace yourself!"

Lakqwi nodded, taking up her hunter's stance as the wind buffeted her buckskin clothing. Sephy felt the gust of wind threaten to blow her over and she sneaked a glance at the sky. The boiling storm hovered over them, sending lightning streaking out in all directions. The crack of thunder sounded just over their heads. Sephy didn't know how the system would react if a transit was executed in a storm like this. The system possessed protection against electromagnetic surges, but this storm might be too much for it. The timer clicked down to twenty seconds.

It took guts to run a company like Willacast Corp. Creating and controlling the only known transit hub made one a target of envy and all that brought with it. Sephy had survived many figurative storms. This one, however, was very literal. The visceral nature of it terrified and invigorated her. She should have waited and found a safer way, but when the chips were down, Sephy Alcott never played it safe.

With three seconds left, Sephy clicked the execute button and, with a deafening blast of thunder, the clearing disappeared.

Chapter Twenty-Four

I roamed the frontier until I found the perfect place to rest. I discovered rest wasn't in my nature. So, I began to build a great city.

—from Chronicles of Galathia by Rafykin, Urey, circa 2640 local planetary calendar.

Kelstone Mountains, Day 002–003, Year 2999 local planetary calendar, Standard Galactic Year 14285

Jay and Saben sat with Myra around her quaint dining table. Bernard bumped around the room, offering tea once again. After he set the service down, he wandered out with an uneven gait. This time, Jay noticed its flavor was not unlike Kaloby's brew.

Saben glowered at Myra.

"Come now, General, don't be so glum. This is not a jail like you're used to," Myra said. "It may feel a bit crowded with the four of us, but we'll make do, eh?"

Jay felt dashed from losing Havoc and seeing Queen Izell's message burned before he could find out what it said. No half-cast prince and no Vinctus Stone. It would disappoint

Kaloby to hear how his encounter with the Oracle had gone. She definitely had the better of him, but he swallowed his pride and tried to rally. "Perhaps if you tell us what Queen Izell's message said, we could—"

"Don't worry about it, young man," Myra cut him off. "The contents of the message were for us women. No need for you to pursue the subject any further."

Jay sat back, defeated. He was stuck here while his gran, his friends, and his queen fought for their lives. It felt maddening to be so useless. Could they sneak past the guards after nightfall?

"What do you have for bunks?" Saben craned his neck to peer into the rest of the house.

"Sir? We're not staying that long, are we?" Jay blurted.

"It will take some time before things calm down out there, Lieutenant." Saben hooked a thumb toward the false window as he dug out his pipe and clamped it into his jaw. "Do you have any lanicina leaf?" he asked Myra.

"Thinking of restarting the old habit?" Myra raised a brow.

Frowning, Saben clicked the pipe in his teeth. "Just looking for a way to pass the time."

Myra shook her head. "You two are a pitiful sight. All right, boys, I have a mystery you can help me with. Follow me." She stood and bustled to the back of the house toward what looked like a cellar door.

Saben and Jay looked at each other, puzzled.

"Well, come on." She spoke over her shoulder as she started down into the darkness.

Curiosity welling up, Jay rose and followed. Saben reluctantly came along behind.

The creaky wooden door opened to a stone stairway dropping into darkness below. Myra led as they descended into a huge, enclosed cavern. A faint glow from the subterranean walls filled the cave with an eerie light. Jay could hear the echoes of water dripping from the ceiling into several isolated pools below. The ripples caused the light to shimmer.

The stairway stopped on a wooden floor constructed above the waterline in one corner of the cavern and anchored upon several stalagmites. An assortment of glowing crystals mounted upon candelabras provided abundant light. Cluttered bookshelves, a chair, a couch and a table holding piles of parchment made the platform look like a study. At the far edge stood a tall stone bust facing away from them, a corner of the platform resting on its shoulder. Beyond the study, cast haphazardly throughout the cave, lay a collection of ancient spears, shields, and random bits of armor in varying states of decay.

A flash of metal glinted from a dark corner, and Jay instinctively placed his hand on his pistol. Reflecting light revealed the outline of the clockwork crow sitting on a freestanding coat rack. Its shining black eye glinted in the dim light, but it didn't move.

"My most recent guest before you two gentlemen came calling." Myra gestured toward the crow. "It appeared here in my study several weeks ago to deliver a message."

"I've seen it before," Jay said. "Your messenger to Queen Izell."

"It's a messenger, but not mine. I borrowed it for that assignment. You now know as much as I do about its origins."

"Some kind of toy?" Saben asked with indifference.

"It's a mystery to me," Myra said, "which is an unusual feeling. My intuition tells me you two might help solve it."

"What could be a mystery to you?" Jay asked.

"I can't scry events protected by Willacast magic."

"This machine has magic from the Three Sister Goddesses?" Jay asked.

"Yes. They added the magic after the machine was built, which has never been done as far as I know," Myra said. "I'm not sure who could do such a thing."

A mystery for the Oracle. Jay raised an eyebrow. Not as all-knowing as Queen Izell believed. He hadn't heard much about magic and the old Willacast religion beyond his gran's occasional references. Kaloby's studies stayed within the realm of science.

"What message did it deliver to you?" Jay asked.

"It told me the Vinctus Stone has reappeared from obscurity and now resides in Aeterna so it might reawaken."

The Vinctus Stone and Aeterna! The race to the ancient city was on, after all. "Does this machine know where to find the Vinctus Stone?"

"I believe the feathered darling delivered it to the ancient city itself," Myra said. "How it found the thing after all these centuries is a mystery."

"And the half-cast prince?" Jay asked.

"A different mystery you'll have to pursue yourself, dear boy," Myra said with a mischievous smile.

"Can the stone really tell the future?" If it had such powers, it could help him find the hidden prince and get him back to the queen safely.

"It has been known to provide guidance to those who wield it, but I do not know if it still has that power," Myra said. "Willacast magic can be unpredictable, but I believe Queen Izell would find it useful."

"Yes, I agree." Jay could not contain his excitement. *I might find it useful as well.* "We should retrieve it. But the door is blocked." Armone dashed Jay's hopes again.

"The crow came to me through the cavern," Myra said. "Passages through the rock lead to a back entry, but it's a long way and there are obstacles."

Saben perked up. "These caves extend to the other side of the Kelstones?"

"Yes. You've been there, General, haven't you?"

"I have." Saben clamped his teeth down on his pipe, brow furrowed in thought.

Jay craned his neck to find another passage out of the cavern. "Are you thinking what I'm thinking, sir?"

"Yes, but I'm also trying to decipher the queen's wishes. She seemed to want us to stay here."

"Did she say that?" Jay asked.

"Not in so many words," Saben said, "but I believe it was her intent."

Jay frowned. "That's not what she told me." In fact, Queen Izell hadn't given any orders about what to do next. She had told Jay to trust the Oracle.

It made no sense for the queen to send them into this dead end. Losing a messenger wasn't too costly, Jay had to admit. However, General Saben was an excellent fighter, effective spy, and proven leader. Jay had to make sure they both got out of here to get Saben back into the war.

"What does the crow know?" Jay asked.

"Let's find out." Myra stepped up to the clockwork crow and gently lifted its wing. A tattoo on her hand lit up with power and she reached under the metal feathers. She traced a similar symbol there, and the machine came to life. It pulled free from Myra's grip and squawked with an echoing sound of a crow's call mixed with grinding metal. Its metallic hackles came up around its head. Myra withdrew her hand with a watchful eye on the bird.

The clockwork crow cocked its head, peering all around the room. It gave Saben a long look and then stared intently at Jay. It squawked and clicked its beak.

"I'm sorry I turned you off, but you're back on now," Myra said to the crow. "We need to talk."

The crow spat a rusty caw and snapped at Myra. It raised metal hackles and let out a low-pitched chortle.

Myra frowned. "That's just rude." Myra turned to Jay. "It will only talk to you."

"How can you tell?"

"It just said so," Myra said with a knowing smile.

The crow coughed, bobbed its head, and opened its beak wide. Within the creature came a furious tapping sound and a strip of paper emerged from its craw. Whirring, it extended about a foot. The crow grabbed it with a talon and yanked down, tearing the paper free with its beak. It snapped up the paper, looking directly at Jay.

Jay approached carefully and held out his hand. The crow dropped the paper strip into Jay's palm. It shook its head and ruffled its feathers. They rang as they brushed against each other. Leaping from the coat rack, the bird took flight. It circled above them and then plunged into the caverns beyond the platform. Its magical light reflected off tunnel walls until it disappeared into the shadows.

Jay watched it go, shaking his head.

"He's a tricky bird." Myra's eyes gleamed with fascination. "Well, what does the message say?"

Jay examined the strip of paper. "It's an old Calonaden battle code." He recalled Kaloby's lessons as he deciphered the blocky letters. "*Aeterna. Here reclaim the half-cast prince.*" Jay's skin tingled. "This means the queen's heir is in Aeterna with the Vinctus Stone."

"Ah," Myra said. "I believe the message means the half-cast prince is ready to be discovered. Looks like you won't be staying here after all. I'll open the way to the ancient city."

Jay vibrated with excitement at the chance to get back into the war. Now it made sense why he had to visit the Oracle. No one could enter Aeterna without her permission. It was the perfect place to hide the most wanted man in the empire.

"How do we get to Aeterna?" Jay asked.

"I believe you have a guide with you, young man."

General Saben nodded. "The old city sits on the banks of the Talindrey River where the Kelstone and Wrayan Mountains converge. I accompanied King Nados during his visit to Aeterna. I know the way once we're through the mountain."

"There's no reason to wait." Myra nodded to Saben.

"I agree. We must leave soon," Saben said. "However, we need provisions. We didn't come ready for such a journey."

"Oh, I can help you with that," Myra said.

* * *

Jay shouldered his heavy pack and adjusted the weight on his shoulders. Unsurprisingly, the Oracle was well prepared to send two men on a long journey into the wilderness.

She walked them to the edge of her cavern while giving

some general directions for traveling through the mountain. They would emerge on the other side of the Kelstones, but with more than one way through, she wasn't sure where.

A crystal strapped to a wooden shaft served as a light for each of them. Jay poked his into the dark tunnel ahead of them. The fissure in the rock opened just wide enough for a man to walk through and remain mostly upright. Moisture throughout the caves made the walls wet and the footing slippery.

"Are there any places to avoid or creatures to be wary of?" Saben asked Myra.

"It has been a long time since I traveled through the mountain. Things may have changed, but the clockwork crow tells us a way through exists."

"Flying is not the same as walking." Saben tucked his pipe securely into his waistcoat.

"True. As far as creatures, the only ones I know of are the stone giants, but you have dealt with them before."

Saben grimaced as he nodded. "Yes, I have."

"Stone giants?" Jay asked.

"I'll tell you later," Saben said.

"You must go, and I have many wards and distractions to prepare to ensure you are undetected for as long as possible. I also must undo a few so you may enter Aeterna." She turned, waved over her shoulder, and walked up the stairs to her dwelling.

"Let's go," Saben said.

"Wait, General. Would you like to explain the stone giants to me?"

"Not really," he said with a sour look, "but I will as we travel. If our luck holds, we won't come across any. Lead the way, Lieutenant."

Jay stepped into the tunnel and Saben followed him in. The general remained quiet at first as they got used to the feeling of damp confinement. After a good hour of hiking, he told Jay a few things. The stone giants resembled Bernard, except bigger and less interested in tea. They had served as allies with Calonade in the war because of a treaty with King Nados. They didn't do well as soldiers outside of the caves but were deadly inside their domain. Nados used them to fortify underground bases along the Kelstone foothills.

"They guard the secret entrance into Calonade. It is said they slumber if left alone. When awakened, they are ill-tempered and unpredictable. It's best to sneak through without disturbing them."

"If they work for the Oracle, why doesn't she just tell them to help us?" Jay asked.

"I don't think they work for her. It's more likely she has a treaty with them as well."

"Could we get them to attack the Galathians in Calonade?"

"They won't fight in the daylight. Don't know why. It's hard to march an army out of the caves in the evening, do any effective fighting at night, and then march them back in again before sunrise."

"So, they're just guards."

"Essentially."

To Jay, they still sounded like useful allies. Jay tried to work out some ways to use them tactically, but Saben would answer no more questions. He preferred not to talk while hiking at their best speed through the tunnels.

As they marched on, each tunnel opened into more caverns followed by new narrow passages. The ceiling of some caverns reached far into the darkness above them. At times, the wind howled through the upper reaches. In other caves, slippery rock formations hung down to the floor, creating a maze of stony columns. Over the musty odor of damp soil, the air smelled vaguely of torch smoke, but Jay saw no sign of light besides their own.

Saben consulted a compass to keep them going in the right direction until they came upon a cavern with more than one passage leading away. Saben examined the choices.

"Do you know the way, sir?"

"Not specifically. I know we need to go north. Pick one, Lieutenant."

The passages angled away from the cavern in different directions. There was no way to tell which would lead to a way out and which to a dead end. "How about the middle one, sir?"

Saben started down the passage. Jay made several more similar decisions before they stopped at one such crossroad.

"We'll camp here." The general dropped his pack. They prepared a cold meal to avoid smoke that might foul the air or allow them to be detected.

"You take first watch, Lieutenant." Saben lay down.

"Yes, sir."

Jay sat down to rest. It had been a long day. His various wounds ached, but his mind still whirled, thinking through all that had happened. In one day, he had gone from messenger to fugitive to seeker of the heir to Calonade. He didn't feel completely clear about his quest, but it felt much better than rotting in Myra's house.

Jay peered around the cavern. Though different from any place he'd ever been, it seemed familiar too. He chuckled to himself when he figured out the irony. He had finally gotten out of the castle to end up in a hole much like its dungeons. Not exactly what he had in mind.

* * *

Jay started awake as Saben grabbed his arm.

"Slide into the shadows," Saben whispered as he shoved the crystal torches under a blanket. "Quickly."

Jay flung himself off the path, leaving behind his sleeping bundle and pack. He scrambled through the muck and ended up behind a rock. The darkness was complete and silent. He couldn't tell where Saben had hidden.

The sound of stamping feet slowly pushed aside the silence as they came closer. Jay could make out voices next. He waited quietly behind the rock, one hand on his sword hilt and the other holding his pistol.

"It was over here." A strange voice, speaking Galathian, echoed from the darkness. Lights flickered from an adjoining tunnel. "At the junction."

"What did you see, Bilford?" a second voice asked.

"Lumps on the path," Bilford answered.

"Are you sure it wasn't a silver bird again?" a third voice asked with a chuckle.

"I did see a bird, but not this time. There were lumps on the path. They weren't there the last time we came through."

A figure carrying a torch stepped into the cavern. The sudden brightness hurt Jay's eyes, and he ducked deeper into the shadows. The figure straightened up and looked around the room with green, glowing eyes. It rose, almost touching the ceiling, at least twelve feet tall. It looked like it wore a stone mask frozen in a fierce, permanent scowl.

As Jay got used to the light, he saw the whole figure was made of stone and its head was the size of a small boulder. The rest of the body looked like a statue of a soldier, complete with sculpted features for a helm, armor, and boots. It carried a burning torch in one hand and a long stone sword in the other with a blade sharpened to a fine edge. Just like Bernard, it had a collection of engravings on its outer surface that looked like the symbols on the Oracle's skin.

"They're here," Bilford said. Like Bernard, the mouth didn't move, and the voice came from inside the creature.

A second one pushed its way into the cavern. "Let me see."

"There." Bilford pointed at the place Jay had been sleeping only seconds before. His supply bundle still lay on the path.

A third voice came from the darkness. "Are you and Clobert going to just stand there, or are you going to smash it?"

"Smash it," Clobert replied. "Smash it!"

Clobert launched past Bilford and charged toward the bundles of Jay and Saben's supplies.

"What if it belongs to the witch?" Bilford asked.

Clobert stopped in his tracks. "The witch?" He ducked his head in fear.

"Don't tell me you're afraid of the witch," the third voice said.

"I'm not, but Clobert is," Bilford said.

"I don't like this part of the mountain, Bobrick," Clobert said. "It's too close to the old witch."

"Oh, be quiet Clobert," Bilford said. "She never hurt nobody."

"She turned Gammer into a statue," Clobert whimpered. "I sees it myself when I had the ill fortune of following Bilford during one of his exploring fits."

"That statue ain't Gammer," Bilford said. "She put that up to scare us. Gammer fell in a hole and liked it so much he stayed there."

"Are you ladies done?" Bobrick poked his massive head through the opening. "Smash the lumps so we can report back to the king."

"I don't want to." Clobert peered in all directions for danger.

"They're not hurting anyone. Let's see what they are," Bilford said.

Bobrick growled a curse and barreled into the passage. He leaped forward and stomped down on the bundles with a reverberating crash. He jumped up and down on the packs until he crushed everything to pieces. It sounded like the cavern was collapsing. Jay had to clamp his hands over his ears to keep his senses.

"There," Bobrick said in mock triumph. "I've crushed their bones. The lumps are no more. The kingdom is safe, and the witch has not appeared to turn me into a statue or anything else. Let's go."

The stone giant stomped toward the exit of the cavern with a rumble of a massive rock fall. Clobert, still hunching fearfully, followed Bobrick.

"Don't you want to keep looking for the silver bird?" Bilford called after him.

"Ain't no silver bird," Bobrick replied. "Nobody else saw it."

"I swear I saw it twice. Once coming in and then headed

out."

Bobrick turned on them. "I'm tired of chasing your ghosts, Bilford, and sick of your quivering as we turn every corner, Clobert."

"Just around the witch is all," Clobert said. "I don't want to be a statue."

"Then let's get moving," Bobrick said, "or we'll be late, and the king don't like that."

They turned and squeezed back through the tunnel. "I do hate these narrow places," Clobert whimpered as the three stone giants pushed back through the way they had come. Jay could hear stone scraping against stone and the curses of the giants fading away.

Saben stepped from the shadows around a corner of a tunnel. "You can put your gun away. It will have no effect on them. All our gear is destroyed," he whispered. "We must follow them or be lost in the dark."

Jay kept on Saben's heels as they tore off after the three giants.

Chapter Twenty-Five

It took me two lifetimes to build Aeterna. Luckily, I had that much time, and much more, to spare.
—from Chronicles of Galathia by Rafykin, Urey, circa 2640 local planetary calendar.

Kelstone Mountains, Day 003, Year 2999 local planetary calendar, Standard Galactic Year 14285

The stone giants crashed through the caverns, making it easy to follow them. The flicker of torchlight and billowing smoke marked the passages they took. Jay and Saben remained out of sight even though the giants remained so intent on moving through the caves they never looked back. Jay suspected he could move along right behind them with little chance of being noticed, but he didn't try it.

When the tunnels grew twice as big and three times as tall, Jay knew they had entered a more central part of the stone giants' underground dwellings. Corridors wound away in all directions, and he felt as if he were inside a huge stone ant hill. He wondered how the mountain didn't collapse.

The light from the torches flickered over the cave walls,

revealing a more regular pattern than in the natural caves. As Jay hurried past, he caught glimpses of carvings running from floor to ceiling.

Saben signaled for him to stop as they rounded another corner. On either side of the passage towered more stone giants, stationary against the walls. Jay swore he heard snoring coming from their fearsome stone masks.

"They're asleep," Saben whispered in a low rasp. He beckoned Jay to follow and continued down the passage.

Jay wondered how soundly they slept. He certainly didn't want to startle any of them into wakefulness. He swallowed his fear and crept after Saben.

After what had to be miles of wide caves and huge tunnels filled with sleeping stone soldiers, they heard more voices. They peeked around the corner and discovered a tunnel widened into a huge circular balcony overlooking a grand underground hall. Great arches of stone reached into the darkness above to hold the ceiling in place. The gentle light of a few flickering torches revealed images of impressive marching armies and battle scenes carved in relief on every surface. Hundreds of stone giants stood in place, leaning against the walls or lying on the cavern floor. Snoring, sleepy muttering, and other sounds of slumber filled the room. Above the background noise, two voices became distinct.

"You cannot say Lord Kriton's victory was assured," a stone giant said in Galathian. He sat on a rock placed on a raised platform at the far end of the hall. "He barely had the advantage of the lay of the land, and he was distressingly outnumbered. Oh, good move, sire."

This speaker was dressed differently than the rest, if wearing a certain sculpting of rock could be called clothing.

He seemed to be in a full-length robe. He even wore a pair of spectacles carved upon his face. However, the figure across from him, sitting on a stone chair, cut a more imposing form. He had the sculpted raiment of a king with intricately designed armor, a robe over it, and a crown upon his head. The crown had no jewels, but the stone had been carved with facets to resemble precious stones.

The two stone giants played a game on a huge stone table placed between them. Each took turns moving stone pieces around on the tabletop marked with black and white squares. The pieces, also made of black and white stone, were sculpted into the shapes of marching soldiers and men on horseback. A tall piece resembled a castle tower, while another figure wore a crown. The size of all the pieces made Jay believe he would struggle to lift them.

"That doesn't matter, Finwald. The training fueled the fighting spirit." The one dressed as a king pointed toward one wall. "Lord Kriton overcame his foe weeks before the battle because of his leadership. He was a talented opponent. One could take a lesson or two from him."

Jay followed the stone giant king's gesture. A tall warrior surrounded by a raging battle scene was carved into the wall. The warrior wielded a great sword as he towered over his foes. On the wall behind the two speakers, a powerful king, flanked by wise advisers, stood over a line of fierce soldiers armed with shields and spears. On the remaining wall, three feminine figures stood together, surrounded by kneeling peasants, soldiers, and kings. Symbols floated around the ladies that looked like the runes inked on Myra's skin. None of the sculpted figures were stone giants. They all looked human.

"If you say so, Your Majesty, but I believe luck may have had some role in the matter. I'll take your knight." Finwald removed a mounted figurine from the board. "Oh, here's our latest patrol. Let's hear what they have to report."

The three stone giants Jay and Saben had been following marched up and saluted the king.

"Let's have it, Sergeant Bobrick." The stone monarch turned away from the game board to focus on his soldiers.

Bobrick straightened to attention. "Nothing to report, sire."

Bilford cleared his throat loudly. Or at least that's what it sounded like. Jay doubted the stone giants had an actual throat to clear.

"What's that?" The king cocked his head to hear better.

"Nothing, sire." Bobrick kicked Bilford in the shin. The crack of the rock echoed through the chamber.

"No, no," Finwald said. "Do not suppress the, um, corporal, is it? Tell us everything, even such things that may not seem relevant."

"We found lumps, sire," Bobrick said.

"Lumps? What sort of lumps?" the king asked.

"Not sure. We smashed them directly." Bobrick pounded his huge fist into his palm, stone smashing against stone.

"We should have found out what they were," Bilford whispered loud enough for everyone to hear, including Jay and Saben in the back of the chamber.

"Hush," Bobrick said. "Turned out to be nothing, sire."

"Lumps appearing mysteriously in the caves." Finwald rubbed his chin with a grinding sound.

"No mystery," Bobrick said. "We smashed 'em good."

"What about the silver bird?" Bilford asked.

Bobrick turned toward Bilford, piercing him with his green eyes, which could only be a stone giant glare.

"A bird in the caves?" the king said. "Not likely."

"I wouldn't put much stock in it, sire." Bobrick glared in Bilford's direction.

"All right, men," the king said. "I'm not too worried about lumps or birds. Just so long as you didn't see any enemies trying to sneak through. Go wake the next patrol. Give them a briefing before you turn in."

"Thank you, sire." Bobrick snapped a salute. The three giants marched away from the king and his companion.

"Now back to our discussion, Majesty. I believe you were expounding upon the virtues of training over strategy. Am I right?"

"No, not quite that," the king answered. "Training is a part of the overall strategy to win, you see."

Saben pulled Jay back from the balcony and into the darkness of the tunnel. "I've been here before," he whispered. "There's a way out beyond this cavern. All we need to do is get through and we're on the other side of the Kelstones. Follow me."

Saben crouched and dashed onto the balcony. He stayed low to the floor and weaved around the statues to keep from being detected by the two below. Jay followed behind him. They made it past the hall and into a large tunnel supported by wide columns. More stone giants reclined haphazardly against columns and on the floor. Saben led him through the slumbering labyrinth. They had to carefully climb over several reclining stone figures. Jay noted they made the sounds of sleeping even though their chests did not rise and fall.

Finally, he spied a massive pair of imposing doors sealing a wide stone archway. A huge lock built into the doors seemed to stare down at them through its oversized keyhole. Jay caught up to Saben as he examined the lock.

"This is the exit," the general whispered. "We just need to find a way through it."

"You could use the key," a voice said behind them.

Both Saben and Jay spun around to see Bilford standing at the other end of the hall. The chamber rumbled like an underground rockfall as every stone giant in the tunnel woke and stood to face them. They stared through the glowing green eye holes hollowed out of their faces.

* * *

"So, what have we here?" the king said. "A couple of Galathian rats."

Jay and Saben stood in the middle of the grand hall filled by hundreds of stone giant soldiers. Several, including the three they had followed through the tunnels, formed a ring around their backsides, holding their huge stone swords toward them. Jay and Saben's weapons had been tossed onto the stage in front of the king, who stared down at them from his raised seat.

"I'm General Saben of Calonade. This is Lieutenant Jay. We are subjects of Queen Izell," he said with all his headmaster gravitas.

"Izell?" The king looked to Finwald for help.

"Queen of Calonade. Married to Nados," the adviser said.

"Ah, yes. The Galathian princess. Young Nados knows how to stir up trouble."

"Technically, she was a Fromeathian princess pledged to marry Emperor Staukard of Galathia. That is, until Nados arrived," Finwald said.

Jay frowned at the Galathian version of the tale. Every Calonaden knew King Nados had saved his true love from the clutches of the tyrant, but Jay kept quiet about it. No need to provoke this hornet's nest any further.

"He's quite the rake." The stone giant king laughed as he turned back to his prisoners. "You expect me to believe you are allies of King Nados when you're wearing Galathian uniforms?"

"We've met before, Your Majesty," Saben said. "Perhaps you remember a young aide to King Nados many years ago."

The king leaned closer to Saben. If his stone face had allowed it, Jay would have expected him to squint. "You do look familiar. How long has it been, Finwald?"

"Twenty-two years, sire."

"That long, eh? Seems like only yesterday." He peered at Saben. "I suppose you could be the man you claim to be. How shall we determine if it's true, Finwald?"

"A test, sire. Something only the aide to Nados would know."

"Ummm, ah, I have it," the king said. "If you are who you say you are, you will be able to tell me what Nados and I used to seal our treaty. Did we toast to a long alliance with red wine or golden ale?"

"Good one, sire," Finwald said.

Saben furrowed his brow, as if trying to recall the moment. "It's a trick question. We had no such toasts. Braving your crushing handshake was the ritual, if I recall correctly."

Murmurs spread through the audience as Jay waited for the king's answer.

"Hah," he said at last. "You are correct, General."

All the stone giants lowered their weapons. Inwardly, Jay let out a sigh of relief. Saben had saved their skins, for now.

"You have a very good memory. Since we were made into stone giants, we have declined to imbibe," the king said.

"More like cannot imbibe," Bilford whispered.

"It's a pity." Clobert sighed behind Jay's shoulder. "I do miss the distilled spirits at times."

"I remember the moment, sire," Finwald said. "The little fellow did well."

"Broke a bone in his hand," Saben said. "But it was worth it to have such formidable allies."

"How is Nados these days?"

"I'm afraid he's dead, Your Majesty." Saben gripped his hands behind his back and frowned. "He was mortally wounded in the Kettlebone Pass fighting the Galathian invasion."

Another murmur passed over the audience, along with several salty oaths of disbelief.

"Dead, you say?" the king asked.

"Dreadfully sorry," Finwald said. "But it does explain the Galathian uniforms. I take it the invasion was successful?"

"Yes, it was." Saben's scowl deepened another notch.

"This is terrible news." The king leaned back on his throne. "Tell me, General, how did you survive?"

"Guile." Saben's expression remained as hard as stone.

"Hmmm, indeed," the king said.

"The death of Nados renders our treaty invalid, sire,"

Finwald said.

"And completely negates our mission to guard the passages under this mountain," the king said.

Murmurs continued throughout the crowd of stone giants as the king absorbed the news.

"What will we do now?" Clobert asked from behind Jay.

"Don't worry," Bilford said behind Jay's other shoulder. "We'll think of something besides sleeping through eternity."

"But I'm so tired," Clobert whined.

"An eternal nap is a bit much, don't you think?" Bilford said.

The stone giants broke from their intimidating formation to discuss their dismay.

"We could renew the treaty." Jay's voice was nearly drowned out by the commotion in the hall.

"What's that?" the king asked. "Who said that?"

The crowd quieted down.

"It was the smaller one, sire," Finwald said. "Lieutenant, uh...?"

"Lieutenant Jay, Your Majesty, messenger to Queen Izell." Jay's voice echoed through the chamber. He swallowed down his nervousness.

"A messenger, you say. Did Izell send a message?" the king asked.

Jay glanced at Saben. The general gave him a withering look. "Not written down," Jay said. "She sent General Saben in person."

Jay looked at Saben and nodded his head toward the stone giant king.

Saben took a breath and rolled his shoulders as he turned to face the king. "King Kormash, son of Klive." He spoke formally and loud enough for the entire hall to hear. "I can offer you a new alliance with Queen Izell. She needs help repelling our Galathian occupiers, and guarding the passages through the mountain is still a critical concern. Will you renew your pledge through me as the queen's representative? With your assistance, we can reclaim Calonade."

"So that's why you've come," Kormash said.

"Yes. I'm meeting with you and other key allies in the Frontier. Will you agree to a renewal of the treaty as it is written?" Saben extended his hand.

"It does continue our purpose," Finwald said. "Without it, we have no reason, well, to exist."

More murmurs flooded the cavern. Kormash leaned toward Finwald in what he probably meant to be a confidential whisper. "Do you think the witch would rescind her magic if we served no purpose?" His words echoed over the chamber, causing more unrest.

"I would rather not find out, Your Majesty," Finwald replied.

The Stone Giant King paused a moment, and Jay held his breath. Saben kept his hand steady before Kormash.

"I heartily accept." King Kormash extended his enormous stone hand to envelop Saben's. Jay heard a bone snap.

Chapter Twenty-Six

There are many ways to control the population of a planet. Religion is one of the most cost-effective. Willacast Corp bet the company on nano-cyber technology for just this purpose.

—from the journal of Sephy Alcott, Standard Galactic Year 11285

Karpathode, Day 022, Year 2017 local planetary calendar, Standard Galactic Year 13303

A surge of pain put Sephy's nerves on edge. Her guts cramped, and she tried to twist her body for relief, but she couldn't move. Her mind knew her corporeal body did not exist during transit. She'd been reduced to a stream of particle waves flowing between matter, but the knowledge didn't help with the pain. Incomprehensible patterns of light blinded her temporarily non-existent eyes. Through the glare, a transit room on the station materialized. Its square corners and glass viewports contrasted with the primitive setting she had just left behind. Sephy panicked at being caught until the station disappeared into the chaos.

Something hard pressed against Sephy's head as the world

re-formed around her. Nausea replaced the gripping pain, and she rolled over to empty the contents of her stomach on a stone floor.

She tried to speak, but it came out as a strangled croak.

"There, there." A light feminine voice spoke in accented Galactic. "You're having quite a day." A cool hand pressed against Sephy's throat. Sephy tried to grab it, but her arm only flopped uncontrollably. Another hand gently returned it to her side. The hand pulled away. "You have a strong heart. Try to relax. I will check on your companions."

Sephy spat out the vile contents of her mouth. Opening her eyes didn't help because she couldn't focus. Portal transit, when done right, felt instantaneous to the brain. Uncalibrated machines could cause flashes of incoherent shapes and a twinge or two like mild electric shocks. This one resembled a train wreck. Her bones felt stretched from their joints and shoved back together. Her limbs had the awkward combination of jangled nerves and numb prickles.

Sephy's vision cleared, revealing a large chamber with a stone floor. Each stone possessed an etched symbol, which glowed with power. She knew them as operating glyphs of a Willacast transit platform. She sat up slowly to look around.

A cone-shaped cavern surrounded the platform. Light snow drifted down through an opening to the sky far above. Semi-precious jewels, seashells, and colored glass embedded in the stone walls twinkled in the platform's glow. Karpath-ode, the ancient extinct volcano converted into a temple, stood as the holiest place of the local religion. It was a bit overdone, but that's what it took sometimes. Sephy's shoulder twinged, and she rubbed it to return feeling into her arm.

Lakqwi stood up and stared about in all directions. "Rolotundra, the Hollow Mountain," she rasped in clear disbelief. "We are here." She knelt and held her hands against her chest in the Shinwate prayer gesture.

A tall human female on the edge of the platform knelt over a child who cried in wretched sobs. The human lifted the child into her arms and Sephy recognized Havaqwi.

"It's okay, dear one." The young woman spoke Galactic. "Kamur is here for you."

Havaqwi shouldn't be here. Something had gone wrong with the transit portal. Well, obviously, it had turned them inside out, but Havaqwi had not been standing on the platform back at the Shinwate village. It had to be the lightning storm. A surge brought an extra passenger. Sephy shook her head. This probably wouldn't end well.

Lakqwi rose from her prayer to stare at the human holding Havaqwi. Her jaw clenched, and she leveled her spear. She took a step, but her knee buckled, and she almost fell. Sephy hauled herself up and stumbled toward the Shinwate hunter.

"Hold up, Lakqwi." Sephy remembered to use Shin as she slapped a numb hand on Lakqwi's arm to point the spear to the floor. "We don't need to start a fight."

The fierce warning in Lakqwi's eyes told Sephy, without a doubt, Daughter of Melrayis meant blood lineage.

The young female helped Havaqwi to stand and took their measure as Havaqwi clung to her. "You are Shinwate."

She towered over Havaqwi and even had significant height compared to Lakqwi. A blue dress with white accents hung to her ankles and comprised sophisticated textiles, including silk and refined cotton. Sephy didn't detect any artificial material and no visible zippers. Instead, a set of laces ran up the sides of the garment. Well-made and cut to reveal her shoulders and neck, the dress spoke to a civilization advanced far beyond the Shinwate.

The woman's blue skin tone grabbed Sephy's attention next. The faint silverish sheen made it appear to be a lively metallic substance. A subtle electric aura emanated around her. The pattern of Willacast symbols tattooed on her skin had no subtlety. They glowed with their own light, some occasionally flickering brighter before fading to dormancy. This being could only be one of three people.

"Hello," she said. "I am Kamur, Maiden Goddess of Urey."

The guardian of peace, innocence, and justice for Urey stood before Sephy in all her splendor. Sephy had to admit she was an impressive specimen of sanctity, and she was definitely going to be a problem.

Lakqwi growled at the sound of her voice. Sephy realized the Shinwate hunter heard Galactic as Galathian and didn't know the meaning.

"She is the Maiden Goddess." Sephy quickly translated for Lakqwi.

Lakqwi snapped her attention to Sephy and stared. "You say blasphemous things."

"No, it's true," Sephy said. "This is why you have problems. She doesn't know she should be on your side."

Lakqwi glared at Kamur. "Tell her to stay away from Havaqwi."

"I do not need a translator," Kamur said in Shin. "The child seems to have recovered from your travels and she may join you." Kamur let go of Havaqwi and nodded toward Lakqwi.

Havaqwi scurried to Lakqwi, who scooped her up into her arms just like a mother would with her own child. While

Lakqwi comforted Havaqwi, Sephy gave them some room by moving toward Kamur. Sephy glanced around to see an empty chamber except for the four of them. A lucky happenstance because security had to be nearby. That Sephy needed a moment alone with an entirely different goddess detracted from her good fortune.

"Hello, Kamur." Sephy used her sales voice. Though Galactic seemed the same as Galathian, she ensured her translator spoke Kamur's native language in case there were any subtle differences. "I'm honored to meet you. My name is Sephy Alcott, and I own this planet."

Kamur laughed, as if delighted to hear a joke. It was a charming little twitter of the sort that annoyed Sephy to no end. She had to ignore it to keep her own charm intact.

"You are very clever for Shinwate," Kamur said. "Tell me how you have traveled into the sacred sanctuary of Karpathode. What magic do you wield?"

This goddess played her role well, with no recognition of an element outside of the boundaries of the acceptable narrative. Excellent commitment to task, but not useful at all.

"I was summoned," Sephy answered. "I am the Prophet Hukindi, and I seek an audience with the Mother Goddess. It is her magic that provides my apparent power."

Kamur displayed her delighted smile again. "You're here to see my sister, Lillain."

"Yes." Sephy matched the insipid smile with her own version. "Can you point me in the right direction to find her?"

"I'm waiting for her, too. She is coming here to begin my training." Kamur gasped, her hands over her mouth. "Are you part of the training? That would explain your sudden presence upon the Well of Ages."

Well of Ages. Sephy liked the curiously mystical name chosen for a piece of technology. The secret to manipulating an entire civilization rested in the wide adoption of a favorable dogma. Mysticism went a long way in supporting that aim and provided an effective disguise for advanced technology.

As Sephy mused, Kamur swept her hand in a flourish to show the circular stone floor on which they stood. "You stand upon the gateway to the Underworld and my true home, Willa."

"Ah," Sephy said with feigned reverence. "It is lovely." Once again, a bit overdone with all the flashing lights, but why criticize if it worked?

Lakqwi and Havaqwi had recovered and stood beside each other at the edge of the transit platform in their own version of parade rest, back to priestess and acolyte mode. Their collective gear rested at Lakqwi's feet, including Sephy's pack. Lakqwi had recovered her spear and Havaqwi held the bow. Neither took a threatening stance, but Sephy could see Lakqwi's effort to remain calm in her clenched jaw.

"Do you still imprison and enslave the Shinwate because they are different from you?" Sephy asked Kamur in Galathian as she considered her devoted companions.

"I do not condone it," Kamur answered with sincerity, "but yes, it is still a practice among Galathians. Perhaps that is something I can change during my tenure as Maiden."

"Let's hope so. How would you go about making such a change?" Sephy leaned her head toward Kamur, a touch to seem as disarming as possible. She found it difficult to imagine this gentle being posing a threat to the Shinwate. The truth, however, differed from Sephy's immediate perception.

"Honestly, I don't know," Kamur said. "I trust it will be part of my training."

Sephy felt her frustration rise, and she forced it back down. This blue star planet had it tragically backwards. Sephy knew the Seeded Human Asset trade well. It had a necessarily cruel facet to it, which she would never deny. The slaving pits, miserable prisons, and who knows what other awful endings should be the fate of humans instead of feminam. This goddess and her sister-triumvirate were supposed to ensure the correct order and station of this planet's inhabitants. Instead, they gave their blessings to a less evolved species.

"The Shinwate are good people," Sephy said. "Worth fighting for."

"You speak as if you are not one of them, Prophet Hukindi." Kamur matched Sephy's gaze on the two Shinwate.

"I'm not," Sephy answered.

The blame for all this, however, sat squarely on Sephy's shoulders. Meliayis would have never allowed the situation to reach this embarrassing state if she were alive. She was not, however, and she had left this place and these people in Sephy's care. They were definitely worth fighting for, and Sephy had a few tricks up her sleeve to get the battle turned around.

"Here is my sister." Kamur clapped her hands together with delight.

A tall human woman entered the chamber through a stone archway. Red lips and cheeks accented her rosy-pink complexion. Blood-red Willacast symbols inked on her skin flickered and glowed with power. She crackled with an electric aura which felt much more potent than that of the Maiden. Her dress, accented with liberal pink and white materials, had the same sophistication as Kamur's in a more elaborate design. The Mother Goddess of Urey strode to the edge of the transit platform and regarded its current occupants with haughty curiosity.

Two of the three members of the goddess triumvirate in charge of this planet found in one place. Sephy lifted a quizzical eyebrow. How had the Galathians monopolized their power? Was the third one here too? Hopefully not. The entire planet needed watching, not just one town.

Sephy noticed Lakqwi and Havaqwi kneel in the prayer stance. Probably a wise move. Sephy, however, stood as tall as her feminam frame would allow. She held herself with a posture just short of defiance without being disrespectful, which she had a lot of practice with over the years of dealing with powerful people on many planets. In those negotiations, she had the ultimate advantage with control over the transit hub. Unfortunately, that trump card wouldn't help her this time.

"Sister." Lillain spoke in a deep, husky voice to Kamur. They bowed briefly to each other. "It is well to have you here in the sacred chamber of Karpathode. Who are our guests?"

Kamur swept a hand toward Sephy and her companions. "Allow me to introduce the Prophet Hukindi and her entourage, who have just arrived using the Well of Ages."

Sephy stooped into an awkward bow. "Happy to make your acquaintance, Your Magnificence." She had to improvise the title, not knowing what was expected, but it didn't matter. Sephy only needed a few minutes alone with the Mother Goddess. "I've come hoping to have a brief private audience with you."

Lillain's penetrating gaze landed on Sephy and bore down

with an intense focus. Even though Sephy knew it was part of the act, for an uncomfortable moment, she felt exposed to the core.

"You are Shinwate," Lillain said.

"Technically, no," Sephy said, "but you can think of me as part of the Shinwate tribe if that helps."

Lillain's gaze didn't waver, and her expression didn't change except to become even more intense. Her electric aura shimmered, and several symbols flashed with power. Sephy felt a bit unnerved despite knowing how Lillain could subtly manipulate emotions using electromagnetics.

"The Willacast do not serve the Shinwate." Lillain used a flat tone that allowed no dispute.

"That's a problem I'm hoping to discuss with you," Sephy replied. Lillain's brow furrowed. Sephy guessed she wasn't used to being defied, even if politely. "You see, your original task was exactly the opposite, and I've come to fix that. It will only take a moment of your time." Sephy glanced around the chamber. It was a single elaborate room, but Sephy didn't know what lay beyond the archway. "Do you have a private room in which we can speak?"

"How did you get here?" Lillain didn't move, but it felt to Sephy as if she grew larger and closer. A low, almost imperceptible rumble emanated from her. Beside Sephy, Kamur's smile melted away to an expression of concern.

"I transported here from another transit device located in the deep forest where the remains of the free Shinwate live in hiding." Sephy used her sales voice, the cheerful antithesis of Lillain's tone.

Lillain blinked, and Sephy knew her words didn't penetrate because they weren't allowed to. At least one safeguard was still in place. "Just a moment alone, Your Excellence," Sephy tried again, "and all will make sense."

"Sister, surely we can hear what the prophet of the Shinwate might have to say," Kamur said in a predictable offer to foster peaceful negotiations.

"No," Lillain said. "There will be no compromise. We do not provide the Shinwate with comfort or succor."

And there it is. The mandate from Melrayis that Sephy had to delete from this goddess' reality. It didn't look like Lillain would allow it to be done in private, which made it risky, but Sephy had never shied away from a gamble.

"Call the guards," Lillain commanded.

Sephy took a breath to speak, but Kamur spoke first.

"Wait, surely no harm can come from—"

"Here is your first lesson," Lillain interrupted as she turned her attention to Kamur. "The Mother is the protector of Urey and that always comes first."

Sephy paused as this interchange piqued her interest. In theory, the tri-goddess controls always cooperated, with the most appropriate one taking the lead. Supposedly conflicts were impossible, and yet here one was unfolding.

Kamur gestured toward Sephy. "Here is an articulate representative of the Shinwate along with her reverent companions. Surely some progress between Galathians and Shinwate is possible. She has made a brave overture to meet with us. Should we not honor it?"

Sephy raised her brows in amused surprise. Advocating for feminkind was the tri-goddess mission. Perhaps Melrayis' inadvertent changes had not reached the Maiden Goddess. Maybe Sephy didn't have to use a heavy hand to undo the damage.

"Second lesson." Lillain raised her hand, palm pointed at Sephy. A red symbol blazed to life and Sephy recognized a disrupter aimed directly at her. "Danger is confronted directly and decisively."

The rapid escalation to deadly violence stunned Sephy for a moment. Before she could react, Kamur stepped in front of her.

"There is no need to kill," Kamur said.

"You don't know who these people are," Lillain snapped. "They traveled here using our magic, which should not be possible. They are clearly a threat. Stand aside."

Lillain glared at Kamur, who stood her ground. The moment, utterly out of Sephy's experience, completely engrossed her. She felt the thrill of everything on the line and let it ride.

"I will not," Kamur said. "I don't need your training to see this is wrong."

"Then I will start solving the problem elsewhere." Lillain swung her arm toward Lakqwi and Havaqwi, the red symbol on her palm blazing with power.

"D–12 Override. Power shutdown!" Sephy shouted.

Lillain dropped her arm and slumped. The disrupter in her palm blinked out along with all the rest of her power symbols. Her electric aura faded, and she slowly toppled to the floor, one leg awkwardly bent under her. Just in front of Sephy, Kamur collapsed onto the platform, her eyes still open and an expression of horror frozen on her face.

"That got out of hand real quick," Sephy said in Shin.

Lakqwi and Havaqwi rose from their prayer stance. They stared at the two goddesses lying prone in eerie stillness. "What have you done?"

"Don't worry. They'll be okay. I'm going to work on them both for a bit. You two guard the entrance and let me know if anyone comes this way." Sephy pointed toward the archway. Lakqwi nodded, and they moved toward the entrance. Sephy watched with admiration. *Good help, those two.*

Sephy pulled the disrupter pistol from her trouser pouch and laid it beside Lillain's limp form. She opened a connection to Lillain's user interface. After entering a security code, she cleared the firewall and accessed Lillain's core memory. The standard D-12-C nano-cyber automaton control codes came up on her neural screen and she flipped to the mission-unique subroutine package. It didn't take long to find Melrayis' adjustments. She had even provided notes in the text sidebars.

The notes revealed a lot of changes. Melrayis had been a genius at coding. The details of the adjustments here were beyond her comprehension, though she got the general gist of it.

Havaqwi appeared by her side. "Lakqwi says guards are forming outside the temple. They will be coming soon."

"This might take a while." The girl scampered away. "Just great." Sephy dived into the programming. The trick was to redirect what was already there. Change a few variable definitions from human to Shinwate, perhaps. Sephy started looking for possibilities. Easier said than done. Melrayis had woven her own set of commands around the core code to change Lillain's mission from protecting Shinwate to isolating them.

The internal AI's attempts to rectify the resulting lack of objectives led to additional lines of code interspersed throughout, some of which corrupted her core memory. That could explain the Mother Goddess' sudden escalation to violence. This was how the benevolent protector of Shinwate became the aggressive protector of humans instead.

Sephy attempted a few simple edits, only to find a growing list of error warnings for each change. Melrayis had woven an elaborate tapestry which might come undone if Sephy pulled too many threads. Her fingers flew over multiple arrays of floating symbols. "You didn't make this easy." Sephy imagined the ghost of Melrayis looking over her shoulder.

Sephy got one set of instructions to compile without errors. *Finally!* She had a method that worked, and she went about making viable changes.

"Prophet Hukindi!" Lakqwi shouted a warning from her place at the archway.

Two Galathian men stood on the threshold with stunned expressions. One wore priestly red robes of luxurious silk that hung to the ground, and the other shining armor with a broadsword on his belt. The priest turned and ran. The soldier drew out his sword.

Lakqwi retreated to the platform with her spear lowered. Havaqwi stayed at Lakqwi's side with bow drawn and ready. Glancing between Sephy and the advancing soldier, Lakqwi said, "We are out of time."

Chapter Twenty-Seven

The greatest war is not against an invading enemy, though those are glorious. No, the greatest war, and the most difficult to win, is fighting ignorance.

—from Chronicles of Galathia by Rafykin, Urey, circa 2640 local planetary calendar.

Frontier, Day 003–006, Year 2999 local planetary calendar, Standard Galactic Year 14285

This time, Jay tended to Saben. They stood in front of the great doors as he lathered the general's swollen hand with lanicina sap and wrapped it with a bandage.

"Sorry about that, sir." Jay kept his voice low. "It's all I could think of."

"I was hoping to get through without stirring up the stone giants, but you did what you had to, Lieutenant."

That was as close to thanks as Jay was going to get from the general.

Using a stone key longer than Jay's arm, Bobrick and Bilford unlocked and pushed the huge barrier open. The screech of the stone pivot spoke to how long the doors had been closed. The doors opened into a mossy cave. Jay could see the sunlight and feel the fresh air flowing in from the outside.

Behind them, King Kormash shouted orders to his soldiers to send patrols through every cavern of the mountains to secure all entries and exits.

"How much of what you said back there was true?" Jay asked.

"In this very spot, I wrapped King Nados' hand like you're doing for me. Queen Izell will be content with renewing the treaty once I explain it to her."

"She doesn't know about the stone giants?"

"Not many do. When we struck the first agreement, only a few officers were present. Most of them are dead. I don't know how much information King Nados conveyed back to the castle, but my impression is that it wasn't much. It's best to keep it that way, Lieutenant. Theirs is a strange magic."

"They seem to guard passage through the Kelstones effec-tively."

"Yes, but they're unpredictable. This situation could have easily gone the other way, and we'd be dead right now. They are best left undisturbed," Saben said.

"Yes, sir."

Kormash strode up, shaking the ground as he approached. "General, Lieutenant, I wish you a safe journey." He gave their weapons back. "I'm afraid the rest cannot be replaced. We have no need for things like bedrolls, dry socks, or food."

Relieved to be armed again, Jay strapped on his sword belt.

"Thank you, Your Majesty." Saben bowed.

"Do take care of this old man, will you?" As Kormash spoke, one of his green eyes blinked off and back on. Jay imagined that to be a wink.

"Yes, Your Majesty."

"Now shove off. I've got to get this door closed before some half-wit wanders in." He turned and stomped away, giving orders to eager stone giants along the way.

Jay chuckled, wondering if he counted as the latest half-wit to wander into Kormash's underground realm.

Saben and Jay hurried through the doors as Bobrick and Bilford drew them shut. The latter gave them a wave goodbye. The doors banged closed, and the lock slammed into place.

They hastened toward the light, stopping at the exit and surveying the surroundings. The cave opened onto the rocky foothills on the northern side of the Kelstones. An expanse of untamed forest spread out across ridges and valleys of the Frontier. A clear and bright midday sky met the horizon.

"If you follow the Kelstone foothills east, they extend to the Wrayans." Saben pointed along the arc of peaks that ran up above them. The craggy hills sloped upward into steep cliffs. White capped peaks of a mountain chain loomed in the distance. "The Kelstones run into the Wrayans, past the Talindrey River. Not far on the other side of the river is Aeterna."

Jay studied the landscape. It looked to be a long trek on foot. He regretted the loss of their horses and supplies.

"The valley is guarded by magic, but with the Oracle's blessing, we should get there," Saben said.

"How is the Oracle assisting us, sir?"

"I don't know how her magic works, but I'm sure it does. All pilgrims to Aeterna sought permission from her before traveling there, including King Nados. She was said to be a guardian or gatekeeper of some sort. Explorers who did not seek her admittance could never find the ancient city."

"I'm glad she's on our side."

"It appears so, but keep in mind, magical people are known for having their own mysterious agendas. We may not agree on what the Oracle thinks of as success. So, stay wary. Eyes front, Lieutenant."

"Yes, sir."

They worked their way down from the mouth of the cave to reach the game trails leading east between the ridges of the Kelstone foothills.

* * *

Jay and Saben watched a curl of smoke drift lazily into the air over the trees. The first sign of civilization after two days of traveling through the deep wilderness had them hopeful and wary.

"Let's have a look, Lieutenant," Saben whispered. "Probably just an isolated farm, but if they have hot food and ale, it would be welcome. Perhaps some news of Calonade."

Jay nodded, and they made their way carefully through the underbrush, avoiding a rough road snaking along the valley. They reached an overhang that provided a view of a clearing with the blackened ruin of ashes around a crumbled chimney. It was the remains of a farmhouse. The skeleton of a nearby barn revealed it had also recently burnt to the ground.

"They've been raided," Jay said.

"Yes, but by whom? I'll cover you while you go down and find out."

"Yes, sir."

Jay crept down to the farmhouse, remaining concealed from any occupants. He observed the place from the edge of the clearing and detected no movement. It seemed abandoned.

With his saber and pistol drawn, Jay stepped into the clearing and approached the remains of the house. The chimney still stood, but the roof was gone. On the far corner, part of a bedroom remained. Blackened bed sheets fluttered over a broken frame. On the exterior of the only intact wall, tacks suspended a parchment.

Jay pulled it down and read the script. Then he waved Saben down to join him.

"It's from the governor," Jay said as Saben appeared out of the woods. "They're hunting down mixed people. Rewards for capture and delivery. Anyone suspected of harboring them will be punished."

"It's a pretext to take what they want," Saben said.

Jay frowning darkly. "This is Armone's doing."

"This is the Galathian Empire, Lieutenant," Saben spat with disgust. "It's what they do."

"Jortica said some of the Galathians in her regiment were out here tormenting people. I didn't think it meant this kind of destruction. What do we do, sir?"

"We stay on our mission."

"What about these people, sir? Someone needs to protect them."

"The best thing we can do for them is to make sure Queen Izell's counterattack is successful. Establishing an heir helps her gather allies. She sent us to the Oracle for a good reason, so let's get it done, Lieutenant."

Saben stepped into the ruined bedroom and kicked open

a trunk that had survived the destruction. Clothing spilled out onto the floor. The soldiers must have left it behind. "I think it's time we got rid of these Galathian uniforms we're wearing. We need to blend in better and not be mistaken for soldiers loyal to the governor while friends might still be found. Besides, you stink."

Jay smelled his tattered coat and realized he hadn't changed since rolling around in the stable muck. "I am pretty ripe." He pulled a change of clothing out to check its fit. "I'm still obviously mixed. That can't be hidden."

"It may help us. People must be harboring those of your ancestry, or they wouldn't be putting up parchments about it. You may have to speak for me. I'm obviously from the north."

Jay scowled. "I guess if we come across soldiers, you can claim me as a captive again."

"It's a good plan, Lieutenant."

"I think you have the better end of thc deal, sir."

* * *

Another day of trekking over rough terrain brought them to a solitary ranch house. A double rail fence curled around the stables behind it. Bales of hay were stacked in the field beyond. Jay crept back from the fence and joined Saben in the shadow of a long, flat boulder.

"This could be it, sir," Jay said.

After two more burned out farmsteads, this was the first intact one they had come upon. And the first possibility of gaining mounts. It was a long journey to Aeterna and getting there sooner seemed worth the risk.

"Could you see any horses?" Saben asked.

"No, sir, but the hay is fresh. Something down there must need it."

"Could be cattle."

"Maybe. Only one way to find out."

"We'll wait until nightfall," Saben said. "Should be dark enough with clouded skies tonight."

"We could ask them for horses instead of stealing them," Jay said.

"What happens if they say no, Lieutenant?"

Jay bit his lip. The general had a good point. It was probably better to keep a low profile.

"I'll drop them some coin," Saben said. "They won't be put out too badly."

At nightfall, a warm glow came from the house. The valley filled with the welcoming smell of the cookfire. It made Jay's mouth water after days of only what they could scrounge. People were home, but whose side were they on?

Jay heard the rider first. He blended with the darkness until the house lights revealed his silhouette. A man on a draft horse dismounted and led the animal into the stable, where a lantern lit the windows. Shortly after, the light faded, and the man entered the house. A few hours later, the light of the house's hearth fire dimmed.

Jay and Saben climbed out of their hiding place and carefully approached. Jay prayed for no dogs to warn the occupants. They entered the stable raising no alarms. Jay found the lantern and shaded it before he lit it. A dim shaft of light revealed no occupants except three horses. They started, but

Saben calmed them before they panicked.

"Find two saddles," Saben whispered.

Jay found them and hoisted one onto the first horse. A lantern flared to life above them. Both men spun around with weapons ready, only to see a child in the loft staring down at them. She wore a simple night dress flecked with straw. A mixture of floral and starburst plinum patterns on her face marked her as mixed descent. She let loose a blood-curdling scream.

The horses panicked, and Saben struggled to keep hold of them with his sore hand. Jay shoved the pistol into his belt and sprinted toward the ladder. "Keep quiet," he whispered.

"Don't take me!" she screamed in Galathian as Jay reached to the top of the loft. "Daddy, don't let them take me!"

"Easy." Jay reached out his hand to calm the child. "We're not going to take you anywhere."

"We just want the horses, lass." Saben spoke as calmly as he could while struggling to keep the horse from rearing. Another horse kicked the wall of its stable hard enough to rattle the roof.

"Don't take me!" she screamed again.

She was thirteen or fourteen years old. "It's all right," Jay said. "I'm like you. It's all right."

The stable doors crashed open and in rushed a man, barefoot and without a shirt, his plinum bands visible from head to torso. The pattern crisscrossed in several places, revealing him as a commoner. Wielding a pike with a long blade on the end, he growled and rushed Jay with all his might. Jay leaped up into the loft. Sprawling backwards, as the blade jabbed up through the floor, he just missed getting skewered. The girl stood over him, holding a dagger. She lunged at his face. He caught her wrist, squeezed loose the weapon and flipped her back into the corner. She landed on a pile of hay and rolled into a ball.

"Stand down." Saben's voice sounded from below.

Jay looked over the edge of the loft. Saben pointed his pistol at the man's chest. The wicked-looking pike lay at his feet.

"Now, we're all going to take a minute and get to know each other," Saben said.

"Don't take my daughter," the man pleaded.

"We're not here for her," Saben said. "My son and I are dodging the empire as well. Come on down, Ben."

Jay hesitated for a moment, then realized the pretense. "Yes, sir." Jay climbed down from the loft with an eye on the girl, but she stayed curled up in the corner.

"My son is lowborn, like your daughter. We have the same enemy."

"What about you?" the man rasped.

"I'm no friend of the empire," Saben answered, "which makes us all on the same side. Am I right?"

"Maybe," the man growled, "but why bust into my stables in the dead of night, giving my daughter a fright?"

"We didn't know about your daughter. Though I understand why she sleeps here. We saw the burnt-out farms on the way through. We're just here for the horses." Saben lowered his weapon. "Now that we know you're a friend, we can be neighborly about it and pay you for them as well." Saben shook the coin purse hidden under his tunic.

At the sound of the money, the man visibly relaxed. "All right, friend. What do I call you?"

"I'm Ben. This is Ben Junior."

"I'm Clem. My daughter, Alyce." The girl peeked over the

loft at the sound of her name. She ducked back down when she saw Jay still holding the knife.

"Ben, you can put that away." Saben nodded toward the weapon.

"Yes, sir." Jay dropped the knife into a nearby feed bucket. "Um, it's all right, Alyce. I'm not going to hurt you." He spoke as gently as he could, still trying to get his heart to stop pounding.

She peeked back over the edge of the loft.

Clem looked them up and down. "You boys seem tired and dusty. Must've been a pretty good journey thus far. Why don't you come into my house and get some food and drink? I don't get many friendly visitors anymore, what with all the soldiers causing trouble."

"All right," Saben said, "but we'll be asking for more provisions and paying a fair price for them."

Clem smiled. "Be welcome guests under my roof and at my table."

Chapter Twenty-Eight

Hiding a planet isn't too difficult. Most rely heavily on the database we maintain. If some busybody finds it on their own, we simply wait a few days before issuing an ambiguous answer to the inquiry. The time dilation overcomes most curiosity.

—from the journal of Sephy Alcott, Standard Galactic Year 11285

Frontier, Day 004–005, Year 2999 local planetary calendar, Standard Galactic Year 14285

It took two days for the storm in her mind to subside. Jortica huddled in a thick patch of underbrush and brambles the entire time, unaware of her surroundings. She could only hear the harsh accusation of the wind in her head. Her squad was dead. All of them gone. Betrayed, and she could do nothing. She played it over repeatedly as the tempest raged. She saw Nackers' taunting smile over and over. Saw her friends die again and again. All at her order to fight.

She had been convinced fighting was the only way. Now, with her friends dead, she wasn't sure. No one but herself remained to tell the world of the fate of the Horse Division.

No one else could bring Legate Armone and his lackeys, like Captain Fauden, to justice. She grasped onto the hope of revenge to survive the storm.

When she finally emerged, she dunked her face in a stream and drank muddy water. She crept through the forest, getting her bearings. She'd lost her way when she ran, paying no attention except to outrun the storm, only stopping due to exhaustion. It took a day to find the road. Jortica remained under the cover of the trees. She saw nothing. No wagon. No bodies. Only a mound of fresh dirt she guessed to be a mass grave. Jortica ground her teeth to keep the storm from rising again. Someday she'd honor her friends properly, but now she needed to find allies.

She had let her guard down because she trusted Fauden. Never again. By sending her team to be killed, Fauden had abandoned all pretense of loyalty to his soldiers. If she found that two-faced Galathian, she'd carve him into pieces. She gripped her saber, thinking of it.

The sword was all she had left. She lost her pistol in the mud when Nackers fell off the wagon. She'd shed her uniform coat, unable to stomach wearing Galathian red. Only her muddy waistcoat remained. Everything else had been tucked in her saddlebags with Calamity at the Outer Gate stables. Would her mare still be there?

Keeping to the trees, Jortica followed the road toward the Kettlebone Pass, trying to work out how to get into Calonade without getting picked off by the Galathians. Had they taken the Outer Gate, or had her fellow soldiers held back the invasion? There had been a lot of enemies on the walls the last time she came through.

Jortica ducked out of sight at the sound of horses on the

road. A troop of Galathians led a dozen riderless horses away from the Outer Gate, presumably toward Thurbush. Jortica spotted Calamity among them. Samos' gelding and the ponies that Eason and Kessa rode were among them too. Jortica grinned, knowing her mount lived, but this also meant the Outer Gate had fallen. Whatever Legate Armone and Captain Fauden had planned, it had already begun.

Near the back, two Galathians had a huge black stallion in tow. It could only be Havoc. The big horse pulled against the ropes, but they held fast. What was Jay's monster doing here? Shouldn't he and his rider be at the castle right now? Had Jay been captured, or worse? Jay would never let Havoc out of his sight if he could help it.

The wind rustled in the back of her mind. How many friends would she lose? She forced the storm back. Jay might be a townee, but he had substance. He had mastered Havoc. He'd turned it close on the Barber. Jay had been training hard, improving himself. Until she saw the earth turned for him, she refused to believe he was dead.

The troop of horses rumbled past her without stopping. Jortica turned away from the road and hustled up the side of a ridge. She scrambled over the rocks and moved in the general direction of Thurbush over the rough high ground, cutting a more direct path than the road.

She reached an overlook of the town as the troop entered. Galathians were working on constructing a log stockade and gatehouses at each end of the town. Twenty red-coated soldiers patrolled the outer boundary of the town. She counted twenty more strolling through the streets or sitting on the covered porches. No civilians braved the outside. The Galathians thoroughly possessed Thurbush. Jortica couldn't just sail into town and take back her horse, so she got comfortable enough to watch the town for a while.

The mounted Galathians herded the horses into the town stable. They had some trouble with Havoc, but with enough hands got him in. Only one Galathian got a kick in the ribs for his trouble.

After a few hours, her muscles stiffening because of the hard ground, Jortica spotted a familiar caged wagon pulling up to the jailhouse. Dark stains marked the sideboards. They hadn't bothered to clean it from the fight. Jortica growled as Nackers dismounted and strolled into the building. The old weasel survived the ambush. Where was his loutish friend, Lunt? The big man had been in the final embrace of one of her friends last she saw him. Had Samos finished Lunt as he died?

Out of the jailhouse poured a group of Galathians manhandling several bound men. They loaded the prisoners into the wagon. All the men were lowborn, the people she had seen in the jail before. The guards escorted another group to the wagon. These were women and children. Jortica growled again. The Galathians had expanded their net to capture all lowborn. Nackers mounted the wagon and cracked a whip. The rolling cage headed out of town and around the bend in the road, out of sight. Jortica kept low and scrambled across the ridges to follow.

* * *

By evening, Jortica caught up with the welcome wagon. She

watched from a perch among the rocky ridges as it entered the gates of a newly constructed stockade surrounding a farmhouse. Nackers waved to the guards and the gate swung open. The wagon trundled into the field near a large barn. Several Galathians waited there.

The soldiers unceremoniously pulled the prisoners from the wagon and marched them into the barn. Even though the people mustered little resistance, the guards were generous with their rifle butts and horse whips. One of the lowborn men took several lashes while hunching over two young children to protect them. The storm in her head blew. A low but ominous wind rushed through her.

Jortica watched until every prisoner had been taken into the barn. Who knew what terrors lurked in there? Nackers talked with his friends as he strutted to the farmhouse. Several Galathian officers greeted him there. Among them stood another familiar figure.

Fauden. The storm in her head ticked up a notch as she burned with a need for revenge.

Taking a breath, Jortica eased away from the cliff and back down the other side. It was time for payback, but first she needed a horse.

Chapter Twenty-Nine

Having experienced the attraction of war, I know it's not solely based on greed. There is more to it. The thrill of epic and deadly conflict runs deep.

—from Chronicles of Galathia by Rafykin, Urey, circa 2640 local planetary calendar.

Frontier, Day 007, Year 2999 local planetary calendar, Standard Galactic Year 14285

Clem introduced his wife, Reah, a handsome Calonaden woman. She returned to the kitchen, leaving the three men to talk. Jay only saw her once more briefly as she brought out bread, meat, and ale for them. Jay thanked her politely, but she made no response. Alyce peeked around the corner once but disappeared again when scolded by her mother.

Jay dug into the food while Saben made the usual small talk that revealed little. Keeping Alyce in the stable spoke to the hard situation for these people. Usually robbers, such as themselves, would approach the stable first. Soldiers would raid the house. They feared soldiers more than thieves.

"We saw three farms burnt out as we traveled through,"

Saben said to Clem. "Can you tell us what is happening?"

"The soldiers come through every few days looking for half-castings like you," he nodded to Jay, "and my girl. First, they said they just wanted to know where all the halfies lived. Then, a couple of weeks ago, they started taking them. Anybody that resisted got burnt out. At first, they were only interested in young men about your age," he nodded to Jay again, "but now they take everyone. None have come back. Rumor has it they're kept in a labor camp."

"Why people of mixed descent?" Jay asked. If Clem noticed the use of the politer term, he didn't show it.

"They won't say. It's just *our orders this and our orders that.* So far, I kept Alyce out of sight, but you never know what might happen."

Jay yawned. The ale settled heavily on his system. Must've been a strong batch.

"There are rumors, though," Clem said. "The biggest one is that Izell hid herself away an heir to the throne. The empire don't like the idea of a child of Nados and Izell popping up just when they finally got rid of them."

Jay jolted into alertness. "Have you heard anything about what happened to Queen Izell?" He tried to seem casual about the question, but his anxiety may have betrayed him.

Clem didn't seem to notice. "What I've heard is the governor tried to do her in, but she got away. Well, for me, that's good riddance. I never did like her much. I mean, she's from good northern stock and all, but she just never stood up to the empire like Nados did. For a raw-cast native, he sure knew how to fight." Clem chuckled. "Ain't many made like he was."

Jay breathed a silent sigh of relief. The queen had escaped.

This welcome news and the heaviness of the ale calmed his nerves.

"Don't get me wrong. I ain't no collaborator, neither. I hate the governor even more now that he's put his own cronies in charge and started hunting people down, terrorizing everyone." Clem spat a curse. "I wish they'd leave us be."

Jay and Saben nodded, and they sat in silence for a while.

Jay heard a quiet voice from the kitchen.

"Mama, can I sleep inside the house tonight?"

"Yes, honey, and I'm sorry you had a fright. I'll take you to bed." The floorboards creaked as Reah moved down the hall.

Alyce's bare feet padded after. "Mama, please tell me the story of Aeterna."

"Sure, honey. Come now, get under them covers."

Jay couldn't remember the last time he heard the old fairy tale. Probably from Gran when he was about Alyce's age.

Saben and Clem returned to talking about the Galathians. Clem had things to say, and Saben just nodded as he listened. Jay cocked an ear down the hall to the unseen bedroom. Reah's resonant voice carried well through the house.

"Once upon a time," Reah said, "there was a king made of metal. His insides were cast iron, but on the outside, he was plated with tin. The king had won great power over his followers."

A door shut, blocking the sound of Reah's voice. It was an interesting story to explain how a northern king and a southern queen could join forces and bring peace to a troubled world. Their son was the half-cast prince, who appeared as a hero in other fairy tales. *What would the real half-cast prince be like?* Jay realized he might find out soon. Would he be a heroic leader, like in the tales, or a frightened boy hiding in the forest?

"Why are you boys on the run?" Clem asked. "I take it that's what you're doing here?"

"Same reason as why you're hiding your daughter." Saben stifled a yawn.

"You boys is ex-military, ain't cha." Clem grinned, clearly proud of his discovery.

Saben rubbed his eyes. "What gave us away?"

"Well, your guns, sabers, and boots. Those say Calonade Horse all over them. I used to be a pikeman in the war. Fought beside King Nados hisself at the pass. That was some battle. We gave them all the hell they could take. Too bad the king fell, or we wouldn't be worried about the empire right now."

Jay couldn't focus his eyes and his head suddenly felt too heavy to hold up. A warm feeling flushed out from his stomach to his limbs, and he discovered he couldn't move.

"What's in this ale, Clem?" Saben slumped in his chair.

Jay pitched forward, his cheek hitting the tabletop. He watched Saben slip out of his chair and flop onto the floor.

Clem got up and stood over the general. "Didn't think I'd recognized you, eh, Captain Turncoat?" He laughed. "I's never forget a face, even after twenty years."

Jay's vision faded as Clem reached down and pulled Saben's coin purse loose. He jingled the coins merrily. "Nothing to worry about, boys. You just go right to sleep and ole Clem will take care of everything."

* * *

Jay came to as someone slapped his face. "Drink this," a low but insistent voice said in Calonaden. A cold liquid was forced into his throat. He couldn't help but gulp part of it down. He spat out the rest. His eyes wrenched open, and he tried to focus. Reah's face floated into view just inches from his own.

"You listen to me," the woman said. "What I just gave you will help you wake up sooner than most. You'll still be caught, but you might be able to help yourself."

Jay tried to lift his arms, but they were bound tight. He tried to talk but could only moan.

"Hush," Reah said. "I only have a minute 'til Clem gets back."

Jay held still and tried to focus on Reah. She continued to blur in and out of his vision.

"Clem's doing this for our daughter. I'm sorry you're catching the short end of it. We have a deal with the local captain. We send you and we get to keep Alyce. It ain't personal."

"Sa-ben." Jay moaned through his numb lips.

"Clem took your pa into the wilderness." Reah leaned out of Jay's sight. "It's his own fault. Shoulda just kept going on past our house. People barging in day and night. Ain't no way to live."

Jay had to go into the wilderness too. "Ae-ter-na," he muttered as he remembered their destination. A dense fog filled his mind.

"Aeterna?" Reah reappeared with her brow furrowed.

Jay tried to tell her about the mission, but all he could spit out was "haff-cass pra—"

Reah put her hand on his mouth. "Hush now. Don't say anything 'til you're fully awake. Then it's best to lie still and listen for a while. You'll be tied up, so you won't be able to do much else, anyway."

"Mama, did he say Aeterna?" Alyce's voice came from beyond Jay's narrow vision.

Reah disappeared. "I told you to stay hidden, girl." He heard them rush away as he floated into a throbbing darkness.

Chapter Thirty

Aeterna stands as a beacon to learning in tribute to the spoils of war.

—from Chronicles of Galathia by Rafykin, Urey, circa 2640 local planetary calendar.

Thurbush, Day 007, Year 2999 local planetary calendar, Standard Galactic Year 14285

The pain of his head bonking on wood brought Jay back to consciousness. The cabin floor shook under him, and Jay tried to brace himself, but felt the bite of the binding around his arms and legs. Whatever Reah had given him made him feel nauseated. The bouncing and rolling of the cabin floor didn't help either. After more insistent hard knocks against the wood, Jay figured he wasn't in Clem's house. Instead, he lay on the floorboards of a wagon moving over a rough road. It had a cover with iron bars for walls.

Jay's swimming vision regained focus on a pattern of stains splashed across the wooden planks of the wagon. His head lay in one patch, his hair sticking to it. It reeked, but not like paint. Jay couldn't place it until the pockmarks along the sides of the wagon provided another hint. Somewhere the war had heated up enough to produce casualties. The cage bars made it clear whose side the recent passengers had fought for.

The wagon halted at a hail to the drivers from somewhere ahead. "We got another halfy for ye," one of the wagon drivers said in Galathian.

Jay tried to sit up, but he was tied too tight to move. Even though he didn't trust the woman, he followed Reah's advice and kept still.

"It's Sergeant Nackers!" a guard Jay couldn't see shouted. "Open the gate for the welcome wagon." Rude laughter followed. The wagon continued bumping along for another hundred feet and then halted. It rocked as the drivers climbed off.

"What you got?" a new voice asked. This one spoke Galathian as well. Despite his pounding headache, Jay thought he sounded familiar.

"Half-casting caught in the wild, Captain," Nackers said.

"Who caught him?"

"Clem," Nackers replied.

"He's been busy. Second one this week from him," the captain said.

Jay swore he'd heard that voice before.

"He's feeling mo'ivated, Captain Fauden," the other driver said.

Fauden! He was going to be trouble.

"I imagine so." Fauden stepped closer to the wagon. "Why didn't you take him to the camp?"

Nackers chuckled. "You'll want to see this one, Captain. Look at his boots. Lunt pointed them out to me. You might notice they look familiar.”

“He’s a boot jockey,” Lunt said.

Jay kept still with his eyes closed.

Fauden moved to the back of the wagon. “Calonade Horseman, yep, he’s the one. Is he alive?”

“He’ll be right as rain in a few hours,” Nackers said. “’Til then he’ll be out cold. Clem’s missus knows a few tricks. This one had a touch of her special ale for unwelcome visitors.”

“Remind me to decline her invitation to dinner,” Fauden said. “Good work, Sergeant Nackers. Sergeant Lunt. Take the prisoner to the holding cell. Plenty of room since it’s been cleared out. I’ll let the commanding officer know he’s here.”

“Yes, sir, Captain, sir,” Nackers said.

Lunt reached into the cage and dragged Jay out by his feet. The burly sergeant grappled him like a bag of feed onto his shoulder. Jay risked cracking open his eyes.

A rutted dirt road stretched out between rustic buildings. Jay spotted a saloon and a stable across the street. Further out, tree trunks had been cut to create a surrounding wall. In the background, the Kelstone peaks rose above the forest. The only people in view were Galathian soldiers. Jay guessed he was in a small Frontier town which had been converted into a fort.

As the sergeant stomped into the jailhouse, Jay closed his eyes, feigning unconsciousness. The rattle of keys and the clank of the jail cell door told Jay he might be stuck for a while, but there was nothing he could do about it trussed up like a pheasant for the stove.

“No need to be dainty,” Nackers said, “just toss ’im in there.”

Lunt obliged, and the floor knocked Jay’s breath out. At

least he landed facing away from his jailers so they couldn't see the grimace on his face.

"What's dainty?" Lunt asked.

"Like it sounds, lad. Like it sounds," Nackers said. "Don't leave behind my good rope."

Lunt undid the knots, stuck a boot into Jay's back, and whipped the rope from under him, burning his exposed skin. Jay stifled a grunt of pain. The sergeants locked the jail cell and stomped out.

Jay waited for the feeling to come back into his arms and legs before he moved. Only his hands still tingled when he turned onto his side. Once his breath came back, Jay almost regretted it because the floor reeked. The jail must be used a lot with little attention to upkeep.

Jay peered up at a barred window toward a scraping noise. A flash of silver caught the light. Between the bars perched the clockwork crow. It regarded him with a shining eye. Jay squinted, trying to make sure he was seeing true. The crow squawked in its metallic voice and hopped out of sight.

The door behind him burst open, and Jay heard two people enter. A familiar voice said, "A half-cast Calonade horseman, you say, Fauden?"

Jay knew that voice anywhere. Gilcres.

"Yes sir," Fauden answered. "Picked up this morning. Could be the man that Armone is looking for, sir."

Was Gilcres in command here? Jay barely kept himself from cursing in disgust.

"Still out?"

"Yes, sir. He'll be down for another few hours."

"All right, let's have a look," Gilcres said.

Fauden opened the cell door, and both men came in. Jay

kept his eyes closed and body limp as Gilcres rolled him over.

"That's him," Gilcres said. "How did he get on this side of the Outer Gate?"

"No idea, sir, but I'm glad we got him."

"Leave the keys and go send a message krike to Legate Armone. He'll be happy to know he can send good news to the emperor."

"Yes, sir." Fauden left the jailhouse.

"Well, well, Lieutenant Jay, it's good to see you again." Gilcres leaned over him.

Jay's eyes popped open. "Good to see you, too."

Gilcres leaped back in surprise. Jay tripped him, and he went down hard on the floor of the cell, his hat flying off. Jay climbed to his feet and stepped forward to stomp Gilcres in the face.

Gilcres drew out his pistol and Jay changed his target. He kicked the gun out of Gilcres' hand. It clattered across the room and into a locked jail cell. Shifting on the floor, Gilcres grabbed Jay's boot and pushed him off balance. As Jay stumbled back, Gilcres sprang to his feet and drew his sword. Jay jumped in close and grappled with Gilcres' wrist. He got the right leverage and bent Gilcres' hand back. Gilcres howled, and the sword dropped from his hand, spinning out of reach. Gilcres tried to punch Jay's face and missed, hitting him in the shoulder instead. They both staggered back.

They circled each other in the jail cell. The blow reminded Jay of their previous fight and gave him a jolt of apprehension. Would Gilcres get the better of him again?

A grin spread over Gilcres' face. "Round two, 'eh, half-casting. No one here to save you this time."

Jay tensed at the insult but kept himself from losing his

temper. He had to think his way through this fight. "Congratulations on your promotion. Enjoying your new assignment out here in the wilderness?"

"It's temporary." Gilcres' grin faded to a frown. "Once I turn in your half-cast hide, I'll be back in the castle commanding the army."

Gilcres charged, taking a swing. Jay saw it coming and ducked under, hooking Gilcres with an elbow and sending him staggering off-balance.

Jay braced for another charge, but Gilcres stood his ground, still grinning. "Not bad. You're learning."

"Pain helps me remember." Jay recounted Commander Kahela's words.

"Get ready to recall a lot."

Jay noticed a gold chain dangling from Gilcres waistcoat. He feigned left and Gilcres bought it, throwing another wild haymaker. Jay spun right and landed a punch in Gilcres' kidney with one hand. His other hand raked over Gilcres, his waistcoat ripping away from the gold chain.

Cursing, Gilcres held his side but reset his stance without looking too out of sorts. "Gonna have to hit harder than that."

"Care to check the time?" Jay brandished the silver pocket watch hanging from the gold chain.

Scrambling to check his empty waistcoat, Gilcres cursed again. "Don't you dare, half-casting. I just had it replaced."

"Could use a winding." Jay twirled the watch and flung it into the adjacent jail cell. With the crack of breaking glass, it hit the far wall and slid to the floor.

Gilcres' eyes followed it and Jay pounced. He placed a wicked kick squarely into Gilcres' ample middle but met solid muscle under the flab. Gilcres absorbed the blow and landed a jab on Jay's cheek, sending Jay reeling back. He kept his footing and remained upright, blood dripping down his face.

Gilcres shifted to the side, forcing Jay to circle with him. "I took your horse, ya know. He's finally learned how to carry me right." Gilcres sneered. "Only took a few whippings to get it into his head."

Jay concentrated on Gilcres' movement, trying to focus. He'd learned how to hold his own against Kahela, who had more skill and grace. He had to do something new against a larger, denser opponent.

"You're not getting out of here," Gilcres growled.

"We'll see about that."

"I'm gonna make sure you hang, you stupid half-casting." Gilcres charged with a swing meant to knock Jay on the side of the head and finish the fight. Jay ducked under it and then grabbed Gilcres by the armpit and elbow, sending him crashing into the bars. Gilcres cursed and spun around with a grunt.

Gilcres lumbered toward Jay, both arms spread wide. Jay bobbed down and Gilcres crouched, expecting Jay to duck under again. Instead, Jay sprang high, split-legged, and caught Gilcres behind the ears. He vaulted himself over the big man, shoving his head toward the floor in a Talistavvi wrestling move.

Gilcres stumbled and smashed face-first into the floor. He slid into the wall, bending his neck at an awkward angle. Bloody and roaring, Gilcres rose to his feet. Jay had time to deliver two jabs to the face before Gilcres could block the third punch and throw one of his own.

It cracked hard into Jay's already bloody cheek and sent him reeling back. He tripped and flopped onto his back, striking his head on the floorboards. Jay's vision blurred.

Gilcres staggered toward Jay and raised his elbow to hammer Jay with his body weight. Jay recovered his focus in time to roll and sweep Gilcres' legs with a kick. Gilcres crashed down onto the floor, missing Jay.

Jay rose and smashed an elbow into the back of Gilcres' head. The big man screamed and flopped an arm out to grab Jay. Gilcres' iron grip clamped down on Jay's ankle, giving it a wicked twist. Jay ignored the searing pain and hit him with his elbow again and a third time, finally knocking him cold.

Pulling himself free from Gilcres' grip, Jay took a minute to catch his breath. His head rang with the heavy throbbing of his bruises. His knee and ankle throbbed. But he didn't have time to nurse any wounds. Fauden would be back soon.

Jay stood at the side of the jailhouse window and peered out into the street. He spied only a few Galathians milling about, and the stable sat directly across the road. Jay needed a ride out of this town.

Jay pulled the red captain's coat off Gilcres and draped it over his shoulders. It fit over him like a tent. He wiped the blood off his face onto the inside of the lapel and retrieved the hat, jamming it down to cover his face. A poor disguise, but it only had to last for a few moments while he escaped.

As he grabbed Gilcres' saber, Jay searched for other weapons. All Gilcres had was the one pistol and there wasn't time to retrieve it from the other jail cell. He grabbed the jail keys and threw them into the adjacent cell. They landed beside the busted pocket watch. He stepped out of his cell and kicked the barred doors shut.

Jay stepped out of the jailhouse and onto the boardwalk. A column of Galathian foot soldiers marched past. The lead officer gave Jay a salute. Jay returned it, but the officer paid no attention. Jay thanked the goddess for the mindless routine of the Galathian military.

No one else seemed to notice him. Jay quickly surveyed the dusty main street. A row of meager storefronts with weathered trim and chipped paint matched those on his side of the road. A sign hanging from a rusty chain announced a saloon and next to it a general store, followed by a barber shop. Now that he wasn't flopped over Lunt's shoulder, he recognized Thurbush, the Frontier town on the far side of the Kettlebone Pass from the Outer Gate.

Jay ground his teeth. Nackers and Lunt had taken him a fair amount in the direction away from Aeterna. If he got out of here, he had a long trek ahead.

A flash of silver drew his eye to the clockwork crow perched on the roof of the stable. If the crow was here, perhaps magic was on his side. He boldly stepped into the street and walked deliberately toward the stable. As he reached the stable doors, the crow hopped off its perch and flew away. Once inside, he closed the doors behind him. No one had followed him, and no one had discovered his absence from the jail. He dashed down the aisle between the stalls to see what mounts were available.

"Stop right there." A harsh voice hissed behind him. Jay felt a cold blade press against the back of his neck. "Drop the sword."

"Easy now." Jay calmly let the sword fall.

"Jay?" The blade withdrew.

Jay turned to find Jortica staring at him in disbelief. "Jortica!"

"You're alive!" She grabbed him and pulled him close in a

fierce hug. He hugged her back, but just as quickly, she jerked back again. "What happened to your face?"

Jay shrugged. "Brawling with Gilcres again."

Jortica smiled. "He deserves it. What are you doing here?"

"Trying to escape. They had me a minute ago. What are *you* doing here?" As unkempt as he had ever seen, a layer of mud caked her uniform and streaked her face. She had her hair tied back with a rough bit of twine.

"Stealing a horse," she said.

"Me too. We don't have long before they notice my absence."

A smirk crossed her face. "Then we'd better get a fast one." She stepped aside, and in the stall behind her stood Havoc.

Chapter Thirty-One

The behavior protocols within a nano-cyber automaton are a sublime combination of AI and feminam creativity, but in the end, they remain only lines of code.

—from the journal of Sephy Alcott, Standard Galactic Year 11285

Karpathode, Day 022, Year 2017 local planetary calendar, Standard Galactic Year 13303

"What's all this?" The Galathian soldier closed on Lakqwi, the sharp edge of his sword gleaming.

Lakqwi held her stance, but the end of her spear shook. Havaqwi fired, and her arrow bounced harmlessly off the soldier's breastplate.

"Hey!" The soldier turned his sword on Havaqwi.

Lakqwi struck hard and swift. Her blade wedged into a joint in the Galathian's armor at the shoulder of his sword arm and pushed him off balance. He grunted and grabbed the shaft of the spear. She tried to pull it back, but his grip held. With a growl of rage, the soldier ripped the spear from Lakqwi's hands and broke the shaft. The spear point remained stuck under his pauldron.

Another arrow from Havaqwi pinged off his helmet. He swung his sword toward Lakqwi, but the spear point jammed his shoulder movement, and the strike fell short. Stepping back and nearly onto Sephy, Lakqwi unsheathed her hunting dagger, which looked like a toy compared to the Galathian's sword.

"Dammit, I don't have time for this." Sephy picked up her disrupter and fired. Luckily for the soldier, it was set on repulse instead of disrupt. The blast sent the Galathian sliding across the floor. He crashed into the far wall and slumped unconscious. Sephy set the weapon down and focused on programming.

Lakqwi and Havaqwi stared between Sephy and the crumpled soldier, his armor smoking. "You have powerful magic, Prophet Hukindi," Lakqwi said.

The disrupter beeped, and Sephy glanced at it. "Only have one more of those." She sighed. "Charge is low." The fouled transit jump must have drained it.

"Assassins!" a Galathian dignitary screamed from the entrance. He ducked out of sight. "Protect the Emperor!" More shouts and screams echoed through the chamber.

"Prophet Hukindi." Lakqwi's voice shook. "How do we escape?"

"Just need another minute." Sephy's fingers flew over the symbols floating around her.

The recoding would take far too long to do right. Sephy searched for another way. She found the source directory for the Mother role package. A growing human civilization had to be checked. Program options existed for such circumstances. Sephy shifted several key parameters to activate a personality subroutine for a new role opposing the active one. A series of commands flickered to life and Lillain changed from Mother to Destroyer. Lillain would no longer provide comfort or succor to the Galathians or anyone else. Quite the opposite, in fact. It was the best Sephy could do within the present constraints.

"Stand aside!" a voice boomed at the entrance to the goddess sanctuary. A large Galathian in resplendent robes, polished armor, and an impressively jeweled helm pushed his way into the chamber. Priests and guards jostled around him.

"Your Majesty, it isn't safe!" one priest shouted, but the emperor pushed his way past them and stood staring at the transit platform.

"Three Shinwate," the emperor said. "Surely you can handle them."

Havaqwi and Lakqwi backed up onto the transit platform on either side of Sephy, eyes wide as more soldiers and priests poured into the chamber.

"But, sire, they have killed the goddesses," a priest squeaked.

"Nonsense," the emperor said. "The Mother and Maiden are immortal."

Sephy waved a calming hand at the crowd without taking her eyes off the displays. "Don't worry," she said in Galathian. "They're not dead. I'll have them back up and running in a moment."

Everyone stared at Sephy, but she paid no attention. She had Lillain's new programming settled. Well, as best as she could do under the current deadline. She activated the reboot sequence and then paused it. The Maiden's code remained a problem. She would resist, which might interfere with the Mother's new parameters. Sephy didn't have time to crack Kamur open for an update. She had to come up with another way to control the Maiden and fast. The only way was containment. Sephy entered a few lines of code in the directory that governed Lillain's relationship with Kamur.

"Lillain! Kamur!" the emperor shouted. "Stand up!"

The emperor started forward when they didn't move, but his knights grabbed him to keep him from harm. He struggled against them, his plinum bands turning a shade pink with dismay and anger. "What have you done?"

"Keep your distance!" Lakqwi shouted in Shin, drawing up her courage. "This is the Prophet Hukindi, and she wields potent magic."

"What is this gibberish?" The emperor shook off his knights.

"She is warning you to stay back," Sephy answered over her shoulder, still punching away at her virtual keyboard.

"Who are you?"

"The Prophet Hukindi, wielder of powerful magic and all that. I'm famous in my own circles."

"This is ridiculous. I am Rafykin, Emperor of Galathia, and I will not tolerate this foolishness. Guards! Advance! Take the Shinwate prisoner. Kill them if they resist."

Twenty armored guards stepped forward and formed an intimidating line of gleaming swords and shields. They advanced toward the transit platform, stomping their feet in unison and shouting a fierce grunt with each step.

"D-12 restart sequence alpha," Sephy shouted over the din. Kamur came to life immediately and sat up. She placed a hand on her head in a human gesture conveying confusion.

Fascinating. A human interaction program upgrade she wasn't aware of, no doubt, but Sephy didn't have time to study it.

Lillain didn't move, but Sephy expected that. It would take her some time to integrate all the changes. Sephy brought up the transit portal controls and started setting a new target. She didn't have time to shield this transport from the station log, so she could only hope no one on the other side watched. It would also be a little tricky to transport just herself and her two companions while leaving the automatons behind, but it was doable. She had to get it set before the soldiers stepped onto the platform. No telling what would happen at that point.

With Sephy's command inputs, the symbols on the stones of the platform flashed with power and pulsed in sync. Lakqwi and Havaqwi knelt and held each other, knowing what would come next, both relief and dread on their faces.

"Kamur!" Rafykin shouted from behind the line of advancing soldiers. "Are you well?"

"I'm fine, Father," Kamur answered.

Sephy paused. *Father?* The D-12 code did not include human-style relationships. Again, she didn't have time to explore this anomaly, but it warranted further investigation later.

With the soldiers at the edge of the platform, Sephy initiated the transport. The platform pulsed and then froze. Error warnings flashed on Sephy's screens. "Oh, crap!"

The transit viability for the Shinwate temple had been overridden because of the lightning surge. The emperor's guards stepped onto the platform with intimidating shouts. She frantically searched for another target. Only one other transit device indicator came up for Urey. It was located far to the south.

She started to key the station as the target for transport, hoping to survive the mess she was about to unleash, when a boot kicked her onto her side. All her neural displays flickered and disappeared. Sephy rolled over and stared up at the sharp end of an enormous sword.

Chapter Thirty-Two

I named my city Aeterna because I wanted it to last forever. I wanted to draw the best minds and most skilled artisans to live in a city made for peace. I wanted it to be my final gift and resting place.

—from Chronicles of Galathia by Rafykin, Urey, circa 2640 local planetary calendar.

Frontier, Day 007, Year 2999 local planetary calendar, Standard Galactic Year 14285

Jortica felt immensely glad to see Jay. Almost as glad as Jay clearly felt upon seeing his horse. He wrapped his arms around the beast's thick neck and whispered in his ear. She understood the feeling. After she'd spent two days hiding from Galathians, she'd broken into the stable hoping to find Calamity. But no luck.

"We've got to get going." Jortica started stuffing Havoc's saddle bags with supplies. Water skins, oats, a rope, whatever looked useful. They both had swords, but no other weapons.

"Right." Jay peeked through a crack in the stable doors. "Still clear, but that won't last."

"How did you get here?" Jortica blurted out. It made no sense. She'd left him in the town where the townees stay. Maybe they nabbed him and brought him up here for the camp. But why? Seemed like a long way to drag a single lowborn.

Jay gave her a guarded look, his eyes wide. The same look she got from him at the officer's mess. "You're right. We should go."

Jortica nodded. Explanations could wait, but when they got loose, she planned on pinning him down and getting the whole story. She doubted Jay could lie straight to her face. Despite being a townee, he didn't have the disposition for it.

"I was going to wait 'til nightfall, but we can't do that now. So, what's your plan?" Jortica asked.

"Impersonating an officer got me this far. You mount behind me. We'll both fit in Gilcres' coat. Then I'll ride us out."

Jortica snickered. "How did you talk Gilcres out of his coat? Never mind. Tell me later. The plan will work if you act as pompous as you can. Gilcres is always impatient with the guards."

"Shouldn't be too hard." Jay pulled his collar up and the hat down. He peered through the stable doors again. "Time is up. Here comes Fauden. We have to go."

Jortica growled at the sound of her former captain's name. He rode around with the Legate's men as if he had always been one of them. Maybe he had. He'd sent his patrol, people who trusted him, into a trap. Jortica still couldn't believe how much she had trusted him. He'd get his. She would see to it.

Jay mounted Havoc, and Jortica climbed on behind him. She wriggled under the coat, wrapped her arms around Jay's waist, shoved her head through the collar, and brushed her cheek against his ear. The odor of male sweat and campfire filled her nostrils. Not the aroma of a typical townee. *Jay's been on an adventure.* Her own journey had been similarly lacking in basic hygiene. Her fondness for him ticked up a notch.

Jay waited for Fauden to enter the jailhouse, then pushed open the door and trotted Havoc out. He steered the big horse toward the gate and put him into a canter.

"Open the gate!" Jay bellowed in Galathian, trying to sound like Gilcres. He rode straight at them, shielding Jortica from sight.

The guards hesitated, staring as they approached.

"Follow my orders, you ignorant fools," Jay shouted as he pushed Havoc into a gallop toward them.

The soldiers saluted and pulled the metal–banded double doors open.

An alarm sounded from the middle of town, and Fauden sprinted toward the gate. "Close the gate! Prisoner is escaping." The guards stood dumbfounded, not sure what to do. Havoc's huge form thundered through the opening without breaking stride.

As they rode, Jortica heard shots firing, but they flew wide of the mark. The path curved east and up a rise, out of flintlock range. She slipped out from under the coat and checked behind them. Through the open gate burst a group of eight riders. "We've got company coming."

Jay nodded and leaned forward. Jortica pressed against his back, making herself as small as possible. Jay sent Havoc flying down the rough road at his best speed. It felt like the race for Top Cadet, except they both rode the same horse.

Jortica realized too late Jay didn't know the terrain. He stayed on the road as it went into a sweeping curve to the north. Their pursuers galloped through the trees to cut them off. Jortica tapped Jay's shoulder, pointing out the problem, and Jay steered Havoc off the road away from the Galathians.

Havoc had to dodge brambles and downed trees the soldiers already knew about. The fastest Galathian caught up with them, brandishing his saber. He howled curses as he charged Havoc from behind.

Leveraging off Jay's shoulder, Jortica pulled a leg under herself and swung around in the saddle. She drew her sword just in time to parry his first swing. His horse faltered, dropping back, but he gave his mount the spurs and rushed in for another go.

Careful not to catch Jay with a careless backswing, she took a swipe and missed. The weight of the saber nearly pulled her out of the saddle. Perched awkwardly behind Jay, it was hard to balance. The Galathian saw his chance and reared back for a deadly strike, but a passing branch fouled his arm, and it came up short. Jortica wrapped a foot around Jay's calf, and he squeezed it against Havoc's side. Then she lunged and stabbed the Galathian in the thigh. Pulling the blade back, she cut through the bridle and slashed the horse's cheek. Horse and rider both screamed and floundered into the brush.

Another rider came up just behind the first, aiming a flintlock pistol at Jortica. She couldn't dodge, so she grabbed Jay's left arm and pulled. He got the idea and yanked Havoc hard to larboard as the Galathian fired. Havoc leaped over a fallen tree and the ball went wide. The rider couldn't cut as hard, and they left him behind in the brambles.

The trail widened onto an uneven road and two riders

came up on either side. Jortica, about to cut the bridle again, recognized Calamity. She checked her swing and parried a blow instead. Jay had his sword out and swiped at the other rider to keep him at bay. Jortica turned her blade to put the flat toward Calamity and stabbed at the horseman. He dodged and pulled Calamity out of range but, overcompensating, plowed back into Havoc. Havoc stumbled and Jortica flopped forward, losing her purchase on Havoc's back.

For a terrifying moment, Jortica flailed in the air, out of control and falling. She crashed into Calamity's rider, shoving a shoulder into his midriff. Air burst from his lungs in a coughing grunt. He punched her in the back with the pommel of his sword. She twisted and slammed an elbow into his temple. He went over, nearly taking her with him, but she held on as Calamity came to a stop. Jay thundered away with more riders on his tail.

Jortica righted herself in the saddle. "Hello, lady." Calamity huffed and snorted with pleasure to see her. Jortica patted the sides of her favorite mount and, to her relief, found she wasn't hurt. Thanks to many training sessions, she'd hung on to her saber without thinking about it. She wiped it clean on her pants. "All right, let's see if we can help the poor townee."

Jortica rode through the woods in the direction she'd last seen Jay. The group wasn't hard to find, crashing through the underbrush, howling at each other, and firing ineffective flintlock shots. Jay had taken a sweeping arc, probably trying to get back to her, the sweet boy. Not the smartest tactic for a person trying to escape capture, but it gave her a great angle.

She leaped across the road, surprising the tail-end pursuer with a sword swipe across his back. He flailed, fell off the chase, and dropped from his horse. Jortica steered Calamity to a hunting trail through a shallow valley. Calamity jumped a slain Galathian lying on the trail and dodged his riderless horse. Within a few strides, she passed another horseman off to the side of the path bent double, gasping for breath, and holding closed a nasty gut wound. Jay fought pretty well for a townee.

Jortica raced over a rise and found Jay just ahead of the last two Galathians. She recognized the one closest to her. *Fauden.* Jortica bared her teeth and gave Calamity her heel. She tore down the hill with just one target, her double-crossing captain.

The rider on Jay's tail had a spear and jabbed at Jay. The galloping horse made it awkward to wield and Jay kept knocking away the blade, but the Galathian remained out of Jay's reach. Fauden hung back, letting the fight unfold. Jay would have to deal with the spearman because Jortica rode straight for Fauden.

Fauden turned just as Jortica reached him. His eyes widened in surprise as he recognized her. She swiped at his face. He dodged the blow and answered with one of his own. His blade rang off hers. The solid hit rattled her arm up to her shoulder. She responded with a backswing, but it only had half-strength, and he dodged it without trouble.

"Jortica!" Fauden shouted. "Stand down!"

She pulled Calamity up close to his horse, faked a swing he tried to block, and gave him a savage kick in the side. He shouted with pain as his horse staggered off the trail and got tangled in the underbrush.

Jortica reined in Calamity and pulled her around. Fauden dismounted, grimacing and holding his side. Jortica slid out of her saddle and marched toward Fauden, blade in hand. Lightning struck in her mind's storm.

"Wait." Fauden held out a hand to stop her.

Jortica leaped at him, saber swinging down to kill. He caught the blade with his and turned it away, shoving her off-balance with his free hand. She fell but flowed with the momentum and rolled back onto her feet.

Fauden stood waiting for her with his hand out, as if calming a wild horse. "Lieutenant, let me explain."

"You killed them!" Jortica screamed.

"I didn't kill anyone," he pleaded. "I didn't know."

"How could you not know? You gave me the orders that led our whole squad into a trap." She shook with rage.

"I swear I didn't know that would happen. The Legate wanted all my riders in Thurbush," Fauden said. "He didn't say why. No one told me about an invasion."

"You're a liar!" Jortica leaped forward, vibrating with fury and swinging for his throat.

He parried, stepping back to give ground. "It's not a lie." Fauden effortlessly blocked her backswing. "I was livid when I heard my entire Calonaden squad was killed. I protested to the Legate himself. He nearly had me executed for treason on the spot, but he explained it to me."

Jortica charged, but he twirled and danced out of her reach.

"I don't care what that tin-striped pile of stable muck had to say." She sprang after him, itching to slice him into chunks.

He dodged and spun out of reach again. He stepped gracefully over the uneven ground, displaying his skill from years of training under Commander Kahela. A small part of Jortica's mind knew she was overmatched, but the storm drowned it out.

"He said the occupation is over. Any semblance of Calon-aden freedom is no more. He said you would fight, and my riders were the best trained and, therefore, the greatest threat to peace."

"Peace," Jortica spat as she lunged with all her strength.

Fauden slipped aside, parried, and caught her blade at an awkward angle. With a flick of his wrist, the saber sailed from her grip. Fauden stood with the tip of his blade at her chest.

She slapped it away and stepped out of reach. He let her go, but they both knew he could have ended her right then.

"Yes, peace."

Jortica scoffed as she prowled left and right, looking for an opening and seeing little chance of one without a weapon.

"As in not war," Fauden said. "Not wholesale death. Your people get to live if you submit. But he knew the Calonaden Horse Division wouldn't. He knew you would never yield. You would lead another rebellion, bring more death. He sent soldiers to capture you but was prepared to kill if necessary."

"If necessary? They killed everyone! Shot them down. There was no mercy." The horror of it cracked her throat. The bodies on the road. The people she knew. Samos, Eason, even Kessa. Serious little Kessa. The wind blowing through her mind rose to a roar.

"I heard you ordered them to fight." Fauden frowned at her with disapproval. "If you had given up, I could have kept them alive. Negotiated a deal."

His words struck home, and she stopped pacing. A vast emptiness opened just below her stomach. She'd given the order to fight. What if she hadn't? Would her friends have wanted some other fate? "You would've made sure they got locked up forever.”

“Yes, but they would be alive.”

Jortica fumed as the storm raged in her mind. It blew with a stronger force with each breath as she stared at Fauden. The chasm under her stirred with its own motion, similar but separate from the storm. Fauden stood calm and waiting, unafraid of anything she could muster. She thought of Eason, Kessa, and Samos. Would they rather be rotting in a prison camp instead of in the ground? Jortica stood frozen between the storm of her rage and the pit of her guilt.

With a crashing of underbrush, Jay and Havoc burst into the clearing. He had a fresh cut across his scalp and blood slowly dripped off his brow, but no one pursued him. He directed Havoc between the two of them and stared down at Fauden, bloody saber tight in his fist. “Captain Fauden. You’re having a rough day.”

Fauden shifted to put some distance between himself and the big horse, but he kept his gaze squarely on her. “Look, Jortica, this is your chance. If you help me bring in Jay, the Legate will let you serve in the Galathian Horse Division. Vassal nations of Galathia provide soldiers and even officers for our armies.”

Jay looked between them, waiting for her answer.

Jortica chose the storm and let the rage break her hesitation. “How can you even ask? Years of training with Kahela and you learned nothing about Calonade.”

“You were the best of my crew. You can have a future.” Fauden glanced toward Jay.

The storm abated a bit as a new question formed. “Why Jay? What is so special about him?”

Jay’s eyes widened with a familiar look of panic. He pulled

on Havoc's reins to get within striking distance of Fauden.

"Stop, Jay!" She held up her hand. Havoc shifted but stayed in place as Jay chewed his lip but didn't interrupt.

"I don't know," Fauden said. "I truly don't, but the reward on his head is substantial. He's not just any half-casting. The Legate is obsessed. He's your ticket to a new life."

"What's in it for you?" Jay asked.

An astute question. The storm paused for an answer.

"Trust," Fauden said. "I prove I'm not a soldier gone native."

"You trained under Commander Kahela. You were one of her best," Jortica said.

"Yes, I'm proud of that and I admire her, but it doesn't matter. Galathia is here. The empire cannot be stopped. You can kill a squad of horsemen. Kill me. Plenty more will come. There's always more. You may win a battle, but Galathia will never be defeated. Please, Jortica, stand with the winners."

Before Jortica could answer, a Galathian war horn echoed through the wood. Another search party, probably dozens strong, had set out from Thurbush.

"We have to go," Jay said.

"Not until I kill this murderer." Jortica stepped toward him.

Fauden stopped her with his blade. "I don't want to, but I'll kill you and then take him."

Jay took his turn to scoff while lifting his bloody saber. "Unlikely, Captain."

"Maybe." Fauden glanced between them. "But you'll watch her die for sure."

Jay's brow furrowed, concern for her all over his face. Again, very sweet, but not useful. She thought about stepping back and letting Jay try him, but she wanted Fauden for herself.

The horns blew again, closing in from Thurbush. Another horn answered from the other side. Jortica took a breath. The storm would have to wait. She strode to the edge of the clearing and retrieved her sword. She marched to Calamity and swung into the saddle.

"There will be another time, Fauden, and you will answer for what you've done." She reined her horse around and led Jay away from the clearing, deep into the Frontier.

* * *

They rode for a long while. Jortica didn't keep track of the time or even their route. She just pushed deeper into the forest, away from any Frontier towns or settlements. As the sun reached tree level, Jay called for a halt.

They dismounted, and Jay offered her a leather skin of water. "You know where you're going?"

"No, just away from that." She waved behind them. The storm still blew through her mind, not blocking out everything yet, but lingering in the background.

"That was intense with Fauden back there," Jay said.

"I wanted to kill him. But it would have taken too long. We'd have been captured and hanged on the spot. Is what he said true? Are the Galathians taking over Calonade?"

"They have," Jay said. "Queen Izell got away, but Legate Armone and Governor Lord Kendric are in charge now."

Jortica clenched her fists. It was wrong, so wrong. She knew the Calonadens wouldn't cooperate. The Galathians would use force, and that meant blood. Would they kill her friends? Would they hurt her father or her sister? "We have to do something, Jay. Wait, did you say *Queen* Izell?"

"Yes, she declared herself queen before she left. Her plan was to rendezvous with Admiral Filcor at sea."

"She's going to fight?"

"Yes."

Maybe there is hope. The fisherfolk like her father would definitely help. Still, something wasn't right. Jay was still a mystery. Jortica peered into his face. "How do you know all this?"

Jay winced. "Um, I'm a messenger in the castle. They tell us things."

His face twitched as he said it. He was lying. The storm rose to a gale. "Don't lie to me, Jay."

Jay sighed and dropped his head. "I'm sorry, Kaloby, but I need an ally." He said the last part more to himself. He reached out and placed his hands on her shoulders. "I'm not a normal castle messenger. I work directly for Queen Izell, and she has sent me on a mission in the Frontier."

At Jay's touch, the storm in her mind fell quiet. Jortica relaxed into the stillness, and her whole body tingled with relief. That had not happened in a long time. Since she stood over her mother's grave, the storm had always been with her, even if far in the background of her mind. In this moment, though, it was gone.

"What's the mission?" she asked in a quiet voice, hoping she wouldn't disturb the calm by speaking.

"I'm to travel to Aeterna and find Queen Izell's hidden heir. Protect him and bring him back to Calonade when the time is right." Jay looked relieved, as if the secret had been burning a hole in his soul. The silence in Jortica's mind deepened and spread. He smiled and took his hands away. Jortica immediately missed his touch, but the storm remained quiet even without it. She smiled back at him, and she kissed him.

It happened before she even thought about it. She pulled him close and kissed him, not even knowing why. Her blank mind suddenly filled with him. The taste of his lips and the salty smell of his sweat. She pushed her body against his, feeling his rough tongue against hers. The kiss took him by surprise, too, but after an initial moment of shock he returned it with an equal passion. She felt his desire—craving the impossible and then getting a slice. She felt it down to her knees. Just as suddenly, she remembered where she was and who she was with. She pulled back, turned on her heel, and stalked away.

"Jortica?"

"Damn it! Just—" She held up a hand over her shoulder to stop him. "Give me a minute."

Why did I do that?

The stillness in her mind lingered, but her heart thundered. She had kissed some boys back home, but this one kissed like a man. Not that she knew the difference, but that had to be it. *But he's a townee.* The most she should ever feel toward him would be respect if he earned it. Had he earned it? He fought well. He had her back. They were in this together, at least for now.

"Sorry." He sounded crestfallen.

"Not your fault." She still couldn't face him. "That was my bad idea."

He waited, probably wondering what in the name of the goddess was going on. Jortica didn't blame him because she didn't know either. And there wasn't time to figure it out. One thing was certain. Getting fresh with a fellow soldier never worked out well. When she turned toward him, she had become professional once again.

"The queen has an heir. That news could shift the tide of the war. We've got to get you to Aeterna."

To his credit, Jay rolled with it. "Right, that's why I stopped you. You're heading north, and I need to go east."

The Galathian horns sounded again. At least they weren't surrounded anymore, but the Galathians would keep coming. "They are persistent. Do you know where the mythical city of Aeterna is located?"

"Yes," Jay said with a shrug. "You want to come along?"

"No," Jortica answered on instinct and then a plan formed in her head. "You need a decoy to draw everyone off your trail. Those hefty rewards will have everyone looking for you. Let's give them a target. Give me your coat."

"This one?" He took off the captain's coat.

"Yes, Gilcres' coat. And we'll need to trade horses."

Jay froze halfway out of the coat. "What do you mean?"

"Our pursuers are after you, not me. If they see someone riding around on your big war horse wearing Gilcres' coat, they are going to think it's you. Meanwhile, you'll head east on Calamity and get to Aeterna without any trouble."

It took a moment, but Jay gave in. "It's a good plan. Kaloby would like it."

"Wait, Minister Kaloby?"

"Yeah, he's the one who trained me to be a spy." Jay shrugged.

"The Minister of Science taught you to be a spy?"

"And Commander Kahela taught me to fight." Jay ducked

his head and looked at her under his brows.

Jortica crossed her arms and peered at Jay with growing respect. "You are full of surprises." She could tell he spoke the truth. The poor townee couldn't lie, which was odd because most could lie so well. The combat training explained a lot, but how was he ever to be a proper spy? Kaloby had his work cut out for him if they all made it out of this mess. "Alright, let's do this."

They split their supplies and rode in opposite directions. Jortica didn't look back as she rode Jay's enormous horse into the brambles. She remembered Jay's crestfallen face and hoped he didn't linger either.

Chapter Thirty-Three

The nano-cyber automaton isn't considered an android because it's not designed to try to become human. It acts on a specific set of instructions to fool humans. It's built far superior to that antiquated species.

—from the journal of Sephy Alcott, Standard Galactic Year 11285

Karpathode, Day 022, Year 2017 local planetary calendar, Standard Galactic Year 13303

Lakqwi and Havaqwi huddled in the corner of the dungeon cell. Havaqwi cried softly, her head buried in Lakqwi's lap. The Shinwate hunter tried to comfort her daughter, but with tears trickling down her own cheeks, she didn't seem in much better shape.

Sephy counted the stones on the opposite wall for the tenth time. Big blocks with heavy mortar in between. A stout barrier, for sure. The ceiling dripped with a thin slime that pooled in a corner. Two lovely stone slabs and a piss bucket made up the furnishings. She'd seen a few brigs in her time, but this one won the prize for perfecting the archetype.

Sephy and her friends had been dragged, none too gently, from the sanctuary and into a holding cell built into the mountain. It made Sephy curious about the reason for building a jail in the cathedral, but the possibilities, such as virgin sacrifice, weren't pleasant to explore. Humans and their weird obsessions.

Sephy sighed and tried to relax into the truth. They were stuck for a while. She still had her neural connection to the transit portal but didn't feel desperate enough to call them for help. Not yet. Accessing the D–12s through the station was possible, but doing so would definitely give her away topside.

While attempting to create a back door into Lillain's core program, Sephy had been rushed and may have screwed it up. Or the Mother Goddess might still be integrating her new subroutines. It had been an extensive and sloppy overhaul. Or perhaps she was out of range. Sephy's local neurals only had so much signal strength. There had been no response on that channel.

The one thing she had was the transit map and the lone remaining on-planet location indicator. There wasn't any record of it in her files for Urey. It could only be an unauthorized transit device. If she could get to it, then she could get home without alerting anyone of her stay here. However, it rested in a group of islands far to the south.

A clang and rattle of the dungeon door interrupted Sephy's thoughts. Finally, a visitor. Lakqwi and Havaqwi shrank lower onto the bed slab, expecting the worst. Sephy assumed this would be a meeting to negotiate her freedom, and she pasted on her sales face.

"I don't think it's a good idea, sire." A gruff voice spoke in

Galathian just outside the door. "We don't know what magic they have."

"Listen, Sergeant," the Emperor of Galathia said. "You're about what? Fifty years old."

"Fifty-five, sire."

"I'm coming up on ninety-eight," Rafykin said. "I know you think you've seen it all, but I really have. Don't worry. This will not be an issue unless *you* make it one."

"Yes, sire, if you say so. Call out if you need me."

The door opened wide and Emperor Rafykin, in all his splendor, stepped into the room. He was a large human, looked about mid-thirties, with a beard, a barrel chest, and matching belly to round it out. He'd changed out of the ceremonial emperor's garb from earlier and wore a simple shirt, tunic, and trousers combination, though made of fine material. The ensemble blended well with the perfectly even pale and dark blue vertical stripes on his skin. With the short cropped blond hair and deep blue eyes, he would make a high value SHA after the customary reconditioning, but this wasn't the time to consider that sort of commerce.

He stepped in, and Sephy stood to greet him. "Good day, Your Excellency. I'm glad you came. Shall we have a chat?" Sephy indicated the slab across from hers. Lakqwi and Havaqwi huddled in the far corner, giving them plenty of room.

"Thank you, Prophet Hukindi, if that is your real name." Rafykin took a seat.

Sephy sat across from him, one hand in her lap and the other behind her hip in her best I-am-more-relaxed-than-you posture. The truth, however, is that her pulse had just increased. Rafykin had learned something beyond the narrative somehow. Leaked by one of the automatons, most likely. "It's not, Your Majesty. My real name is Sephy Alcott. Have you perhaps heard of me?" Sephy probed to find out the extent of his knowledge beyond Urey.

"No, I cannot claim I know that name. However, I am aware you are from the Underworld," Rafykin said. "What do you say to that?"

Sephy stopped herself from breathing a sigh of relief. He didn't know all that much then. She strained her face to look like she'd been caught. "I'm shocked you would say that, Your Honor. As you can see, I'm no ghost." Sephy assumed the Underworld had something to do with the ultimate destination of the dead, a typical trope.

"I can see you are real. My wife Lillain is also real and so is our daughter. Their origins are the Underworld, and they are the only ones who could use the Well of Ages, until you came."

Sephy had to keep from choking. The automaton-human family anomaly took on a whole extra dimension. At least one of the automatons, and likely both, were corrupt. A dangerous sign. When Sephy got back to the station, she would have to explore this unfortunate outcome. If she got back. Her next destination depended heavily on this interaction, and Sephy felt the familiar thrill.

"What you say is true, Your Worthiness." *Why lie when he's got a lie of his own?* Sephy just needed to exploit it for her own gain. "I am able to use the Well of Ages."

"How do you use it?"

Sephy could tell she had his interest. She just had to make his intent match her own. "I have magic. It's why these Shinwate villagers think I'm a prophet." She waved a hand at

Lakqwi and Havaqwi, who cowered in the corner. They kept their eyes lowered and heads down, oblivious to the content of the conversation.

"What can you do with the Well of Ages?" Rafykin leaned in, concentrating his entire attention on Sephy.

What does an emperor want that the goddesses won't give him? A toy perhaps. "That depends on what you want me to do with it, sire."

Rafykin leaned back, considering Sephy. He tapped a contemplative finger on his chin. They both waited, each daring the other to flinch. The moment stretched long enough for Sephy to wonder if Rafykin enjoyed the thrill of lives hanging in the balance like she did.

He laughed. "A mistake is easy to make in a situation like this. I don't blame you for trying to make one happen in your favor."

Sephy's insides froze, but she kept her sales face intact. "Excuse me, sire?"

"The mistake is yours," he said, still smiling. "You assumed I don't have full control over the Well of Ages and think you can offer me something beyond what I already have. You presume to believe my wife can hold something back from me because she is divine, and I am a mere mortal. She may remain asleep under your spell, but I can activate the power myself."

"No, sire." Sephy rolled the dice one last time. "I simply think you don't know the full capability of the Well of Ages."

"Nonsense!" Rafykin stood, jabbing his finger down at Sephy. "I know all about it. It is my tool for domination of life and the afterlife. I am almost one hundred years old and will live as long as I desire. You have no leverage over me." He stopped shouting and laughed again. "A band of Shinwate trying to swindle me! I have to admit, it's been an entertaining day. The last act of your little theater will be the three of you hanging on my mantel by dinnertime."

Sephy's mouth dropped open at the magnitude of her miscalculation. "Uh, wait, sire. I—" She couldn't think of anything to say.

Rafykin dismissed her with a wave and stepped to the door, but as he reached for the handle, the door swung open on its own. A bright rosy light filled the dungeon and Rafykin took a step back with a shocked expression on his face. "Lillain, what are you doing here? I mean," he stammered, "I'm glad you're up and about. You seem much better now."

The Mother Goddess of Urey stepped into the dungeon cell, forcing Rafykin, Emperor of Galathia, to take a step back into some muck. "Hello, Rafykin. I do feel better. I have come to meet the Prophet Hukindi and set her free."

Sephy stared back and forth between them both.

"What? No, dearest of them all, you must not," Rafykin pleaded. "These Shinwate tricksters are simply trying to manipulate us. Their use of the Well was likely an illusion."

"It was not an illusion." Lillain spoke in a serene voice. "This one has the power to use the Well of Ages." She swept a hand toward Sephy in a regal gesture. "And her companions bravely protected her. They are on a divine mission and must be allowed to continue. We shall set them free and send them on their way."

"What about their crimes? They accosted you and Kamur. They hurt one of my guards."

"They are pardoned of any crimes as of now." Lillain used her most regal tone. It even echoed a bit in the dank dungeon.

"All of their possessions shall be returned, and they shall have passage to any part of the empire or beyond as they so choose."

Lillain turned and glided out of the prison cell.

"Wait! Wait," Rafykin called as he stumbled after her. "Please reconsider."

"I have decided," Lillain said, and they were gone.

As Lillain moved out of range, Sephy closed her neural feed and allowed the set of symbols floating near her hidden hand to dissipate into mist. With the hand behind her back, she had set a simple program in motion. Only a few lines of code and it worked. The thrill dissipated to relief. "That was a close one," she said in Shin with a wink at Lakqwi and Havaqwi.

"Are we free?" Hope dawned on Lakqwi's face. Havaqwi peeked out from her mother's bosom, wiping away tears.

"We can continue on our mission," Sephy said. "Our possessions will be returned along with some traveling money. A ship waits for us at the dock. We sail south at the next tide."

Chapter Thirty-Four

I outlived Aeterna. Peace, it turns out, is not popular. The city lost its use once wars began again, and the people slowly abandoned it.

—from Chronicles of Galathia by Rafykin, Urey, circa 2640 local planetary calendar.

Aeterna, Day 010, Year 2999 local planetary calendar, Standard Galactic Year 14285

The bark on the tree next to Jay exploded. The boom of the long rifle followed shortly after. Jay cursed and swung Calamity off the trail and into the cover of heavy brush, pushing Jortica's horse ever eastward. How far he had to go he didn't know. Fauden still had his trail. With only a sword in hand for a weapon, Jay had no choice but to run.

Three days of cat-and-mouse with the Galathian Horse Division officer had taken a toll. Calamity breathed harshly, and Jay felt weary to his bones. Fauden had pressed them mercilessly. Jay dismounted and led Calamity up a slope to reach the top of a ridge. He skirted over the peak and stopped on the opposite side to peer into the valley behind. Fauden pushed his shaggy mountain horse through the underbrush, following the signs Jay had left behind. Fauden slowly gained, but no other Galathians kept up the chase. As Jay watched, Fauden looked up and spotted him. Jay felt too tired to duck away.

"Jay!" Fauden shouted, his voice echoing through the valley. "I know it's you on Jortica's horse. Your ruse didn't fool anyone."

Jay smiled. If that were true, Fauden would have a lot more help. Jay could tell he and Jortica had outfoxed all the Galathians except for this one. Jay turned and glimpsed flowing water in the valley ahead. The Talindrey River wound through a bend and meandered northwest. Hope rose in Jay's chest. Finally!

"We're almost there, girl," Jay muttered to Calamity. The horse dipped her head down and back up, eager for a drink of water. Jay mounted Calamity and pointed her down the slope. "We have to get across the water before Fauden gets to this spot or we're sitting ducks."

Calamity whinnied and stamped a forefoot. Jay touched her flank with his heel, and she leaped forward, pitching down the slope. They rode hard down the rocky ridge, Calamity picking her footing with rapid precision. More agile than Havoc, she sprinted down the slope at full speed. Jay leaned as far back in the saddle as he could to help with balance. Every footfall held and they made it into the clearing at a full gallop. The riverbank rushed up, and Jay reined her in.

The roar of the water deafened him as it crashed down a mountainside waterfall and rushed through a gorge, marking the boundary between the Kelstone and the Wrayan Mountains. Crossing through this current would be impossible, even if he had Havoc to carry him over. Calamity, even fresh, didn't have a chance. On the far side, he couldn't see a path, any sign of a city, or anything else besides the dense trees and underbrush.

The sand erupted nearby. Fauden sat atop the ridge behind them, reloading his flintlock long gun. The sound of the water had drowned out the report of the rifle. Jay saw little choice, but he didn't have to risk Calamity. He dismounted and stood at the water's edge, knowing the current would sweep him far downstream and perhaps beyond the way into Aeterna.

Just as he prepared to jump into the river, a silver streak wheeled overhead. The clockwork crow flew by Jay and landed on a nearby tree branch. The crow coughed a rusty caw loud enough to be heard over the crashing water.

Jay peered at the curious messenger. "You following me?"

Almost immediately, it leaped into the air and landed on a twisted root exposed by the water's flow further down the bank.

No, you want me to follow. Jay mounted and moved Calamity toward the crow's perch. The bird took flight and led them northward, following the current.

A rifle shot sang as it bounced off the rocks along the water's edge. Jay spurred Calamity to a canter. Fauden, though out of range, could get lucky. As Calamity ran along the beach, Jay monitored the clockwork crow, flying ahead and leading the way.

The river opened from the narrow gorge into a sweeping curve of water, still too fast and far for Calamity to cross, but the mechanical bird soared out over the expanse. Jay brought Calamity to a halt and peered over the water. Jay could just make out an opening in the foliage directly across. A trail cut a thin path through the trees. Standing in any other spot along the riverbank, it could not be detected. "This must be the place, Calamity, but how do we get across?"

As if in answer, a platform floated up from the shallows. It seemed to be made of stone, but rested on the surface of the water, just like a ferry barge. It was the right size for horse and rider.

Has to be Myra's magic. Jay dismounted and stepped onto the platform. It held firm, so he brought Calamity onboard. The craft floated across the river. Jay leaned over the prow and found a thick and rusty chain below the surface. It pulled them along, using some unseen mechanism on the far side. Jay wondered about the age of the device he had trusted, but it seemed better than waiting for Fauden to catch up.

When they reached the halfway point, Fauden appeared on the riverbank in the same spot the boat had docked.

"Jay!" Fauden's voice echoed over the water. "Stop!"

"You know I'm not going to."

Fauden aimed his rifle again. It was another long-range shot of the kind he'd struggled with all along, but Jay stepped in front of Calamity just in case. Couldn't let Jortica's horse get hurt. She'd never forgive him.

Fauden lowered the long gun without shooting. "She won't last long." He shouted over the water. "Gilcres will capture her, and I won't be able to protect her. You can prevent that if you come back as my prisoner."

"You're a fool if you think Jortica needs protection." Jay felt a twinge of guilt. She was taking a tremendous risk for him.

"Please, Jay. What can you do out here?"

"I have my orders," Jay answered.

"From a deposed and defeated queen? Come on," Fauden pleaded. "See reason."

The barge bumped to a halt, and Jay led Calamity onto dry ground. "I can only do what I think is right, Captain Fauden. What about you?"

Fauden dropped his head, and Jay thought he might turn away to go home. Instead, he plunged his horse into the water and swam hard, angled into the current. The mountain horse made good progress until roughly the center of the flow. The water surged and swept Fauden and his mount farther and farther downstream until Jay could no longer see them.

Jay admired the man's persistence and commitment. It was too bad he was on the wrong side of this war.

Jay led Calamity over a thin trail while following the clockwork crow as it flew from branch to branch of the dense surrounding wood. Though bone weary, Jay didn't feel he could stop moving until he found the mythical city.

The slow pace allowed Jay to think for the first time in days. The feeling of Jortica's kiss still lingered on his lips. It had happened so fast he barely had time to respond. Then she'd been angry and called it a bad idea. Jay hoped it wasn't the usual reason people thought of him as a bad idea. He didn't mind being hated by the Galathians. It hurt when Calonadens dismissed him because of his mixed origins.

Kaloby liked him, Commander Kahela respected him, Queen Izell trusted him. They were powerful allies. Gran had always been in his corner. General Saben, of all people, had stood up for him. Most of the population might shun him, but the people who counted didn't care.

A heavy regret lingered at the thought of his old headmaster. Saben had been caught in a trap meant for Jay. Clem likely slit the old man's throat. Only weeks ago, Jay would never have longed for the presence of the notorious headmaster, but now he wanted nothing more. The best thing to do, as Saben would advise, was to keep doing his duty, so Jay pushed on.

Jay's thoughts wandered back to Jortica as he followed the meandering trial. She'd kissed him hard. No dainty kiss from her. Jay doubted anything about her would be delicate or halfway done. He couldn't puzzle out why she'd pounced on him and then stalked away. He shook his head. Despite the confusion, he'd like another chance at it.

The path opened to an overlook of a valley. Below, the ruins of a city pushed up through the trees and vines. It seemed a stout wall with several watchtowers along its circular length had once protected it, but the fortifications had not kept the forest at bay. Several of what must have been impressive structures within the walls had collapsed and clumps of trees grew in the rubble. A dry canal and cracked roads left hints of the city's orderly design. Silence and desolation spread in equal measure across the valley.

Aeterna. Long ago, the mythical stronghold must have been a prosperous place, positioned at the foot of both the Wrayans and Kelstones with the Talindrey as a thoroughfare to the rest of the Frontier and eventually the sea. What had brought this ruin? Only signs of great age and its utter abandonment betrayed any trouble.

The clockwork crow soared over the valley and circled downward, calling out a few times. Only the echo of its rusty voice disturbed the valley below.

A switchback path of carved stone steps, some of which had been turned askew or washed away, was the only way down. Jay hitched Calamity to a sturdy tree with plenty of grass within reach.

He descended until he reached the valley floor and the remnants of a brick road. Though covered by moss or torn up by trees, Jay could see it had once been a major thoroughfare leading into the city. The undergrowth grew thickly at the edges of the road, and the tree canopy above blocked out the sun, leaving what seemed like a tunnel through the forest.

Jay followed the road to the city wall and its arching gate. A thick stand of growth that seemed impenetrable filled the entryway. In fact, every gap in the stone wall had been filled with some vegetation to make it an impassable barrier.

An impressive statue of a fifteen-foot-tall man wearing plate armor, holding a huge stone greatsword, stood on one side of the gate. The tip of the sword rested between the statue's feet and the blade was tarnished with age, but still sharp. The visor of his helm opened to reveal a set jaw and a glare for anyone who dared approach.

The clockwork crow soared into view and landed on the shoulder of the statue. The bird fluffed its metal feathers and peered at Jay with one of its shining eyes.

Jay, now leery of statues, approached it carefully. No snoring came from it. No sounds at all. It must truly be a statue. He noticed an antiquated Galathian script etched into the sculpture's base. Jay cleared away the obscuring vines. Kaloby had taught him some Old Galathian. He couldn't make out all of it, but the overall meaning was apparent.

The crow hopped off the statue and glided down to the ground to land near Jay's feet. It cocked its head toward the inscription.

"You want me to read it?" Jay asked.

The crow bobbed its head.

"It says something like, *Traveler, beware. To enter the*—I'm assuming that word is *mystical* or might be *magical*—*city, you must obey the law with heart and mind. Knowing yourself and speaking the truth are the keys to this gate. Forsake any heart shadow*, which I think means lying, *and speak your true name or suffer the wrath of Lord Kriton, Guardian of Aeterna.*"

Jay recognized the statue as a figure in the relief sculptures of King Kormash's hall. Jay wondered if Lord Kriton was friend or foe to King Kormash.

"The Guardian of Aeterna." Jay considered the statue. "Myra said she cleared the way, so if I speak my name, the door opens."

The clockwork crow answered with a sharp squawk.

"All right, keep your feathers on." Jay stood before the entrance and said in a clear voice, "I am Jay of Castle Calonade, Lieutenant of Queen Izell's Guard and her personal messenger."

Like a strike of thunder, a giant greatsword smashed into the ground in front of Jay. He jumped back to see the huge warrior had leaped off his base and planted the sword in his path. His fierce eyes glared down upon him.

"You lie!" the statue shouted.

Jay stumbled backward. He grasped for his saber as he backpedaled into a tree trunk. "What in the name of the goddess?"

The giant lifted his sword and swung it around in a fluid motion, stopping the tip inches from Jay's heart. "You will not lie to me and live!"

Panic gripped Jay, but he controlled it. This creature wasn't like the stone giants or the Oracle's half-machine companion.

He seemed suddenly made of flesh. His face reflected every emotion a man might have. Kriton appeared indignant and angry, but his eyes were watchful.

The Oracle had cleared the way, hadn't she? This must be a test. *All I need to do is figure out the riddle.* "Who are you?" A question for a question. A good tactic to stall for time.

"I am Lord Kriton, Guardian of Aeterna, the eternal city, and will suffer no liar to enter. Now, tell me the truth. Who are *you*?"

The truth would get him killed for sure. "Wait, I've heard of you. King Kormash mentioned your name."

"Kormash!" Lord Kriton sounded enraged, but he withdrew the sword. "I can see that you tell the truth about my old enemy. So Kormash lives."

"Yes, he has a lovely kingdom under the mountains." Jay wasn't sure if this was helping, but the sword no longer pointed at him, which he took as a good sign.

"Kormash is a coward," Lord Kriton growled. "He never could stand against me in battle. Always maneuvering away from a fight."

"He seemed to have a high opinion of you. He mentioned learning the importance of training from your example."

"Did he?" Lord Kriton peered into the distance, vaguely toward the Kelstones. "Perhaps he was paying some attention while I defeated every other army that dared march into the realm of my liege. Kormash is the only one to escape my grasp." The giant leaned casually on his sword and rubbed his chin. "Perhaps revenge is at hand. If I could raise an army, then I could...No." He shook his head. "That was long ago. I have a new assignment." He turned back to Jay.

He had already leaped forward. Jay ran straight at the

giant's foot, brandishing his saber. Lord Kriton roared and jumped away, swinging wildly with his sword. This set him off balance and stumbling. Jay rushed past him and made it to the gate. With all his might, he chopped into the vines blocking the way. A layer fell. He chopped again, and a second layer fell, but many more waited.

Lord Kriton regained his balance and charged the gate. Jay leaped aside as the giant's sword swung down upon the vines. It crashed through at least twenty layers but still didn't fully penetrate the barrier. The sword stuck fast between two thick roots, and Kriton struggled to free the blade.

Giving up on the gate, Jay scrambled to the side and climbed a tree growing against the wall, hoping to get over the barrier before the giant could regain his weapon.

With a mighty heave, Kriton pulled the sword free. He spun around and slashed the tree just under Jay's feet. The tree splintered and fell, and Jay fell with it. At the last moment, he pushed away from the falling timber and sprawled on the road in front of the gate.

Towering over him, Lord Kriton raised his sword. Jay rolled. Bricks erupted from the walkway where the giant sword smashed down. Jay scrambled to his feet and dashed along the path away from the city entrance. The magic must have a boundary. Surely Lord Kriton wouldn't chase him all the way through the Frontier.

The greatsword flew past his head, missing by inches. Jay stumbled as the weapon smashed into the base of a gigantic oak. The tree toppled, crashing down to block the road.

Jay spun around to see Lord Kriton pull a dagger, as long as Jay's saber, from his belt. A determined grimace spread over Kriton's face. "You won't get away that easily."

"I'm not lying!" Jay shouted.

"Every liar says that!" Kriton shouted back.

Jay charged Lord Kriton. He feinted right with his blade and dodged left. Kriton blocked the feint, swaying off-balance and leaving an opening. Jay dashed under Kriton's legs and scraped his blade across one of the statue's knees. Sparks flew as the metal scraped on stone, but the sword didn't leave a mark.

Kriton howled and leaped away as if wounded. He grasped the spot on his leg, cringing. Jay stood staring as Kriton acted as if he were staunching blood, but Jay could see none. Again, Kriton roared and lunged forward. Even hurt, he moved fast. Jay blocked the strike with his sword, its metal squealing on the stone dagger until it splintered. Kriton's fist hit Jay on the shoulder and sent him sprawling.

Jay rolled and scrambled to his feet. He fought to regain the breath knocked from his lungs. His shoulder throbbed and his neck ached. The blade of his sword was gone. Kriton spun around, still favoring one leg, though no wound had appeared. Jay couldn't tell if he was pretending or if the wound was invisible. Either way, Jay's bruises were real. Another solid hit and the fight would be over.

"Are you done, boy?" Lord Kriton shouted.

Jay flung the hilt of his broken saber at Kriton's head. He surged forward behind it, stepped up on a boulder, and leaped into the air.

Lord Kriton batted the sword hilt away, exposing the back of his arm. Jay grabbed hold of Kriton's shoulder pauldron and pulled himself onto the stone giant's back. Lord Kriton spun, roaring with rage. Jay nearly lost his grip as his feet flew outward, but he arched his back and legs, pulling himself up. He landed straddled on Kriton's shoulder and flung an elbow into the giant's ear, hitting the statue with a sickening crunch of bone.

Both Jay and Lord Kriton howled in pain. Kriton dipped his shoulder, bucking Jay off like a wild horse. Jay tried to land on his feet but ended up flat on the ground.

Lord Kriton loomed over him, holding his ear with one hand and pressing his dagger onto Jay's chest with the other. Jay was pinned and disarmed. Pain lanced up from his elbow and his sword arm was numb.

"Well done," Kriton said. He checked his hand as if he expected to see blood on it from his ear. "I concede you can fight. I haven't been wounded in battle for many long centuries. As a reward, I will give you one last chance to tell the truth."

"I am Queen Izell's messenger, and I am here by her order." Jay gasped for breath.

"I care nothing for orders from any sovereign but my own," Lord Kriton growled as he poised to strike Jay's heart. "Tell me your name or die."

Chapter Thirty-Five

Humanity's expansion into the stars saved us and changed us forever. Some say we're ruined, and others claim we've evolved. I think we've done and continue to do what we have to.

  —from the journal of Sephy Alcott, Standard Galactic Year 11285

Frontier, Day 010, Year 2999 local planetary calendar, Standard Galactic Year 14285

Jortica did her best to give Havoc a brush down with Jay's well-used grooming brush. The big warhorse had gotten her out of another scrape, and they hid in a narrow gully filled with thorn bushes under a creaky wooden bridge. A vigorous creek rushed over the pebbles of a streambed, the noise of the water masking Havoc's occasional snort of disgust. His skin trembled as she pulled briars from his hide, but he kept munching on a tuft of grass. Poor fellow looked a little rough after crashing through the better part of the Frontier, leading the Galathians on an epic chase over the last few days. He needed a rest. Jortica wiped her sweat-stained brow. They both did.

She pulled off Gilcres' oversized red coat and shook the wet from it. Giving it a critical eye, she needed to make some alterations besides rolling up the sleeves. The thing draped on her like a tent. She stuffed it under her bedroll to keep from being spotted.

The rain went from sprinkle to patter. It had been misty and cold all day, and Jortica doubted anyone had the stomach for more of the chase. A makeshift shelter would be the next chore. Maybe she could risk a small fire.

The crack of breaking wood made her freeze. At the far end of the gully, she heard someone curse in Galathian. Trusting Havoc to stay put, Jortica crept through the scrub and peered through the soggy vegetation.

Below her, the gully sloped through a wash and into a clearing, like an oddly shaped bowl. Mud gathered into a sodden mess at the center where a very familiar caged wagon sat. The pockmarks of musket shot still graced its sides. None other than its infamous driver hunched at one side, shoving a thick branch under the axle.

Nackers. Jortica bared her teeth and squeezed the hilt of her saber. The storm in the back of her mind lingered just beyond her inner ear.

Hooves on the bridge brought her head around. Four Galathian horsemen crossed over where she'd tucked Havoc. She crouched deeper into the bushes as they approached along the side of the gully. The four riders, armed with swords and flintlocks, outmatched her saber and pistol with wet powder. This was definitely a trap, but she'd stumbled into it too soon for them.

Nackers kept on with his act with the wagon, pushing and cursing, trying to work it free, but making no progress.

"He really committed to this charade," one rider said in Galathian. Jortica couldn't risk a peek to see the speaker, but she could hear him just fine.

His companion spat into the gully, narrowly missing her. "He thinks the Mad Captain is the girl who escaped. Thinks he's got the right bait to bring her out."

The riders laughed and exchanged a few rude comments about lady soldiers. Jortica ignored them as she fought off a leg cramp.

"The Mad Captain is tucked into some collaborator's warm cabin, Lieutenant Dothery," another rider whined. "He ain't coming to this wet hole in the ground."

"I think you're right, Sergeant. Let's head back and see how long it takes for Nackers to figure out we left."

They all laughed again as they ambled their horses back to the road and disappeared into the mist. Jortica stretched her protesting leg. The storm in her head receded as she pushed through the brambles and into the gully. She hiked down the wash to the valley, staying out of sight from the wagon.

When the gully filled with rushing water to her shins, she climbed out onto the open field. She had no cover, but sheets of rain obscured the wagon and its occupant. Nackers flipped a hood over his head to protect against the rain and hunched against the supposedly stuck wagon. Jortica dropped all pretense of stealth as she marched through the mud toward her target.

Halfway there, Nackers saw her coming. He didn't even bother with his flintlock, drawing a dagger instead. Jortica pulled free her saber and let the rain splash off its shining blade.

"Lieutenant Jortica, nice to see you again," Nackers called

out loudly as she approached. He smiled as if they were the best of friends, but shifted his stance with a practiced grace Jortica hadn't seen from him before.

She charged him, slashing for his throat with no intent of mercy. He leaned back to dodge the blow and rocked forward with a vicious, underhanded thrust meant to gut an aggressive attacker. Jortica pivoted, and he stabbed the air beside her ribs. She swept past him and slashed with her blade but hit the side of the wagon as Nackers ducked low. The blade stuck fast in the wet wood. He tried to elbow-punch her sword arm, but missed and hit the wagon instead, howling with pain. Jortica wrenched the blade free and staggered back, dodging another slash of his dagger.

"So, you're not a weak little girl, after all." His grimace slowly changed to a pained smile as he rubbed his elbow.

"And you have no friends." Jortica shot back with a glare. "They left you to rot in the rain."

Nackers peered through the downpour, trying to make out the wooded ridge where the Galathians should have been waiting to spring the trap.

"No one is there." Water dripped from her brow as her matted hair flopped loose from its tie and drooped around her face. The rising storm in her head drowned out the deluge surrounding her. The storm that killed her mother and blinded her father felt much like this. No salt sprayed from the ocean, but her mind howled with wind.

Nackers had it right. No longer did she cower in the wreckage of her home. She'd never again be the wounded child in need of rescue. This time, a warrior faced down her enemy.

"You killed my friends!" she screamed like the thunder of

a cresting storm.

Nackers laughed. "Maybe you haven't noticed, but war comes with a lot of killing. It's just a job." He shrugged. "None of it's personal. The lucky," he tapped his chest with a fist, "become old men and the unlucky," he nodded toward her with a wide grin, "don't last very long."

She leaped at him, taking the bait. He knew she would and swung his knife to turn its blade and trap her in a close embrace for the killing blow. Her sword rang hard against the dagger hilt. Rattling up his arm, the force of it stopped his lunge short. He barely kept hold of the knife, and his eyes popped wide with surprise.

She kicked his knee, and he dropped into the mud. She slashed down with all her strength, again and again, upon the dagger Nackers held in front of his face. Jortica smashed down with power fueled by rage at every man who'd ever insulted her, belittled her, made her feel wrong or small or worthless. She hammered again and again for her friends who died too soon. Eason, Kessa, and Samos stood with her as she struck their killer with all her might. The storm raged with her, and she screamed as loudly as its terrible wind.

She lashed out at Fauden's face as it took Nackers' place. She raged against his betrayal with every part of her which had ever trusted him. As she reared up for the final blow, her father's face replaced Fauden's. She stared down at the silent disappointment in his blind eyes. She held the blade back as the storm crested, then waned.

When she straightened, her father's visage was gone. Nackers lay in the mud, bleeding from deep cuts to the neck and chest. Jortica staggered away, panting for breath and shaking. As she leaned against the wagon, the storm in her mind still roared, but the worst had passed.

A shadow moved through the pouring rain. Jortica sprang back as a gleaming ax cut through the water. It smashed into her side and cracked into the wet wood, pinning her. Dropping her saber into the mud, she tore her eyes away from the wound to see the bulky figure of Lunt lumber into view.

"The lady officer," he grunted.

Jortica stared into his soulless eyes. New wounds festered on his face and bald head. "You. Alive?" she rasped with all the air remaining in her lungs.

Lunt nodded. "Only just. Your friends were tough."

Jortica dropped her head and watched her blood seep from the wound in her side. Samos. Eason. Kessa. Her squad would not be avenged after all. The storm in her mind eased into a dull howl in the distance.

"Help me, idiot." Blood spattered from Nackers' lips as he cursed.

Lunt stepped away from Jortica and bent over his friend. "Doesn't look good, boss."

Jortica grasped the ax handle, and the storm in her mind picked up a notch.

"What kept you?" Nackers coughed.

"Rain is too thick. Didn't see the girl."

Jortica pulled the handle and worked the blade one way and another. Pain flared through her side and down her legs, but the wind in her mind suppressed it. The storm sucked air into her starving lungs.

"You had one job," Nackers wheezed, the remaining color draining away from his face.

"Sorry, boss."

The storm in Jortica's head reached a raging tempest as she pulled the ax free. Her legs fell out from under her, and she slumped into the mud beside the dirty metal of her blade. She grasped the hilt and her focus moved to her enemies.

Nackers peered into Lunt's face with unfocused eyes. "How will you subsist without me?"

Lunt cocked his head. "What is subsist?"

"Like it sounds, lad. Like it sounds." Nackers released his last rattling breath.

Lunt stared down at his friend. His hands flew up to each side of his bald head.

Jortica levered herself to standing with the help of her saber and clamped her free hand down on the wound in her side. She wobbled but remained upright. She wanted to raise her blade and kill the remaining murderer, but she didn't have the strength.

Lunt collapsed to the wet earth, leaning over Nackers. He shook his friend gently and then with more force. "Boss?"

The rain let up, changing to a spitting mist. Jortica could see the water on Lunt's face came from his own tears. "He's gone."

Lunt screwed two enormous fists into his tiny eyes. "Who will tell me what to do?"

"Stay here and rot beside him." Jortica turned and staggered away from the wagon. She didn't bother to check her back. She knew Lunt wouldn't follow.

As she slowly dragged herself up the wash, the storm receded to the back of her mind. Would she ever be free of it? It was a connection to her worst day. A manifestation of her greatest loss she could never escape. But maybe, like the storms of the sea, a power lived in her inner tempest.

Dragging her sword, she limped toward the trees where Havoc waited.

Chapter Thirty-Six

As my city slid from glory to neglect, I tasked my most loyal general to ensure no one except those of the purest heart could enter.

—from Chronicles of Galathia by Rafykin, Urey, circa 2640 local planetary calendar.

Aeterna, Day 010, Year 2999 local planetary calendar, Standard Galactic Year 14285

Jay tried to push Kriton's blade away from his chest but felt weak as a kitten. The monstrous guardian of Aeterna casually pinned his arms with the breadth of his free hand. "Tell me your name."

Saying his name would get him killed. "Myra sent me." It was all he could think of.

Kriton pulled the dagger away from Jay's chest. "You speak the truth regarding the Eldest Sister Goddess of Urey. Only my emperor holds more sway."

Jay frowned. *Eldest Sister Goddess. Myra, a Willacast goddess?* The Oracle didn't seem like a divine being. Jay didn't know what a divine being should look like. Maybe she was. What–

ever the case, it seemed best to keep Kriton talking while he figured a way out of this. "Who's your emperor?"

Kriton cocked his head at Jay and frowned. "You are clearly uneducated. The emperor I serve is the legitimate leader of the Galathian Empire and builder of Aeterna, Emperor Rafykin."

Rafykin? Who was that? "Isn't Staukard the emperor?"

"I suppose someone must keep the seat of power warm in Galathia, but Aeterna is the rightful place of the true emperor. Rafykin the Conqueror, Husband of the Mother Goddess, the Maker of the Holy City." Kriton swept his arm dramatically to show the ruins behind him.

"Wait, isn't Rafykin dead by now?" Jay recalled a story about the king who built Aeterna, but that was hundreds of years ago. The ruins proved the story authentic.

"Of course not," Kriton said. "Rafykin married Lillain, Mother Goddess of Urey. He's the begetter of the Maiden Goddess Kamur. He can't die like a normal mortal."

Jay wanted to scoff but suppressed it. The evidence of beings existing far beyond the limitation of normal mortals currently held him against the ground.

Kriton let go and stood up. He shook his dagger at Jay as he paced away and back. "We're not here to talk about me. I need to know who you really are."

"I've told you already." Jay sat up, wincing from his bruises. He hoped Kriton would keep talking while he regained his strength.

"Yes, but that was a lie." Kriton didn't shout with indignant anger this time. He folded his arms, dagger dangling from his grip, and rubbed his chin. Stone ground against stone, but Kriton didn't notice. "I'm thinking you don't know who you are. Who is your father?"

Jay ground his teeth. "The subject of ancestry is a personal matter."

"If you want to enter Aeterna, you have to know the truth about yourself and tell it to me. Who is your father?"

"Fine." Jay sighed. "My father is dead. He was a Galathian soldier named Duncan."

"That is false, but I sense your sincerity. Curious."

"I'm not lying." Jay changed his mind about the value of this conversation. Sword fighting with an insane magical statue might be better. He just needed a weapon.

"Who is your mother?" Lord Kriton asked.

Jay really hated this. "My mother is also dead. She was a servant in the Calonade castle named Olivia."

"False." Kriton's brow furrowed as he examined Jay. "You are an interesting puzzle. How did you get this far, not knowing who you really are?"

"I know who I am," Jay spat.

"Is Jay your true name?"

"Of course it is!"

"False again."

"Who I am doesn't matter!" Jay shouted. "To some, I'm a castle rat, not worth a daily meal. Others know me as a messenger, barely deserving a uniform. To many people, I'm a half-casting, malformed trash. Better to be rid of. No one has much cared about my name. However, to Queen Izell, I'm an officer sent on a mission. And I'll be damned if I let an old magical statue get in the way. So, step aside or kill me, but get on with it."

Jay held his breath, and Kriton slowly knelt and leaned in close. His face stopped inches away, but his dagger remained limp in his grasp.

"That's the truest thing you said to me." Kriton spoke in a low rumble without malice, but still dangerous. "But I wonder, Messenger, have you thought about why Queen Izell sent you to Aeterna to find her hidden heir?"

Chills ran up Jay's back. "I never said anything about a hidden heir."

"Myra prepared the way, did she not? You are in my realm where truth is the key to access. No secret is hidden from me." Kriton's rumbling voice dropped to a harsh whisper. "Why would Queen Izell entrust the welfare of her only child, the true heir to Calonade and the key to the survival of its people, to you? A lowly half-casting, as you put it."

Jay paused as thoughts of escape dropped away. He'd lost the race for Top Cadet and yet the Queen of Calonade had picked him to be her messenger. Why? Gran having influence didn't hold up to scrutiny. Even if he had won, why didn't Izell send a proven champion on this vital mission? Kahela! Why wasn't Commander Kahela facing down this overgrown Galathian knickknack?

"I don't know."

Kriton leaned back. He got to his feet and regarded Jay with a half-smiling expression. "You truly don't see it."

"See what?"

"The child of King Nados and Queen Izell would be a half-casting, would they not?"

"Yes, he's of mixed descent," Jay said, "and he'll likely be run out of town on his first day as royalty. Not that it matters. My mission is to give him a chance at a first day. What does me being mixed have to do with it?" Jay's eyes popped wide. "Wait. You think I'm the half-cast prince?!"

Kriton lifted a knowing eyebrow.

"Have you been talking to Gilcres?"

Kriton frowned. "You are the first visitor to these gates in a generation."

"Nevermind. Look, I'm too young by more than a year. King Nados was long dead before I was born. You're the one lying now."

"I never lie." Kriton grimaced and ground his teeth as if to stave off the sour taste a lie would leave in his mouth.

"Myra cleared the way for me to retrieve the half-cast prince from Aeterna. Now you're trying to distract me from doing my job."

Kriton groaned and sheathed his dagger. He crossed his arms and studied Jay with an intense curiosity. "Lies surround you, but you carry truth within. My opinion of you evolves. I feel a duty to unravel these falsehoods."

Jay played along. "What falsehoods?"

"There is only one resident of Aeterna, and he isn't the heir to Calonade."

"Then explain the message that brought me here," Jay said.

"From the silver bird?"

Myra must have told him about the crow. "Yes, it said I would find the half-cast prince in Aeterna."

"Do you still have the message?"

Jay dug the strip of paper from his waistcoat and read the scrawl. "*Aeterna. Here reclaim the half-cast prince.*"

Kriton considered the text. "Curious. Notice the use of the word *reclaim*. Not the same as *find*."

"What does that matter?" Jay snapped.

"Tell me, how do you know how old you are? You have no memory of the moment of your birth."

Jay rolled his eyes. "I had no parents, but my gran looked after me. I helped bake the pies she used to make for me for each birthday that I can remember."

"What lovely memories." Kriton's voice carried an edge of sarcasm. "It would be easy, would it not, to substitute one age for another? Adjust your history slightly, even in your own eyes, especially when you were young."

"Excuse me." Jay rose to his feet, despite the ache in his bones. "Are you calling my gran a liar?"

Kriton stared at Jay with the impatience of a teacher trying to instruct a slow student. "She is a co-conspirator."

Jay bared his teeth. "I *know* you're lying now."

Kriton rose to his feet and glowered down at Jay. "Did you not hear me? I am the guardian of truth and I never lie!" he roared.

Jay flinched but did not back down. "My gran would have told me."

"And what would have happened on that day?" Kriton sneered. "The whole scheme to keep you safe would have crumbled." Kriton pointed an accusing finger. "By your own reckless words or thoughtless acts, you would have doomed your mother, yourself, and your servant guardian to death. Your kingdom would have lost its future, and the people would have been cast into the mechanisms of the empire as grist."

"Liar!" Jay shouted, pointing at Kriton's face. "If my mother were alive…" Jay's voice cracked. "If she were alive all those years, she would have…" Jay froze. Memories surfaced of his days as a cook's boy, forced to accompany his gran on her duties. Izell hovering in the halls, just around the corner. Izell sneaking a glance under the dining table where he hid. And more recently, Izell giving him his first message to deliver. Izell confiding in him she had a son. "She would have been there for me," he finished, voice quavering.

"The truth is finally revealed." Kriton's voice dropped low, the danger gone. "Your mother has always watched over you. She couldn't be a mother in any other way. A trusted servant claimed the role."

"No." Jay's stomach clenched. "Gran is more than that. I know it."

"She loves you, but she is not your grandmother."

"No." Jay's eyes burned. It couldn't be true. His gran was all he had. His mother and father were gone. Always had been. Hadn't they?

Kriton knelt to look Jay in the face. "The complete story lives within you. Lurking, unknown until now. Her every move watched by the oppressors, your mother did what she had to do to save the kingdom. She refrained from ever touching you with the love she felt, while another acted in her stead. Izell sacrificed the most precious thing in her life to save you and her people."

Jay gasped as the invisible veil shielding him from the truth ripped away. He reeled from the sheer magnitude of the lies. His whole life was a treacherous web, but necessary to preserve a people in continuous danger. Terrible and beautiful all at once.

"Myra only sends future sovereigns to this place." Kriton spoke gently. "There is no other half-cast prince than you. Every ruler before you claimed guidance and wisdom within the gates of Aeterna. For you, it is a reclaiming. To enter, all you need to say is your true name."

Jay sagged at the words. "I don't know it."

"Jados!" came a voice from the road.

Both Jay and Kriton looked toward its source. At the edge of the clearing stood Saben. *He's alive!* Jay's jaw dropped open. *The old man came back from the dead.* More likely he'd turned Clem's knife back on the wielder. He had never been so glad to see his headmaster.

"Careful, sir." Lord Kriton's fierceness returned. "You are interrupting a sacred ritual, one that is more important to me than my life."

"I am merely here to shed light upon the truth." Saben raised his hands to show he was unarmed. "Isn't that what you want?"

"Then say the truth now. Who are you?"

"I am Saben, once of Galathia and now of Calonade."

"I remember you. The truth rings from you like a sacred bell, Saben of Calonade," Lord Kriton said. "You have been granted safe passage and not for the first time. But this one still carries a shadowed heart." He nodded toward Jay.

"It's not his fault," Saben said.

"Normally, I would block entry of a person who doesn't know their truth," Kriton said. "Such people should not enter Aeterna. But in this case, the truth has been kept hidden as protection. You may enlighten the boy."

Saben cleared his throat. "Lieutenant, your name is Jados. Your parents were kept apart by the war while the queen was pregnant with you. As the king's aide, I dictated the letters in which Nados and Izell agreed on your name."

Kriton looked down at Jay. "If you are ready to enter Aeterna, tell me your true name."

Jay looked at Saben and then back to Lord Kriton. It couldn't be true, could it? Had the queen sent him here to face Lord

Kriton's test and discover the secret? Was he the half-cast prince, hidden in plain sight? He was the one Armone hunted, after all.

If true, it was the greatest deception ever pulled on the Galathians. Queen Izell and Minister Kaloby were the masters of disguise and trickery. Only they could accomplish such a deceit. And Gran had joined them. Even though what they did was appalling, he trusted Gran, and she trusted them.

"Jados Justinkeel," Jay whispered, still not confident of the truth.

The giant warrior stepped onto his pedestal, and his greatsword floated back into place. "You may enter." With that, he became an immobile statue once more.

Chapter Thirty-Seven

We left Earth because we had to. We evolved to one gender because we had to. We exploit the SHA because we have to. We deceive and enslave entire planetary populations to survive. This, unfortunately, must be the basis of our moral code.

—from the journal of Sephy Alcott, Standard Galactic Year 11285

Aeterna, Day 010, Year 2999 local planetary calendar, Standard Galactic Year 14285

Jay chewed a piece of lanicin bark as Saben wrapped his shoulder with strips of cloth torn from his own stolen shirt. Saben had fashioned a sling for his elbow as well. Jay had been sitting on a boulder just outside the entrance to Aeterna for a few minutes, trying to take in what Lord Kriton said. The guardian stood motionless on his pedestal, but the thick tunnel of briars and thorns had parted, revealing a long passage through the gateway and into the city. Jay couldn't have hacked his way through, even with Lord Kriton's sword.

"You all right, Lieutenant?" Saben asked.

The relief of surviving a duel with a giant magical creature had faded to embarrassment. Jay had just claimed to be heir to the throne of Calonade. "Was any of that true, sir?"

"Let's get inside before Lord Kriton asks for more truth." Saben pulled Jay to his feet and led the way over the crumbled road into the abandoned city. The cobblestone street within wasn't in much better shape. The gaping openings of the crumbling buildings stared at them as if sightless. Weeds and tangled vines covered the ornate architecture. A central fountain had become a dry bowl of dust.

Saben cleared off a spot to sit on the stones of the fountain's edge. He pulled out his pipe and clamped it into his teeth.

"How did you escape from Clem?" Jay took a seat beside Saben.

"He spared me. Has a soft spot for Galathian turncoats. Told me to get lost. So, I came here looking for you." Shaking his head at the empty fountain, Saben pulled a waterskin from his belt, took a sip, and handed it to Jay.

Jay took a swig as he gathered his thoughts. "What happened back there?"

"Your real name is Jados."

Jay stared at Saben. The general's stony expression seemed entirely sincere. Jay clenched his fists. He didn't want to be the heir. When he said the half-cast prince would likely be run out of town, he held out some hope the offspring of Izell and Nados might turn that tide. But if he was the true prince, how disappointed everyone would be. Thoughts raced through Jay's mind to find a way out. "You're saying I'm the hidden heir. The half-cast prince."

"I didn't say it. You did. In front of Lord Kriton, no less. And you lived."

Jay's body tingled from head to toe, but he still couldn't

believe it. "So, some magical madman says that I'm a prince, and that makes it true?"

"That's not how it works," Saben said. "Lord Kriton is the Guardian of Aeterna. Only those who speak the truth may enter. Only future rulers are invited."

"I'm not a prince! I'm just a lieutenant." Didn't Saben understand? No one would let him rule anything.

"You are Jados Justinkeel, the only son of King Nados and Queen Izell and heir to the throne of Calonade. *And* you are a lieutenant of the Calonade Guard."

Jay stood to face Saben, his anger rising. "You can't order me to be a prince, sir!"

Saben calmly brought himself up to his full height. "Lieutenant, you are the prince. *And* because I'm your commanding officer, I can give you any orders I want. That's how Calonade works."

Jay felt his knees buckle like a fresh cadet in the face of Saben's burning glare, but he stood his ground. "I don't want to be a prince!" Jay shouted. "Who would ever want to be? Especially a prince of Calonade with the whole Galathian Empire trying to have his head on a pike."

"You came on this mission to protect such a person. That could cost you your life."

"That's the duty of a soldier, which I would gladly die for. Being the prince is different."

"How so?"

"Because it is!" Jay shouted. "A prince is not a soldier."

"Every sovereign is a soldier for their people." Saben's voice did not rise to meet Jay's. He remained stone-faced and steady.

"You're saying Queen Izell is a soldier."

"Yes."

"Was King Nados a soldier?"

"The best I ever served with."

This made Jay pause. King Nados probably had been one hell of a soldier.

He paced away from Saben. "My whole life is a lie. What about Olivia, the mysterious daughter of Gran? A lie. And Dunken, the fallen Galathian turncoat hero. Also, a lie."

"Olivia was Sedia's daughter. I didn't know Dunken. Perhaps they were a couple, but they were not your parents."

Jay shook his head in disbelief. He had gone to the cemetery with Gran on Remembrance Day for years. He had helped carry and arrange flowers. Gran had cried actual tears.

His entire life was built on a lie. Kaloby had tutored all the castle orphans, but he was only teaching one of them. Izell had chosen him as messenger, not because of how he rode in the race, but because he was her son. Kahela had trained him, not as Izell's protector, but as her successor.

Jay spun to face Saben. "Did you know?"

"No, but I suspected it when you nearly won the academy cup. The way you rode that horse. It was so..." Saben's voice broke for a moment, but he stiffened. "It was so much like your father. And Havoc was sired by your father's horse, Mayhem. It was as if I saw the two of them again that day."

"That's why you made sure I would keep Havoc."

Saben nodded. "Your father would have wanted you to have him."

King Nados, the father he never knew, had reached from beyond the grave to ensure he would ride Havoc. The enormity of it was only outweighed by the web of lies woven around him. "Were all the lies really necessary?"

"After your father's death, the Galathians sent a conquering force to Calonade's doorstep. Queen Izell parlayed in exchange for a treaty. She saved many lives, including yours, by keeping your true identity a secret." Saben slapped his pipe into one hand as if clearing it of debris.

"So, it was a strategy." A brilliant and calculating one. The Galathians would have disposed of a Queen Mother and her brood. A childless dowager who held influence over the Calonaden masses would be seen as useful. Izell secretly brewed a future rebellion in the family cauldron. A cold and efficient solution built on unspeakable secrets.

Jay reeled. "The *queen* is my *mother*?" He sat down, the old hurt of not having a mother welled up. Jay rubbed at the ache in his chest from the loss of something necessary and precious. But his mother had been nearby all his life.

What did he know about Queen Izell? She was a crafty lady. He had been afraid of her during his childhood. She was mostly detached and frosty, though that was probably because she was Fromeathian, a stoic people from a cold place. She had always been nearby, watching him from a distance.

He also knew something else. "She lied to me. Right to my face."

Saben cocked his head. "When?"

"She told me to come here and find her son. To bring him home safe." Jay slapped his own forehead. "I offered to play the part, to draw the Galathians away."

"Here you are." Saben cast a wary eye around the ruined city. "Mostly safe."

"Why didn't she just tell me then?"

Saben's focus returned to Jay. "Would you have believed her?"

"No. Not sure I do now."

Saben tucked his pipe into his waistcoat. "Queen Izell split you from her by sending you on this mission, increasing the odds one of you will survive to ensure Calonade's future. This has been the situation for your whole life. The secret of who you are kept you and your mother separate, but also kept you both and all of Calonade alive."

That's a big secret. It's not only my whole life, it's a whole city's. A whole nation's. Jay paced to the fountain and sat down. Saben joined him.

"But, sir, I'm lowborn. A half-casting." Jay lowered his head. *Broken, malformed.* Everyone had an insult to throw his way. It was the reason he wanted to leave Calonade. "No one would ever accept me as their prince."

Saben's expression softened. He reached out and grasped Jay's shoulder. "Having mixed ancestry hasn't always been a curse. Mixed people lived in Calonade for generations without any discrimination. Before the Galathians invaded, King Nados, Queen Izell, and all Calonade eagerly awaited your birth. When the Galathians arrived, they poisoned that well, and I'm afraid many of our countrymen drank from it."

"So, I will be a prince for people who despise me?"

"No, you will be their king."

Realization slowly dawned on Jay. The reason the tales of the half-cast prince endured was because Calonade almost had one. They still might if all this were true.

"What now? Go rally Calonade?"

"Not yet." Saben looked around the square as if seeking someone. "You still have a mission to fulfill."

"The Vinctus Stone. I nearly forgot."

"I don't know much about magical stones, but I know

you're here for a different reason. The same reason your father came here. Future monarchs visit this place."

"Kriton mentioned that. Kaloby said something about it, too. Why?"

Saben chewed the stem of his empty pipe. "I don't pretend to be a political animal, but *you* have to be. Visiting Aeterna gives you legitimacy with Parliament."

"Parliament? They're the worst. Collaborators and Galathian lackeys."

"Not all of them," Saben said. "Most will do what's best for Calonade."

"They threw you in jail for killing the king."

"That's how I know." For a moment, shadows fell across Saben's dour face. He stood up and paced away from the fountain, peering down at the city streets converging on the square.

Jay's mind spun. He held both histories in his mind—the lie to protect him and the truth, according to Saben and Kriton. Jay focused on the one detail that was the same in both stories.

"My father is dead," Jay said.

"Yes, and I am sorry for it," Saben said. "I would have given my life for his if I had the chance."

King Nados was his father. Somehow, that was harder to accept. Like thinking of oneself as the son of a gravestone. Instead of dwelling on the cold of a tomb, he returned to a warmer thought. "My mother is alive." For the first time, the troubling emptiness he carried within had a glimmer of hope.

"Yes, as far as we know. She is in peril, and we must act."

"Well, I guess we have found the hidden heir to Calonade." Jay looked down at himself, trying to get used to the idea.

"Why didn't *you* tell me?"

"I was afraid I was hoping too much, but Lord Kriton's test is not to be doubted. Anyone who knows of this place will understand if you can enter Aeterna, then you are genuine."

"What if you had been wrong? What if I really was just Jay, the former castle boy turned soldier with a sword pointed at my chest?"

"Then there would be one less messenger in the world." Saben didn't smile.

"Yeah, either way, mystery solved."

"That's the spirit. Now, Lieutenant, the sun is setting, and it's time for you to meet someone."

Jay looked around the ruins and then remembered Aeterna had a single resident. "Kaloby said a ghost lives here."

"He's the former emperor of Galathia. All the rulers of Calonade talked with him. I'm told he gives sound advice, and my feeling is that we need some."

Jay stared at Saben. Somehow the revelation Saben believed in ghosts ranked as high as the previous ones of the day.

"I don't pretend to know how the magic works, but going through the rituals lends influence and power," Saben said.

"Is that why Myra wanted me to enter Aeterna?"

"I don't know what that old crone wants, but it's a brilliant stroke to ensure your legitimacy. Maybe gaining your favor is the motivation. Doesn't matter right now. The meeting matters, and you have to do it alone."

"You're not staying with me?" Jay's voice rose a touch. He didn't believe in ghosts, but Saben seemed to be serious about it.

"No," Saben said. "No one stayed with Nados either. I left him at this fountain, so I know this is the right place. I'll take your horse, go back across the river, and wait for you there."

"How long will it take?"

"Nados took all night." Saben looked around, squinting at the empty buildings as if he expected to find one occupied after all. "I have to go. Find out anything you can that might help us regain Calonade. Good luck, Lieutenant."

Saben strode out through the archway without a backward glance. As the crunching of Saben's boots over the broken stones faded, Jay felt the silence of the abandoned city descend upon him. The long shadows from the setting sun pitched the city into twilight.

"Quiet as a graveyard," a voice said behind Jay in Galathian.

Jay spun, his hand flying to his saber and grabbing air.

An old man stood on the other side of the fountain with both hands raised in surrender. "I'm unarmed."

"Who are you?" Jay asked.

Torches placed in sconces Jay hadn't noticed lit up. Fire-light filled the town square surrounding the fountain.

The old man had neatly trimmed gray hair and a full beard along with perfect plinum bands down his face. Despite his age, Jay could still see the muscles of a warrior in his arms and shoulders. He wore a silk robe with gold trim belted around the middle.

"I am Rafykin, Emperor of Galathia, or at least I was about a thousand years ago." His eyes twinkled with mischief. "You are my guest today, and I welcome you to my final resting place."

Chapter Thirty-Eight

With the Willacast Corporation as the galactic monopoly control-
ling interstellar access, our place at the top is secure. Our only
fear is pirated technology in the hands of an unregulated rival.
    —from the journal of Sephy Alcott, Standard Galactic Year
13303

Aeriemuchawi Island, Day 064, Year 2017 local planetary calen-
dar, Standard Galactic Year 13303

The way the boatmen dumped her onto the abandoned pier
of the island made Sephy wonder. Her translator had picked
up strange references to witches in snatches of muttered
conversation. And the men rowed away at double time to
return to their ship.

    The farewell from Lakqwi and Havaqwi weeks before on
a similar dock a few hundred miles to the north had been
just as brief, but much more poignant. They had gotten to
know each other in the month of sea travel from Galathia to
a quaint little fishing village called Calonade as passengers
on a merchant ship. Neither of them had wavered from their
roles as priestess and acolyte throughout the journey, despite

Sephy's tendency to invite more casual conversation.

She procured a map to guide them home and advised them to acquire a new SHA for the village on the way. A specimen young and virile no one would miss. "You are the prophet, Hukindi," Lakqwi had said in her unflappable voice. She bowed with the respect due to a tribal chieftain. Havaqwi waved a tentative goodbye behind a shy smile. Lakqwi turned and strode toward the shore, tapping the butt end of her spear on the deck boards as she walked. Havaqwi peered past the bow and quiver of arrows slung over her shoulder. Sephy knew they'd never meet again and hoped their trek across the continent would be more interesting than the sea voyage.

Sephy knew when she reached this island it would get interesting, but she hadn't expected a huge Roman villa, not on this planet. She stood at the entrance of an impressive two-story manor house complete with circular cobblestone drive, decorative fountain, and sculpted vegetation providing tasteful accents. A stout wall surrounded the whole compound. The natives on the nearby islands were living in huts and yet, here was this monstrosity. Had she found another Willa Corp expat, living in obscurity?

Sephy strolled past the open gate. She kept her neural map running. A symbol flashed, showing her the location of the unauthorized transit device inside the manor house.

She walked up the steps and straight to the ornate double doors. Shrugging, she banged the door knocker. No one came. She pounded on the door again. Still nothing. Sephy tried it and it opened. *Not locked.*

The inside felt airy thanks to vaulted ceilings and sparse furniture. Poor attempts at art occupied the occasional corner. Overall, it felt empty.

Sephy strolled through the rooms and corridors of the first floor, finding no signs of life. A layer of fine dust covered everything. Sephy searched for the transit indicator as best she could, taking a few wrong turns, until stepping out a side door and finding an extension to the manor house with a domed roof. A single nondescript door was its only entrance. Her beacon pointed to a spot inside the walls of the structure.

Hoping to find no one else in this part of the manor, Sephy tried the door, and it opened with ease. She peeked in and immediately noted the difference between this room and the rest of the house. Clutter of all sorts filled several tables spaced throughout the room. Papers commingled on several stools and chairs. Tools and machine parts littered the tabletops and corners. Overflowing bookshelves pressed against the wall. A metal staircase led to a platform where a huge telescope suspended from the ceiling. Its massive lens pointed through a gap in the dome.

A half-finished structure, appearing to be the framework of a man combined with a horse, stood along a wall. Its insides comprised cogs, springs, and gears. More components littered the floor at its feet.

A far corner glowed red and Sephy felt heat coming from a brick hearth. In front of it stood a man with his back turned. A long mane of curly ginger hair flowed from his head. He held up a heated metal part with a pair of tongs and examined it, turning the object in all directions for a good view. He placed it on a traditional anvil and tapped it with a hammer. Sephy watched his precise movements. By the look of things, he was an excellent, if somewhat disorganized, craftsman.

"Hello," Sephy called out over the tapping sound.

The man spun around, tongs still in hand. He pulled a set

of heavy-lensed goggles from his face and stared at her.

Sephy stared back because this man was no inhabitant of Urey. He had the pinkish cream skin tones of a person exposed to a yellow star, not the blue one they orbited. An off-planet male human with access to an unauthorized transit device spelled trouble. Transit pirates were a tremendous concern. Dozens of laws across the galaxy protected against them.

A huge smile creased the man's face. "A guest!" he boomed in accented Galactic. "How nice. Come in, please." He set the smoking part on a metal bench and took off the blacksmith's goggles and apron. "My name is Huygens." He waved Sephy to come closer. "Have a seat anywhere. How can I help you?"

He held a genuinely cheerful smile, and Sephy relaxed until a warning flashed on her neural display. The person in front of her had no detectable life signs. He wasn't human. Sephy realized exactly what he was and knew she had an even bigger problem.

"Hi, I'm Sephy." She pulled out her disrupter and pointed it at Huygens. "I'm armed."

Huygens froze for a second but raised his right hand, palm out. A small barrel protruded from his wrist. Not a standard Willacast repulser, but a more primitive weapon. Sephy guessed it was a compact needle gun which could expel tiny explosive darts using compressed gas. Though not as fancy, they could make you just as dead as a disrupter.

"Put it down," Sephy said, "or I will tear a hole in you. I know you're a machine. All I want to do is talk."

The barrel of the needle gun retracted, and Huygens lowered his hand. His smile evaporated, and a bland expression took over his face. "How do you know what I am?" he asked in a monotone.

"You can keep your personification program active," Sephy said. "I prefer talking to a personality, even if it is simulated."

Huygens smiled again. He really drew her in. Nice piece of programming for an outdated model. This had to be a D-4 model before the adaptive nanostructures were introduced. Its interior assemblies, including the needle gun, consisted of fixed components.

"What would you like to talk about?" Huygens asked.

Sephy's neurals provided her with a set of verbal commands to try. "D-4 passivity protocol."

"I'm not going to attack you," Huygens said with a shrug. "At least not yet."

"D-4 power shutdown."

"You won't have any luck with standard Willacast command protocols. They've been deleted from my processor."

"Fine." Sephy sighed. "I had to try." She kept her weapon leveled at Huygens. A D-4 automaton running around without safeguards was an immense problem. This situation just kept getting better.

"I'll get right to it," Sephy said. "You have an unauthorized transit device, and I need to use it."

Huygens cocked a quizzical eyebrow. "Aren't you with the Willacast Corporation? There must be an authorized transit platform somewhere on this planet."

"There is, but I'm not using that one," Sephy said.

"I see. I *do* have a transit device, but it's not working. I'm stranded here along with you."

"What's wrong with it?" Sephy asked.

"If I knew that, I'd fix it."

Sephy glanced around the room at all the tools. *It must*

be really broken. But that made little sense. She still had a healthy ping to track. The device was nearby. "All right, how about I have a look?"

"Sure, on one condition."

Sephy nodded toward her disrupter. "You're not in a position to bargain."

"Do you really believe your reflexes are faster than mine?" Huygens asked. "You're still alive because you interest me."

"Fair enough." Sephy pocketed her pistol. "What's the condition?"

"Send me back to Earth."

Sephy snorted before she realized he wasn't kidding. "Why would you want to go there? It's a mess."

"It's home."

Sephy frowned. No one called Earth home. No one living, that is. Technically, this automaton wasn't living, so it might feel right at home on Earth. "All right, you have a deal. Where is the transit device?"

Huygens pointed toward a piece of canvas covering a lump on the far wall. Sephy maneuvered through the lab and pulled back the cover to reveal a wall clock. Willacast symbols were carved into its wood panels. The clock face sported two sets of numbers. One was old Earth Roman numerals, and the other was their equivalent in Willacast glyphs.

Sephy pulled open the front panel and studied the insides. Several schematics popped up on her neural feed as she did so. The issues preventing operation became clear and would be easy to fix. This, in itself, was interesting because any self-respecting D-4 automaton should be able to repair this device unless something prevented them from detecting the problems. Huygens had been trapped here on purpose by someone who knew Willacast programming. Sephy tapped her chin as if working out a complex issue. She reached inside the device to look like she was doing something.

Who wanted this D-4 on ice, and who removed its safeties? Who made it in the first place? Mysteries Sephy didn't have time to solve. Nor did she need to. There was no way in hell she was going to send an unpredictable automaton to Earth. Not even considering the proprietary technology that would be compromised, Willacast automatons were too powerful to be left unsupervised. Her present situation being an excellent object lesson.

She couldn't leave him on this island either, but that didn't mean he couldn't go somewhere else. Huygens was effectively blind to anything she did under the hood, so she cooked up an idea and set the innards of the device. After transmitting a set of instructions into the clock's auto send buffer, she was done.

"That should do it. Check it for yourself, Huygens."

Huygens peered into the clock. Sephy pondered how the blocking program worked. Did he see nothing and pretend? Or did the program have him see something other than what was there?

"Very good. Nice work," he said.

Sephy wouldn't know unless she had time to crack him open, which she didn't. "All right, let me set your destination." She manipulated the hands on the clock face. "You first. Then I'll reset for my transit. You won't be keeping the clock."

"That's fine. On Earth I won't need it." Huygens checked the clock face setting, which was accurate, but Sephy couldn't tell if he knew it or not.

Sephy pointed at the Willacast power symbol. "Do the honors?"

Huygens frowned. "I can't. No nano-cyber capability. Can you do it?"

"Oh, that's right." Another reason the D-4 was trapped. He couldn't provide the nanites needed to construct the power conduit configuration which activated the device. Only a D-10 or later model could. Or a technician with a power stick. She fished out her penlight. The glowing end had a crystal constructed from a collection of power nanites. She popped off the protective cover, stuck the crystal into the groove, and traced the power symbol. The microscopic nanites sluffed off the penlight and linked to do their job. The transit device lit with power. All the Willacast symbols flickered and glowed.

"Nice." Huygens admired the clock. "It's been a long time since I've seen it power up."

Sephy scooted a table, some chairs, and other random items out of the immediate vicinity of the clock. "Last chance to change your mind," Sephy said, deadpan.

"No, I've been waiting for this longer than you know."

Sephy activated the transit sequence. The clock vibrated with a low rumble that spread across the room. Every loose piece of metal hummed along with it. A ribbon of light formed in the space in front of the clock. It split open into a mid-air threshold like a hanging doorway. Through it Sephy saw a stretch of desolate wasteland and a pattern of stars in the sky beyond.

"Earth." Huygens took a step toward the portal. "Beautiful."

Sephy had seen some powerful delusion programs, but this one could win awards.

The vibration of the clock rose in pitch, screeching through the room. Loose metal rose into the air. The hands on the clock spun and clicked to a new setting. The scene through the portal blinked and changed to a deep red background. One Sephy now knew all too well—the inside of Karpathode.

"What is this?" Huygens turned, raising his palm toward Sephy. A cord of light whipped around Huygens from beyond the threshold. It slammed tightly around him, pinning his arms. Lillain stepped into view, holding the other end of the lightning whip.

Sephy raised an eyebrow. That was new. Most likely a manifestation of Lillain's weather control program. Well, at least the updates were taking hold.

"Thank you, Mother Goddess." Sephy bowed. "Please hold this heretic for as long as you feel necessary."

Lillain glared down at Sephy as she reeled the fruitlessly struggling Huygens through the threshold. "I do not wish to see you again, Prophet Hukindi. You disrupt the peace of my sanctuary."

"My apologies. This will be my last request." Sephy slapped the clock and severed the connection. The threshold dissolved and the metal bits dropped to the floor.

Sephy breathed an enormous sigh of relief and sat down. Mission accomplished, at least for now. For a moment, it felt peaceful, like a vacation should. Sephy peered around the lab. It was an interesting place, but she had no time to indulge. She'd been absent from the station far longer than planned. She got up and reset the clock after disengaging the component that would automatically change the coordinates.

She moved both sets of hands to midnight and activated the clock. The portal opened again, revealing a long tunnel of light. The way home yawned like an endless pit before her. With no real reason to do it, she took a deep breath. Hoping this transit device would be gentle with her insides, she stepped through.

Chapter Thirty-Nine

All the people left Aeterna except for me. I couldn't go back to the capital because it's the place I lost my wife and child. I lost them both when Mother cast Maiden into exile beyond even my reach. All I can do now is wait and prepare for the cycle to renew.

—from Chronicles of Galathia by Rafykin, Urey, circa 2640 local planetary calendar.

Aeterna, Day 010, Year 2999 local planetary calendar, Standard Galactic Year 14285

"You're a ghost?" Rafykin didn't look like a ghost to Jay. No faded edges or misty limbs. No blood from death wounds. He looked like a living person.

"No, I just keep on living. I know I have an end, but not yet." He peered at Jay intently. "It draws closer, however. Meeting you is a milestone."

"What do you mean?"

"Never mind. I enjoy these meetings with prospective monarchs." He groaned as he eased himself down to sit on the edge of the fountain. "Immortality is not kind. So, you represent the royal House of Justinkeel, like your father before you."

Jay stared for a moment. He had to get used to being a member of House Justinkeel. Queen Izell's various relatives and hangers-on were generally idle and spoiled. Some spent their time plotting a revolt against Izell. Others were collaborators with the Galathians. None were company he cared to keep.

"I am from Calonade."

"Then things have changed. Has your father been killed?"

"You knew King Nados?"

"Of course, didn't the young aide, what's his name? Saben? Didn't he tell you?"

"You know General Saben is here?"

"I know to whom Lord Kriton has allowed access to the city," Rafykin said. "You, son of Nados, and Saben, your personal aide."

"He's my commanding officer, not a personal aide."

"As you wish." Rafykin held up his hands in surrender, but the knowing smile never left his face. "I don't think you would be here if Nados were still alive."

A long list of things would be different. Jay stopped himself from thinking about it. "He was killed a long time ago. Queen Izell claimed the throne in his place."

"Too bad, too bad." Rafykin shook his head. "I admired the young man. So, how does your mother fare as ruler?"

Jay, still getting used to thinking of Queen Izell as his mother, took a moment to answer. "She made a deal with Galathia to avoid war. In exchange for lanicin, we lived in peace under a Galathian governor. Recently, an attempt was made on Queen Izell's life, followed by full occupation. I believe she has escaped to the south seas, but I don't know her whereabouts." *Nor would I reveal them if I did.*

"Ah, you must be having a bit of an adventure of your own, eh? Well, if Queen Izell lives, she'll be back." Rafykin spoke with confidence. "If she is anything like the Fromeathians of my day, then I know she is a fighter and master strategist."

"She is the shrewdest person I have ever met," Jay agreed with a wisp of pride.

"Indeed," Rafykin said. "So Galathians have oppressed Calonade for a generation and now they're trying to take full control. Well, if you're here, then they haven't succeeded, have they?"

"No. I suppose they haven't."

"What will you do next?"

Jay hesitated. Should he answer this Galathian? His next move was obvious to even the lowest-ranking officer, and he couldn't share any tactical information because he didn't have any. Saben had told him Rafykin's insights had been valuable in the past. Jay trusted him. "I will have to find the queen and help her retake Calonade."

Rafykin nodded. "Yes, but tell me, do you think the people of Calonade, the Frontier, the south seas, and other allies will rally to Izell?"

"Why wouldn't they?" Jay was puzzled by the question. Anyone loyal to Calonade would aid her.

"Because she is not Calonaden." Rafykin held up a finger. "She is Fromeathian, and it may also be argued she is the cause of all the trouble. By leaving Staukard at the altar for your father, she has brought the wrath of the empire down upon Calonade."

Jay frowned. The Galathian version of events differed—the foreign prince stole the fair maid from the emperor on their wedding day. It fueled Galathian oppression for many years, so Jay doubted it was true. The version of the tale in which Izell left with Nados of her own accord, days before the wedding, was also romanticized. Whatever the actual events, Jay wondered about Izell. She ended up as Queen of Calonade rather than Empress of Galathia. How could such a reserved person have such a dramatic past? He was collecting many questions to ask his mother the next time they met. If there was a next time.

"That was a long time ago." Jay struck on with his counterpoint. "She defended Calonade, built up its defenses, remained the head of the ruling family, and gained the favor of the Parliament."

"All of that is dust as well." Rafykin's eyes gleamed fiercely.

"The alternative is the Galathian Governor, Lord Kendric. No one wants that."

"Correct. Even the emperor probably doesn't want that," Rafykin said. "He will strive to install a more capable puppet on the throne and do so by making many sweet promises to the people of influence. Queen Izell cannot combat such an outcome. The Calonaden people need a new leader, one of their own. They need the son of King Nados."

"But I'm just a—"

Rafykin held up a hand for silence. "Your lineage is compelling. The people will flock to you. You will embody their hopes and dreams for freedom. Your people have been oppressed for a long time. If you claim your father's inheritance, you could raise an army that wouldn't be easily opposed. Where Nados failed, you might succeed."

The old man's advice put him in Saben's camp as far as his own future. The glint in Rafykin's eye made Jay wary.

"Why would you encourage me to do that? You're Galathian."

"Yes, but things have changed since I was emperor." Rafykin clapped Jay on the shoulder. He felt as solid as anyone alive. "I would have been honored to take the field against you and the courageous Calonadens in an earlier age, but now my people seem more intent on clandestine deals and assassination. It weakens them. I admire your people. Calonade has risen from an unknown fishing village to a power great enough to challenge the empire."

Rafykin looked wistful for a moment. "Besides, I haven't seen anyone from Galathia here in a long time. They must have forgotten me." He paused, shoulders slumping. A heavy sadness surrounded him, but after a moment, he shook it off. Straightening, he looked out over the landscape.

"You see this city?" Rafykin gestured all around them. "This was supposed to be for them. A place where ruling pow-ers might negotiate for peace instead of choosing perpetual war. I conquered them all to stop the fighting. I charged Lord Kriton, my greatest general, to ensure only those committed to the truth could enter. This place was once full of sovereigns, scholars, and peacemakers. All were welcome. Yet no one from Galathia comes here anymore. I wish you could have seen it in its day. Now, the entire city is a doleful memorial to one man's failure. I am glad, however, to be of service to you, my boy." As he spoke, a sad smile flashed across his face. "Calonade is worthy of honor."

"Is that why you sent me a message?"

"Message? What message?"

"The one that came in the clockwork crow," Jay said. "Saben thinks it really came from the Oracle, but I don't. To me, she seemed genuinely surprised by it."

Rafykin peered at him, puzzled. "Describe this messenger."

"A bird made of metal and clockwork gears. It has magical symbols on its sides. It delivered a message summoning me here. And it led me through the jungle to the entrance, so I thought it came from you."

"The symbols. Did they look like this one?" The old man revealed an intricate tattoo on the back of his hand.

Jay felt drawn to it without knowing why. "Yes. And like the ones on the Oracle's skin."

"The Oracle, yes. Do you know her as Myra?"

"I do. She lives in the Kelstone Mountains."

"Interesting," Rafykin said. "I hate to disappoint you, but the message wasn't from me. I think the clockwork crow and Myra are working together. Such a messenger seems very much like Willacast magic."

"Myra mentioned Willacast magic." *It's cropping up everywhere.*

"Yes, she is one of the Three Willacast Sisters. There is a Maiden, a Mother, and a Crone. At times, they are powerful. Every millennium the cycle renews—the Maiden becomes the Mother, the Mother becomes the Crone, and so on. We are near one of those times now. In fact, you can see it in the stars."

The torchlight faded at a gesture from the old emperor, and he gazed at the sky. The dampened light revealed a wide span of stars. "There." He pointed at three bright ones forming a slightly crooked line. "The Three Sisters. Each one represents one of the Willacast—Myra, Lillain, and Kamur. The brightest is the mother, Lillain, and the other two are the maiden and the crone, Kamur and Myra. They wander about the fixed points of light that surround them. Once in a thousand years, they align."

Jay vaguely recalled a lecture from Kaloby on the wanderers during one of their late-night study sessions. Jay had been so tired he couldn't remember their significance.

"The wanderers are close to alignment." Rafykin traced the line of wandering stars in the sky. "The turning of the cycle is nigh."

"What cycle?" Jay asked.

"Have you not heard of the Willacast cycle?"

Jay shook his head. Gran was devoted to the Three Sisters religion but had mentioned nothing like that.

"It could be a teaching lost to the ages. Much has been lost." Rafykin peered at the sky in deep thought. "I was hoping for a fellow Galathian, but the time has arrived. You are a powerful lad with capable allies, and my descendants have forsaken me. You will have to foster a renewal for the world."

Jay considered Rafykin, puzzled. The old kook had some interesting insights, but the talk of cycles, goddesses, and magic detracted from his credibility. Jay knew the outcome of this conflict would have a profound effect on Calonade and Galathia, but Jay had seen Kaloby's maps. The influence of these two realms was hardly the entire globe.

Rafykin stood up and gestured for Jay to follow him. "I want to show you something."

The old man seemed harmless, and Saben said it would take all night. Even though he felt tired, curiosity kept him alert. He followed the old emperor out of the dark courtyard.

The path led further into the city. Torches along the way lit as they passed and faded as they moved away. After a few twists and turns, they arrived at another courtyard. A large obsidian mausoleum appeared before them in the torchlight. Two huge marble lions stood as guardians on either side. Vines and moss grew into the cracks and over the surfaces, giving the statues a sense of movement in the breeze. Jay had the eerie feeling their eyes were tracking him.

A tomb rose abruptly out of the ground, its front archway blocked by a dark slab of stone. Carved into its rock face was a series of symbols that looked remarkably like those he saw light up on Myra's skin.

"This is Willacast magic." Rafykin indicated the symbols. "I learned some of it as a young man. I use it to protect my most precious possession."

Rafykin traced the symbols with a finger. Each symbol glowed and faded. As he did this, Jay noticed the tattoo on his hand light up and glow briefly. The ground below them rumbled and the stone slab shuddered loose. Slowly, the door to the tomb lowered into the ground. The sounds of rusted gears turning emanated from the darkness as the stone lowered out of sight.

Rafykin stepped in, gesturing Jay to follow.

Walking into a tomb with a ghost might not be the best idea, but a whisper of wind from inside the tomb caressed Jay's cheek, calming his nerves. He felt no fear as he stepped over the threshold and followed Rafykin down a series of cracked slabs of stone. The passage opened into a large, round chamber.

Dry leaves littered the room. In the center sat a massive sarcophagus with a stately figure carved into its top. It looked much like the old man standing in front of him.

"This is where I will be laid to rest. It's comforting to have a final destination after all these years." He smiled. "It's also a door to a secret place, protected by magic. Besides myself, only Myra can access it. It's impenetrable unless you have the key."

The old man bent over the sarcophagus and traced more symbols, the light on his hand glowing each time. He stepped back and a seam at the base of the coffin slowly cracked open. Air thick with ancient dust streamed out as the coffin slowly slid across the floor, revealing a stairway descending below the crypt.

"Follow me," Rafykin said.

Jay, too far along to quit now, followed him down to the bottom. Still, he felt no apprehension, no matter how spooky the place seemed. In fact, the deeper he ventured, the more welcome he felt.

Crystals placed inside torch holders lit up as they climbed down the stairs. They were like the glowing crystals Myra had provided in the caves. They reached the bottom and entered a long, dust-covered corridor carved through stone. Footprints marked the floor, and Jay noticed they matched the sandals of his guide.

Rafykin led the way through the corridor until it opened into an arched chamber. It remained empty except for a standing clock placed in the center. Rafykin crossed to the other side, where another archway entered a second corridor, but Jay stopped to examine the timepiece. It looked a lot like Myra's clock, though built squatter and more solid. It had a collection of ornate Willacast symbols carved into its wood panels, which glowed faintly. Etched on its face, a set of Galathian numbers mingled with a set of Willacast symbols.

"Myra has a clock like this."

"Yes, well, it is a useful tool to keep up with what's happening across the realm but ordinary compared to what I wish to show you in the next room."

At the mention of the next room, Jay's attention left the clock, and he caught up with Rafykin. They walked through the final corridor and stepped into a room with a circular floor and a domed ceiling made of stone bricks. Each brick had a Willacast symbol carved into it that hummed with power. The runes flashed in a pattern of silver light. More bricks created an altar in the middle of the room. On the altar sat a single oblong stone about the size of a chicken egg. It had a rough exterior that glittered in the light. A low vibration seeped up through the floor and into Jay's feet. He felt it in his bones.

"This is the Vinctus Stone. It is most precious to me," Rafykin said.

Tingles surged over Jay's body. He'd won the race to the Vinctus Stone. This was far better than the race for Top Cadet. Jay couldn't wait to see Kaloby's face when he plopped it into his old tutor's hand.

"You have come at an auspicious moment. The stone was lost to me until recently. I feared it destroyed. The last time I saw it, many years ago, the magic within was gone. When it reappeared here in its proper place, the magic revived."

The old man stared at the Vinctus Stone with palpable longing. "Such appearances and disappearances are typical with Willacast magic. I am glad, however, to see it again. It is not valuable in itself, but it is powerful. The person who forges a strong relationship with it may wield power beyond measure. This is the heart of Willacast magic."

And the key to winning the war. How did a magical stone advise a battle commander or a queen? "A relationship with a stone? How does that work?" Jay asked.

"Well, it's not the stone. It's what lies within. I don't know how it works. In fact, it has not worked for me. I am merely its protector, but you may play a different role."

"Did my father wield this stone?"

"Oh no, I'm afraid not. In fact, you are the first and only person besides myself to enter this sanctuary. Your father may have been able to receive the stone, but he visited me a generation too early. You have the fortune, or perhaps misfortune, of arriving at the right moment."

Jay gave the old man a sharp look. "Why would it be misfortune?"

"Power does corrupt, you know. Look at me. I provide a clear example of that."

"I haven't studied very much ancient Galathian history."

"Ah well," Rafykin said, "perhaps someday you will read my chronicles. They are quite entertaining. I'm having a grand time writing them. But I digress. The more immediate reason this could be unfortunate for you is that the Vinctus Stone must accept you as its new protector. I don't know if it will."

"What happens if it doesn't?"

"I don't know that either. All I know is that it accepted me long ago, and I survived the process."

That sounds ominous. Jay studied the stone. It wasn't an ordinary rock. It emanated power and felt as if it were regarding him similarly. There was a hint of intelligence to it. He almost felt like meeting someone new. Someone glad to see him.

"How do I find out if it accepts me?" Jay asked.

"All I did was grasp the stone, and I knew. I imagine the

same would work for you."

Jay turned and regarded the old emperor. The piratical gleam in his eyes had returned. "If this stone is so precious to you, why are you letting me do this?"

"Because my time is done. A new era starts soon, and you can lead it. All you have to do is take this stone and return to Myra. She'll do the rest."

So that was it. None of this was really about lineage or who might rule. It probably had nothing to do with Calonade at all. This was all about the Oracle's hidden agenda, and Jay was just a convenient messenger.

But Jay didn't get angry. A warm feeling rose to counteract Jay's suspicion. "If Myra wants the Vinctus Stone, then why doesn't she just come and get it? She's the goddess who protects this place, isn't she?"

"She could, but she doesn't need it," Rafykin said. "You do. That is why it has returned and reawakened in this place. And why Myra sent you here. Working with it, however, is tricky and there are forces that don't want that to happen. Myra can help you and show you what to do."

More mystery, how surprising. Jay turned away from Rafykin as he thought about what to do next. This could be an attempt on his life, but it sure was an elaborate assassination. Even though he questioned the motives of Rafykin and the Oracle, the feeling he got from the stone was different. The only word Jay could put on it was purity.

Several symbols on the bricks flashed, and suddenly Jay was somewhere else. Havoc was under him as he raced through the lanicina groves headed for the castle. He was there, but he was also standing in Rafykin's cave. Cannon fire erupted ahead of him, and he knew a battle raged in Calonade Bay.

He looked at the Vinctus Stone sitting on its altar only a few steps away. He was in both places at once.

Mounted soldiers, all around him, galloped into the fight. He felt the Vinctus Stone in his waistcoat pocket. Jortica rode ahead of him. She looked back and flashed him a bold grin. Her scar mirrored the smile. She wore a Calonaden uniform and held a rippling banner with Calonade's sigil as they thundered over the road. He never felt so free, so alive.

Just as quickly, the vision was gone. He stood before the Vinctus Stone in the quiet of the tomb.

"What did you see?" Rafykin asked.

"A battle," Jay murmured, still stunned.

"You have glimpsed the future, or at least one that is possible. It is a common occurrence with the Vinctus Stone."

"Charging into battle is an amazing feeling."

"Ah, yes," Rafykin said. "Turning points and key moments happen around battles. I remember them well."

Jay peered at the old man. "Is this what it's like to be king?"

Rafykin nodded. "At times, yes."

Jay focused on the stone. Everything he had just felt told him he could do it. He could be the man Calonade needed him to be and change the course of the war. He could bring victory to Queen Izell and Calonade. His lineage mattered, but his appearance did not. And Jortica was there with him.

Jay took a step toward the altar. More symbols on the bricks flashed.

"Is this a good sign?" Jay asked.

"I don't know. I'm very curious to see what happens next."

Jay waited but didn't feel any fear. He tingled with eagerness and anticipation. His hand itched to grasp the stone.

He took another step. More symbols flashed around him.

He took the last step to stand in front of the altar. Flashing symbols accompanied his advance. The stone lay within reach, but he waited.

A new feeling appeared, and Jay knew it came from the Vinctus Stone. Loneliness, like he used to feel when thinking of his parents, washed over him. In his chest, he felt the old ache of loss and he knew the Vinctus Stone felt the same. As he reached out, the ache eased for both of them.

"May I touch you?" he whispered to the stone. It seemed only right to ask first.

A warmth flowed through his body. The old emptiness he had always carried filled with promise. He smiled and touched the stone.

Blinding pain shot through his arm, stabbed his heart, and crashed into his head. Everything went dark.

Chapter Forty

The key to my success and the future of feminkind is secrecy.
—from the journal of Sephy Alcott, Standard Galactic Year 13303

Alcott Station, Standard Galactic Year 13303

Sephy sat up on the transit platform, rubbing her head. The abandoned transit portals in the old section of the station provided a convenient way to conduct unauthorized travel. She'd secretly kept Portal 7 in Sector 41 operational, even though it gave her a headache. At least she didn't feel like puking.

"Tough day?" the intercom crackled.

Dammit. So much for stealth. Looks like her secret was blown. It was probably too much to ask after all the unauthorized transit shenanigans.

Sephy dragged herself up to standing. In the adjoining room, Sub-Director Fyley peered at her over a floating console and through the glass. Willacast control glyphs danced around her wrinkled bald head. No security guards or transit investigators were with her, which was a good sign.

"Took longer than I planned," Sephy said.

"Almost three hours gone. That's over forty days in the maintime. Must have been a hell of a party." Fyley gestured at her clothing. "I see you went native. Get any good SHA?"

Sephy brushed off the Shinwate animal hides. "Naw." Maybe no one knew where she'd been. "Just a lot of drinking with unsavory business partners who love hunting." A lie to test the waters.

"Sounds pretty boring. Please tell me you got in some pleasure."

"There were some fun bits."

"You should have more fun bits," Fyley said. "You never take a break. That's why I checked up on your logs after you were gone for more than an hour. I've been keeping an eye out for your return."

Sephy smiled. In truth, she was exploring business ventures, but this time not for Willacast Corp. Well, not directly. A positive outcome with Urey would benefit the company too. "Catch me up on the latest."

"Several reports of unauthorized transits," Fyley said. *Here it comes.*

"But no one traced them down yet. Minor stuff. You want a priority on that one?"

Sephy sighed inwardly with relief. "Send them to me in a confidential file."

"Yes, boss."

Good ole Fyley. Never questioned her. Her best trait.

"That's it, boss. Quiet day."

"Thanks, Fyley." She actually looked forward to getting back to work. Maybe her little adventure really had been a bit of a vacation.

"What do you want done here?" Fyley gestured at the

equipment around the transit platform. Low flickering lights showed it ran at low-level power. This whole layer of the station had been abandoned in place because of upgrades on transit stations on the outboard decks. No one traveled into the center hub anymore. She could leave it up and running, ready to go back to the Shinwate paradise any time.

Sephy shook her head. That didn't sound as appealing as it once had. The blue star had enough life in it to let Urey sit for a while. She needed to give Lillain time to turn things around. Sephy smiled as she considered the nasty surprises in store for Rafykin and his cronies. The Shinwate also needed time for incubation to further their genetic rehabilitation. Maybe a few hundred years would do the trick.

"Shut it all down," Sephy said. "I'm done with this for now."

Fyley nodded and shut off the power to the transit portal.

Sephy stepped off the transit portal platform and joined Fyley in the control room. "All right, my friend, let's get back to work. This galaxy won't run itself." They walked out of the transit room, leaving a single error light blinking in the darkness.

Chapter Forty-One

Besides a final home to rest my bones, only one purpose remains for Aeterna. To provide a safe place for my daughter to reside.
—from Chronicles of Galathia by Rafykin, Urey, circa 2640 local planetary calendar.

Aeterna, Day 012, Year 2999 local planetary calendar, Standard Galactic Year 14285

Jay woke lying on the bricks beside the altar. Vertigo seized him as he sat up. When he got his bearings, he discovered he still grasped the Vinctus Stone. He peeled his grip loose, and the stone clattered onto the cavern floor. He saw no signs of Rafykin.

The rune stones around the altar remained dark in the dim light. A chill seeped in from all directions. Jay could feel the dankness of the tomb, no longer a welcoming place. His head ached and his chest hurt, but the pain slowly faded.

Panic seized him. Jay leaped up and rushed toward the corridor. He emerged in the room with the Willacast clock and found it dark and still. Even the clock no longer glowed.

He started for the exit, hoping he wasn't trapped, but his gaze returned to the Vinctus Stone. He didn't feel a presence from it anymore, but he couldn't leave it either. Something about it pulled his eyes back each time he looked away.

He knelt beside it and patted it. The stone didn't shock him this time. It felt cool to the touch, like an ordinary rock. Whatever had happened seemed to be over. He grabbed the stone and stuffed it into his waistcoat pocket. He'd figure it out later. Right now, he had to get out of this strange place.

He hurried through the next corridor and rushed up the steps. With relief, he found the way out still open. As he climbed into the crypt, the sarcophagus slid back into place. With a clanking of unseen gears, a huge stone door rose from beneath the floor to seal the tomb. Jay leaped through the opening in time to turn around and see the door seal itself. After the dust settled, it looked as if no one had been near it in years.

The late evening sun slipped down toward the trees. Jay had no idea how much time had passed. He ran back to the gateway courtyard to find the torches doused and the fountain abandoned.

He called out for Saben but received no answer.

With the clicking of branches and groaning of wood, the heavy vegetation around the gateway began to close. Jay rushed through the shrinking passage. On the other side, he watched as the vines and trees knit themselves together, thoroughly blocking the entrance.

Lord Kriton stood stationary on his pedestal, glaring down at any pilgrims daring to approach Aeterna. Jay climbed over the fallen oak and rushed down the trail out of the valley. The foliage wove into an impassable thicket behind him. As he hiked up the narrowing path, the trees closed behind him. He turned once at the overlook to watch the ruins of Aeterna disappear into the undergrowth and mist.

Back at the banks of the Talindrey, the stone ferry rested against the sand and the water rushed swiftly past the bank.

Campfire smoke caught his eye on the opposite bank. General Saben sat tending the fire with Calamity hitched to a nearby tree. The delicious smell of roasting meat greeted his nose, and he suddenly felt urgent hunger pangs. Jay jumped on the boat and rode it back across the water. It sank below the surface as he stepped off. He hurried to Saben's camp and fell on the food like a starving wolf.

After eating enough to feel human again, Jay told Saben what happened. At least, what he thought happened. He didn't mention the vision from the Vinctus Stone because it might not be real. It had been two days since they had parted at the fountain. He must have spent most of it unconscious.

"The whole thing could have been a magic spell." Jay ended his narrative as the sun set.

"Rafykin did appear to King Nados, but he made no mention of going anywhere beyond the fountain courtyard."

Jay showed Saben the Vinctus Stone. Except for a slight flicker of firelight reflecting off the mineral deposits on its surface, it looked ordinary. "I'm supposed to take this to the Oracle."

Saben regarded him with his empty pipe stuck between his teeth. "Are you going to?"

"I don't know. The magic might help the queen, but we don't know where she is. Rafykin said it was for me, but Myra could help me sort it out. I'm still not sure what it does."

"Perhaps you'll find out more as we go along. In the meantime, we have more urgent matters. Rafykin is right. You must make yourself known. If you can create an opportunity for people to rally around you, then we can help Queen Izell win this war."

"What did Rafykin tell Nados exactly?"

"He said Nados could never win a war with Galathia, but he could strike a bargain for peace using lanicin."

"Did he try it?"

Saben clicked the pipe in his teeth. "No. He tried to win. Queen Izell is the one who bargained."

"King Nados went against Rafykin's counsel." Jay cocked an eyebrow. His father married someone else's bride and ignored magical advice. He persuaded his people to go to war with a bloodthirsty empire. Jay was learning quite a bit about his origins. "He must have been quite convincing."

"Yes. We all believed we could win until your father fell. Then, I think, we all fell with him."

Jay wanted Rafykin to be wrong as well. The old ghost had outlined an intimidating agenda. Jay might get used to being Jados Justinkeel, but it was more than a name. He had to become a prince and then a king. He had no idea how to do any of it. Plus, he still doubted the people of Calonade would accept him.

"There was one other thing," Saben said. "Rafykin told King Nados to prepare his heir. He said that it was his heir who could defeat Galathia."

"Did King Nados believe that?"

"I don't know, but Queen Izell must have."

Jay reclined against a log for a long time, thinking about what had happened in Aeterna. Rafykin said he could lead the people of Calonade to a victory over Galathia, but everything changed when Jay mentioned the Oracle. Suddenly it was about the world, not just Calonade. He looked at the little stone sitting innocently in his palm.

Jay jolted upright, remembering Jortica's plan to help Jay bring home the heir of Calonade. She was still out there on the run, pretending to be Jay. "Have you seen Jortica?"

Saben shook his head. "Not since the race. Why?"

"She created a distraction to get me loose from the Galathians. Only Fauden saw through it." A queasy fear settled in his stomach. "I hope she's not..." He couldn't finish the thought out loud. *Hurt. Dead.* She was a soldier, he reminded himself. She was doing her duty and a soldier's duty, at times, was to face death. Still, he couldn't bear the thought of her dying for him.

He had a vision, though. They were supposed to fight together. It meant she wasn't dead, right? At least not yet. Rafykin had said it was a *possible* future, so he still didn't really know.

"What are you talking about, Lieutenant?"

Jay pulled away from the dreadful thoughts and told the story of his capture, escape, and Jortica's mission.

Saben nodded, clicking his pipe between his teeth. "You're right. She's probably still on the run."

Thinking of the consequences of Jortica's bold ruse, a heavy dread settled around Jay.

Saben must have sensed it. "She's a capable fighter with the best mount in Calonade. She's likely out-foxing those fools every day and night."

Jay tried to let that thought console him, but it wasn't much to go on. So much had changed in the last few days. What would she think of him being a prince? Well, at least he had a clear career path now.

His gaze focused on the Vinctus Stone once more. Firelight

glittered over its surface. No, he wouldn't be Rafykin's messenger and take it to the Oracle. At least, not yet. Jay grasped the stone and put it back in his waistcoat. As he did, an idea occurred to him. "How many frontiersmen are our allies, do you think?"

"Most of them, I'd say, the way the Galathians have been burning towns and homesteads. They aren't good at making friends."

"You're right," Jay said. "I think we can do a better job. Tomorrow, we start a fresh rebellion."

Epilogue

The most sublime programming known to feminam exists within planet-governing automatons. They control nearly a thousand seeded planets with little to no direct oversight. What happens if that simulated sentience becomes real?

    —private communication from Melrayis Valdez to Sephy Alcott, Standard Galactic Year 11247

Kelstone Mountains, Day 026, Year 2999 local planetary calendar, Standard Galactic Year 14285

With a ringing of metal, the clockwork crow landed on the coat rack in Myra's cavern and shook its feathers. Glowing crystals illuminated a set of bookshelves, an antique desk, and an aging couch. The crow peered into the shadows and barked a rusty croak to announce its arrival. Only silence answered.

After a moment, the clockwork crow stretched its mechanical wings out to either side and cried out again, louder this time. Its cough echoed through the cave.

"Keep your feathers on, I heard you the first time." An oil lamp flashed to life, revealing a figure descending a set of stone stairs. "My bones take a moment to get going these days." Myra stepped onto the far side of the platform and raised the lamp.

The crow's mechanical eye whirred as it focused on the hunched old woman. Faded runes shone green on her ancient skin.

"So," she said, "the mysterious messenger returns. The stealer of magical stones himself. You've got some cheek coming back here."

The crow bowed, a feat of balance on the coat rack. It broke into a series of warbles, beak clicks, and head bobs. A rusty chortle ended the outburst.

"That *is* promising. Tell me, where are Jados Justinkeel and the Vinctus Stone now?"

The crow cocked its head sideways, staring at the old woman with one onyx eye as it clicked its beak.

"Don't get snippy with me. You watched them after they left Aeterna, didn't you? How long until they get here?"

The crow puffed up, extended its hackles, and cawed with decent volume. It ruffled its feathers again and settled back onto the coat rack as if speaking proper crow took some effort.

"Hmm. That's a wrinkle." The old woman frowned. She placed a finger on her chin and closed her eyes. Several symbols on her skin glimmered with power. On her forehead, a shape like an eye, lashes swirling around it, burned a fierce green. "I see him. Jados has the stone. He and Saben are going to Thurbush." She shook her head. "A pity, but it's not the first time a Justinkeel ignored good advice. I imagine they'll stir up a bunch of unnecessary trouble, as men are prone to do. My sister will get wind of it if she hasn't already." The runes on the old woman's skin faded to a glimmer and went dark.

The crow barked again and followed up with another set of hoots and cackles.

"Yes, I know all about Armone. He will lure young Jados into a foolish attempt to regain Calonade. But magic protects the entrance to the city. The Outer Gate will be nearly impossible to overcome."

To that, the crow squawked with an impatient tone.

Myra pointed a crooked figure. "No, I will not help. I could care less who rules Calonade or any other city of Urey. There are larger concerns than such petty conflicts." Myra paced across the platform and idly traced her finger along the spines of several ancient tomes.

"Calonade's impenetrable wall has its part to play. Jados must crack the grip of the Vinctus Stone to release what sleeps within. Grinding his flesh against such a formidable barrier may be the only way."

The crow cackled, its hackles rising.

"I can't use my sight to predict my sister's actions, but it's safe to say she's distracted in Galathia for the moment."

In response, the crow fluffed its feathers and settled onto the coat rack.

The old woman balled her fists to her hip. "You can't stay here. This is your fault, you know. If you had brought the stone to me in the first place, we wouldn't be at the mercy of that foolish boy. Get back out there and keep your crow eye on things, or I'll take control of your gear-stuffed head again. Now shoo!"

The crow squawked and leaped off the coat rack. With the sound of honing blades, the machine flapped away from the platform and dove into the dark tunnel, its glow lighting the way.

Grumbling, Myra trudged up the steps. At the top, she opened the door and doused the lamp. Light from the room beyond streamed around her silhouette. "Humans and their toys." She shook her head with amusement, stepped through, and shut the door.

Glossary

Aerietaga: Group of islands to the south of Calonade.

Aeterna: Ruins of an ancient city hidden in the Frontier near the intersection of the Kelstone and Wrayan Mountains.

Alcott Station: A space station orbiting a rogue black hole called Willa. Headquarters of the Willacast Corporation and founded by Sephy Alcott. Center of the transportation network spanning the galaxy.

Ametrine Grasslands: Plains east of Galathia.

Aquerl Sea: Body of water to the west of Calonade.

Calonade: Coastal city in an equatorial region of Urey.

Cleavicon River: River that runs through Galathia.

Feminam or Feminkind: Humans with genetic damage from exposure to generations-long space travel. Characteristics include gray wrinkled skin, average height is 4'3", only the female sex, and lifespans averaging 120 years.

Fenduer Forest: Large impassable forest between the south–

ern border of Galathia and the northern reaches of the Frontier.

Fillaquill River: River that runs through Calonade.

Fromeathia: City in the far northern icy regions. Vassal of Galathia.

Galathia: Refers to both the dominating northern empire and its capital city.

Half-casting: Slur used for mixed ancestry people, usually Galathian-Calonaden. Origin is a broken or malformed machine part that is useless and typically discarded during the manufacturing process.

Half-cast: A descriptor of a person of mixed ancestry. Used as a slur.

Halfy: Another slur for people of mixed ancestry.

Highborn: High society Galathians.

Ireya: Calonaden name for the planet.

Karpathode: Underground city built into an extinct volcano located just to the north of Galathia city and used as a prison. Also called Rolotundra by the Shinwate.

Kelstone Mountains: Rugged mountains that form the northern border of Calonade.

Kettlebone Pass: The only way through the Kelstone Mountains and the only land passage into Calonade. Site of many battles between Galathia and Calonade.

Krike: A nocturnal bird with black feathers and red eyes used to send messages.

Lanicin: Healing products made from the sap, leaves, bark and roots of the lanicina tree.

Lanicina Tree: Tree that grows only in Calonade.

Lowborn: A less insulting term for those of mixed ancestry, but still considered impolite.

Mixed: The term used by those of mixed descent to refer to themselves.

Outer Gate: Calonade's fortification built to guard the Kettlebone Pass.

Plinum: A term used for pale skin features that take the shape of bands of pale blue hue running vertically along a person's body, usually Galathians. Results of generations of controlled breeding.

Raw-casting: Slur used for indigenous people that are not Galathian. Origin is a machine part that is formed correctly but lacks any polish or finish.

SHA: Acronym that means Seeded Human Asset. A primitive

human that has been conditioned to work in servitude to feminam is known as a SHAsha. Most feminam refer to all humans as SHA, whether conditioned or not.

Shin: Language of the Shinwate.

Shinwate: Feminam living in primitive isolated tribes on Urey.

Talindrey River: A river that runs through the Frontier.

Talistave: An independent city-state north of Galathia.

Thickets: Several hundred acres of thick brambles and briar patches in the Frontier near Thurbush.

Thurbush: Frontier town just to the north of Calonade.

Tin-striped: Slur used for people with pale- skin features, usually Galathians. Refers to a process of using thin strips of tin plating, usually shiny, to cover up corroded parts or structures.

Urey: Galathian name for the planet.

Vivigossic Ocean: Body of water to the south of Calonade.

Willacast: Three goddess sisters—Maiden, Mother, and Crone—are known as the Willacast sisters and are the source of Willacast magic. Also, the name of the Corporation that controls the main transport hub for the galaxy.

Wrayan Mountains: Rugged mountains running north-south, intersecting the Kelstone Mountains to the east of Calonade, and forming the eastern boundary of the Fenduer Forest.

Yawate: Moving trees associated with Shinwate villages.

Yawa-lee: Trees ridden by the Shinwate.

Acknowledgments

I started this novel long before I possessed any writing skill. It has seen so many iterations, Joseph Campbell can't keep up with all its faces. Many people helped along the way. My wife, Amy, has been a constant presence throughout the process, lending her critical eye and steadfast support. My kids read versions along the journey with the expected "meh" reaction, inspiring me to ratchet up the pace, increase the stakes, and deepen the characters. Hopefully this version turns them around.

Many beta readers, critiquers, and editors have helped me tremendously. Thanks to Steve Vincent and Christina Thomas for working over the whole series chapter-by-chapter. The love story between Jay and Jortica would not be what it is without them.

My sister, Stacey, read an early version and gently re-directed my efforts into better description instead of endless dialogue. I love dialogue a little too much.

Editors Melissa Prideaux, Jeff Seymour, Brittany Elges, and Renita McKinney shaped the story and writing. Beta readers Laura Kjosen, Pat Pierce, and Zawdie Ekundayo provided great feedback.

A special thanks goes out to the Rocky Mountain Fiction Writers. I've been a member since I started writing twenty years ago. The talented people of RMFW have been a constant source of support. Special thanks to the following for their encouragement and inspiration: Susan Mackey Smith, Aaron Michael Ritchey, Janet Fogg, Jason Evans, Amy Rivers, Veronica Calisto, David Slayton, Kate Jonuska, Cheryl Fallin, Linda Ditchkus, Paul Martz, Mindy McIntyre, Evon Davis, and Dani Coleman.

Andre and Natasha Gonzalez deserve a lot of credit. They welcomed me into their writing family and have guided me along way. This book wouldn't exist without them. I'm grateful to be with such excellent people on this writing adventure.

Subversive

If you enjoyed this first book of the Violet Sky series, don't miss out on the free short story, Subversive, in the same universe.

Download your free copy of Subversive.

https://BookHip.com/NDRVKXG

Enjoy this book?

We hope you enjoyed this release from M4L Publishing.

Reviews are the most helpful tools in getting new readers for any books. We don't have the financial backing of a New York publishing house and can't afford to blast our books on billboards or bus stops.

(Not yet!)

That said, your honest review can go a long way in helping us reach new readers. If you've enjoyed this book, we'd be forever grateful if you could spend a couple minutes leaving it a review (it can be as short as you like) on the site you purchased this book from, or on Amazon if you bought it in-person.

Thank you so much!

About the Author

Collin Irish is an engineer-storyteller. Both halves of his brain get a workout each day. With over twenty-five years of experience as a mechanical engineer he can believably explore the breadth of science fiction from pre-industrial to fantastical technology. He volunteers as a storyteller for youth mentoring groups using mythological imagery for emotional development. He lives in Lakewood, CO, where his wife and two children claim the third half of his brain, and his whole heart.

Also by M4L Publishing

Replicate *Andre Gonzalez*
The Burden *Andre Gonzalez*
Insanity *Andre Gonzalez*
Erased *Andre Gonzalez*
Followed Away *Andre Gonzalez*
Followed East *Andre Gonzalez*
Followed Home *Andre Gonzalez*
A Poisoned Mind *Andre Gonzalez*
Snowball: A Christmas Horror Story *Andre Gonzalez*

Stoner Comedy:
Blue Dream *OG Haze*

Children's:
Lying Monster *Natasha Gonzalez*

www.ingramcontent.com/pod-product-compliance
Lightning Source LLC
Chambersburg PA
CBHW071958190726
48293CB00001B/74